WHAT
SHE LOST

SUSAN ELLIOT WRIGHT

**SIMON &
SCHUSTER**

London · New York · Sydney · Toronto · New Delhi

A CBS COMPANY

First published in Great Britain by Simon & Schuster UK Ltd, 2017
A CBS COMPANY

Copyright © Susan Elliot Wright, 2017

This book is copyright under the Berne Convention.
No reproduction without permission.
® and © 1997 Simon & Schuster, Inc. All rights reserved.

The right of Susan Elliot Wright to be identified as author of this work
has been asserted in accordance with sections 77 and 78
of the Copyright, Designs and Patents Act, 1988.

1 3 5 7 9 10 8 6 4 2

Simon & Schuster UK Ltd
1st Floor
222 Gray's Inn Road
London WC1X 8HB

www.simonandschuster.co.uk

Simon & Schuster Australia, Sydney
Simon & Schuster India, New Delhi

A CIP catalogue record for this book
is available from the British Library

Paperback ISBN: 978-1-4711-3452-4
eBook ISBN: 978-1-4711-3453-1

This book is a work of fiction. Names, characters, places and
incidents are either a product of the author's imagination or are
used fictitiously. Any resemblance to actual people living or
dead, events or locales is entirely coincidental.

Typeset in the UK by M Rules
Printed and bound by CPI Group (UK) Ltd, Croydon, CR0 4YY

that is n   aper
Stewards   rt the Forest
Our   n organisation.
                                                    ied paper.

**London Borough of
Hackney**

03 / 2017

91300001023189

Askews & Holts   CLA

AF   £7.99

                         5339930

For Collette, James and Mia McGowan,
Jessica Allott and Henry Sinclair-Smith

PROLOGUE

Marjorie, October 1967

Marjorie didn't know how long she'd been in labour. There were no windows in the delivery room so she couldn't tell if it was day or night. It had been twelve hours with Eleanor, but she felt as though she'd been here twice that long already. She wondered if it was still pelting down with rain outside. When they said on the wireless this morning that there was likely to be some flooding, she'd gone straight downstairs to check the basement. Sure enough, there was already about an inch of water pooling in the area at the bottom of the back steps, so she took the stormboard from the old scullery and tried to wedge it up against the back door. Her bulk made it difficult to manoeuvre and the rain pounding on her back felt sharp and cold. She should have waited and let Ted do it, but she was sick of being huge and slow and useless, and she wasn't going to be beaten by a silly plank of wood, so when, after the fourth attempt to fix it in place, one side popped forward again, she put her hands on the door frame to steady herself, drew back her right foot and gave the board a sharp kick, slotting it perfectly into place. Whether it was the violent movement or whether it would have happened anyway, she didn't know, but it was then that she'd felt the unmistakable gushing between her legs.

There were three midwives in the delivery room now, and a doctor, too. 'We need Baby out, Marjorie.' This was the older midwife, the one she trusted. 'I want you to use all the strength you have. You've done this before, so you know you can do it again.'

'I can't,' she whimpered. She didn't want them to have to cut it out, but she couldn't go on any longer, she just couldn't. She wondered if Ted was still outside, pacing the corridor. Or maybe he'd gone back home to see to Eleanor. They'd dropped her off at Peggy's on their way to the hospital. Eleanor had been more excited about sleeping at Peggy's house than she was about the new baby. That seemed like days ago now. Another pain started to build, and she knew that within moments she'd be in its grip, consumed and unable to speak. She needed to say this quickly. 'Can't do it. Please. Caesarean. Just get it out.'

'Nonsense,' the midwife said. 'Come along, one more almighty push.'

Then more voices: *Push! Come on, push! You can do it, push!* So many of them shouting at her; she wanted to scream at them to shut up, but she didn't have the energy.

'I *can't*,' she cried, dragging the word out. Had they no mercy?

Just as she was certain she couldn't take any more, she felt the intense burning she remembered from before.

'Okay, that's the head. Stop pushing now and—'

But all at once she felt the little body slip out in a watery rush.

'That's it! You've done it!' The midwife sounded triumphant. 'Your baby's here. You have a little boy.'

A boy. Ted would be pleased. They'd call him Peter. If it had been another girl, they'd have called her Eloise. Eloise and Eleanor. She'd have quite liked another girl, but it didn't matter; so long as it was healthy.

She craned her head to see, barely aware at first of the hush that had fallen over the room. Then she realised her baby hadn't made a sound. 'Is . . . is he breathing?'

Before anyone could answer, the silence was broken by a weak cry, more like a kitten than a baby. He was alive. She fell back against the pillows, relief flooding through her. Why didn't they bring him to her? They were on the other side of the room, clustered around him, speaking in hushed voices. 'Can I hold him?' she asked. 'What is it? What's wrong?' She could hear his grizzled cry and her arms ached to hold him. One or two of the faces looked across at her, but still no one said anything. Then the older midwife – she was called Lily, Marjorie remembered – came to her side. She wasn't smiling. 'Baby . . . Baby has some mucus in his airways, so we need to clear that out for him, help him breathe a bit more easily.'

'Oh, I see.' She strained to see what they were doing. But it looked as though they'd finished clearing his airways. 'What are they doing now?'

The midwife opened her mouth then closed it again. Marjorie saw the anguish in her eyes, saw that her face was heavy with bad news.

'Tell me,' she said. 'Tell me what's wrong with my baby.'

The midwife nodded. There were tears in her eyes. 'One moment, Mrs Crawford,' she whispered.

It was the doctor who brought the baby to her, wrapped in a shawl. She could see a tuft of dark blond hair sticking up from the top of the bundle. She held out her arms to receive him. 'Mrs Crawford,' the doctor said, 'I'm afraid your son appears to have some . . . some problems.'

'Let me hold him.' She almost had to pull her child out of the doctor's arms. She saw it instantly. Those same frighteningly wide-spaced eyes she'd seen once before, a very long time ago. She looked into them in order to greet him, to welcome him to the world the same as she had with Eleanor nearly four years ago. She remembered that moment as if it were yesterday, the way Eleanor had looked back at her when she'd said, *Hello, baby*; the look in those moment-old eyes that said, *I know you; we are connected*.

But these tiny, too-round pools of blue were shallow and empty. She unwrapped the shawl. His scrawny body was too small in proportion to his puffball head, and the skin was pale and opaque-looking, with a delicate network of blue-green veins showing through. She ran her finger down his right leg to his foot, where the two middle toes were joined by a stretch of pink skin. She moved to the other foot, which was completely webbed, making him look like a little mer-child. He started to cough, his fragile chest heaving.

'He ... as you can see,' the doctor was saying, 'this baby has a number of ... abnormalities. There's likely to be a degree of mental handicap as well. We'll need to take a proper look at him.' He stopped speaking and seemed at a loss as to what to do next. Marjorie wrapped her limp-limbed baby in the shawl again, swaddling him tightly so he'd feel safe. He was still making that weak grizzling sound. 'Is my husband here?'

The midwife appeared at the doctor's side. 'Mr Crawford's gone home to try and get some sleep. He was dead on his feet. But he said he'd be back at about nine.'

'Are you on the telephone at home?' the doctor asked, and Marjorie nodded. He turned back to the midwife. 'The number will be in the notes,' he muttered. 'Get someone to ring him up and tell him to come and see me as soon as he arrives. I'll break it to him.'

Marjorie looked down at the child in her arms. If she kept her gaze away from his face and focused on the white, shawl-swaddled bundle, she could kid herself for a moment that he was normal, like any other newborn.

'Doctor needs to have a proper look at Baby, dear,' the midwife said, her voice so much softer now. 'I'll bring you a nice cup of tea in a minute, and then we'll get you onto the ward. You need to get some rest yourself.' She patted Marjorie's hand. 'You've had a ... Well, it's been a long night, hasn't it?' She tried to smile, but failed.

*

Marjorie was sure she wouldn't be able to sleep, but somehow she did, deeply and dreamlessly. When she woke, not on a ward as she'd expected but in a room on her own, Ted was sitting in the chair next to her, his face twisted with distress. On the end of the bed was a large bunch of white chrysanthemums, wrapped in blue paper and tied with matching ribbon. She hated chrysanthemums, and she felt momentarily annoyed with Ted for forgetting. But then she remembered why she was here.

She couldn't bring herself to look at Ted properly just yet, so for a moment she allowed her gaze to rest on the paper the flowers were wrapped in. It was so pretty: a soft, dusty blue covered with storks in flight. From each strong beak dangled a brilliant white nappy with a pink, plump, perfect baby nestled inside. Tears blurred her vision.

Somehow, eventually, she managed to lift her heavy eyes to Ted's. 'Have you seen him?'

Ted nodded.

She wondered now whether she should have told Ted about Maurice. But there was nothing to be done about it, so what was the point? Until today, she'd managed to do what Mother told her the one and only time she'd met him: *Now you must forget about this, Marjorie, and promise me you'll never, ever tell anyone. Never, do you promise?*

Ted was sitting in the chair beside her bed, not looking at her, turning his pack of Embassy over and over in his hands. He looked up when the door opened. The doctor from the delivery room attempted a smile but then allowed it to die on his lips. He sat down in the chair on the opposite side of the bed. 'I understand how difficult this must be for you, Mr and Mrs Crawford, but you have yourselves and your daughter to consider. There are some excellent establishments that can care for Peter. It's unlikely he has much awareness of his surroundings, or indeed that he will survive beyond early childhood. My advice is to go home, try to put this behind you and look to the future. You're both young – plenty of time to have another child.'

She closed her eyes and leant her head back against the pillow, but she could feel Ted looking at her. Another child. How could she possibly risk another child? She took a breath and opened her eyes again. 'No. We'll take him home.'

'Marjorie . . .'

'I can do it; I've experience, after all. It was my job. I was a nurse before I had my first, and I worked with plenty of retarded children.'

'Mrs Crawford,' the doctor paused. 'I'm sure you were a highly competent nurse, but I fear that caring for your own child in your own home, where you would be "on duty", as it were, twenty-four hours a day, well, it's a rather different kettle of fish, don't you see?'

She turned her head to the pillow. 'I'm tired. Please, I need to sleep.'

She heard the doctor sigh; Ted, too. With her eyes still closed, she pictured the look that was probably passing between them. Then she heard the doctor's chair move as he got to his feet. 'I'll come back when you've had some rest,' he said.

And he did come back, twice more, to try to persuade her to let them find somewhere suitable for Peter to be 'cared for'. 'Your intentions are admirable, Mrs Crawford, that goes without saying. But I urge you to consider the effect on yourself and your family.'

There were some very good places these days, he told her, but she didn't believe him. Things were better than in Maurice's day, and there were some kind and dedicated people working at the home where she'd been a nurse, but nevertheless, she'd seen children neglected, lying on their backs in their cots for hours, tied to the bed if they were restless, even slapped for emptying bowels over which they had no control. No, she had seen it too often. Her son was not normal, but he was still human.

Eleanor: the present, Scalby, North Yorkshire coast

Conscious of her hand trembling, Eleanor takes a breath and pushes the door open. She hasn't needed a hairdresser since she was eighteen years old, and coming here now, more than thirty years later, is something she has both dreamed about and dreaded. She looks around the salon as she hands her coat to the receptionist. Everyone else looks so relaxed, so at ease. The stylist, Gaby, has shortish hair that is three different colours: blonde, a chestnut brown and a bright pink – like a Neapolitan ice cream. She's very young – they all are – but when Eleanor explains the situation, Gaby listens closely, her expression serious. 'Okay,' she nods. 'Let's see what we can do, then, shall we?'

Eleanor can feel the stares, people assuming she has cancer, trying not to look. She is used to that, and to the well-meant assurances that it would *soon grow back*. At one point, when she was still angry, she'd drawn some perverted satisfaction from saying, *No, it won't, actually,* but she'd got over that fairly quickly. It wasn't quite true, anyway; what the specialist actually said was that it was by no means unheard of – a case of 'wait and see'. And then he'd laboured the point that hair loss triggered by trauma was relatively rare, which had only made it feel even more personal, more like a punishment.

Gaby catches her eye in the mirror, smiles and mouths, 'Trust me.'

She smiles back, and then tries to adopt a neutral expression as she puts herself in the hands of this pretty young girl, who is probably used to working with rather more hair than this. After years of battling with wigs that itched and scarves that slipped, she now managed to do a pretty good impression of someone who didn't mind being bald. Big earrings helped, she found, and holding your nerve and looking people in the eye, even when she could see them studiously trying to avoid letting their gaze drift higher than her eyebrows. When tufts of new downy hair began to appear unexpectedly when she was in her early thirties, she couldn't stop herself from touching it, stroking it, wondering how soon she'd be able to brush it again. But the regrowth was patchy and short-lived. It had grown again since then, on and off, but it hadn't ever held for more than a few weeks. Until now.

She can't bear to look too closely at what is happening to her hair as the stylist snips away, a millimetre here, a millimetre there, so instead she watches Gaby's face in the mirror. Her brows are knitted together; the tip of her tongue pokes from between her lips as she concentrates. Given that there is so little to work with, Eleanor had assumed it wouldn't take long, but Gaby seems to be treating this as a work of art as she gently combs and cuts, combs and cuts.

She glances around the salon. There are a couple of women with heads a mass of foils, looking like truncated Medusas as they flick through magazines and wait for their colour to take. One woman is having her sleek dark bob blow-dried, and there are three others having cuts. Eleanor watches as their shorn hair falls to the floor, mostly a couple of centimetres here and there, but in one case, three-inch strands of lovely coppery hair lie around the base of the chair. It is no wonder people are looking at her; the hair she's managed to grow isn't anywhere near as long as some of the hair that's drifting carelessly to the floor all around her.

A teenage boy pushes a wide broom behind the cutting chairs. She wouldn't mind betting that most of these women abuse their hair all the time, drenching it in chemicals or clamping it between heated metal plates and searing it to make it straight. They probably complain about *bad hair days*. She doesn't blame them, though; everyone takes their hair for granted.

After half an hour, Gaby's expression relaxes and she catches her eye in the mirror. 'Nearly done.' She makes a few more snips. 'There.' She leans down so her face is level with Eleanor's and appraises her work in the mirror. 'How's that for you?'

Eleanor allows herself to look properly. 'It's . . .' She struggles to find her voice, still stunned by the transformation. 'It's amazing.' She turns her head this way and that. 'I don't know quite how you've done it, but you've actually made it look longer.'

Gaby flushes. 'You like it?' She picks up a hand mirror and holds it so Eleanor can see the back.

'I love it.' The cut makes her cheekbones stand out and it emphasises the shape of her eyes. She turns and smiles. 'I can't thank you enough.'

After she's paid and collected her coat, she finds Gaby, presses a substantial tip into her hand and thanks her again. 'Hopefully I'll be back in a few weeks, but I don't want to jinx it by making another appointment.'

'You know where I am,' Gaby says. 'Fingers crossed.'

*

Twenty minutes later, Eleanor parks the car opposite the beach and picks up her heavy-duty work gloves and the roll of extra-strong bin liners, then she takes her wellies out of the boot and puts them on. She hurries down the steps, keen to get this done and get back to the community farm. The February wind pinches her cheeks as she gathers armfuls of seaweed and stuffs it into the bags, which she's doubled up for even more strength. Seaweed is brilliant for enriching the compost, but she wishes it didn't stink so much. Before long she has six bags, each about a third full but still so heavy that she has to lug them to the car one at a time. Her back and arms are aching by the time she's finished. She slams the boot shut, but instead of getting back in the driver's seat, she locks the car and heads back down to the beach to look at the sea for a few minutes. She walks across the wet sand to the water's edge and stands, hands deep in her pockets, looking out towards the horizon as the lacy froth washes over her boots. As usual, she finds herself mesmerised. There is something about the hypnotic movement of the waves that always makes her feel a little gloomy, but still she finds it hard to tear herself away.

It's starting to rain. As she heads back to the car, the salty wind stings her cheeks and makes her eyes water, but she can feel it moving the hair on her scalp, and it's a sensation she wants to fully soak up, just in case.

As she drives back to the community farm, she's aware of looking in the rear-view mirror rather more often than she needs to. Her sudden gloom is lifting again now, and she is actually smiling as she turns onto the track. The helpers have put the new signs up while she's been out, but instead of being at the bottom near the main road, they're about halfway up, which is a fat lot of good. The whole point is to try to attract more takers for the various classes they're running, and anyone who actually drives up the track will know what's available already. She slows down as the car shudders over the cattle grid, a relic from the days when this was a traditional working farm. Ah well, it won't take long to move the signs. It's probably her own fault for not spelling it out.

As soon as she's unloaded and emptied the bags of seaweed, she heads for the kitchen.

'I'm back!' She takes her jacket off and hangs it on the back of a chair. A fresh, earthy smell fills the room as Jill chops peppers for a vegetable chilli. There are four new volunteer helpers arriving today and six already here. Good home-made food is part of the deal – the helpers provide manual labour, the farm provides food, accommodation and social contact.

'Wow!' Jill puts down her knife and wipes her hands on her striped butcher's apron. 'It takes years off you.'

'Great, isn't it? That hairdresser's a genius.' She pauses. 'I just hope it stays this time.'

'Fingers crossed.' Jill takes off her apron to reveal a long, blue-and-orange kaftan-type dress. She always wears this sort of thing for cooking. If she's working outside, she usually wears a pair of David's jeans, tied up with a bit of old rope for a belt and one of his oversized shirts. Jill and David tell all the new volunteers about how they met as carefree young hippies in the sixties. 'And now,' they add proudly, 'we're carefree old hippies in our sixties.'

'Before I forget.' Jill hands her a mug of tea. 'Two things to tell you and a favour to ask. First, your mum phoned.'

Eleanor's heartbeat quickens and she feels a tickle of shame as she realises she hasn't spoken to her mother since Christmas Day, almost two months ago.

'Everything's okay, but she said there's something she needs to tell you. Said it was very important.'

'That's weird. She hardly ever calls me. I wonder what could be so important?'

'Only one way to find out. Use the landline.' Jill passes her the handset. 'I need to get the cabins ready for the new helpers anyway.'

'Thanks.' She starts to key in the number, then pauses. 'You said there were two things?'

'Oh, yes. And a favour. Favour first – can you take my yoga class for me tomorrow? I've pulled something in my back sorting out those bloody cloches.'

'All right, if your group don't mind.' She's taken the yoga classes before, but she isn't as good at it as Jill, who at sixty-eight is more than eighteen years her senior, but is tall and slender and can do things with her body that would defeat most women half her age.

'Of course they won't; they love you.'

'And the other thing you had to tell me?'

'Ooh, yes. Postcard from Dylan.'

There is a tiny skip in her stomach.

'It's on the corkboard. He'll be here sometime in May or June, he says, and he'll probably stay until late autumn, if we can use him, which, of course . . .'

'We most definitely can.' She smiles as she reads his postcard, which has a picture of Tower Bridge on the front; he's in London again. Dylan never uses the telephone; doesn't even own a mobile, never mind a tablet or even a laptop. He has no need of such things, he says.

She feels lighter as she goes back to keying in her mum's number.

'Hello?'

'Hello, Mum. Jill said you phoned. Is everything all right?'

'Who do you wish to speak to?' her mother says in her most formal telephone voice.

'Mum, it's me. Eleanor.'

Silence. It must be one of her bad days. 'Mum, are you there? It's Eleanor. You rang earlier; you said you had something to tell me.'

'Eleanor? Oh, hello. Nice to hear from you. How are you keeping?'

'I'm fine, Mum. You called me, this morning. Do you remember?'

'Did I? No, I don't think so. I seldom use the telephone these days. I can never remember the numbers. They've all changed.'

'You don't need to. I put them in your phone last time I was down, remember? You just need to look at the list on the front and you'll see which number you have to press for which person.'

'Last time? When was that? I don't remember.'

For a moment, she thinks her mother is being sarcastic; after all, although she tries to phone every couple of months, she hasn't actually seen her mum for over two years. Probably more like three, now she thinks about it. 'It's been a while, I know. But when I came, I put the important numbers in for you, and if you look on the front of the phone, there's a list. Have a look now. Can you see it?'

Silence.

'Mum? Peggy's mobile should be first, then—'

'I don't need Peggy's number.' She sounds irritated. 'She's only upstairs, and we've got an extension.'

'I know, I meant her mobile. In case she's out and you need to talk to her. It should be my mobile next, then I think it's the landline for here, but if you—'

'I'd better go,' her mother says. 'Peggy will be down for coffee presently. I'll tell her you called. Bye, darling.' And she's gone.

Eleanor sighs. She ought to go down again soon. Her mum and Peggy have been friends since they were teenagers, but it isn't fair to rely so heavily on Peggy; after all, she's only two or three years younger than Marjorie, although Marjorie often seems much older. It was Peggy who'd rung to tell her about the diagnosis, more than three years ago now. 'Your mum didn't want to worry you,' she'd said. 'But I told her not to be so bloody stupid. She's struggling to take it all in, but I said I'd let you know.'

She'd called her mother the next day and asked exactly what the doctor had said.

'Well, they're almost certain that's what it is. There's no blood test or anything, but they did some memory tests ... like being at school. They had me counting backwards in nines, or was it sevens? I had to draw something – a clock, I think. And lots of silly questions – what

year is it, who's the Prime Minister, that sort of thing.'
She sighed heavily. 'They think I've had it for a while. I'm
always forgetting things when I go shopping, or leaving
my keys in the front door. But I forget people's names
now, too. And things that have happened.' She paused.
'Even big things.' For a moment, Eleanor had wondered
if she might finally mention the 'big things' that had
defined their lives, coloured their relationship. But then
she sounded brisk again. 'Anyway, it's not too bad at the
moment, but it'll get worse. I'll just have to learn to live
with it.'

Ever since then, Eleanor has made sure she keeps in
touch more frequently in an attempt to move some way
towards being a dutiful daughter. She's been meaning
to arrange a visit for ages, in fact; she thinks about it
every few weeks. But the weeks and months have quietly
stretched and become years, and somehow all this time
has passed and now it seems the disease is starting to
crank up.

*

Eleanor is working in the kitchen this week. Jobs on
the farm are allocated on a rota system for the sake
of variety, so if you're in the kitchen one week, you'll
probably be working in the grounds the week after,
either on gardening duties – digging, weeding, planting; anything associated with growing food – or you
could be on maintenance and repairs. That can mean

things like repointing, replacing broken tiles, securing loose guttering or perhaps repainting the house and the cabins – the salty sea air tends to eat through the exterior paint quickly. If you have a particular talent or skill, that'll be taken into account, too. Bread-making is one of her regular duties, and she and David take turns because they both seem to have the knack for it, whereas Jill can make cakes but is, in her own words, *completely bloody useless with yeast!*

They bake two or three times a week, depending on how many volunteers they have, and she's always trying out new things. She loves the smell of newly baked bread and the sight of the table laden with fresh loaves, rolls and baguettes, and she revels in the warm appreciation of the volunteers, especially those used to limp supermarket sandwiches grabbed on the way to the office. And although she hates to admit it, she likes it when the volunteers – with their homes and families, their proper jobs, their mortgages and pensions – look at her properly and say things like, *Where did you learn to bake like that?* Or, *What a wonderful skill to have.*

She has just started mixing water into a mound of flour and yeast on the kitchen table when her phone vibrates in her pocket. 'Shit,' she mutters. This is not a point at which she can stop, so she carries on mixing with her fingers until she has a loose dough, then she pulls what she can off her hands before washing them and getting her phone out of her pocket. It's her mum again. At least that means she must have remembered how to use the stored numbers. There's a voicemail. 'Eleanor?' Her voice sounds hesitant. 'Is that you? It doesn't sound like you.' There is a pause, then she hears her mum make a tutting noise. 'Oh, it's the machine, isn't it? Are you there, Eleanor? Pick up the phone if you're there.' Eleanor has explained voicemail again and again, but her mum can't seem to hold onto it. Marjorie is seventy-four, so not exactly old. Well, not *old* old, anyway. *Next new message.* 'Eleanor, it's me again. I need you to telephone me.' She doesn't sound upset exactly, but there is an undercurrent of anxiety in her voice. 'There's something I need to tell you. It's very important, so I must speak to you.' Pause. 'Yes, so ring me, please.'

She calls back immediately. It's less than twenty minutes after her mum's message, but by that time, Marjorie has completely forgotten what it was she wanted to tell her, or that she'd even called.

Eleanor

Over the next three days, there are two more 'I need to tell you something' voicemails, but each time, by the time Eleanor calls back, Marjorie can't even remember phoning.

'I'm worried about her,' she says to Jill as they dig in the rich, seaweed-enhanced compost ready for the start of planting next month. 'I need to visit soon. In fact, I might have to start going down quite regularly, depending on how bad she is.'

'Of course,' Jill replies. 'You don't need to think about this place, you know that.'

She smiles. 'True.' She always tells people it's the very 'no ties' aspect of the farm that has kept her here so long, but in truth it's a long time since she's considered leaving. 'It'll only be for a couple of days this time, anyway. I should have gone down before, but I suppose I've been putting it off. It's never easy.'

Jill pauses to brush a strand of hair out of her eyes, a gesture Eleanor always notices. 'Do you have to go? I mean, it's not as though you're close, is it? And if—'

'That's the problem, though. If I can't make some sort of connection with her, I don't know ... I suppose I always thought there would be time to sort things out.'

'You never know; she might even feel the same way. Did you ever find out what it was she wanted to tell you?'

'No, she couldn't even remember phoning. I don't suppose she really has anything to tell me – it's probably the Alzheimer's.' Even as she says this she wonders if she might be mistaken – her mum had sounded quite distressed in the voicemails.

'It might not be all that bad. I mean, we all forget things, don't we?'

'Not my mother.' She tips out more compost from the wheelbarrow. 'At least, I don't think so. I don't know for sure because she never bloody tells me anything.' She is fairly sure her mother recalls everything that's ever happened to her, whereas Eleanor herself still has gaps in her memory. Maybe some things *are* better forgotten, but she wishes she'd been given the choice. Instead, her parents took her to a psychotherapist. *A quack, more like*, Dylan had said when she told him. Her mother wasn't sure where they'd got the idea – possibly from an article in *Reader's Digest* – but the gist of it was that children could be made to forget traumatic events by being taught to symbolically dispose of bad memories. Every time the young Eleanor remembered anything that made her unhappy, she was to imagine herself throwing the upsetting memories into a dustbin and putting the lid on tight. Then she was supposed to think of something nice, because if you filled up your head with nice memories, there would be no room for the nasty ones.

So she spent a lot of her early childhood thinking about picking sweet peas in different colours, stroking a fluffy kitten or being given a whole box of Smarties at Christmas.

*

Most of the drive to south-east London isn't too bad, but the drizzling rain turns to a deluge, and visibility is so poor that she has to crawl the last twenty miles as her wipers thrash uselessly at the flooded windscreen. By the time she arrives it's mid-afternoon, the rush hour has started and traffic in the centre of Lewisham is heavy. The road layout seems to have changed since she was last here, or maybe it's that she is so disconnected from who she was when she lived here that the place feels alien to her all the time now. She passes Lewisham Hospital and indicates to turn left. The shops all look so different now. She notices that the pub has gone, although the Chinese takeaway is still there, and the little general store where she and her friends used to buy Jamaican patties after school; they still sell them, according to the board outside, along with curried fish or goat.

Her stomach shifts as she pulls up outside the huge corner house where she grew up. This is one thing that doesn't change. At least, her mother's half of the house, the topsy-turvy part where you go downstairs to bed instead of up, has barely changed since she left.

Pulling her coat up over her head, she goes up the steps to the main front door and rings the bottom bell. She waits for a minute and rings again, but there's no reply. Perhaps her mum is upstairs with Peggy. When she was growing up, it felt as though it was one house instead of two maisonettes. The inner front doors were often on the latch so she could go up or down without having to ring the bell, and she'd taken advantage of this as a child, spending much of her time up at Peggy's.

She tries the top bell but there's no response to that, either. A sense of unease begins to creep through her. She leans across to look through the rain-lashed bay window into the living room, but there are no lights on, no sign of life. Maybe her mum has forgotten she's coming. She goes down the steps and along the side alley into the garden. If her mum is downstairs in one of the bedrooms a light will be on somewhere – you need electric light down there on all but the brightest of days. But the basement is in darkness. An image flashes into her head of her mother lying unconscious on the floor, but she rejects it almost immediately. After all, physically, Marjorie is far from frail.

She climbs the steps to the veranda, where she'll be able to see through into the kitchen. Again, no lights, no sign that anyone's around. There is a shock of cold wetness on the back of her neck as water starts to seep through her coat. Why hadn't she thought to bring her Barbour? She feels the faintest stirrings of panic as she gets back into the car, but when she checks her phone she sees there are two texts: *On our way. Be about 10 minutes P x* Thank God. She scrolls up to the previous text, which came through half an hour ago. *Not sure what time you're arriving, but we'll be back soon. P xx* She texts a reply, *Am here, see you in a bit*, then sits back to wait.

The house is Victorian and could reasonably be described as imposing. Her parents bought it while it was undergoing conversion from a single dwelling into two maisonettes. Her mum told her that when they first viewed the lower part as newlyweds, there was still a row of servants' bells in the basement. She looks up at the black windows. The Dralon curtains that still hang in the living room were once a deep red, but they're badly faded now, almost pink with darker stripes in the folds where the sun can't reach. She looks down at the bay window to her mum's bedroom, half sunken beneath ground level. Those curtains haven't changed either: an oatmeal colour with sprinklings of insipid lilac flowers. Her eyes flick up to Peggy's windows: tasteful wooden blinds for the living room; curtains in the bedrooms at the top – huge red poppies on a white background – very Peggy.

She remembers how thrilled she'd been the day she heard that Peggy and her husband Ken had bought the upstairs maisonette. She must have been only five or six, because it was about the time her mum was in and out of hospital. The first she knew of it was when Peggy came round with Martin and Michael after school one day to tell them that it had all gone through at last and that, as from Saturday fortnight, she, Ken and the boys would be their new upstairs neighbours.

Eleanor had felt her grin stretch across her face, and her dad had ruffled her hair. 'That's good news, isn't it, Ellie-belly?'

Then Peggy smiled at her. 'It'll make babysitting easier, won't it, sweetheart? Not that you're a baby any more, obviously.'

Eleanor always went up the road to Peggy's when her mum wasn't well. She liked playing with the twins, although they were boys, of course, and a bit older. Mainly, though, she liked being with Peggy. She liked looking at Peggy, too; she felt guilty thinking it, but her mother wasn't as pretty; she was thin, with a pale, dry face and a frown that stayed around her eyes even when she smiled, which wasn't often. But Peggy had wide-awake eyes and a mouth that always looked as though it was about to laugh. Her cheeks were peachy pink, and they were ripe and juicy.

Peggy leant forward with her hands on her knees. 'Tell you what, Ellie, when we move in, how would you like to come up and help me and the boys unpack?'

She'd nodded vigorously, and when the day came, she reminded her mum that Peggy had said she could go upstairs to help. Her heart sank when her mother said she would come too, but to her amazement, once they were up there, surrounded by more cardboard boxes than she had ever seen, her mum was soon chatting and laughing with Peggy as they tried to work out which box the kettle was in.

She'd wondered whether it was partly the house itself that was causing her mother's malaise. Her mum spent too much time in the dingy basement where revolting, squirmy silverfish lived in the carpets and you dared not move anything in case you disturbed them. Maybe simply being in a higher, brighter part of the house cheered her mum up. Downstairs, misery built up like mould in the rooms; the very bricks and mortar were steeped in it. She'd known even then that something bad had happened, and she had an inkling that she'd been part of it, but she couldn't remember what it was. Sometimes, just as a ray of sunlight might illuminate the dust motes in a stuffy old room, a chink of light would fall upon a buried memory, causing it to brighten and glow in her mind: herself, sobbing as she ran barefoot down the garden; Peggy's face as she dropped her shopping bags, oranges rolling across the grass. But nothing stayed long enough for her to make sense of it. Sometimes she wished she could find that imaginary dustbin and take all her memories out again, even if they weren't very nice.

The drumming on the roof is easing off now, although the sky is still dark. She is about to look at her watch again when Peggy's little blue Fiesta pulls up behind her. The driver's door opens and Peggy gives Eleanor a tense smile. 'Hello, sweetheart. We've had a bit of an adventure.' Then Marjorie climbs out of the passenger side, looking wet, cold and slightly bedraggled.

'Hello, Mum,' she says. 'I thought you'd forgotten I was coming.'

Marjorie looks at her blankly for a moment, as though she doesn't know who she is. But then she smiles and says, 'Eleanor! You came.'

'Of course I came. We spoke on the phone last night.'

'Did we?' Her mother shakes her head in irritation. 'I don't remember, I'm afraid.'

'Come on,' Peggy says, 'let's get in out of this sodding weather.' She lets them in at the main front door, and then, using her own key, the inner door to the downstairs maisonette. 'I'll put the kettle on, Marjorie. Give me that shopping.'

Eleanor follows her mother into the chilly living room, hoping Peggy won't be long – Peggy always helps to fill the space between them. With its high whitewashed ceiling and enormous bay window, you'd think there would be a feeling of light and space in this room, but instead it is gloomy and claustrophobic, especially as it's almost dusk now. Her mum has walked straight past the light switch, and there are no lamps.

'Bloody hell, Marjorie,' Peggy says, setting the tea down on a side table and flicking on the overhead light. 'It's as dark as a dog's guts in here.' The light is inadequate against the dark, patterned carpet and chocolate-brown vinyl wallpaper, which has been up for as long as Eleanor can remember. Why change it, her mother argued, when it was perfectly serviceable?

She realises Peggy is looking at her hair. 'I didn't notice at first. You look lovely, Ellie. Not that you don't always, but ...'

Eleanor smiles and shrugs. 'I don't know how long it'll last.'

Marjorie, who is still standing uncertainly in the middle of the room, turns to look. 'It's awfully short, darling. I think I preferred it longer.'

'Yes, but that was a wig, Mum. This is real.'

Marjorie seems about to say something, then hesitates, looks slightly puzzled, and turns away again.

Now she can see her mother properly, she notices that she's a little thinner and her hair is greyer, but apart from that she appears to be reasonably well and is dressed much the same as always in navy trousers and an apricot roll-neck jumper. Peggy is wearing black jeans, a scoop-necked black sweater and bright red lipstick, set off by her softly styled hair, now a silvery blonde. She's always looked striking. Her figure is more rounded than Marjorie's, not fat but fleshy, well covered. The first time Eleanor sat on Peggy's lap as a child, she noticed how comfy it was, how she couldn't feel bony knees like she did when she sat on her mum's lap.

'You're both looking very well.'

'You want your eyes tested, Ellie.' Peggy peers critically

in the spotted mirror that hangs over the mantelpiece and prods at her face. 'Should have gone to Specsavers.'

Marjorie sits in the armchair and gestures towards the coffee table on which is a large, half-completed jigsaw puzzle on a wooden board. 'I have to try and stop my brain from rotting too fast. Hence the jigsaw. And,' she picks up a book from the arm of her chair and waggles it, 'I'm getting to be a whizz at chesswords. Aren't I, Peg?'

'Crosswords.' Peggy smiles. 'You certainly are.'

'Crosswords.' Briefly, a cloud crosses Marjorie's face. 'A whizz at crosswords.'

'Bloody things,' Peggy says. 'I couldn't do one to save my life.' She sips her tea. 'I'll fetch that cake in a minute. Marjorie, tell Eleanor what happened. Just now, before I picked you up.' She turns to Eleanor. 'It's good for her to exercise her memory.'

'I am *here*, you know.'

'I'm only explaining. Don't get your knickers in a twist.'

Marjorie tuts, but it's good-natured. 'Well,' she says to Eleanor, 'I got lost, is the long and the short of it. Coming back from the Co-op, if you can believe that. Good job I had Peggy's spare phone.'

'They're digging up the road round there again,' Peggy says, 'so it all looks different, especially when it's raining so hard you can't see your hand in front of your face. It's a bloody miracle you remembered to use the phone, though.' She turns to Eleanor. 'Eventually, anyway – but by that time she'd walked the whole length of Hither

Green Lane and was in the middle of Lewisham, right down by the clock tower.'

'I knew where I was, but couldn't remember what bus to get.' Marjorie sighs. 'With all this carry-on, I've not had a chance to go shopping or I'd have bought a cake or something.'

Eleanor and Peggy exchange glances.

'You've just bought one at the Co-op,' Peggy says. 'Remember? Victoria sponge. I wouldn't mind, but you bought exactly the same thing from the baker's yesterday.'

'The same thing? You mean … I've bought two Victoria sponges?'

'One yesterday and one today.' Peggy smiles. 'So I think we'll be all right for cake.'

Eleanor smiles too, but is then horrified to see her mother's eyes fill with tears.

'Oh, Peg,' Marjorie murmurs. 'Whatever's happening to me?'

*

It's strange being back in her old bedroom. It's been painted – white – since she was last here. But it makes very little impact. Gloominess is inevitable in a basement room where the only natural light comes from a tiny window that gives on to an alleyway.

It's freezing in here, the same as it always was, despite the electric fire she switched on earlier to take the chill off. The hot, burnt dust smell combined with the slightly mouldy dampness that is so familiar sends her hurtling back thirty years. In winter, the smell was so strong it would sometimes keep her awake. She remembers one or two of her school friends being envious that she had a room all to herself. She'd tried to explain that it wasn't as nice as they thought, but she hadn't been able to put into words quite how bleak she found it, and how lonely. She'd been envious of them because they had siblings. She'd often lain awake wondering what it must be like to have a brother or sister. Sometimes, especially when things were difficult upstairs, she'd become quite tearful thinking about it. If only she'd had a sibling to talk to, perhaps she would have minded less about not getting on with her mum.

A deep sadness wells up inside her as she thinks about Marjorie, and about what happened to her today: getting lost on her way back from the shop she's visited two or three times a week for as long as anyone can remember; using the wrong words so many times this afternoon; her distress when Peggy told her she'd bought a cake yesterday and again today. How horrible this disease is; how unsettling to have no recollection of something you've done. But then she realises that she knows how that feels. Obviously Alzheimer's is a different type of memory loss, but yes, she knows only too well what it feels like not to remember your own actions. As a teenager and even as a young woman, she'd felt manipulated, foolish for allowing the psychotherapist to dictate what should happen to the thoughts inside her head. She'd been angry with her mother. How would her mum feel if it was she who'd had to throw her memories in the dustbin, she used to wonder? But she took no pleasure now in witnessing Marjorie's diminishing memory. With maturity came acceptance that her parents had genuinely thought they were doing the right thing, and her anger had given way to an empty feeling – not quite grief, not quite sadness, but a void of which she was perpetually aware.

Now, as she lies shivering in the darkness, a single tear leaks out of the corner of her eye, and she isn't sure whether she has shed it for her younger self, or for her poor, fading mother.

Marjorie, May 1970

Marjorie and Ted stood on opposite sides of the room as they prepared for bed. Ted was wearing just his pyjama bottoms – it was too warm to wear a top tonight, he said. Marjorie glanced quickly at his chest then looked away again. Was it her imagination, or did he look thinner? She'd lost weight herself these past two years, but she hadn't noticed the change in Ted until tonight.

'You look tired, love.' He looked at her with concern as he took off his watch and put it on the bedside table, laying it on top of a paperback he hadn't picked up in months.

The book looked dusty; Marjorie struggled to keep on top of the cleaning these days.

Ted switched on the radio alarm. 'How have things been today?'

'Not too bad, I suppose.' Marjorie sat at her dressing table, opened a pot of Pond's Cold Cream and dotted tiny blobs over her cheeks, nose and forehead. She hardly ever bothered, but she'd noticed how dull and lifeless her skin was looking, and while she was in Boots today picking up her tablets, she spotted a display of Pond's and remembered seeing an advert saying it would 'melt away tired lines', so she'd bought a pot. This meant she cared what she looked like, she realised. Perhaps she was getting better. She'd certainly felt better since she'd been back at work, and Eleanor seemed perfectly happy going to Peggy's in the afternoons. It was a godsend having Peggy and Ken up the road, and it would be even easier when they moved in upstairs, at least until Peggy went back to work. 'It's just this tiredness. I know I'm only doing a few hours a day, but by the time I get home and pick Ellie up, I'm good for nothing.' She paused, caught Ted's eye in the dressing-table mirror. 'I wish ... I wish I could do more with her, Ted. I was watching her today, playing with her dolls as happy as anything, and I wondered if I would ever be able to ... if I could bear ...' She put a fist to her mouth and bit her knuckle hard to try to stop the tears.

Ted was across the room in two bounds and enfolded her in his arms. 'Shush, it's all right, love, it's okay.' He stroked her hair. 'Remember, one day at a time.'

She nodded against his chest, comforted by the warmth of his body and the clean, laundered smell of the cotton vest. She sniffed and wiped her eyes.

Ted kissed the top of her head and stroked her hair. 'It'll get better, in time. And we're getting there, aren't we? Slowly.' He kissed her head again. 'Just keep trying, step by step.' He knelt down next to her and held her face in his hands. She caught a whiff of whisky on his breath.

'I know it seems impossible, Marjorie, but you mustn't give up.' He searched her face with his eyes. 'I haven't; it's hard for me too, you know.'

'I know.' She let out an involuntary sob. She understood that it was hard for him, of course she did; but it was different, and no matter how kind and loving he was, she would never be able to explain that to him.

'We'll get through this, love, the three of us.' She could see tears in his eyes. 'We just have to take little steps.'

She looked into his dear, kind, sad eyes. She leant forward and kissed him lightly on the lips. He kissed her back, a firmer, more lingering kiss. She touched his face with her fingers. 'Ted,' she whispered, feeling the tiniest flutter of desire.

He kissed her palm, then reached for her other hand. 'Come on,' he murmured, pulling her slowly to her feet. She allowed him to lead her to the bed where he pulled back the blankets and gently, gently, kissing her all the while, pushed her down so that her head was on the pillow. He slid under the covers and lay next to her, kissing her neck, kissing her shoulder.

'Ted, hold me,' she murmured.

He put his arms around her and gathered her to him, kissing her harder now. His hand slid under her nightgown and he began to pull it up, exposing her thighs, her stomach, her breasts. She held her arms up automatically

36

as he pulled her nightdress up over her head and buried his face in her breasts. 'I've missed you so much,' he said, kissing and kissing, I've missed *us*. Oh, Marjie, darling Marjie.'

But although in her head she ached for him, it seemed her body was betraying her. Just seconds ago she'd been almost ready, caught up in the forcefulness of his desire, yet now she felt almost repelled by his nearness, the whisky on his breath, the slight roughness of his chin. She pulled away from him and sat up. 'I'm sorry.' She could feel the tears on her cheeks. 'I'm so sorry.' Ted stopped and searched her face. 'What is it? Why? What's changed?'

She shook her head, crying properly now. 'I don't know. It's just ... I can't. It doesn't seem right that we should ... I'm sorry.'

Ted seemed frozen for a moment, then he sighed heavily and swung his legs out of bed. She looked at his beautiful broad back, the smooth skin she used to run her hands over while they made love. She wanted to touch it now, to soothe him, tell him how much she loved him and how much she really did want him. Because she did, she truly did. But she couldn't do it, not yet. 'I'm sorry, Ted. I ... I think it's still too soon.'

'How can it be too soon?' His voice sounded hard. He was sitting on the edge of the bed with his back towards her. 'It's getting on for two years, Marjorie. I thought being in that place ...'

He always referred to it as 'that place', she noticed. But

then it was virtually impossible to name it without dragging up awful connotations. In fact, many moons ago, before her life twisted out of shape, she'd joked about it herself. She could almost hear herself playfully scolding Ted for trying to waltz her round the kitchen while she was cooking the dinner, or Eleanor for lying in bed singing the chorus of 'The Old Woman Who Swallowed a Fly' over and over at the top of her voice instead of going to sleep: *You'll drive me round the bend one of these days*, she'd say, laughing. *I'll end up in Bexley.* But she wasn't sure if she was actually mad now, or just sad. Maybe it was a little of both.

'I thought that a few weeks' rest was supposed to make you better.'

'I am better, Ted; much better. I just don't . . . not yet.'

He sighed again.

She looked at the sprinkling of freckles across his shoulders. Oh to reach out and touch him! But the silence was blocking her way; it may as well have been a raging ocean between them. She tried to slip her nightdress back on discreetly, so he wouldn't notice the action and see it as an insult, as further evidence of rejection. She wasn't rejecting him, though. It was something about herself she was rejecting.

Eleanor: the present, south-east London

Her mum is already making breakfast when Eleanor goes up to the kitchen in the morning. The ancient central heating has come on but it isn't very efficient and she doesn't fancy showering in the icy bathroom just yet.

Marjorie turns and smiles when she comes in. 'Did you sleep well?'

'Yes, thanks. I was very tired – driving always knocks me out.'

'Well, you can have a nice rest today. Sit down and I'll make us some toast.' She takes four slices from a loaf of white bread and puts them in a red, modern-looking toaster, a little out of place in this shabby kitchen with its mismatched units and fluorescent strip light.

'Nice toaster,' Eleanor comments. 'Is it new?'

'Peggy made me buy it. Fair enough, I suppose. I kept putting bread under the grill and forgetting it, and she got fed up with the burnt smell drifting upstairs.' She pours water from the kettle into two mugs, then pauses, looking at them before turning to Eleanor. 'I know I shouldn't have to ask, but I can't for the life of me remember whether you take sugar.'

'No, no, thanks.'

Marjorie puts the toast onto plates. 'Peggy'll come down for coffee at eleven, and then I think she said we could go up to her later for ...' She becomes perfectly still as she concentrates. 'Oh, for goodness' sake, what's it called? Not breakfast – the other food time, the middle one.'

'Lunch.'

'Lunch. Yes, that's it. Lunch.'

*

By the time she's showered and dressed, has washed up the breakfast things and allowed Marjorie to walk her round the wintry garden, it's time for coffee. Peggy is already in the kitchen when they come up the steps to the veranda. They can see her through the French doors, pouring water into a cafetière. 'Morning.' She smiles. 'I thought we'd have a proper coffee, Marjorie.' She winks at Eleanor. 'Instead of that instant muck you usually give me.'

'So rude,' Marjorie mutters as she picks up the tray Peggy has prepared. 'Let's go into the dining room, it's warmer in there.'

The dining room is only slightly warmer than the

kitchen. The sideboard is virtually hidden under an assortment of papers, books and other stuff that's piled on its surface along with a glass fruit bowl and two ashtrays. Eleanor has a sudden mental picture of her father sitting in the armchair, half hidden by a cloud of choking blue smoke, a Senior Service in the nicotine-stained fingers of one hand, a glass of whisky in the other. When she thinks of her father, she remembers first the smell of whisky and cigarettes, but it wasn't always like that: she has an earlier, much vaguer memory of him smelling of peppermint creams, coffee and Wrights Coal Tar soap.

Marjorie stands in the middle of the room as though she can't recall why she's come in here. 'Are you all right, Mum?'

'Yes, I think so.'

'Sit down now, Marje,' Peggy says. 'You're making the place look untidy. Speaking of which,' she tuts and gestures towards the sideboard. 'I blitzed it in here for her the day before yesterday, but you wouldn't know it. Why do you keep emptying all the drawers and cupboards, Marjorie?'

'I keep telling you, it isn't me.' She turns to Eleanor. 'The trouble is, when you've got this senile dementia thing, they can accuse you of all sorts, and you can't argue because you can't remember.'

Peggy rolls her eyes again. 'Sometimes, Marjorie Crawford, you really push your luck.'

Marjorie sticks her tongue out and they all laugh.

'Seriously, though,' Peggy says when Marjorie leaves the room to go to the loo. 'This keeps happening, and she's told me a few times that she's looking for something. Sometimes she says it's a letter, but she doesn't know who from, and sometimes she can't remember what she's looking for. But what's a bit odd is that now and again I get the impression she does know what she's looking for but she doesn't want to tell me.'

Eleanor feels a beat of interest; she knows so little about her mother's life now.

Peggy sighs. 'I'm probably imagining it. She's probably after a shopping list from 1975 or something.' She laughs and starts gathering up magazines, utility bills, recipes, postcards.

Eleanor picks up one of the postcards and turns it over. She recognises her own handwriting:

Dear Mum, just to let you know I am in Buxton now, working and staying in a pub. The landlord and landlady are nice but they said the job is probably only for the summer. I am still feeling very sad but I'm all right. Please give my love to Peggy and say sorry I haven't sent a separate card but I'm being careful with money. I hope you are OK. E x

She looks at the picture on the front. She can barely remember the landlord there, but she'd worked in so many different pubs and cafés at that time, they sort of merged into one. She can see a couple of other postcards in the pile Peggy is straightening. 'I'm surprised she kept them,' Eleanor says, flipping over the cards and finding similar messages.

'I think she kept them all. I still have mine, too. We were both so worried about you, Ellie, driving round the country in that motorhome thing you used to have – what did you call it? Dolly?'

'You mean the old camper – Doris.'

'Doris, that's right.' Peggy shakes her head. 'You were so young, and you were in such a dreadful state.'

'I'm sorry. I never wanted you to worry.' She plucks a couple more from the pile. 'But I suppose I didn't really think ... Oh, look at this one, this was a nice place.' She shows Peggy the picture of the little tea rooms in Bakewell where she'd worked for a few weeks.

'Ah, yes, I think that's the one where we drove up to try and find you.'

'Sorry?' She thinks she's misheard. 'You—'

Peggy reads the back of the card. 'Bakewell. Yes, that was it. Pretty little town. You didn't stay there long, though, did you? We just missed you.'

'You ... you and Mum went to Bakewell?'

Peggy nods. 'I think it's the furthest your mum had ever driven. She was nervous about going all that way on her own, so I said I'd come with her. Truth was, I wanted to see for myself that you were all right. We'd missed you by two days, the lady in the café said. She told us you'd only been there to cover holidays, and she didn't know where you'd moved on to. We didn't have a clue where

43

to start looking, so we bought a Bakewell tart and drove back home.'

'But ... you went all the way up there to look for me? She drove?' As far as she knew, her mother never drove further than Lewisham shopping centre; Bromley if she was feeling adventurous.

'You didn't know?'

'I had no idea.'

'I thought I'd told you. But I suppose we weren't in touch very often at that point, were we?' She smiles. 'That's not meant as a dig; I know you were in a bit of a mess. But your mum said she wanted to talk to you; that was why we came.'

'Talk to me? About what?'

'We'd had a bit of a chat, me and your mum.' She looks at the postcard again. 'Ellie,' her voice is soft, 'your mum knows things would have been easier if she hadn't been the way she is. She was coming to realise it at about the time you left, but of course she knew it was too late by then. It was good that you sent postcards – at least we knew you were alive. But you never gave us your address at first, and then when this one came with the picture of where you were,' she fans the air with the card, 'well, your mum reckoned there couldn't be that many tea rooms in Bakewell, and off we went.'

Eleanor's hands suddenly feel cold for some reason. 'You went all that way,' she mutters.

'As it happened, she was wrong about that – there were a *lot* of tea rooms in Bakewell! Took us ages to—' She breaks off as Marjorie comes back in. 'Do you remember, Marje? Traipsing round all those bloody tea shops in Bakewell. '

'Bakewell?' She turns to Eleanor. 'Weren't you living there at one time?'

'That's what we're talking about. That day we drove up there, you and me. Looking for Eleanor. Remember?'

'Looking for Eleanor?' Marjorie looks thoughtful. 'Yes, yes, that's right. But we never did find her, did we?'

'Mum, I didn't . . .' She feels a lump of emotion swelling in her throat. It's hard to speak, and when she does, her voice sounds thin and weak. 'I didn't know you came looking for me.'

Her mother leans forward. 'Sorry, Eleanor, I didn't catch that.'

She clears her throat. 'I said, I wish I'd known you drove all that way to Bakewell.'

'Bakewell? Weren't you living there at one time?'

*

Eleanor had intended to set off first thing, but her mum forgot she was leaving today and bought ingredients for a vegetarian lasagne, so she ends up staying longer. Her mum spends all morning preparing the lasagne but then forgets to light the oven, so everything is later than anticipated, and by the time Eleanor puts her bags in the car it's gone six. 'Mum, don't stand out here in the cold – I've got to scrape the windscreen yet so I'll be a few minutes.'

45

'Go in and put the kettle on, Marje,' Peggy says. 'I'll be with you in a bit.'

'I think I will if you're sure you don't mind. It was nice to see you . . .' She pauses.

Eleanor realises immediately. *She's forgotten my name.*

'Yes, very nice to see you. Safe journey.'

This is the moment where any normal mother and daughter would embrace. Eleanor hesitates. If she's going to do it, she needs to do it now. 'I'll try and come down again soon,' she says, stepping forward, but Marjorie is already turning away. 'I'll give you a ring, Mum.'

'Right you are, darling.' Marjorie waves her hand briefly as she makes her way up the steps.

'You'd better go in too, Peggy. It's freezing out here.'

'No, I'm all right. I see your mum every day, but I don't get to see you very often, so I'm not sitting in there while I could be out here chatting to you. And anyway, I've got more meat on my bones.'

Eleanor smiles and goes back to scraping frost off the windscreen. 'I'm sorry it's been such a brief visit. I hadn't realised how much you were having to keep an eye on her.'

'It's not that bad, really; not yet, anyway – she has good days and bad days. I'm just glad I can help out a bit.'

Eleanor tosses the windscreen scraper onto the passenger seat and turns to Peggy, who pulls her immediately into an embrace. 'I'll look after her, pet, and I'll keep you posted.'

Peggy's hugs are always tighter and warmer than

anyone else's, and they last longer. They make Eleanor feel about six years old again, but in a good way.

'Thanks for all you're doing,' she says, affection for Peggy surging through her. Then comes the familiar pang of sadness at the realisation that, while she always has Peggy's full attention, her own mother usually seems distracted. Sometimes she still feels like a child, desperate for her mum's attention and approval.

Peggy kisses her cheek. 'Drive safely, sweetheart,' she says, finally releasing her. 'Text me when you get in or I won't sleep a wink.'

'I promise.'

As she sets off, she realises she didn't ask after Martin and Michael. Peggy doesn't see much of them these days, and doesn't seem to expect to. 'They're boys,' she'd shrugged last time Eleanor asked. 'Daughters are closer to their mums.' Then she'd looked uncomfortable and changed the subject. It wasn't the only time she'd said something like that. Her boys weren't interested in cooking, she said once when a very young Eleanor was helping her in the kitchen, then she'd sighed and muttered, *Your mum's so lucky to have a girl.* She said it so quietly, Eleanor wasn't sure she was supposed to hear, but she realised that it meant Peggy really did like having her around and wasn't just 'looking after' her to help out.

Eleanor: 1973, south-east London

The first Christmas after Eleanor's dad died, Peggy and Ken invited her and her mum upstairs to spend Christmas with them and the boys. Eleanor was relieved. She'd been dreading it just being her and her mum on Christmas Day. She couldn't even imagine how it would work without her dad. He was the one who carried the turkey in on a big plate and then carved long, thick slices for everyone; and it was he who poured brandy over the Christmas pudding and set it alight so that blue flames danced around it. They always turned the lights off for that bit. It was bad enough last year when he was staying at Granny Crawford's and she hadn't been able to show him what she'd got in her stocking when she woke up, but at least he'd been there for Christmas dinner and had stayed the night. He'd gone back to Granny's on Boxing Day, though, and she'd cried when he said he'd see her next week.

This year, it was much worse because she knew she would never see him again, and she kept feeling sad when she remembered things, like helping him decorate the tree. He would put the fairy lights and the tinsel on, but he always let her hang the baubles. Her mum said she could help this year, but she only let her hang the ones that weren't glass and it wasn't much fun. The worst thing was when she was making her Christmas-present list and, without thinking, she wrote the list in the same order as always: *Mum, Dad, Peggy, Grandma*. She'd bought him a shaving brush last year, and there was a tiny moment when she wondered what to get him this year before she remembered. She couldn't bear to cross his name out, so, eyes blurred with sudden tears, she tore the page from her notebook and wrote a new list: *Mum, Peggy, Grandma . . .*

Her mum seemed extra sad as it got nearer to Christmas, and on Christmas Eve, although she felt a bit guilty leaving her on her own, Eleanor couldn't wait to go up to Peggy's to help get everything ready. She spent most of the day in Peggy's kitchen, singing along to the radio – Peggy knew all the words to 'I Wish It Could Be Christmas Every Day' – and helping to make mince pies and cheese straws. Then Peggy showed her how to make Marmite whirls: after you'd made the cheese straws, you gathered up the left-over pastry, rolled it out and spread it with a thin layer of Marmite, then you rolled it up like a Swiss roll, cut it into slices and cooked them until they were crisp.

When they'd finished baking, Peggy brought out the

Christmas cake, which she'd said Eleanor could help decorate. She'd put the marzipan on and made the royal icing already, so Eleanor got to do the best bit: spreading the thick white icing over the top and sides of the cake and forking it up so it looked like snow. Then she carefully pushed silver balls into some of the peaks where they sparkled like frost when they caught the light. Finally, she arranged the three plastic Christmas trees and the Father Christmas on top, then stood back to admire her work. 'Perfect,' Peggy said, smiling. 'You've made a lovely job of that, Ellie.' After they'd tidied the kitchen and put everything away in tins, Peggy made them both a cup of sweet tea, then took a new loaf from the bread bin and, holding it in the crook of her arm, deftly sawed off two chunky slices. She spread them thickly with pale yellow butter and sprinkled one slice with demerara sugar, then put the other slice on top and cut it in two. 'There,' she said, pushing the plate towards Eleanor. 'Special Christmas treat – a sugar sandwich.' Eleanor had never heard of such a wondrous thing. The combination of the crunchy sugar crystals, the soft bread and the cool, creamy butter was delicious, easily the nicest thing she had ever eaten.

*

They started doing cooking at school one cold and miserable February afternoon. They were to bake rock cakes, and Eleanor was excited about making something all by herself. She remembered what Peggy had told her: *Read the recipe carefully and follow the instructions – you won't go far wrong.* So she read the recipe twice and made sure she didn't rush anything. She kept rubbing the butter into the flour until it 'resembled fine bread-crumbs'; she made sure she stirred the mixture until the fruit was 'properly incorporated'; she was careful to grease her baking tray properly. When she took her cakes out of the oven, they looked exactly like they did in the picture. Miss Miller pronounced them 'nigh on perfect' and gave her a gold star. She couldn't wait to get home and show her mum and Peggy, so she hurried along the icy pavements, holding her satchel steady against her hip so it didn't bounce too much and damage the newly baked cakes.

As she opened the main front door, she caught a hint of a rich, meaty smell and assumed it was coming from upstairs, but when she opened the inner door, the savoury scent enveloped her. She shouted 'Hello' as she hung her coat and satchel on the hall stand. The living-room door was open. There were no lights on, but she could see her mother lying on the settee. 'Hello, Mum,' she said more quietly, but her mother didn't stir.

She went through to the kitchen, which was warm and steamy, and Peggy was there. Eleanor immediately felt better.

'Hello, sweetheart.' Peggy was washing up. On the stove, a steak-and-kidney pudding wobbled about in a saucepan of boiling water, the lid clattering away on top as the steam tried to force its way out. Peggy wiped her hands on a tea cloth. 'That's good timing – I was just about to put the kettle on. Mum's having a bit of a rough day and the boys are at their grandma's, so I thought I'd come down and do dinner for the three of us.' She filled the kettle and lit the gas underneath. 'How was school?'

'Quite good. We did cooking – look what we made,' Eleanor held up the white paper bag containing the rock cakes.

'Ooh, what a treat! Your mum *will* be pleased! You take some plates out of the cupboard and I'll make the tea.'

As Eleanor opened the paper bag, the warm, fresh-baked cake smell rose up to greet her. She put a cake on each of the plates. Then Peggy put two of them on a tray together with cups and saucers. She smiled at Eleanor as she poured boiling water into the teapot, replaced the lid and set it on the tray. 'I'll have mine in here, pet. I've got to keep an eye on that pudding.' She pronounced it 'pud'n'.

Eleanor tried not to look disappointed.

'But I can't wait to try this.' She took a cake and turned it round to look at it properly. 'It certainly looks like the real thing.' She took a bite and looked thoughtful as she chewed, then she smiled. 'That, young lady, is the best rock cake I have tasted in all my born days!'

Eleanor felt a smile spread across her face. Happily, she picked up the tray and took it through into the living room.

'Oh, hello.' Her mother pushed herself up into a sitting position. She didn't smile. 'I didn't hear you come home.' Her hair was all flat on one side, and her face looked creased. It must be one of her bad days; she'd told Eleanor the last time she came out of hospital that she felt much better in herself, but that she still had good days and bad days.

There was nowhere to put the tray down because the coffee table was covered with things – a newspaper, her mum's cigarettes, lighter and ashtray, a cup and saucer. 'Just a tick.' Her mum leant forward, pushing her hair back off her face, and moved everything to make space.

'Where's Peggy?'

'She's keeping an eye on the pudding, so she's having hers in the kitchen.'

Her mother sighed.

Eleanor poured the tea, then chose the plate with the best cake for her mum. As she waited for her to say something, she became aware of the clock on the mantelpiece ticking loudly and the faint sound of raindrops starting to hit the window. She bit into her own cake, enjoying the way her teeth broke through the crisp outer surface and sank into the soft, slightly chewy middle. It tasted wonderful, even if she said so herself. She watched her mum break off a small piece and push it into her mouth, then take a sip of tea, her eyes cast downwards as usual.

The best rock cake I have tasted in all my born days, Peggy said. So why was her mum only picking at it? Eleanor

53

took another bite, but she suddenly felt self-conscious. When she swallowed, she found her mouth had gone dry, and the cake made a hard lump in her throat. Her mother had broken off another piece but hadn't eaten it yet and was just sitting back, sipping her tea. Eleanor was working up to asking, *Do you like it? What do you think?* but her throat had begun to ache and she was worried she might cry.

Her mum ate another tiny piece, little more than a crumb, really, then she put her cup and saucer back on the tray and looked up at Eleanor as though she'd forgotten she was there. She smiled. 'Good day at school?'

Eleanor nodded.

'Good. Do you have any homework to get on with?' She'd picked off another piece of cake, but was just crumbling it between her finger and thumb.

Eleanor felt the tears brimming. She blinked them away and cleared her throat. 'Yes, we're supposed to write up the recipe and method for making the cakes.' She waited.

'Off you go then. I'll call you when dinner's ready.'

Eleanor: the present, North Yorkshire

As the miles roll away beneath her wheels, little things keep dropping into her head: how her mum appeared to forget her name when she was seeing her off; how, when Eleanor had asked what time it was, Marjorie had looked at her watch intently. 'I can't tell,' she said. 'I can't remember how to say it.' She seemed restless, too, opening drawers and cupboards and rummaging through them. When Eleanor asked her what she was searching for, she looked down at what she was doing. 'There was something I wanted to show you. Or tell you, or something.' She paused. 'No, it's gone again.' It was the third or fourth time she'd said this in two days, Eleanor realised. And there were the phone calls, too. At first, she wondered if it was something that happened in people with Alzheimer's, some sort of tic, perhaps. But her mum seemed so lucid when she said it, the effort of trying to remember creasing her forehead every time. What could it possibly be? It must be quite important, given the urgency, the desperation almost, with which she was rifling through those papers. Eleanor is beginning to realise that she doesn't know her mother as well as she thought she did – she's still reeling from the discovery that Marjorie drove to Bakewell all those years ago to try to find her.

She bites her lip. What could her mum be looking for? And what is it that she needs to tell her? Could it really be that after all these years with so little to say between them there is finally something her mother wants her to know?

She hears herself sigh. Although she feels almost desperate to be back in Scalby, where the daily rhythms of life are familiar and soothing, she is now aware of the insistent pull of her old life. Her mother is disappearing: she has a progressive disease that will slowly rob her of her memory and reason, and then she will die. It will be too late.

It's nearly midnight when she turns into the yard and parks the Renault next to Doris. The ancient Volkswagen camper hasn't been roadworthy for a long time, but Eleanor can't quite bear to part with her. After all, Doris was her home for almost two years, and for a long time she'd had the idea that one day she'd renovate the camper and take off again. Poor old Doris – her tyres have perished and there's ivy growing over her roof and in through the passenger door. Eleanor knows her attachment is ridiculously sentimental, but Doris was what she'd needed at the time. There was something about the smallness of the living space and the fact that nothing was expected in return; she'd felt protected, as though there were arms around her. Doris was a tiny, safe place to crawl back to when the effort of a day of normal living had left her raw and drained. Her mum had no doubt tried her best, but living with her at that time had seemed impossibly painful.

She looks along the row of cabins. Only the outside lights are on now; everyone is in bed by the look of it. There's not much wind at the moment, and all is quiet. She sighs as she looks up at the clean, clear sky, where the stars shine like glass chips in the velvet darkness. She loves the landscape itself: the dark, scalloped coastline, the wind that whistles around the farm and haunts the chimneys day and night; she loves the salty North Sea air and the long, plaintive cry of the seagulls. In fact, she loves everything about her life here, especially the friends she's made. Her stomach gives a little jump as she remembers that Dylan will be coming again soon. Dylan – she loves him for all he is and all he will never be.

A quiet sadness inches through her and she realises how much she'll miss this place if she has to leave, but the reality of the situation is drumming in her head; time is running out.

*

Despite being exhausted from the long drive, she sleeps fitfully. The wind has got up again and its howling seems particularly loud. At one point she wakes with a start as something is hurled against the front of the cabin. She is just drifting off when it happens again, so she gets up and opens the door, bracing herself against the gust that nearly wrenches it from her hands. She picks up the battered wooden crate that has blown up against the door and brings it inside so it doesn't crash around the yard any more. She is about to shut the door when she glances over to the main house and sees a light on in the kitchen. She reaches for her dressing gown and slides her bare feet into her shoes. With some difficulty, she pulls the door closed behind her and then battles her way across the blustery yard to the house.

Through the window, she can see Jill standing by the Rayburn, pouring water from the kettle into a mug. She taps gently on the window and waves, then pushes the door open, allowing a gush of dried leaves into the room. 'Shit!' Jill says. 'For a minute I thought you were Cathy's ghost come looking for Heathcliff.'

'Sorry. It is a bit Gothic out there, isn't it?'

'Want some chamomile tea? Can't sleep with this din going on.'

'Please.'

Jill fills another mug and hands it to her. 'So? How did it go?'

She feels all the remaining energy drain from her body. She puts her mug on the table and slumps onto a rickety wooden chair. 'I think I'm going to go back down for a few weeks, see how bad things really are, get a few things sorted out – her paperwork's all over the place and she can't find anything. Well, she can't find what she's looking for, anyway.'

Jill sits down opposite, her hands cupped around her mug. 'Makes sense. She'll manage better if things are more organised to start with.'

'That's what I thought.' She sips her tea. 'I'd rather be here, though, especially at such a busy time.'

'Listen, we'll cope. I hate to tell you this, Eleanor Crawford, but you are not indispensable!'

'I bloody am, you know.' She smiles. 'David'll have to do all the baking. And who's going to do the accounts?'

'Ah. This is true. How long do you think you'll stay?'

She shrugs. 'I honestly don't know. I was thinking maybe three or four weeks initially, but it may turn out to be a lot longer. I suppose it depends on what happens and how she is.'

The kitchen is quiet. Jill takes another sip from her mug then wrinkles her nose. 'God, that chamomile tea is bloody disgusting.' She gets to her feet and starts opening cupboards. 'I thought it might help me sleep, but I'm sure alcohol would do just as ... Ah, here we are. Port.' She pours them each a glass. 'Cheers. So come on, tell me. Was it awful?'

'Not awful. It's mixed, to be honest. One minute she doesn't seem any different, and the next she can't remember something you said ten minutes ago. Peggy says it's worse when she's tired or upset.'

'David's mother was like that. She'd change dramatically

59

from one hour to the next, and she was definitely worse in the evenings when she was tired.'

'She gets confused, puts things in the wrong places, uses the wrong words. Each thing on its own isn't a big deal, but I keep remembering more – like when I found her trying to fry an egg that was still in its shell. The awful thing was that when I pointed it out, she looked mortified.'

Jill sighs. 'So it's getting worse.'

'Definitely. And we don't know how long she had it before she was diagnosed.' She sighed. 'So really, this is my last chance.'

'Last chance for what?'

'To try and get a bit closer, maybe. If she'll let me. I was thinking the other day, I can't remember ever being that nice to her, even when I was little. I just avoided her. She seemed to be in hospital for ages, but she was still depressed, even after she went back to work. Or she was too tired or preoccupied to talk to me. But I wasn't ever sympathetic.'

'You were a little kid. It wasn't your job to be sympathetic.'

Eleanor shrugs and takes another sip of port, surprised to find she's nearly emptied her glass.

'I feel like I don't even know her. I found out while I was down there that she'd actually come to look for me once. When I was living in Doris.'

'Really?'

'Yes, and I had no idea. I'm not sure I'd have felt any better at the time – I don't remember much about that couple of years, to be honest – but it's made me think maybe there's more I don't know. And she keeps going on about there being something she needs to tell me.'

'That's what she said when she phoned here.'

Eleanor nods. 'She keeps saying it, and when she's going through all the cupboards and drawers, she says there's something she wants to show me. It might be nothing, but she obviously feels it's important. Thing is, it's only now that it's beginning to hit me properly; she's actually losing her mind. If we're ever going to say what we need to say to each other—'

'You need to say it soon.'

'Exactly.' She rests her elbows on the table and takes the weight of her head in her hands. 'Maybe we won't ever be able to talk properly, but one thing's for sure – it won't happen if I never see her. God, I'll miss this place, especially if I end up staying for any length of time.'

'You can always drive back up now and again. It's a long way, but I do it every six to eight weeks and it doesn't kill me.'

'True.' She'd forgotten that Dawn, Jill's daughter, lives in Greenwich now.

'And there's always the phone. And email. And Skype!'

She has to smile. When they first set up this place, Jill had been so anti-technology that they could only just about get her to use a calculator. And when they first bought the old Amstrad, you'd have thought it was an instrument from hell the way Jill avoided it. Now she's practically a computer nerd.

'Also true.'

'I don't know what I'd do without Skype now Alex is living on the other side of the bloody world. At least Dawn didn't follow in her brother's footsteps – Greenwich is bad enough, but at least I get to see the grandchildren.'

Poor Jill. Alex has four kids now, and Jill has only ever seen the youngest on Skype.

'Greenwich isn't far from your mum's, is it? Perhaps you and Dawn could meet for coffee.'

'Good idea. Might help keep me sane!' She glances at the kitchen clock. It's coming up for two and her alarm is set for seven. 'I suppose we should try and get some sleep.' She stands up. 'Thank you. For the port and the chat.' She leans down and kisses Jill on the top of her head. 'Night.'

The wind has dropped a little, although, as she walks over to her cabin, she can still hear it whistling around the buildings, moving things and making its presence known. She yawns as she climbs back into bed. Now she just has to decide when to actually go. She wants to be here when Dylan arrives, but that isn't for another few weeks at the very least. She hasn't seen him for almost eighteen months. She can't wait, this time, partly because of her new hair but also because, apart from Jill and David, he is the one person in her life here that she's allowed herself to become close to, even though it's only for a summer at a time; maybe *because* it's only a summer at a time.

She thinks about the two of them taking a walk along the clifftop, perhaps scrambling down to the small, rocky beach where they sometimes look for fossils or collect seaweed for the compost. She pictures them walking along the coastline as they usually do, although it'll be chilly; windy, probably. Maybe she'll wear a scarf and whip it off later as a surprise. It's a shame the weather isn't warmer. On those summer walks, they might take a hastily gathered picnic of hard-boiled eggs, newly baked bread, strawberries and white wine, then eat it sitting on the rocks at the bottom of the cliffs, gazing out to sea and enjoying the sound of the waves lapping gently around them.

In her head, she follows the clifftop all the way along the coastline. Sometimes she goes too near to the edge, giving herself vertigo as she looks down to the dark water below, mesmerised by its beauty and the unsettling sense that it is pulling her towards it. Her heart beats faster and her breath catches as she thinks about how, when swimming, she has occasionally forced herself to stay underwater until her breath runs out, just so she has some idea of what it would be like to drown. She pushes the thought away and tries to relax into sleep, concentrating instead on the gentle movement of the waves. As she watches, the water changes: it isn't the sea any more, but a thick green pond, choked with weeds; and then she is about five years old, sitting on a vast beach in glorious sunshine. Her mother is standing a little distance away and is looking around frantically.

Eleanor shouts, 'I'm here!' She waves. 'Over here!' Her mother turns and looks at her. 'Who are you?' she says, and starts to walk away. But Eleanor can't follow her, because all around there is quicksand and if she starts to sink, there won't be anyone to pull her out. She feels the panic start to rise, but then she tells herself she is only dreaming; she makes herself feel the pillow under her head and the duvet over her shoulder; she tries to open her eyes, but still she can't make herself wake up properly. She thinks she hears the wind outside, but then realises that she's standing on the edge of the cliff again, with her back towards the sea this time. A few yards away stands a tall, faceless figure who turns towards her and suddenly, from nowhere, produces a bundle which Eleanor knows instantly is a baby. Before she can speak, the figure throws the baby towards her. Instinctively, she puts her arms up to try to catch the child, which has now slipped from its bundle of clothes and is hurtling naked towards her outstretched arms. She feels its slight weight land in her hands, the bare skin wet and slippery, but then she wakes with a start as the baby slithers straight through her fingers.

Eleanor: summer 2002, North Yorkshire

Eleanor had been into Scalby village to post a birthday card to her mum. She always felt better when she'd sent a card with a couple of lines of news inside; it eased her conscience. As she drove the old camper van back up the track, she wondered how much work she'd have to do on Doris if she were to take to the road again. She suspected the camper would need some serious attention first. She could do minor repairs herself – she'd replaced brake pads, the fuel pump, even put a new clutch in – but the gearbox was sticking every now and again and the engine didn't sound right. The cattle grid shuddered and banged as she crossed it, then she parked in the yard and turned off the ignition. As she climbed out, she realised that the sudden quiet emphasised just how noisy the engine had become.

Would she really want to live in the camper again? She wished she could remember more about that couple of years before she came here, but much of it was still a blur. She wasn't sure why she was even considering leaving this place she loved so much, but every few years her attachment to the farm, to these people who had become her family, would cause her to panic slightly, because she knew that with love came responsibility.

'Ellie.' Jill was walking towards her, squinting against the sunlight. 'I was hoping you were back. Can you sort out the new volunteer for me? He's in the kitchen. I've made him a cup of tea but I need to help David in the polytunnel, so I said you'd look after him. Do you mind?'

'Course not.' She automatically put her hand up to her head, which she'd wrapped in a black scarf, turban-style, for her trip to the village. She hated wearing wigs in summer, but, although she frequently told herself it wasn't her problem if people were offended by her bald-ness, she chickened out of displaying it when meeting someone for the first time. 'I'll sort my head out and go straight over.'

'Thanks. Seems a nice bloke. Name of Dylan. Says he's a painter – very young, early twenties, I should think.' She leant in to Eleanor. 'And quite fit.'

'Jill!' Eleanor laughed. 'You're going to have to stop lusting after young men soon.'

'Darling,' Jill said, 'I'm fifty-four, not eighty-four, and I'm only human.' She waved as she strode off to join David.

Most of the volunteers were fine once they knew, but there had been some horrible reactions over the years, so she was always aware of how she looked at a first meeting. She stood in front of the mirror in her cabin. She was wearing a white vest top which looked good with her strong, tanned arms. Her jeans were old and scruffy, but they were clean on this morning, so she didn't really need to change. She sighed as she pulled the wig properly into place. It was dark blonde, close to her natural colour, and it was quite short, so at least it wouldn't make her neck hot. She turned her head to the side. Bloody thing. It felt too tight, too noticeable; it was as if she was walking around with some huge, sharp-clawed creature clutching at her scalp.

As she made her way over to the kitchen, she tried to let the tension slip from her face. So the new volunteer was a painter. That would be useful. The cabin doors and windows all needed painting soon or they'd start to rot, then it would cost a fortune to sort them out.

Dylan was sitting at the kitchen table with a mug of tea, leafing through the volunteer information folder. He looked up when she walked in. 'Hi.' He smiled and extended his hand. Jill was right: there was something instantly attractive about him.

'Hello, I'm Eleanor.' She shook his hand; it felt smooth and warm. 'Welcome! Jill's asked me to show you around. Finish your tea first, though.' The kettle on the Rayburn was still hot, so she made herself a cup and pulled out the chair opposite. He smiled again. She wasn't sure whether he was trying to nurture a beard or he just hadn't shaved, but the sandy-red growth on his chin and upper lip suited him and made his face slightly less boyish. His shoulder-length hair was straight and smooth. It was a rich reddish brown, and the sunlight that was coming in through the kitchen window made it shine like a fresh conker. It was beautiful hair. She instinctively put her hand to the back of her head. She was glad the wig she'd chosen today was a decent one. They were all pretty good these days, though, not like the horrible things she'd had to wear when it first happened.

'Are you one of the owners, then?' he asked.

Eleanor gave a half-laugh. 'Good God, no. I can't be trusted to look after myself, never mind anything else. I'm what they call a "resident helper" – means I haven't got round to moving on yet. I was here at the start, though. Moved here with Jill and David and their children, Alex – he's got two kids of his own now – and Dawn. We set the place up between us.'

'Cool. How long ago was that?'

'Almost sixteen years now.'

His eyes opened a little wider. Then he nodded. 'Sixteen years; that's a long time. It can't be that bad here, then. How long do people usually stay?'

'Not usually as long as that! The minimum's five nights. Some people only come for a short while at first, but quite a lot stay for several weeks. They tend to come back, too – we've got quite a few regulars. Anyone who's here for more than a month gets a share of profits from the farm shop, and when things are tight here, we all do other bits and pieces – there's plenty of work in the pubs and hotels locally. No one earns a lot, but if you're living here, you don't need a lot.' She smiled and took a mouthful of tea, burning her tongue. 'How long do you think you might stay?' She tried to sound casual.

'Do I need to decide now? Because I'm not really—'

'No. No, sorry. Apart from the five days' minimum, there is absolutely no commitment, although if you can give us twenty-four hours' notice before you leave, that would be good.'

'Cool. I was thinking three or four weeks at least? Maybe longer. I'm hoping to get some work done while I'm here.'

'Well, that's kind of the point.'

'I know, sorry – I meant painting.'

'Oh, there are quite a few things that need ...' She realised immediately, but it was too late to pretend she hadn't misunderstood. *Just admit it.* She looked straight at him and smiled. 'You don't mean as in "painting and decorating", do you?'

He grinned good-naturedly. 'No, but I'm a dab hand with a three-inch paintbrush as well.'

'I'm an idiot; ignore me.' She stood up. 'Come on, I'll give you a guided tour and show you the ropes. Grab your bag and I'll take you over to your cabin first. We call them "cabins" because they weren't much more than

69

wooden sheds when we first set up, but they're actually much more robust than they sound.'

He stood to follow her, and she thought how slender and delicate his body was, without being remotely weedy. 'So you're an artist?' she said as they walked together across the yard.

'I hope so. Sort of. I'm studying Fine Art at Goldsmiths in London – mature student, obviously.'

'Goldsmiths? I grew up not far from there. Lewisham.'

He turned towards her, grinning. 'Lewisham? No kidding! That's just down the road. Do you go back there much?'

Eleanor paused. 'Not much, no. So, are you enjoying it? Your course?'

'Yeah, it feels right. I worked my arse off for a few years after I left school so I could save some money. I knew it was what I wanted to do, but I didn't have parental support, so I've kinda learnt to be a jack of all trades to support myself. I've still got some savings put away, but I don't want to rely on that, so I thought I'd do the "work for the summer" thing, you know, keep some cash flow going.'

'Good idea. We get quite a few students, though most of them are young.' She glanced at him. 'I mean, younger – really young. Not that you're not young, because you are, clearly. You're really young as well.' She heard a silly laugh escape her lips. 'I didn't mean ... I just meant ...' God, what was the matter with her today? 'Sorry, I mean—'

'I know what you mean,' he said from behind his curtain of hair, his voice full of amusement. 'I'm twenty-four.'

She felt a beat of disappointment. Not that he was likely to be interested in her anyway. What would an attractive twenty-four-year-old artist see in a bald permanent volunteer of thirty-eight, even if he wasn't fourteen years her junior?

He tipped his head towards her and she was sure she could feel his breath on her ear. 'And I'm mature for my age.'

*

Not since she first met Jill had she found herself in such easy company as Dylan. They chatted amiably and laughed often as they worked side by side all day in the sunshine. In the evenings, she found herself next to him at mealtimes, and again when they all gathered in the main living room after supper. When it was clear that they would be lovers, she told him about her hair. But instead of being taken aback, he asked if he could see. He was sitting on her bed as she removed the wig slowly with her back to him, then turned to face him. He stood up and came towards her, his eyes roving over her naked scalp. He reached up, then paused and looked into her eyes. 'May I? Do you mind?'

'Be my guest.' His palm was cool and smooth. He stroked the top and sides of her head, above her ears and below; he ran his fingers along the base of her skull briefly before cupping it in his hand. Then he held her gently by her shoulders and turned her round to face him. She closed her eyes as she felt him touch her head again. His fingertips were silky smooth as he moved them lightly over her scalp, allowing them to rise and fall with the curves, the little dips and bumps, as though he was tracing out a pattern that only he could see beneath the surface.

'Beautiful,' he whispered. 'You have a beautiful, complex, fascinating head.'

It flashed through her mind that he was taking the piss, but only briefly, because his tone made it clear that he wasn't.

'I mean it.' He stood back slightly and looked at her again. 'Your eyes look bigger without the wig, more almondy; they have more definition. Your eyebrows look better, too. So many women mess about with their eyebrows. Yours are a perfect shape, but the wig covers them up.' He stepped behind her. 'I love that I can see tiny veins under your skin. I keep thinking if I look hard enough I might be able to see what's going on inside your head.'

'I bloody hope not.' She laughed. No one had ever said anything so flattering about her head. Most of the men she'd slept with accepted it, but one or two had touched the bare skin and jumped back as if they'd been burnt. They'd apologise, but the whole thing was ruined anyway. One man actually asked her to put the wig back on before they had sex. 'Or a scarf, if it's easier.

Just something to cover it up.' She'd opened the door and told him to get out. 'And if you see me around the place during your stay,' she'd added, 'do not come *anywhere* near me.' Then she'd slammed the door quickly so he wouldn't see her tears.

Dylan was looking at her again. 'There's a little bit in the middle that you probably can't see. It's right here,' he said, touching it with his fingertip. 'It's so smooth that the light bouncing off it makes it look as though there's a diamond or something sparkling there.' He smiled. 'Eleanor, you have a beautiful head. I'd love to paint it sometime. Will you let me?'

'I suppose so. If you really want to.'

Then Dylan kissed her, and kissed her again. And she found herself kissing him back and, for the next hour or so, she felt more desirable than she had for a long time.

They slept briefly, then woke and made love again in the darkness, more languorously this time, before falling back into a deep sleep.

*

The following morning, she woke early as the sun forced its way through the thin curtains, warming the cabin and bringing out the comforting smell of the wood. She turned to face Dylan. He was a beautiful-looking man, and for a moment she lay there, admiring his peachy complexion, the elegant length of his spine, the dark brown hair which glinted copper in the sunlight.

She wriggled closer and allowed herself a few more moments of comfort with her cheek resting against his bed-warmed skin.

Her whole body ached, but it was hardly surprising, given the size of the drainage ditch they'd dug yesterday. It was a good ache, born of honest hard work. Dylan stirred, then turned over, put his arm around her and kissed her nose without opening his eyes. 'Morning,' he mumbled. Then his face creased as he shifted position. 'Ow, ow, ow. God, I feel like I've been trampled by a herd of cows.'

'You'll live. And anyway, it's Sunday, so at least it's an easy day.'

He opened one eye. 'Can we lie in bed reading the Sunday papers? Or are we going to spend the morning shagging and then go for a quick pint before the roast beef and Yorkshire pud?'

'Neither, you silly arse. For one thing, we rarely take whole days off here, only afternoons and evenings – I did warn you. For another, the Sunday papers are too bloody expensive, and for another, Jill and David are vegetarian, so you can forget about roast beef!'

'You're no fun any more,' he grumbled playfully, throwing the covers back and sitting up. He winced as he did so. 'Ooh, my back! You were more fun in the old days,' he said, 'back when we first met.'

She smiled. 'Tuesday was a lifetime ago. Come on, you lazy sod. Just because it's going to be an easy day doesn't mean you can waste half of it lying in bed.'

'You're a cruel woman, Eleanor; a cruel woman.' He stood up gingerly, then stretched his slender limbs. 'I'm not built for this sort of work, you know. I'm more the delicate type – better at painting flowers than planting them.'

'You're more likely to be planting cauliflowers than pretty flowers. You do realise that, don't you?'

'Yeah. I suppose so.' He yawned and rubbed his scalp vigorously. 'So, what is this "easy day" of which you speak? Please tell me it doesn't involve digging, or the words "drainage" or "septic".'

'No, we'll be working in the polytunnels today, thinning out lettuces, and so on.' She loved working in the polytunnels. The warm, moist air; the smell of green things growing. Sometimes, when she'd finished the day's work, she would take her book and sit there feeling all that new life around her. She pulled on jeans and a t-shirt, then chose a sunflower-yellow scarf and wound it around her head. 'I'm going across to the kitchen. Can you collect the eggs on your way over? You'll find a little basket just outside the coop.'

'Okay.' Dylan yawned again and began pulling on his clothes.

It was Eleanor's turn to set out the breakfast things on the huge kitchen table, so she laid out the bread she'd baked earlier in the week – a mix of white and wholemeal loaves and a big basket of rolls – as well as honey from the hives, a cluster of the assorted preserves that Jill made every year and, of course, eggs from the hens that wandered all over the site.

'Morning,' Jill said. 'Ooh, nice scarf! Not often we see you in bright colours.'

'I know.' She smiled. 'But I feel bright yellow today.'

*

'When you said you wanted to paint my head,' Eleanor said, 'I thought you meant you were going to paint a picture!' She was sitting on a wooden chair in front of the cabin window while Dylan knelt on the floor next to her, his paintbox open beside him. He had one brush in his hand, another behind his ear. 'I did, but only after we've got you all flowered up.' He tilted his head to one side thoughtfully. 'I'm going to go mainly for pinks and purples with a touch of yellow. And greens, of course, for the leaves, and perhaps a sort of vine. Okay?'

'Okay.' It felt slightly absurd, letting him decorate her head with painted flowers, but she couldn't deny she was flattered. It wasn't every day that someone found her head attractive.

'Ready? Brace yourself.'

'Ooh, it's cold,' she said, flinching.

He laughed. 'Don't be such a baby.'

She could feel the brush, cool and wet, sliding down towards the nape of her neck and then flicking around in little whorls. 'It tickles.'

'Ignore it; think about something else.' He picked up the damp flannel and she felt him wiping just above her ear. Then there were more flicks and whorls, then firmer strokes and blobs. She pursed her lips and tried to concentrate on not wriggling or laughing. She could feel his warm breath on her scalp and soon she found herself relaxing as he continued to work away. 'Right,' he said after a while, 'I'll do the vines now.'

She sat upright as she felt the cold brush snake across her skin, over, down, round and up, then more tiny flicks. 'Fronds,' he explained.

He sat back on his haunches. 'There,' he was clearly pleased with his work. 'Hang on, let me show you.' He sprang to his feet and lifted the round mirror off the wall. 'Well?' he held it in front of her. 'What do you think?'

She turned her head sideways. 'It's—' She automatically put her hand up.

'Don't touch!' He made to grab her wrist. 'Sorry, but it'll smear if you touch it too soon.'

She nodded again. 'It's ... it's really colourful.'

'You don't like it.' He looked crestfallen.

'No, I do. It just ... takes a bit of getting used to, I suppose.'

He sighed, sitting down heavily on the bed. 'You can wash it off – I won't be offended.'

'No,' she said, 'I don't hate it; and I'll certainly make an entrance when we go over to the house for dinner.' She forced a smile. It was a pretty design, and if she'd seen it on some fabric, perhaps, or even wallpaper, she'd probably like it. Poor Dylan. He was so excited a couple of minutes ago, and now she'd burst his bubble. 'Hey, let's take a photo of it!' she said.

He looked up at her, the brightness returning to his eyes. 'Really?'

'It'd be a shame if there was no record of it. I mean, it's bound to wear off, isn't it?'

Dylan nodded. 'Yeah, it's not that long-lasting; it'll be gone by next weekend.'

Or sooner if I get caught in the rain, Eleanor thought, looking hopefully out of the window.

Eleanor: the present

Despite having been up in the middle of the night drinking port and talking to Jill, she wakes before her alarm goes off. She trudges over to the kitchen, collecting a basketful of eggs on the way. She makes toast and coffee, boils a couple of the eggs and takes it all back to the cabin on a tray. Before she can change her mind, she calls Peggy to tell her she's thinking of coming down for a while.

Can she afford to take all that time away from the farm, Peggy wants to know? Will she still get paid? Will they hold her job? Peggy has never quite understood how the farm works. Eleanor assures her there's nothing to worry about on that score, though privately she wonders how long her meagre savings will last if she ends up staying in London for more than a few weeks. Peggy tries to sound as though it doesn't matter one way or the other, but the relief in her voice is unmistakable;

SUSAN ELLIOT WRIGHT

so much so that Eleanor feels guilty she hasn't suggested it sooner.

'Have you telephoned your mum yet?' Peggy asks.

'I thought I'd ask you what you thought first. In fact, I was wondering if perhaps you'd mention it, see what she says. I don't want to come barging in on her life if it's going to make her feel uncomfortable having me there.'

Peggy doesn't say anything for a moment. Then she speaks softly. 'Eleanor, she'll be pleased, I'm quite certain of that. She doesn't always show it, but you mean a great deal to her, you know.'

Eleanor's throat tightens. Sometimes she is still surprised by the sudden threat of tears, the way her throat constricts painfully as she swallows them back. Deep down, she knows her mother loves her, but it's more of an intellectual knowledge than a tangible sense of being liked. She remembers asking Peggy one day whether she thought it was possible to love someone without liking them. Peggy had laughed and said it must be; she'd cut out her heart for Martin and Michael, but they were both little sods and they didn't half get on her nerves. Eleanor would have been about eleven at the time, so the boys must have been thirteen or fourteen. She can't remember now what had made her ask the question, but she remembers feeling none the wiser afterwards, because at that point, the twins came in and Peggy spontaneously flung her arms around them, laughing as they shook her off in disgust and then stomped moodily up the stairs to their room. She remembers thinking how she wouldn't dare behave like that with her mum, and she envied the boys – it was clear that they felt safe, that they knew their mother would still love them even when they behaved badly.

Eleanor paces the cabin with the phone, the floor-boards creaking beneath her as she moves. 'I suppose you're right,' she says. 'I should speak to her myself.'

'I think that would be best. You'll feel better, apart from anything else.'

'Okay, I'll call her in a minute.' She pauses; she feels like a child again, relying on Peggy to tell her the truth. 'Peg, what if she doesn't want me there?'

'Trust me, sweetheart, she will.'

*

Throughout her life, Eleanor has felt guilty for being more comfortable with Peggy than with her own mother. But Peggy has always been so much easier to talk to, so much more approachable. It was Peggy who'd helped her through most of the difficult points in her childhood and teens; occasionally, she'd secretly pretended that Peggy was her mum and the twins were her brothers. And then she'd felt guilty for that, too, and for not turning to her mother more when she needed help or advice. But on the other hand, if it weren't for Peggy, she'd quite likely have started her periods with very little idea of what was going on.

She'd gone upstairs one Saturday morning to see if Peggy and the twins were going swimming. She loved going to Ladywell pool on Saturdays, but her mum hated swimming, so she wouldn't go with her.

'Sorry, Ellie,' Peggy said. 'I meant to tell you – the boys are at their grandma's for the weekend. They won't be back till tomorrow night.'

'Will you come, then?'

'I can't, pet, I've got my Visitor this week.'

'Oh, I didn't know you had a visitor. Who is it?'

'No, I don't mean an actual person,' Peggy chuckled. 'I meant I've got the Curse.'

Eleanor was mortified.

'You do know all about that, don't you?'

She knew that the Curse involved bleeding from your privates, and was to do with having babies, but that was about it.

Peggy put her hand on Eleanor's arm. 'Ellie, it's nothing to be embarrassed about. Has your mum explained to you about periods?'

Reluctantly, Eleanor shook her head. 'I know a little bit, but I was home with a cold when they did it at school.'

Peggy sighed. 'You should know all this before you start at secondary, if nothing else,' she muttered. 'I'll have a word with your mum, get her to explain it all before it's too late.'

'Can't you . . . I mean, would you be able to tell me?'

'It's not really my place, sweetheart.'

'*Please*,' Eleanor said.

Peggy hesitated. 'No, I think you should ask your mum. She'll explain.'

But although Eleanor rehearsed in her head what she'd say, she couldn't bring herself to ask her mother about something so personal. In the end, she pleaded with Peggy to tell her what she needed to know.

Peggy sighed. 'I suppose your mum's got enough on her plate, all things considered. All right. Sit down.'

And she'd explained. She made Eleanor giggle by holding up a sanitary towel by the loops and swinging it from side to side. 'We used to call them "mouse hammocks",' Peggy said, laughing. She showed Eleanor how to fix the loops to a sanitary belt, then she wrapped one in a paper bag and told her to keep it with her all the time, along with a couple of safety pins, which she could use to fasten it to her knickers if needs be.

Three weeks after her thirteenth birthday, Eleanor started her periods in the middle of a maths lesson in a stomach-hollowing gush. She fixed a sanitary towel as she'd been shown, but instead of feeling confident and grown-up, she felt awkward and conspicuous, as though she was walking around with a bath towel rolled up between her legs. When she got home, she changed into clean knickers, screwed up the bloodied ones and pushed them to the bottom of the dustbin. The school nurse had given her two more towels, but she'd need more soon, so she'd have to ask her mum. Her stomach went over at the thought of talking to her mother about such an intimate thing; so instead, she told Peggy.

'Have you told your mum? Peggy asked.

'No,' she admitted. For some stupid reason, she felt

as if she was about to cry. She swallowed 'I just ...' She pretended to cough to disguise the tears that had sprung to her eyes.

Peggy looked at her for a moment. 'Would you like me to tell her?' she asked gently.

Eleanor nodded.

When she came home from school the next day, her mum came in from the garden, took her gardening gloves off and put them on the draining board. 'How's everything?' she said. 'Are you feeling all right?'

'Yes, okay. Why?'

'I ... I just wondered. I've left something for you in your room.' She looked as if she expected Eleanor to say something. After a moment, she continued, 'Well, if you have any questions, or if you need anything – a hot water bottle, or an aspirin, anything – you must come and ask me, all right?'

'Okay,' she mumbled, and turned to go downstairs to her room.

'Ellie?' Her mum's voice was soft. She didn't usually call her 'Ellie'. And she sounded a bit sad. 'You will ask me, won't you? If there's anything else you need to know?'

Eleanor said, 'Okay' again and scurried downstairs before her mum could say any more. On her dressing table were two packs of Kotex, a little box containing a pink sanitary belt and a booklet called *Becoming a Young Woman*. She didn't really need it now, but at least her mum had got it for her. She went back upstairs to say thank you, but as she stood looking through the kitchen window, watching her mother pulling up the weeds that had taken hold after the wet summer, she lost her nerve. She didn't see her mum again until dinner time, and that didn't seem appropriate, then the next day slipped past and somehow the time never felt quite right. But every month from then on, two packs of Kotex appeared in the bottom of her wardrobe like magic.

*

How confused will she be today, Eleanor wonders as she waits for her mum to answer. But Marjorie's 'Hello?' is strong and confident. Relief. 'Hello, Mum, it's me,' she says, adding quickly, 'Eleanor.'

'Hello, Eleanor,' her mum says immediately. 'Did you have a good drive back?'

'Yes, thank you. Listen, I've been thinking. What with this horrible Alzheimer's thing, well, I was wondering ... I thought it might be a good idea if I were to come and stay with you for a few weeks. Help you get things organised so you don't have to rely on Peggy all the time.'

Marjorie doesn't say anything. So Peggy was wrong; her mum still doesn't want her around. 'It was just an idea, anyway.'

There's a pause, then her mother says, 'That's awfully kind of you, darling. And I have to admit, it would be a help. Peggy's marvellous, you know, absolutely marvellous, but I think she's getting a bit fed up with me. When do you think you could come?'

It's a moment before she takes it in: her mother *wants* her to come; she sounds happy about it. 'In a couple of weeks, I should think. There are a few things I need to do here, but probably before Easter.'

'Before Easter. Right you are, darling. I'll write that down. Now, what was it . . . ? There was something I had to tell you but I can't for the life of me . . .' There's a pause. 'I expect it'll come back to me at some point.'

Eleanor

A few weeks, she tells herself, that's all. Just to get some idea of what arrangements might need to be made in the future. She deliberately doesn't bring much with her – clothes and toiletries, obviously; her laptop, a few books – but once she's unpacked, she wishes she'd brought more, just a few more things to dot around her bedroom to make it look a little less bleak.

For the first few days, her mum seems fine. So normal that if you didn't know, you wouldn't guess anything was wrong, and she begins to wonder whether she really needs to stay for more than a few days. But then she walks into the kitchen to find Marjorie diligently putting the contents of her handbag into the freezer.

'Mum, what are you doing?'

'If you don't put it all away as soon as you get back from the shops, it'll start to thaw, then you can't use it, you see.'

'You've already put the shopping away, Mum. You did it as soon as you came in – I helped you unpack everything.'

Marjorie looks at her blankly.

'Look.' She reaches into the freezer and takes out her mum's purse. 'This isn't shopping.' Next, she hands her the frost-covered foldaway shopping bag she always carries, then her hairbrush, her powder compact, half a tube of fruit gums.

Marjorie looks bewildered at first, then she bites her lip. 'I'm sorry, darling. I suppose it's this Alzheimer's.' She shakes her head. 'I knew it would make me forget things, but I didn't realise it would make me so stupid.' She sounds so distressed, Eleanor's irritation evaporates.

'You're not stupid, Mum. It's the illness. Come on.' She gently pushes the freezer door shut. 'Go and sit down and I'll bring you another cup of tea.'

She thinks about something Peggy said the other day: 'I know it sounds awful, but in a way I think it'll be easier for her when her brain goes completely. Then at least she won't feel daft every time she makes a mistake.' Eleanor had been shocked. Of course she knows that Alzheimer's is progressive, that her mother's brain function will gradually deteriorate. But hearing it put so starkly had jolted her. She thinks again about Marjorie needing to tell her something; she has always hoped that eventually she and her mum might be able to talk properly about what happened, and about the grief they have in common. But maybe there won't be an *eventually*.

*

Her bedroom is cold, and the bed feels slightly damp when she gets into it. It's a good half-hour before she feels comfortably warm, and she's only just dozed off when something wakes her with a start. She lies still and listens; there's movement upstairs. She gets out of bed, pulls on a jumper over her pyjamas and goes up. Her mother is sitting hunched over the kitchen table in her thin, sleeveless nightdress, weeping quietly. She isn't wearing any slippers and the room is freezing.

'What is it?' Eleanor says. 'Whatever's the matter?'

'I . . . I forgot, Peg,' her mum says without looking up.

Eleanor is about to correct her but stops herself. She takes her jumper off and drapes it around her mother's shoulders.

'I woke up, and I saw he wasn't there. He often gets up, you know, when we've had words. I know we haven't been getting on.' A fresh wave of tears overtakes her. 'I mean, we *hadn't*. I couldn't get over it, you see. Because there was more to it. I think I must have blanked it out. Poor Ted. He was very patient . . .'

'Mum,' she speaks as gently as she can. 'What do you mean, *more to it*? What did you blank out?' She can feel her heart thudding hard in her stomach. 'Mum? When

89

you say you couldn't get over it, are you talking about what happened to Peter?'

'I wasn't being fair to him, Peg.'

'Mum, it's me. Eleanor.'

Marjorie turns to look at her, but her eyes are teary and vacant. Then her bottom lip trembles. 'I forgot, you see. Just now, when I woke up. I thought I'd come up and talk to him, try and explain. I thought he'd be sitting here with a whisky, like he used to, but he's gone, isn't he? I forgot.'

Maybe what she's talking about has nothing to do with Peter. 'Yes, Mum. Dad died quite a long time ago. But what did you mean just now? When you said there was more to it?'

'He wasn't even forty when I lost him.' The tears are rolling down her face. 'How could I have forgotten such a thing? To think I wouldn't let him come home after all that had happened. And it was my fault, you know.'

'What was, Mum?'

'No one thought it at the time, but I know it was my fault.' And then she makes a long *ohhh* sound that is so sad, so full of anguish, that Eleanor can hardly bear it. She wants to know more and is tempted to probe, but this is not the time. 'Come on, Mum,' she says gently. 'Let's get you back to bed.'

Marjorie, September 1972

There had been a spectacular thunderstorm overnight, but it didn't seem to have cleared the air at all, and Marjorie could feel the pressure building behind her eyes. She'd considered calling in sick this morning, but it was only a headache; maybe she could just work it off. The ward was stuffy and airless and her head was thumping so much that she was actually glad to get out into the sluice room, where at least no one was moaning or fitting or needing to be fed or toiletted.

She and Ted had argued again last night, and she wondered whether that was what was making her head scream.

He'd still been awake when she went down to bed, even though she'd sat up reading *Woman's Realm* from cover to cover until gone midnight, then spent ages checking all the doors were locked, writing a note for the milkman and putting out the milk bottles. She'd tiptoed across the floor to switch off the light, and when she pulled the chain in the bathroom, she put the seat down and sat on it to muffle the sound of the flush. The bedroom light was off and she could hear him breathing. She was glad she'd let Peggy talk her into buying one of the new continental quilts – if she'd had to untuck sheets and blankets she'd almost certainly have disturbed him. Gingerly, she lifted the corner of the quilt and slipped in beside him, careful not to let her arm touch his. She lay on her back and closed her eyes but as soon as she began to feel her muscles relax and her breathing slow, she felt him turn towards her, and then the warmth of his arm as he curled it around her waist. Instinctively she turned towards him, desire fluttering in the base of her stomach. But if she put her arms around him, if she responded in any way and then couldn't continue with what she'd started, things could be worse than if nothing had happened at all. So she stayed still, trying not to hold her breath. Perhaps he wasn't properly awake. Perhaps, as long as she didn't move, he'd drift off again. But then he whispered, 'Marjie? I've been waiting for you.' She sighed. 'I'm sorry, Ted.' She felt his body tense, and then he turned over so abruptly and violently that she bounced on the mattress. He snapped the bedside light on and sat up, throwing back the covers and swinging his legs round to the floor. 'We can't go on like this,' he said. 'At least, I can't.' He turned to face her. 'You've changed. You always used to enjoy—'

'Of course I've changed, after what happened.'

'No, no; that doesn't explain this. It happened to me too, remember? But I still love you, and I still want to show you in the same way I always have. You might even find it a comfort.'

A tear leaked out of the corner of her eye and rolled down her face into her ear.

'It was one of the things I loved about you, how you were never coy, how you weren't afraid to enjoy sex.' He sighed. 'Do you remember how we used to spend whole days in bed when we were first married? And even before, that time at Keston Ponds. It was you who started it, for heaven's sake. I never tried to force you. Never tried to get you to go to bed with me before you were ready, not like some men would have.'

Keston. That was the night she lost her virginity, three days before their wedding. And when she walked up the aisle on her father's arm, her stomach gave a thrilling little flip as a memory of that night skipped into her mind. At that exact same moment, Ted, standing at the altar, turned round and beamed at her. As she paced regally towards him in her long white dress, she had to shake away a vivid image of the two of them lying on a blanket in the back of Ted's Morris Traveller, sharing a cigarette and giggling like children because they felt so naughty – they'd actually done it and they weren't even married yet! And she remembered her certainty that nothing could possibly go wrong. They loved each other, and she had never in her twenty-one years experienced such pure and utter joy.

'And now you make me feel like some insensitive brute because you've decided you don't like it any more.'

'It's not that, Ted, honestly. It's just that I find it difficult to ... relax, I suppose. And it doesn't seem right that I should be enjoying myself, not after what happened to Peter.'

'Marjie,' he said, his voice quieter now, more gentle. 'We've suffered a terrible tragedy, but everyone deserves to be happy again. You have a right to some pleasure, you know.'

Oh, but I don't, she thought. I truly don't.

She was so lost in thought that she hadn't noticed the ward sister coming into the sluice room behind her. 'Are you feeling all right, Marjorie?' It still felt odd, being addressed by her name, even though she was only a nursing assistant now.

'It's only a headache, Sister.' Marjorie straightened up and tried to make herself look efficient as she finished dealing with the umpteenth bedpan she'd had to wash that morning. Usually, the sights and smells didn't bother her, but today she found herself fighting repeated waves of nausea as she worked. Maybe Ted was right; maybe she shouldn't work on this particular ward, not after Peter. But on the other hand, at least she was doing something to make the lives of these poor wretches more tolerable. Some of them were so bad it was hard to know whether they were aware of anything that was being done for them, but despite what some of the other nursing assistants said, Marjorie preferred to assume that they felt every touch and understood every word. Just because some of them were mute didn't mean they didn't hear the jokes and insults being bandied around above their poor misshapen heads.

'You've gone a shocking colour,' Sister said. 'Maybe you should sit in my office for five minutes if you're feeling a bit queer.' Her voice had a concerned tone that Marjorie hadn't heard before. No one here knew about her breakdown, so that couldn't be the reason. Everyone at home – Ted, her parents, even Peggy – they all talked quietly, as though they were afraid they might accidentally wake her from a deep sleep. And in a way, she did feel as though she was stuck in some sort of sleep world, still wading through a nightmare she couldn't quite pull herself out of.

'Thank you, Sister, but I'll be all right in a minute. Perhaps I'll just . . .'

One of the other nursing assistants came in with a used bedpan and Marjorie felt herself sway as she glimpsed the contents, then she became aware of Sister's arm on hers.

'We can't have you collapsing on the sluice room floor, Mrs Crawford – you'll be in the way. Come along and sit down for a few minutes until you feel better.'

But even after sitting down, she didn't feel better. In fact, she started to feel worse, and in the end, Sister let her go early, which was virtually unheard of. It was raining heavily when she stepped outside. The nausea was still washing over her and her head was pounding.

She craved fresh air, but not the polluted, grey air of Lewisham High Street. She made her way back through the corridors and out of one of the service entrances at the rear of the hospital, and then she slipped through the gap in the fence so that she was in Ladywell Rec.

The grounds were almost empty apart from a few determined dog walkers who trudged stoically through the wet fields, huddled into their anoraks. Rain falling on grass seemed less aggressive, somehow; softer. The grass was a vivid, emerald green and for a moment, she thought absurdly that it was too green, too healthy, too vibrant and alive. She walked alongside the Quaggy, which was running high and fast today. She shuddered. The last time it was this high was just before those terrible floods the same year Peter died. Within a few hours, the whole park was a lake, and she'd got home to find Ted bailing the water out of the back door and her slippers floating along the hallway. She looked down at the brown-tinged froth that was building up along the edge of the riverbank as the current surged along, sweeping twigs and leaves as it went. Her nausea was beginning to subside, but the pounding in her temples was becoming even more intense. She needed to get home, make a nice cup of tea and lie on her bed. At least she wouldn't have to cook as soon as she got in. Eleanor was going to her friend Karen's after school because Karen's mum was taking them to Brownies, picking them up afterwards and dropping Eleanor back later. Ted would be home, but he wasn't expecting her until gone six, so he'd be sprawled in an armchair, snoozing under a copy of the *Evening News*.

By the time she was back on the high street, she was drenched, her hair dripping and her coat wet through. She crossed over and started to walk up Mount Pleasant Road, cursing herself for not picking up her umbrella that morning. Rain was running down the gutter towards the main road like a miniature river. Even her sensible lace-up work shoes couldn't cope – her right foot was completely wet and water was beginning to seep into the left one, too, and she could feel cold splashes up the backs of her legs. When the house came into view, she felt her body relax. Soon, she'd be rubbing a dry towel over her hair while the kettle boiled. Maybe she'd treat herself to a couple of slices of hot buttered toast as well.

She let herself into the house quietly, not because she was trying to catch anyone out, but because her head felt so fragile that even the sound of the door closing was like an explosion in her skull. Her coat was dripping, so she hung it on the hook, then spread a newspaper underneath to stop it making a wet patch on the carpet. She took her shoes off, saw that her tights were spattered with mud and took those off too, then she started to make her way downstairs. When she heard the low moaning and whimpering, her first thought was that maybe Eleanor had been sent home from school, poorly. Was it this morning she'd complained of tummy ache? But surely they'd have telephoned her at work? Just as

SUSAN ELLIOT WRIGHT

she realised it didn't sound like Eleanor, the moaning stopped. Marjorie sensed the sudden change in the air. There was at once an intensity, a sort of crackling static, like last night just before the thunderstorm. And she knew. She wasn't sure how she possibly could know, only that she did. She turned the handle and pushed open the door and there they were, a ludicrously contorted tangle of flesh. She tried to take in what she was seeing. The girl, vaguely familiar, her hair a wanton mess; Ted's naked back, pale and slightly pudgy. At least he wasn't on top of her, so perhaps she should be thankful for small mercies. The look on their faces was one of absolute horror, and for a split second she had to fight down a perverse urge to laugh.

The three of them looked at each other for what seemed like a very long time, then the girl closed her eyes and put her hands over her face. Marjorie stood on the threshold, part of her wanting to grab the little trollop's hands and pull them away from her eyes so she could see her properly, another part wanting to use her own hands to blot out what she was seeing. Then it came to her; this was Jeannette, the girl who'd helped out with Eleanor while she was in hospital, the one who'd answered Ted's advert. They'd needed someone for when Ted and Peggy were both working. Marjorie had only met her a couple of times.

Ted sat up, carefully arranging the continental quilt so it still covered his lower half. 'Marjorie . . .'

'Don't, Ted.'

She closed the bedroom door calmly and went back upstairs, her headache miraculously fading into the background. She walked into the kitchen without knowing why, then went back out into the hall and put her bare feet into her wet shoes. She could hear movement from downstairs. They were out of bed, getting dressed, perhaps. Of course they were getting dressed. They weren't going to come upstairs naked, were they? She didn't want to be here when they came up, clothed or otherwise. Maybe the girl would leave through the downstairs door. But she didn't want to see Ted anyway, not yet, so she opened the front door and went back out into the rain, not even bothering with her coat.

She walked quickly, wanting to put as much distance as possible between herself and what she had just seen. There was a number 54 at the bus stop; she started to run, but the conductor reached up and rang the bell. She was on the verge of tears; why would nothing go right? But then the conductor, who was standing on the platform, appeared to take pity on her. 'Hurry up, love.' He rang the bell again four times to stop the driver moving away. 'Room for one more inside.'

She got off in Blackheath Village and started walking, quickly finding herself up on the heath. It was too muddy to walk on the grass so she kept to the paths, feeling better for moving forward, putting one foot in front of the other. The rain was easing off now, and soon she was walking through a persistent drizzle which somehow seemed just as wet as the earlier downpour. A blanket of grey dampness shrouded the heathland; she paused by the pond across the road from the Hare and Billet and stood looking into its dark waters. There was a movement to her left, and she saw a blackbird struggling to pull a worm from the sodden earth. She looked back at the water. She'd found her husband, her dear, patient, beloved Ted, in bed with another woman. It was difficult to take in, but it had actually happened. She could feel the tears building up inside her, but for some reason she couldn't quite let them go. There was a flutter to her left as the determined blackbird gave one last tug and half of the worm came away in its beak, the other half glistening and pulsing in the ground.

Her back was beginning to ache from standing still. She began walking again, and when she glanced at her watch she was surprised to see that she'd been out for over an hour. She felt sick at the thought of going back into the house. The girl would be gone, of course. Ted would be apologetic. But what happened now?

*

Ted was sitting at the kitchen table with a glass in his hand and a half-empty bottle of whisky in front of him. Surely that had been a new bottle yesterday? He looked older, wearier. She had an absurd desire to put her arms around him. He looked up. 'I didn't hear you come in.'

'Obviously,' she said with as much contempt as she could muster.

He dropped his gaze again. 'I meant just now.'

She took a breath. 'How long have you been fucking her, then?'

He flinched; he actually flinched.

'Oh, Marjorie, that's such an ugly word.'

She grabbed the kettle and filled it from the tap, water splashing all over her hands, before slamming it onto the stove and lighting the gas. She realised she was shaking now. 'What would you prefer? How long have you been screwing her? Banging her?'

'Shut up!' Ted jumped up from his chair, making her start, but then he sat down again and put his head in his hands. 'Oh, God, I don't ... I don't know what to say.'

'You can start by telling me how long it's been going on.'

'It was ... it's never happened before. She came round to drop off something for Eleanor – a book she'd promised her, or something – and we got talking. She started telling me how she'd fallen out with her mum and then she got upset. I ... put my arms around her to comfort her and ... I don't know how ... I didn't mean it to happen, it was just—'

'You didn't mean it to happen?' It came out as a shriek. 'So you're trying to say you fucked her by accident?' There was something vaguely comforting about using this language she'd always abhorred. 'You accidentally fucked her in our house? In our *bed*?'

'Marjorie, please. I'm sorry, truly, truly sorry. It was wrong. I'm not trying to justify—'

But before he could finish she was standing over him, hitting him, pounding him with both fists. Tears were there now, but she didn't want Ted to see them so she shut her eyes tightly and pummelled away, with no idea which bit of him her fists were making contact with.

The next minute, she seemed to be a long way away from what was happening. She'd experienced this before, that strange sensation of standing outside of herself, watching her own actions from a distance. Part of her was appalled; another part was fascinated. The only person she'd ever deliberately hurt before was herself. She had a brief memory of standing in the kitchen that day, pulling at her own hair then banging her fists against her forehead over and over until Ted managed to get hold of her and pin her arms to her sides. She remembered seeing Eleanor hiding under the table, her terrified little face peeping out from under the tablecloth.

'For Christ's sake,' Ted said now, bringing her back to the present. 'Calm down!'

She carried on hitting him, lashing out wildly.

'Marjorie!' He managed to get to his feet and grab her wrists. 'Now listen.' He struggled to hold her still. 'I've done a bad thing and I'm sorry. You'll never know how sorry. You can hit me if it makes you feel better, but not until you've listened to me. I didn't plan it, it just happened – no, don't interrupt me. You can hit me again in a minute, but I want to talk to you first.'

She opened her eyes as she felt his grip on her wrists loosen. She could see the helplessness in his face, the redness around his eyes. He'd been crying. She felt herself sag, all her energy suddenly draining away as though someone had pulled the plug out. She allowed him to lead her to a chair. He sat opposite her and poured more whisky into his glass, and then held the bottle up and raised his eyebrows in query.

She flicked her head. 'Tea. I just want a cup of tea.'

He got up. 'You stay there,' he said quietly. 'I'll make a pot.'

His cigarettes were on the table, so she reached across and took one while he made the tea. He poured them both a cup and brought it to the table, then picked up the whisky bottle and poured some into his tea before topping up his glass. 'Are you sure you won't have a drop? It'll settle your nerves.'

She fought down a bubble of anger and shook her head.

He looked defeated, deflated. 'Marjorie, you have to believe me; I've never even looked at Jeannette in that way. I just ... it was stupid, thoughtless. Oh, God,' he muttered. 'What have I done?' She thought she heard a crack in his voice. 'I'm sorry.' His face was stricken. 'How can I make it up to you? I do love you, Marjorie, you know that, don't you?'

She did know that, deep down. And she loved him. But she couldn't say it, for some reason. Hadn't been able to for a long time.

'Can you forgive me?'

'I don't know, Ted.' She felt a familiar sense of panic

at the way her thoughts were tumbling round in her head, all coiled up and tangled. Every time she tried to straighten the thought out and read it, it just got jumbled up with all the others again. 'I can't think properly.' But she wanted to make sure she remembered this clearly so she could decide how to deal with it. She made herself think the words: Ted has gone to bed with another woman. She called up the image and there it was, that intimate shape of the two of them together, Ted looking over his shoulder, caught out – guilty, guilty, guilty. And her, Jeannette. At least she had the decency to look guilty, too, and upset and embarrassed. But even with those emotions rippling across her face, even with all those things that should have weakened her somehow, what Marjorie noticed was how thoroughly healthy and alive the girl looked, almost as if you could see her heart pumping and the red blood running through her veins. The girl was young, but Marjorie wasn't that much older, and back in the days when she'd paid attention to her appearance, she'd have said she was no less attractive. But where the light in her own eyes had dimmed four years ago, Jeannette's eyes shone. And where Marjorie's lips had settled into a thin, pale line, Jeannette's were full and pink. Jeannette, Marjorie realised, was a normal, properly functioning woman. That was what Ted wanted, and he'd taken it. She looked at the pot of tea he'd made, and for a fraction of a second she imagined herself throwing the hot tea into his face; Jeannette's too. Briefly she allowed herself the luxury of picturing them both screaming, blinded by the scalding liquid, properly punished. But Jeannette was gone, and she doubted she'd see her again. When she looked at Ted, she could no longer tell whether she loved or hated him. Again she had the sense of watching herself from a distance as she stood up, stretched her arm out across the table and swept everything onto the floor. Ted jumped up, pushing his chair back and knocking it over. 'Marjorie, for God's sake,' he yelled.

But she was on her way out the door again, hot tears pouring down her face. She paused on the threshold before slamming the front door as hard as she could. It was only once she started walking that her arm began to sting and she realised that it was she who'd ended up scalded.

Eleanor: the present, south-east London

Eleanor leans back and stretches. Thank goodness she can do some of the farm's admin while she's down here. The work feels like a refuge, and of course it means there's some money coming in. There's more admin than ever now, mainly due to the expansion in the number of courses they run. It used to be just yoga and aromatherapy massage, but this year they're offering fourteen different courses, so Jill is paying her to keep on top of the accounts, advertising, social media, and so on. It's a connection with the farm, too.

She glances down at the corner of the screen. It's gone four, and she's been working at the kitchen table for almost two hours. Her mum was watching an old film, but it must have finished by now. She saves the spreadsheet and shuts down the laptop. The living-room door is open but Marjorie isn't there. 'Mum?' She finds her in the dining room, frantically rifling through one of the sideboard drawers. There are papers everywhere. Again.

'What are you looking for, Mum?'

Marjorie whirls round as though she's been caught doing something she shouldn't. She looks at the paper-strewn carpet and a puzzled expression settles around her features. 'Do you know, darling, I'm awfully sorry, but I'm not entirely sure. It'll come to me, though. It always comes to you if you don't try to think about it, doesn't it?'

'Come on, let's go through it together again, and perhaps you'll remember.' Every time this happens, she wonders whether, even if they can't find what Marjorie's looking for, there might be a photograph or a letter or something that'll jog her memory. But she gives only a cursory glance to each item Eleanor passes to her before dismissing it with a wave of her hand.

'Mum,' Eleanor ventures, 'do you think ...? Look, don't take this the wrong way, but you know you said you're looking for something you wanted to tell me about, or show me?'

Marjorie nods, her eyes still focused on the clutch of papers in Eleanor's hand.

'Well, do you think it's possible that it's something you've already shown me or told me about, and that you've just forgotten? Alzheimer's can make you forget things, can't it? And it can make you confused.'

Marjorie looks blank.

'Do you think it might be that?'

'Might be what?'

'The illness, Mum. The Alzheimer's.'

Marjorie looks as though she's struggling to follow, then she nods. 'Yes,' she mutters. 'They said I've definitely got Alzheimer's.'

*

They are having lunch upstairs with Peggy today. Peggy's kitchen is bright and modern, with cream-painted units and an oak worktop; red and yellow mugs hang on hooks under the wall cupboards and there are colourful prints on the walls. The room is directly above Marjorie's kitchen, but it feels warmer and sunnier somehow, even though the window is smaller.

'You look tired, pet,' Peggy says. 'How are you coping?'

Eleanor is slicing a French stick and piling it into a basket while Marjorie sets the table in the other room. 'It's not too bad, but she's definitely getting worse. Yesterday she trailed around after me all day for no apparent reason, and she still says she's looking for something. I went through it all again with her this morning, but—'

'Nothing?'

She shakes her head.

'It might just be the Alzheimer's, like you said. It's a complicated disease. And not easy to deal with.' Peggy stirs the leek and potato soup she's made for lunch. 'I bet you're missing your friends up North, aren't you?'

'A bit.' She was thinking about the farm the other night as she sat with her mum, watching *The King's Speech* for the third time since she's been here. She bought the DVD after Peggy told her Marjorie loved it so much they'd seen it twice at the cinema in Greenwich. She doesn't mind watching television, but when she's sitting with her mother in that vast, chilly room, she finds her thoughts straying to evenings on the farm. Usually people gather in the kitchen just before seven. Sometimes the helpers are so tired they're practically nodding over their food, but often, once the dishes have been cleared away and the kitchen tidied, people drift to the main sitting room to drink David's home-made wine and chat, read or maybe play an instrument. It always used to be guitars or mandolins, but these days there are a lot of ukuleles appearing out of rucksacks. Dylan might join in with his treble recorder, a deeper, richer-sounding version of the horrible squealy thing most people expect – there are often groans when he mentions the recorder, until they hear him play, that is.

'I miss Jill and the others, but I think it's the day-to-day life I miss more. More than I thought I would, actually. And I had a text from Jill yesterday to say she's had another postcard from Dylan – you know, the guy I told you about who comes every year? He says he'll be there in two or three weeks.'

'Well, you must go back and see him, of course.'

'No; I can't leave you to look after her twenty-four hours a day, it's not—' She stops as Marjorie walks back into the kitchen.

'I'm only in the next room, you know. There's no reason at all why you shouldn't go back to your farm, Eleanor.' She sounds completely normal again. Sometimes it's as though the old Marjorie has popped in for an hour or two and replaced the one with Alzheimer's.

'That's nice of you, Mum, but I'm not sure you—'

'For goodness' sake. I don't need constant supervision like a naughty child.'

Peggy puts her hands on her hips. 'Then stop bloody well behaving like one, you cantankerous old cow.' And they both end up laughing. Eleanor feels a familiar pang. Why can't she laugh with her mum like that?

'You need to recharge your batteries,' Peggy continues. 'Having you here these last few weeks has done me a power of good, never mind your mum. I'm sure we'll be all right for a while.'

'Let's wait and see,' Eleanor says. 'I don't need to dash off immediately, whatever happens.'

*

During the afternoon, as she listens to her mum and Peggy chatting easily and normally, she begins to day-dream about going back up to Scalby. Even if it's only for a couple of weeks. Her fingers are almost tingling with the desire to get back to the digging and planting. She longs for the fresh green smell of things growing, the feel of the crumbly soil between her fingers. Not to mention the clean, salty sea air, the walks along the clifftop and the sound of the water lapping at the rocks below. And, of course, Dylan. Has he ever seen her with any more than a few sparse patches of hair? She doesn't think so. It's long enough to comb now, although she only does so tentatively. Perhaps she'll go and see Gaby again when she goes back.

Much later, after they've had their evening meal and Marjorie has gone into the living room to watch television, Eleanor refills the plastic medication organiser and clicks down the lids. The only trouble with this system is that it relies on the user knowing what day it is. She only realised a week ago that her mum had been forgetting to take her pills, and since then she's been putting them in her hand three times a day and watching her swallow them. She sighs, wondering if it's really feasible for her to go back to Scalby.

Marjorie isn't in the living room, though the TV is still on, showing yet another old episode of *Friends*. 'Mum?' She opens the dining-room door and there is her mother, on her hands and knees in front of the sideboard once more. The three drawers are open and their contents spread out on the carpet around her. Eleanor catches sight of old utility bills and shopping lists among the photos, cards, envelopes and scraps torn from notebooks.

'Mum, what are you doing?'

Marjorie doesn't look up but shakes her head. 'I'm

trying to find ...' She opens one of the cupboard doors and begins pulling things out. 'There's something I need to show you.'

Eleanor kneels down beside her. 'Mum,' she says gently, 'we went through everything in here this morning.'

Marjorie sits back on her heels, a wad of papers in her hand. She flicks through them, then tosses them back on the pile and picks up another handful.

'Mum, are you sure it isn't something you've already told me about?'

Marjorie picks up more papers and sifts through those, too, then she looks at Eleanor, her expression suddenly puzzled. 'Do you know, I can't ...' She looks down at the papers in her hand. 'It's something I've been meaning to tell you. Or there's a letter to give you. Something I wanted you to read, I think.' She flicks her head in irritation. 'Shit. I can't remember. Why can't I bloody remember?'

Eleanor does a double-take. Her mum never swears, not even mildly. She catches a glimpse of one of her postcards among the papers. She still can't get over the fact that her mum and Peggy drove up to Bakewell that time. *She wanted to talk to you.*

'Mum,' she hands her the postcard. 'Could it be ...? I'm just wondering if what you wanted to tell me, was it anything to do with, you know, when I was living in the camper? Or when I was little? When Peter died?'

Her mum's expression is blank, as though she has no idea what Eleanor is talking about. But then her eyes focus and she says, 'Better to *not* remember, that's what they said. And now I *can't* remember.'

'No, Mum, it was me they were talking about when they said that. Your memory's bad because you have Alzheimer's disease.'

'Mr Greenfield; he said we'd all get over it sooner. He came highly recommended, you know.'

The psychotherapist; she remembers him. Remembers sitting on a wooden chair in the huge, high-ceilinged 'consulting room' in his expensive-smelling house in Sevenoaks. *We take the bad memories and we put them in a dustbin, then we put the lid on tight so they can't get out. Do you see, Ellie?*

She remembers her four-year-old self being indignant at his familiarity in calling her 'Ellie'; she remembers the deep red colour of the new Start-rite sandals she was wearing, and staring down at them to avoid the shame she felt crawling around in her stomach when Mr Greenfield looked at her.

But even though she now knows more or less what happened that day, she still can't remember it properly, not like she should be able to. All she has are vague details from her mother, who's never been clear about it herself, and odd scraps of memory. Being in the garden, the heat of the sun on her head and shoulders, her mum's stricken face; *You stupid, stupid child.*

'He was a modern thinker, you see; we followed his advice to the letter, your dad and me; to the letter. Your father said there was no point in going to all that trouble to see one of the top chaps and then not follow his advice.'

'Mum,' Eleanor says as softly as she can, the way she would talk to a frightened animal to avoid startling it. She doesn't want to jolt her out of this train of thought. 'I know you did what you thought was best, and I'm not angry about it any more, but maybe we could talk about ...'

But her mum has turned her attention back to the papers. She grabs something from the top of the pile, rapidly runs her eye over it then tosses it aside, then does the same again, her movements increasingly frantic. She can't possibly be taking in what she's seeing.

'Mum, you just mentioned Mr Greenfield, and how he—'

'Shush. There's something I need to find ... need to tell you ...'

It's too late; the moment has gone. Disappointment comes crashing down so hard she has to make a conscious effort not to snap. 'Yes, but *what*, Mum? You keep saying this, but what is it you need to tell me?'

Marjorie doesn't look up from her task. 'I'll know it when I see it. I'm sure I will.'

Eleanor: summer 1982, south-east London

Eleanor had been going out with Ray Bedford for three months, and while she wasn't madly in love with him, she liked the fact that he was keen on her and wasn't the least bit embarrassed about holding her hand in public or even kissing her in front of his mates. But he was a year older, and already at university. Although he was still living at home, he was used to coming and going more or less as he pleased, so she felt stupid and childish having to tell him she had to be home at ten thirty.

'No,' her mother said. 'Half past eleven is much too late, certainly on a school night.' Eleanor was drying the dishes as her mother washed. She banged the casserole lid she'd just dried down on the table. 'I'm nearly eighteen,' she said. 'And after that I can do what I want.'

'Not while you're living in this house, young lady.' Her mum wiped her hands on a tea towel. 'And mind you don't smash that dish – it's Pyrex.'

'I don't even *want* to live in this house,' Eleanor yelled, throwing the tea towel onto the table. 'I hate it here. It's dark and messy and cold.'

'Messy?' Her mum put her hands on her hips and nodded towards the mound of school bag, jacket and shoes which Eleanor had dumped on the kitchen floor when she'd come in a couple of hours ago. 'I wonder why that would be?'

'I didn't mean that, I meant ... Oh, never mind.' She grabbed the jacket and put it on, then picked up the shoes and bag. 'I'll put these on the stairs and take them down when I get back. I'm going up to Peggy's.' She opened the door.

'No, you're not, not tonight.'

Eleanor did a double-take. 'Why not?' She asked, genuinely wondering if Peggy was working late and she'd just forgotten.

'No,' her mum said, 'you can stay in with me for once.'

'But ... It's *Sapphire and Steel* tonight.'

'We do have our own television, you know.' Her mother's voice had an edge to it now. 'I'm getting a bit fed up with this. You spend more time upstairs than you do down here.'

'What's wrong with spending time upstairs?'

'Nothing, if it's in moderation.' Her mum started busying herself around the kitchen, putting things back in cupboards and straightening things on the worktop. 'But you're up there far too often. They must be sick of the sight of you.'

'Peggy likes me going up to see her. She said so.' She had to resist a childish urge to add, *So there*.

'Well, I'm sure Ken would rather you weren't there quite so often when he comes home from work, especially as he has to work away so much.'

She was about to argue when it flashed through her mind that Ken had asked her once or twice whether she had any revision to do. Maybe she did overstay her welcome sometimes. 'But I told Peggy I'd be up at seven. She'll wonder where I am.'

'I'll ring up and tell her.' Her mum filled the kettle and switched it on. 'You can stay here tonight for a change. It won't kill you. And you won't be able to go running to Peggy every five minutes once you start university, so you might as well get used to it now.'

'But that's not until October. Why should I have to stay here every bloody night? It's not fair.'

Her mum stopped what she was doing and turned towards her. 'Eleanor, that's enough! You are not going upstairs this evening and that is final.'

She wished she'd never got into this stupid row now, because not being allowed to go up to Peggy's was worse than not being allowed to stay out with Ray for another hour on Thursday. She searched her brain for something hurtful to say, and then, before she'd really considered it, she heard herself shout, 'I wish it was you who'd died instead of Dad!' Her mother flinched as if she'd been struck, and Eleanor braced herself for the retaliation. But instead, it was as though her mother suddenly deflated, as though someone had taken all the air out of her. She sank down onto a kitchen chair, leant forward with her elbows on the table and put her head in her hands. 'So do I,' she murmured without looking up. 'I've wished it more times than you could credit.'

Eleanor was frozen; she hadn't meant to say something so cruel, but now that she had, why wasn't her mother screaming at her? The effect of her words was unexpected, and now she didn't know what to do or say. Suddenly her mother looked paler, smaller, more fragile. The more she tried to think of something to say, the more her throat seemed to tighten. She felt as if she couldn't move. Her mum looked up at her. 'Your dad was a good man, Eleanor. He wasn't perfect, which is why we separated, but no one's perfect, are they? Certainly not me, and maybe not even you.'

'Mum, I know I'm not perfect.' She had to swallow then, because she was afraid she might cry. 'I'm sorry. I shouldn't have said what I said.'

Her mum nodded. 'We all say things we shouldn't say; and sometimes we don't say things we should say. And then . . . sometimes it's too late to put things right.'

'I'm sorry,' she said again, but her mum was looking down at the table.

Finally regaining her ability to move, she crept quietly from the room and made her way downstairs.

That night, as she lay in bed, it played over and over in her head: *I've wished it more times than you could credit*. She couldn't ever remember having been quite so frightened by something her mum said. She stayed awake for a long time, wondering whether her behaviour was really so dreadful that her mother wanted to die.

*

The next day, her mum wasn't home when she got in from school, and she knew Peggy was on early shifts this week, so she went straight upstairs to tell her all about the argument.

'It's not to do with you, Ellie,' Peggy said, 'I promise.' She put two mugs of coffee on the table. 'It's made with hot milk, for a treat.' She sat down opposite. 'You see, your mum still gets depressed sometimes. She probably always will do, and that can make her say things that, well, things she hasn't properly thought about.'

'But does that mean she really wishes she was dead?'

'No, I'm sure she doesn't. She told me you'd had a row, and that she'd been a bit upset about you coming up here so much.' Peggy sighed. 'The thing is, Ellie, she's still your mum, and naturally she wants you around. She sometimes feels bad about having had to send you to me so often when you were little.'

'But that's what's so unfair. She sent me to you every day when she didn't want to look after me, but now she's trying to tell me I'm not allowed to see you. And I'm practically a grown woman.'

There was a beat before Peggy replied, and Eleanor felt a ripple of foolishness for saying that.

'I'm sure she's not saying you're *not allowed*, pet. And it wasn't that she didn't want to look after you; she was very poorly, you know. Hardly surprising, I suppose.' Peggy's eyes fluttered as though she was embarrassed, or she'd been caught out.

'What? What was hardly surprising?'

'Oh, nothing. Just that ... she had a lot on her plate, that's all.' She took a couple of sips of her coffee. 'Your mum went through a lot.'

'Yes, but *what*?'

Peggy sighed. 'It's not for me to say, sweetheart.'

'But—'

'Your mum didn't want ... Well, she's one of those people who doesn't like to dwell on unhappy things; it's her way of coping. Bad things happen to everyone at some point, and we all cope in different ways. Your mum, she prefers to try and forget.'

'I wish you'd tell me what it was.'

Peggy looked uncomfortable. 'I shouldn't even tell you this, because as I say, it's not my place to talk about your mum's ... about private things. But one thing I do know is that she felt guilty about your dad. She blamed herself for not making it up with him before he passed away. She still loved him, you know.'

She remembered the night her dad died. She'd been sitting at this very table, eating fish fingers and spaghetti hoops with Peggy and the twins. Her parents were living apart at that point and her dad was staying at Granny Crawford's, but she'd assumed he'd be back any day. She heard Peggy's front door open and her mum running up the stairs, then the kitchen door burst open and her mum was there with her car keys in her hand, breathless and looking scared. 'Can you hang onto her for tonight, Peg? I've got to go to the hospital; Ted's been rushed in, apparently. His mum thinks it might be his heart. She's probably overreacting but you know how much he's been drinking lately, and the smoking . . .'

'Don't worry about anything, Marje. We'll look after Ellie, won't we, boys? She can stay the night if necessary.'

The boys groaned, but only in a jokey way.

'Off you go,' Peggy said. 'Ring me if you can. And don't worry about Ellie.'

'Thanks, Peg.' Her mum turned, and with barely a glance at Eleanor, disappeared back down the stairs and out into the night.

Eleanor had been so happy to stay at Peggy's that the following morning she'd completely forgotten why she was there until she went into the kitchen. She'd smelt the cigarette smoke from upstairs, but in the kitchen it was so thick it made her cough. Her mum and Peggy were sitting on opposite sides of the table, their packs of cigarettes and lighters resting next to them and an overflowing ashtray in the middle. They both looked up when she came in. Her mum's face was blotchy and red and her eyes were puffy. Peggy looked as if she'd been crying, too.

'Eleanor,' her mum said in an odd, squeaky voice. 'I am afraid I have some very bad news.'

Even now, when she thought back to that night, she remembered the icy-cold feeling that had quickly filled her stomach and the way her knees had gone all watery so that she couldn't stand up.

Shivering a little at the memory, she took another mouthful of her coffee and sighed. 'I wish I hadn't said what I said.'

Peggy reached for her hand. 'You didn't mean it, sweetheart. And your mum knows that.' She gave her hand a squeeze.

'I wish I remembered more about my dad. I know he used to call me Ellie-belly, and he used to bring me home a packet of Opal Fruits on Friday nights. I can't remember what he looked like, though. There aren't any photos around.'

'I think she put them away. She'll have one somewhere – you should ask her.'

Eleanor, summer 1982

She was supposed to be going to the pictures with Ray tonight, but she wanted to look for a photo of her dad while her mum was at work so she phoned him and cancelled. She could have just asked her mum. It was a perfectly reasonable request, after all. But she didn't want to risk another argument after that row they'd had the other night about her staying out late. She made up a Vesta chow mein for her dinner and ate it while she watched *Top of the Pops*. She wasn't that keen on Bananarama, but watching them made her wonder whether to dye her hair so it was proper blonde instead of her boring mousy colour.

After she'd eaten, she opened the sideboard and took out the small suitcase she knew was full of photos. It was slightly bigger than the one she'd had when she was little, the one she'd once packed in preparation for running away from home. She was probably six or seven at the time, and she remembered carefully packing her Sindy doll, a clean vest and knickers, a brand-new brushed nylon nightie that Peggy had bought her for Christmas, a lemon curd sandwich and her purse containing the money from her piggy bank – six shillings and four-pence. She'd even walked out of the house, but Peggy had been looking through her kitchen window at the time and spotted her trotting down Aldworth Grove, the road that ran between their one and the next. Peggy had persuaded her to come back home and give it another week before deciding whether she wanted to leave for ever. She'd agreed only after Peggy promised not to tell.

As she opened the case, the familiar old photograph smell wafted up from inside. Some were still in their Kodak envelopes with the negatives, and there were some in cardboard frames, but most were loose. A few were in colour, but a lot of them were black and white, taken before her dad died. As she leafed through the many pictures of her mother as a young woman, and her mum with herself as a toddler, she remembered her father explaining that there were hardly any of him because he was usually the one behind the camera. There was one of her and her mother sitting on a blanket in Greenwich Park, the Observatory high on the hill in the background behind them. There were a couple of shots of elephants and chimpanzees – a day at the Safari Park, she vaguely remembered. She was sure her mum and dad's wedding photos were in this suitcase last time she looked, but they weren't here now. She lifted out a pile and set it aside. At the bottom there were snaps of Granny Crawford, and Eleanor and her mum at the seaside, but all of these were taken when she was tiny. In fact, it seemed that the only later pictures of herself were the school portraits in cardboard frames, where she was smiling, gap-toothed, hair in bunches, trying to do as the photographer instructed. There must be others somewhere, surely? And where were the wedding photos?

Her mother's bedroom smelt fusty, with a hint of apple blossom talcum powder. Clothes that had been worn were piled on the chair in front of the dressing table, and there was a pair of tights on the floor. She hesitated at the threshold; she felt awkward entering this room, as though she was being watched by some secret camera. It was never very light down here, but it was a bright day and she could see dust motes spinning in a ray of sunshine that was coming in through the bay window. The sun illuminated the layer of dust on the dark wood dressing table with its three mirrors. She hated the three mirrors and what they reflected – three snooping daughters. She went straight to the built-in cupboards that stretched across the back wall. The bottom shelf was stacked with sheets, blankets and pillowcases, but the other shelves were a bit of a jumble, with boxes of face powder, various bits of costume jewellery and a bunch of dusty red plastic tulips mixed in with assorted handbags, gloves and neatly folded scarves. She moved things carefully so that it wasn't obvious they'd been disturbed. Towards the back were two shoeboxes, which she lifted down. The first was stuffed with papers – her old school reports, her mum and dad's marriage certificate, a letter to her dad about National Service. She closed the lid and opened the other box – bingo! The wedding photos were right on top. Her dad, smiling and clean-shaven, didn't even look like her dad in these pictures. But as she thought about him, she realised she couldn't remember exactly what he'd looked like.

Lots of these shots were similar to those in the suitcase upstairs, but mostly taken earlier. There were a few of her mum as a young girl. She'd forgotten how pretty she'd been with her clear, almost luminous skin and long, dark blonde hair. There were quite a few pictures of her mum and Peggy as student nurses, then one of them dressed up and ready to go out, by the look of it, both laughing, both wearing full-skirted dresses, hats and light-coloured gloves. Her mum looked so happy. There were two snaps of Peggy and the twins when they were babies. She looked so young in these, and a little bit frightened. There was one of Ken with the babies, too – even he looked about twelve here, though she knew they were both eighteen when the twins were born. Then she found one of her dad looking more like she remembered him. He had the beginnings of a moustache and his hair was sticking up at the back as it always did if he forgot to use Brylcreem. He had his arms folded and was leaning back, half sitting on his motorbike and squinting at the sun. She'd forgotten her dad had a motorbike; she remembered her mum saying they used to go out for long rides to the coast when they were courting. She closed her eyes for a moment so she could picture him. What would life be like now if her dad were still alive, she wondered?

She slipped the photo into the pocket of her jeans and was about to put the lid back on the box when she noticed another cardboard frame near the bottom. It was a professional portrait of her parents in evening dress: her dad, handsome in a dinner jacket and bow tie, her mother, looking not unlike a young Princess Margaret, in a long, dark-coloured evening dress and with a double strand of pearls around her neck. They were both smiling softly at the camera; her dad had his hand on her mum's shoulder, and she was touching his hand with her own. They looked more recognisably themselves than in most of the others. It was nice; why hadn't she seen it before? After only a moment's hesitation, she decided to take it for herself. The fact that her mum had put all her wedding photos away up here meant she probably didn't intend to look at them any time soon. Slipping her fingers inside the cardboard frame, she took hold of the photograph and tried to slide it gently out. It would be smaller and easier to conceal in her room without the frame, which she'd throw away somewhere later. She expected it to just slip out, but it snagged on something. Another, smaller picture had got stuck to the back of this one and was caught in the frame. Carefully, she peeled it away. It was a snap of her mum and herself in the living room. They were sitting on a stripy settee, her mum holding a baby wrapped in a shawl, a smiling Eleanor wearing a tartan pinafore dress and with her hair in bunches holding the baby's hand. Her mum was smiling here, but she looked tired and thin, as though she'd been ill. The baby was tiny, although you couldn't see its face. She wondered vaguely whose it was. The other children she remembered being around when she was small tended to be older than her, not younger. She put the photograph back; she'd been kneeling too long and she was getting pins and needles in her legs. But something made her pick it up again.

Back upstairs in the dining room, she sat at the table staring at the snap with the little baby. It had unsettled her, and suddenly seemed of much more importance than having a photo of her dad. Her mum would be home from work any minute, and her stomach felt as though there were eels swimming around in it. The palms of her hands were sticky and she could feel sweat trickling under her armpits. She wouldn't admit to having gone through things in her mum's bedroom; she'd swear blind she'd found this in the little suitcase which was still open on the table. She heard her mum's key in the door and took a deep breath.

'Eleanor? Are you in?'

'In the dining room,' she called back. 'I was just looking through these,' she said when her mum came in. She held up the picture of her parents in evening dress. 'You look lovely in this, can I keep it?'

Her mum looked at the suitcase. 'Oh, I didn't realise ...' She looked at Eleanor. 'What made you get these out?'

'I've not seen them for ages. And ... and to be honest, I wanted to find a photo of Dad. I didn't want to ask you in case it upset you.'

Her mum sighed and shook her head. 'Oh, Eleanor.'

'Would it be all right if I kept this one?'

'Of course. You could have asked me, you know. I wouldn't have been cross.'

Say it now, Eleanor told herself. *Before it's too late.* 'And by the way, whose baby is this?' She held up the snap.

The colour drained from her mum's face. 'Where ... ?' Her voice was barely a whisper. 'Where did you get this?' She snatched the photo from Eleanor's hand.

Eleanor had never seen anyone's skin go so pale so quickly. Her mother's face was ashen.

'It was ...' She pointed towards the box as she started to speak, but she couldn't say any more, because the idea that had twinkled for a fraction of a second in the back of her mind was starting to flash again. 'Mum? Whose baby is it?'

Eleanor, the present

If the sitter works out, Eleanor should be able to go back to Scalby for a while, even if she has to come down again in a couple of weeks. Part of her is desperate to be there. It's May, the sun is shining, there's work to be done on the farm, lots to be planted or thinned out. Things will be growing already; little green shoots bursting with life will be stretching their leaves up through the rich soil. And Dylan should be there by now, although Jill hasn't texted to say so.

The sitter, Jenny, is a semi-retired nurse who doesn't want to stop working completely. She enjoys sitting with people with dementia, she tells Eleanor; it's usually straightforward, and all she has to do is make sure they remember to eat their dinner and take their medication – and that they don't burn the house down, of course. Eleanor stays in the house for the first couple of nights, but everything goes swimmingly. Jenny is easy to get along with and has a reassuring air of capability about her.

On the third night, Eleanor goes to Bromley to see a film, but sleeps through the whole thing. She hadn't realised just how exhausted she was. When she gets back, Peggy is there and the three of them are playing cards in the kitchen and giggling like schoolgirls at something Peggy said. They seem to be getting on so well that Eleanor feels distinctly surplus to requirements.

On the fourth night, she decides to take advantage of the warm evening and go for a walk. After half an hour or so she finds she is almost in Greenwich, so she carries on towards the river then walks along the Thames path up to the Trafalgar Tavern. She orders a large glass of Sauvignon blanc and, as it's still fairly early, manages to bag the table by the huge bay window directly overlooking the river. At high tide, the water laps at the brickwork a few feet below, making it the most coveted table in the pub. She remembers crowding around it on summer nights with the girls from school, long before the days of identity cards, and drinking vodka and lime by the open window as they watched the boats going up and down and fireflies dancing in the warm breeze. She'd taken all this for granted when she was a teenager; but then, you never really appreciate the place where you grew up until you've left it.

As she sips her wine, she watches the sunset, just as she does on summer evenings back on the farm. While the streaks of colour in the sky change from orange to apricot to pink, she feels a curious mix of affection for this place where she was born, and a profound homesickness for the place where she's lived for so many years; the place that, despite her years of reluctance to admit it, she thinks of as home.

Over the last few days, being here has felt less onerous. Maybe it's because she knows she's going back soon; or maybe it's to do with the tiny chinks appearing in her mum's armour of silence about the past. They've talked about her dad a few times now, and Marjorie even mentioned Peter once, although she clammed up again as soon as Eleanor asked a question.

She finishes her drink and sets off back along the path, down towards the town centre, past the restored Cutty Sark, or as Jill calls it, 'that boat in a car park'. It's one of the many tourist attractions she's never been to. People are always impressed to hear that she grew up in London. They seem to imagine that she must have spent every spare minute visiting museums and art galleries, going to the theatre or watching the changing of the guard. In reality, she rarely did any proper 'London' things when she was growing up here. She went to the Tower of London once, but that was on a school trip. Grandma Crawford took her shopping in Oxford Street a couple of times, and to the theatre to see *Fiddler on the Roof* on one of her birthdays. It made her cry and she was embarrassed because she couldn't explain why she was crying, but instead of saying so, she'd turned away, unable to answer, and her grandmother had been cross and thought she was being ungrateful.

She looks over the wall down to the river. There is

a faint salty-sea smell in the air tonight, so different to how it was when she used to come here in her teens. The Thames was a nasty brown chemical soup back then, and rumour had it that if you fell in they'd have to pump your stomach. These days, it's possible to catch salmon in its waters, but Eleanor still has a horror of falling in. There is something about deep water that both repels and attracts her, and even now she feels a certain fascination which draws her towards it like iron filings to a magnet. Perversely, she steps up to the railing, slides her fingers around the cold, rusty metal and leans so far over that everything but the deep, dark water is outside her field of vision. This has the effect of concentrating her fear, exposing her fully to it and making her stomach go over and over so that her whole body ripples with adrenalin-filled terror. Don't let go, she has to tell herself; stand up, stand up.

A brightly lit pleasure boat makes its way upriver, the wash causing the water below to rock and chop, twirling its frosting of discarded styrofoam cups, plastic bottles and other unidentifiable detritus. It jolts her out of her frozen state. She forces herself to straighten up and waits for the nausea to subside before setting off again, her legs and hands slightly shaky as they always are when this happens. She often finds herself doing the same thing near the sea at home, and on a rare day out at Whitby last year she'd been drenched and nearly knocked off her feet by a heavy wave when she'd stood much too close to the slipway at high tide, despite the signs, which were pretty clear: EXTREME DANGER FROM WAVE ACTION DURING ROUGH WEATHER. Her relationship with water is a complicated one, which is why she has always found herself unable to stay away from it, despite the compulsion to pit herself against it being almost overwhelming. Away from water, she never even thinks about it. She certainly doesn't feel suicidal, not now, and even during that terrible time when she'd briefly considered ending her own life, her chosen method would have been gentler, more cowardly. Pills and whisky, probably, with the hope that she'd just go to sleep and sink into blissful oblivion. But maybe water is her destiny; maybe that is how she will die.

*

Lost in the past, she barely notices the walk back, and it is almost completely dark by the time she arrives. Her mum is in the living room, watching one of the David Attenborough DVDs they got from the library. She appears mesmerised by the weird and wonderful sea creatures that billow and undulate across the screen, accompanied by a haunting underwater soundscape to which their movements seem perfectly choreographed.

'Hello, Mum,' Eleanor says. 'Everything okay?'

At that point, Jenny appears in the doorway. Her hair is dishevelled and there are two livid scratches down the side of her face. 'We've had a bit of an eventful evening, I'm afraid,' she says. 'Any idea who Jeannette is?'

Eleanor, the present

As she sits on her bed, waiting for Jill to answer, Eleanor catches herself absent-mindedly fingering her hair, probably subconsciously testing it for stability. She stops immediately, terrified that the very act of touching it will cause it to loosen and fall.

'Ellie! At last. How's your mum?'

'Bit of a nightmare, to be honest. Listen, I don't think I'm going to be back this weekend after all.'

'Oh, no. Did the sitter not work out?'

'No, she's great, but we had a bit of a drama last night and I think I need to be here until I can be sure everything has calmed down.'

'Shit, what happened?'

'She went for the sitter – started hitting her in the face.'

'Oh my God!'

'Quite. I'll tell you more when I see you, but anyway, she – Jenny, the sitter – is being really good about it. Says

135

SUSAN ELLIOT WRIGHT

it's one of those things that happens sometimes and not to worry about it.'

'Well, then, if she's not worried . . .'

'Yes, but . . .' She sighs. 'She doesn't seem too bad today, I suppose. But then she's often fine in the mornings, so it's hard to tell.' She can still hear her mum moving around in the kitchen upstairs. 'Maybe I'm overreacting. Oh, Jill, I just don't know what to do for the best.'

'I wish I could come up with a solution.'

'I feel as though I'm being pulled in two directions. I really, really want to be there, but I know I should be here. Part of me *wants* to be here.'

There is a pause before Jill says, 'Are you sure it's not just duty?'

'I don't know.' More than once, Jill has asked Eleanor if she loves her mother, and it's not an easy question to answer. It's definitely there, but it's a love that she has often pushed down in order to protect herself. 'Maybe it's partly that. But she's clearly grateful that I'm here, and that in itself . . .'

'Well, make sure you look after yourself, that's all. You sound like you need a break – and soon. Why not come back for a few days and then go down again if you need to? We're longing to see you.'

'The feeling's mutual. God, Jill, I'm not sure I can do this. Not indefinitely, anyway.'

'We'll all have a good old chat about it when you come; see what we can come up with.'

Eleanor is about to say there isn't another option,

but instead she just agrees. Jill's mother walked out on her and her two younger sisters when Jill was thirteen, leaving a fiver under the biscuit tin – which was empty – and a note saying sorry, but she wanted her life back. Jill managed to look after the other two for almost three weeks before social services came along and took them all into care. It was several months later when their father and his new wife finally turned up to claim them. Hardly surprising that Jill has a dim view of filial duty.

'By the way, has—'

'Not yet,' Jill says. 'I reckon he'll be here at some point in the next couple of weeks, so see if you can time it right!'

Eleanor pretends to be indignant. 'I might have been going to ask if David has fixed the roof on number six yet.'

'But you weren't, were you?'

Eleanor smiles. 'No.'

'There you are, then. Go on, see what you can do.'

'I'll think about it. I'll see how it goes this week, and I'll give you call.'

When she goes back upstairs, her mother is pouring milk onto branflakes that she's spread out over a dinner plate. 'Mum, what are you doing?'

'I'm having my … what's it called?' She looks at the plate. The milk has splashed over the edge and onto the table. 'The morning one.'

'Breakfast,' Eleanor says. 'But you've already had your breakfast. We had it together, about half an hour ago. You were supposed to be clearing the things away.'

137

Marjorie looks at the box of branflakes and the carton of milk. Slowly she picks up a jar of marmalade and stares at it, then puts it down again. 'I thought ... oh dear ...'

'It's all right, Mum, don't worry. Here, look.' Eleanor takes a bowl out of the cupboard. 'If you're still hungry, you need to put your cereal and milk in this. So it doesn't spill.'

Marjorie looks at the mess on the table and shakes her head. 'No, no, I'm not hungry.' She sighs. 'It's getting worse, isn't it?'

She seems so defeated and vulnerable that Eleanor almost wants to put her arms around her. 'We'll talk to the doctor again soon,' she says softly. 'Try not to worry. Why don't you go down and get dressed while I put this lot away?'

Her mum nods and goes downstairs, appearing again five minutes later dressed in an ancient baggy jumper with holes in the sleeves and men's trousers tucked into wellington boots, of all things. Eleanor's heart sinks. 'Oh, Mum, what on earth ...' She stops herself. 'Tell you what, shall I come and help you choose some clothes?'

Marjorie looks down at herself with a puzzled expression.

'Sorry, Mum, but what you're wearing ... it's not really appropriate.'

Marjorie tuts and moves towards the French doors. 'I haven't gone completely doolally, you know. These are my gardening things, for heaven's sake. There's so much needs doing out there. I might as well take advantage while the weather's good.' And in no time she's out of the French doors, down the steps and striding across the lawn towards the shed.

*

The sideboard has been emptied and there are papers strewn all over the table and floor again. Marjorie hasn't even been in here this morning, so she must have done this during the night. What on earth is she looking for? Eleanor sighs and start picking things up, pausing occasionally to read one of the postcards she sent all those years ago. Many bear no clue at all as to where she was staying at the time, apart from the picture on the front. It had been a deliberate decision not to tell her mum or even Peggy where she was, because she was afraid they'd try to find her. Or maybe she was afraid that they wouldn't.

When Marjorie comes in to have coffee, she chats happily about what she's achieved in the garden this morning and what she hopes to get done this afternoon. Then she asks if Eleanor can take the trousers she bought in Bromley last week back to Marks & Spencer's to change them for a smaller size.

'Yes, of course,' Eleanor says.

'Thank you, darling. And could you pop into the garden centre on your way back? I need another bag of bark chippings – that fat tabby from next door uses the

139

patch by the rhododendrons as a toilet and scatters the bark all over the place.'

She sounds completely and utterly normal. How can this be the same woman who flew at the sitter in a rage last night? 'Yes, sure. If you'll be okay on your own for a couple of hours, I'll pop into Lewisham and get some shopping, too.'

'Good idea, I think we're low on eggs.' Marjorie drains her coffee cup, picks up her gardening gloves from the draining board and heads back down into the garden.

Normal. Normal, normal, normal.

On her way out, Eleanor pops up to see Peggy, who is just unpacking her own shopping. 'I was wondering if you're around for a few hours, and if you could pop down later to make sure she takes her pills and remembers to eat her lunch. I've got to run a few errands and do a bit of shopping.'

'Of course! I've said before, just ask me any time. How is she today?'

'Good. In fact, if you saw her now, you wouldn't think there was anything wrong. I'm not complaining, but it's hard to know where you are with her.'

'Tell me about it! It's been like that for a while. Sometimes she's so much her old self that you honestly wonder . . .' She pauses. 'Well, I used to wonder, anyway. You know, whether they'd got it wrong. Not so much now, though, obviously. There are a lot more bad days now.'

'It's not even whole days, though, is it? She was all

over the place this morning, and now she seems fine. It's worse in the evenings. Which reminds me – do you know anyone called Jeannette?'

'Jeannette?' Peggy looks up from the bag she's unpacking. The recognition on her face is instant.

'Yes, I was going to tell you – she had a bit of a set-to with Jenny last night.'

'Really? I thought she liked Jenny.'

'She does, but I think she mistook her for this Jeannette, and she went for her. Hit her in the face and tried to pull her hair.'

Peggy looks at her for a moment, then shakes her head and carries on unpacking the next bag. 'Oh dear.'

'Jenny's being very reasonable about it, thank God – says she's had far worse to cope with than a bit of hair-pulling.'

Peggy shakes her head again. 'Why didn't she phone me? Jenny, I mean? She knows about the extension. And she's got my mobile number. I'd have come down straight away.' She balls up the carrier bags she's just emptied and shoves them into a drawer, then she pulls out a chair and sits down. 'You don't remember Jeannette, then? She babysat for you a few times while your mum was in hospital.'

'I don't remember that. I thought you looked after me. I remember coming up here after school. And even going up to the other house when I was very small, before you moved here.'

'That was the first time, when the boys were little and

I was around more. This was later, when I was back at work. I still looked after you when I could but if I had a late shift, and your dad was at work and your grandma couldn't come over, that's where Jeannette came in. She'd pick you up from school, give you some tea and stay until your dad got home.'

Eleanor has a sudden flash of memory; sitting on the pouffe in front of the fire, eating Marmite toast and watching *Blue Peter* and feeling shy because she barely knew the pretty lady in the red blouse who was looking after her.

'Hang on, it's coming back to me now.'

'It probably wasn't more than a dozen times all told. Seemed a nice enough girl.'

'So if my mum went for Jenny because she confused her with Jeannette, what happened?'

Peggy looks away. 'They had a bit of a falling-out. I don't know exactly what happened, but I think she blotted her copybook in some way.'

Eleanor has been thinking about what Jenny said: *Called me a filthy trollop.* She has her suspicions. 'Was it something to do with Dad?'

The way Peggy's eyes flicker and look away more or less confirms it. 'I'd rather know; it won't upset me. I barely remember him now, to be honest.'

'I don't suppose it makes much difference, not if you can't remember him.'

'I think I've guessed anyway.'

'You may have. Your mum came home from work one day and found the two of them in bed.'

Eleanor sighs. 'Thought so. So that's why they split up.' How strange it was to feel ever so slightly relieved to find out that your dad was an adulterer. It isn't great, but maybe it helps explain things; maybe her mother's depression was partly due to that betrayal rather than entirely because of what happened with Peter.

'I don't think that was the main reason, but it didn't help, of course. Don't judge your dad too harshly. I'm sure it was a one-off – not like Ken.' She shakes her head. 'No, your dad loved your mum, but she wasn't easy to be around, especially when she was poorly.'

'That's one thing I *do* remember. You're so good to her, Peg.'

'Thing is, she's always been there when I needed her, especially when I had the boys. Being young, unmarried and in the family way was frowned upon much more back then than it is now, or even than it was when ...' She catches Eleanor's eye. 'Well, at least young girls now don't have it as bad as we did.'

'No,' Eleanor agrees, 'I hope not, anyway.'

Peggy's face takes on a faraway expression. 'My parents disowned me, as you know, even though we were engaged, but your mum stood by me the whole time.' She looks thoughtful. 'And then all those years later when I found out about Ken and his bloody harem all over the country, well. I'm not sure what I'd have done without her.'

'That was such a shock. About Ken,' Eleanor says. It had all happened not long after she took off in the

143

camper, so she didn't hear about it until she was in touch with her mum again. 'I couldn't believe it when Mum told me.'

'No one could, that was the point. Ken was always so charming to everyone else that some people thought I'd made it up. But your mum was a brick. She sat up with me the night I found out – the whole night! I couldn't sleep, so we just sat at this very table smoking ourselves silly. You know, if it had been just one woman, I could probably have let it go, but four of them, Ellie; I mean, why would one man need that many women?' She sighs. 'And what a hypocrite. He'd been deceiving me for don- key's years, and then he had the bloody cheek to get on his high horse about you and me keeping things from your mum.'

Eleanor looks thoughtful. 'I've never forgotten that, Peggy; it was a lot to ask.'

Peggy shrugs. 'It was, but I can see why you felt the way you did. Anyway.' She smiles. 'I suppose that's why I've stuck around your mum for so long, even when she's being a pain in the arse. And because of you, of course.'

*

She is only out for a couple of hours, and is loading the rest of the shopping onto the back seat because the bark chippings take up most of the boot space, when her phone beeps a text: *Mum absolutely fine but is upstairs with me, so come here first when you get back. X*

Her stomach tightens. Why would Peggy be reassuring her that her mother was fine if there wasn't something wrong? After she's returned her trolley, she sits back in the car and calls Peggy. No answer. Oh, well, she'll be there in ten minutes anyway.

She parks outside the house, relieved there are no fire engines, ambulances or police cars lining up in the street. Perhaps there really isn't anything to worry about. She grabs the bags with the frozen stuff so she can put that away before she goes upstairs. As soon as she unlocks the inner door the smell hits her: damp, slightly musty, like wet carpets. She loads the frozen food into the freezer, then checks the dining room and living room before opening the door to the bathroom. It is still warm. There are no windows or fan in here, so the air is still moist, the mirror misted with steam. The floor is wet, although by the look of the heap of sodden towels in the bath, attempts have been made to mop up. Some of the cork floor tiles have started to lift and she can see water sitting beneath them. It looks quite bad.

She opens the door to the basement. The downstairs hallway looks okay, but as soon as she opens the door to her mother's bedroom, she feels cold water seeping through the sole of her right shoe. The carpet in here is completely sodden. The curtains are still closed so she flicks the light switch, but nothing happens. She feels her way around the bed to the window so she can pull the curtains, her feet squelching as she walks. Once she's let some light in, she looks up and sees the extent of the damage to the ceiling. There is a hole about the size of a tea tray where the paper has come away completely, exposing the lath and plaster beneath. Drips are still forming on the laths, and some of the debris has fallen onto the bed – chunks of saturated plaster with the ancient whitewashed paper attached. This is going to take some putting right.

*

Marjorie is sitting at Peggy's kitchen table, in her gardening clothes, her hands clasped around a mug of tea as if it were a life raft. Her face is streaked with mud where she's wiped away tears with soil-encrusted hands. She is rocking back and forth like a child and doesn't even look up when Eleanor comes in.

Peggy looks upset, too. 'Ellie, I'm so sorry, I should have gone down sooner. I was chatting to Michael and Chrissie on Skype and I—'

Eleanor waves her apology away. 'No, it's not your fault. It's only a bit of water, anyway. It could have been worse.'

'I was on my way down to check on her when I heard the taps running. I turned them off and chucked the towels on the floor but the water had seeped under the tiles by then. And after you asked me to pop down, too. It's my fault.'

Eleanor puts her hand on Peggy's arm. 'Honestly, it's no one's fault. No one's hurt, that's the main thing.'

Another tear rolls down Marjorie's face. 'It was my fault, you know. I fell asleep.'

'No, you didn't,' Peggy says. 'You were pulling up nettles when I came down. You just forgot you'd left it running, that's all. It wasn't your fault.'

'If I hadn't gone to sleep,' Marjorie says, 'it would never have happened. I shouted at her, but it was all my fault, you see. Right from the start.'

Eleanor, the present

With Marjorie happily installed in Peggy's spare room until everything dries out and is repaired or redecorated, Eleanor can head back to the farm for a while. They called the insurance company, but apparently there had been no response to the renewal letters, so the policy lapsed several months ago. Fortunately, Peggy knows a good, reasonably priced painter and decorator. He came to do a quote within a couple of days and while he was there, he helped Eleanor take up the wet carpet. It was so ancient there was virtually no pile left to hold the water, so it wasn't as heavy as they expected, but that meant the water had run straight through and soaked the floorboards. Once she'd scraped up what was left of the underlay and plugged in the dehumidifier, the whole thing didn't seem quite so bad.

The drive back up to Scalby is a nightmare – there's an accident on the M18, then miles of roadworks on the A1, and by the time she arrives, exhausted and slightly frazzled, it is past midnight. The cattle grid shudders beneath her as she crosses it slowly to reduce the noise. The farm is still and quiet. All the lights in the cabins are off but the whole area is bathed in such bright moonlight that the sensor light which flickers on as she passes the main house hardly seems necessary. An owl hoots, puncturing the silence. The sound of the owl and the familiar hush surrounding it feel soothing after the noise and urgency of south-east London, and she can already feel the tension starting to slip away. She closes the car door quietly and, leaving her bags in the boot for tonight, makes her way across the yard. Right now, all she wants is a cup of tea and her bed. She could do with a slice of toast as well, but she doesn't want to disturb anyone by going over to the main house and crashing about in the kitchen. She opens the door to her cabin and flicks the light on. On the desk-cum-table is a tray covered with a tea towel. There's a note on top: *Fresh milk in fridge. Kettle filled, but thought you might need more than tea! Welcome back! Jx* She lifts the tea towel. Jill has laid out an individual cottage loaf, probably baked today, a disc of goat's cheese and a tiny dish of butter. Next to that, a small bowl of strawberries and sliced melon and, poking out from underneath the bowl, a Snickers bar. There's also a miniature bottle of David's elderberry wine. A surge of gratitude and affection swells inside her as she kicks off her boots, pours the wine and climbs onto the bed with the tray of food.

*

149

Eleanor's relief at being back at the farm is tempered by the knowledge that she'll have to go down again before too long, despite Peggy's assurances. But for the time being, she feels good. The weather's warm, things are growing, everything is bright and cheerful and the familiar routines of daily life here feel almost nourishing.

As of this morning, they have three new hens. It's the same old story – a family who'd fancied the idea of a constant supply of fresh eggs without really thinking about the work involved or what would happen when they went on holiday. 'At least they've been well looked after,' Jill says as she opens the back door to the yard where all the hens – eleven of them now – are fussing and clucking, sensing that food is imminent. 'There we are,' she points out the new arrivals. 'That one's Joni Mitchell, that's Petula Clark, and the one at the back having yet another dust bath—'

'Dusty Springfield?' Eleanor suggests.

'How did you guess?' She turns and points back into the kitchen. 'There's some stale cake in that tin, so you can mix some of that in with their feed if you like – don't give them the coconut one, though. Remember last time?'

'Ha! I certainly do.' A whole slab of coconut cake, lovely when fresh, had been forgotten and allowed to go stale; they'd fed it to the chickens, who'd gobbled it up greedily, and for the next two or three days all the eggs had tasted of coconut. In the kitchen, she crumbles up the plain cake, mixes it into the bucket of chicken feed and sets out again to feed the 'girls'.

She smiles as she scatters the food, and is thinking how she's missed their funny little ways, when she spots a figure coming through the gates. She recognises Dylan instantly, even though she hasn't seen him for ages. His hair is short now, and he's still slim, though no longer the gangly youth he'd been when he first started coming here. He's smiling as he comes towards her, slightly bent under the weight of his enormous backpack – she'd told him before it was like Mary Poppins' travel bag. The first time he stayed here, she'd watched him unpack and had been enthralled as, after pulling out the usual clothes, washbag and camping gear, he'd then produced a sketch pad, pencils, charcoal, paints, brushes, a collection of poetry – Christina Rossetti – and a treble recorder. Her heart gives a little skip.

'Hey.' Dylan smiles broadly as he walks towards her. His skin has a tanned, weathered look; he must have been living outdoors again. His usual designer stubble is now a definite beard, short and neatly trimmed, lighter than his red-brown hair. She isn't usually keen on beards, but it suits Dylan. He swings the backpack off his body and lets it fall to the ground so he can embrace her.

'Hey, yourself.' His skin feels cool and he smells of spearmint with a hint of tobacco underneath. She can feel herself smiling already; Dylan always makes her smile. 'It's good to see you.'

'Likewise,' he says, his eyes darting straight up to her scalp. 'What's . . . ?'

'You remember I told you it grows every so often? It usually falls out again fairly quickly, but this time, well, so far so good.' She turns her head one way and then the other. 'I can't exactly flick it yet, but I can run a comb through it.'

He holds her away from him and steps back to get a better look.

'May I?'

She nods, and feels his cool hand, so familiar now, as it cups the back of her skull, then strokes her hair which is now a good three centimetres long.

'It's so soft,' he says, still looking at it. 'Downy, almost. It looks great. I know you've said before that it grows sometimes, but I didn't realise it would be so silky.'

'This is the probably the best it's been. It's usually a bit patchy and dry. And as I say, well, I'm not getting my hopes up, but it's been four months this time. Longest so far.'

'Well, you look beautiful. No more beautiful than when you don't have hair, but ...'

He pauses and she wonders whether he is trying to work out how to pull that remark back to the compliment she knows it was meant to be.

'... but differently beautiful. I've always thought you have a beautiful head, as you know, but now you look ...' His eyes flick over her head and face again. He smiles. 'You know, I think that hair makes you look pretty as well as sexy. I don't know many women who can do that.'

'God, you are such a flatterer! Keep it up.'

He laughs and looks down at the chickens, who crowd around his feet as if they're pleased to see him too. 'Hello, girls,' he murmurs. Then he bends down to pick up his backpack again. 'So, what's new?'

'Quite a lot, actually. Come on, let's go over and get some coffee. I'll tell you all about it.'

*

When Eleanor finishes speaking, Dylan sighs. 'I don't know what to say. You're brave, taking all that on.'

'Either brave or stupid.'

'You know, growing up without parents is shit, and I wouldn't wish it on anyone, but when I hear about people having to put their lives on hold—'

'I don't *have* to.'

'You know what I mean. At least that's something I'll never have to worry about. I was so young when my grandad died that no one expected me to take any responsibility anyway.'

Eleanor puts a hand out and squeezes his arm. 'Sorry, I shouldn't moan. You had it much tougher than I did.'

'Not really. I had a few rough years, but it taught me to look after myself. Anyway, do you think you'll actually move back? Aren't there special homes where—'

'Yes, but not until it gets a lot worse. She wants to stay in her own home for as long as possible.'

'Understandable, I suppose. But does she need you down there full time?'

SUSAN ELLIOT WRIGHT

'Maybe not full time, not yet. But I think I feel like . . . like this is it.' She drains her coffee cup and turns to him. 'It's my last chance, Dylan. She's losing her mind, basically. So I need to try and, not put things right, exactly, but maybe talk about it all for once; make *some* sort of connection before it goes completely.'

'How long?'

'It's still coming and going at the moment, but it'll get worse over time. They say she'd probably had it for quite a while before she was even diagnosed, and that was nearly four years ago.'

He looks thoughtful for a moment. 'Bit ironic, isn't it? Your mum losing her memory when she was so keen for you to lose yours.'

'It is, isn't it?' I sometimes wonder whether she's aware of that herself.' She sighed. 'It was always so simple with her – forget it ever happened; if you don't think about it, it can't hurt. Talk about burying your head in the sand.'

'I suppose it's not that unusual, is it? And when you think about it, you may have repressed that memory anyway, even without that quack and his screwed-up ideas.'

'Yes, that's possible, I suppose. I used to be so angry about it. When I was younger, I used to think it would serve her right if she lost her memory. But you grow up, don't you? And it wouldn't change anything; what happened, happened whether we remember it or not.'

*

Later, as they lie in bed with the early evening sunshine pouring through the window and bathing the room in a golden glow, he runs his fingers ever so gently through her new hair. 'Funny how things change, isn't it? And odd that it's happening to both of us at the same time, given how we've both managed to avoid much responsibility up until now.'

'It's a bit different, though, isn't it? You're going off to Italy to do the thing you love.'

'Not quite. It's not real art – most of my designs will probably end up on wallpaper. But I take your point; I've got the better deal. I suppose what I meant was, we're both moving on, both finally doing grown-up things instead of . . .' He looks at her. 'Sorry.'

She smiles. 'Don't apologise. You're right. I've avoided being grown-up, too. And for far too long. You're still young enough for it to be reasonable. I'm . . .'

'Not exactly ancient.'

'But definitely old enough to know better.'

'Eleanor,' he turns to face her; he looks serious. 'You will come out and see me, won't you? No strings, just . . . you know, it was weird last summer, not seeing you. Made me think. Do you realise that apart from last year and that year I was ill, we've spent every summer together? Sometimes the autumns as well? We've probably spent more time together over the last thirteen years than a lot of married couples.'

She laughs at the comparison. 'Possibly.' At one time, when she was a teenager, she just assumed she'd be part of a married couple one day, and then she'd have children. Two, or maybe three. She sits up and swings her legs over the edge of the bed before the sadness can engulf her. 'Come on, lazybones. We need to get over to the house for dinner.'

Marjorie, November 1972

Marjorie stood in front of the dressing table, wishing she hadn't drunk so much gin with Peggy last night. It was a good job Eleanor was away with the Brownies – she couldn't have coped with her today. It wasn't fair that Ted got smashed on whisky night after night without any ill effects, while the one time she allowed herself to get a bit tipsy she ended up feeling awful all day. She looked at her reflection; she hated how the three mirrors showed her from different angles so she was forced to see herself as others saw her. Ted used to say she was beautiful, but he couldn't possibly think that now. Something had happened to her face, making her look permanently cross. She had no figure to speak of; she'd never had a particularly big bust, but she'd lost weight over these last four years and now she was virtually flat-chested. Her neck was too long, and her face too sharp and angular. Ted was due in a few minutes, and although she'd applied some mascara and a little lipstick, she lost her nerve now, grabbed a paper handkerchief and wiped off the lipstick, which was too pearly anyway and didn't suit her.

She recognised the distinctive sound of Ted's Hillman Imp pulling up outside. She sprinted across the room and switched the light off because she didn't want to let him in down here, where he'd have to walk past the bedroom. She hurried upstairs and along to the main front door. He still had his key, but so far he hadn't used it and she was grateful.

'Tea?' She said as he drew out a chair and sat at the kitchen table. He'd shaved, she noticed, and his hair looked recently trimmed. She could smell Vosene shampoo.

'Please.' He took out a pack of Senior Service, put one out for Marjorie and lit his own.

'Thanks,' she said, picking it up after she'd set the teapot down and leaning towards him for a light. Things felt almost normal. It was quiet, the silence broken only by the sound of a slow drip plopping into the bowl of water she'd left in the sink. The washer in the cold tap must have gone again. Perhaps she could ask Ted to fix it.

'So,' he said, 'what are we going to do, Marjorie?'

'What do you mean?'

'What the hell do you think I mean?'

She realised it sounded simplistic. 'Well, do you mean about the immediate future, or do you—'

'That would be a start.'

She sighed. 'Ted, you sound so cold.'

'What do you expect?'

He looked more sad than angry. She lowered her eyes. 'Sorry.'

'Look,' he ran his hand through his hair, 'I'll say my bit first, then you say yours, all right?'

She nodded.

'What I want is to move back in here to be with you and Ellie. I know I've done wrong, Marjorie, but we've been over that again and again; I've apologised until I'm blue in the face.'

She sighed. 'I know you have, Ted.'

'I don't know what else I can do. I hate this, stuck living at my mother's like a flaming teenager, seeing my daughter for a few hours a week. I want to come back, Marjorie.' There was a catch in his voice. 'I don't like sleeping in a single bed.'

'I see. It's all about bed again, is it?'

He rolled his eyes. 'Of course it isn't.' He stubbed his cigarette out and immediately took another from the pack, then offered one to Marjorie. She shook her head. 'You know,' he said after he'd lit the cigarette, 'maybe it *is* about bed. After all, that's why we're in this mess, isn't it? I went to bed with someone else. I shouldn't have, and I didn't plan it, but … It was one time, Marjorie. One miserable, lonely time in four years. Did you realise it's been that long?'

'Of course I realise how long it's been. Do you think the date isn't etched on my memory?'

'I meant since we—'

'Same thing,' she snapped.

He sighed. 'I know you'll never get over it properly; I don't suppose I will, either. But you have to carry on living, not only for my sake, but for yours as well. And Eleanor's. She needs you too, you know. And you can't go on blaming her.'

'I don't blame her; truly I don't. It's just . . .' Just what? She couldn't even analyse it herself, but she knew what he was getting at. She knew she hadn't mothered Eleanor properly since that day. Perhaps it was that she no longer felt she had the right to *be* a mother.

'I want to come back, Marjorie. But I can't live as though we're . . .' He looked around as if the words he wanted might be written on one of the walls. '*Companions.*' He said it with distaste. 'I want to come back as your husband.'

'By which I suppose you mean sex.'

'Why do you say it as if it's something wrong? Something dirty?' He looked at her for a moment, then he banged his fist on the table. 'Christ, Marjorie. It's not normal.' He stood up roughly, knocking the table so that the tea spilled into the saucers. '*You're* not bloody normal.'

She saw the instant regret on his face, but it was too late, he'd said it, and the comment scared her because she could feel it setting her free to say whatever she wanted; she could shout now, insult him, hurt him – anything goes. It was as exhilarating as it was terrifying. 'You say I'm not normal, but what about *you*?' she yelled. 'How normal can it be for you to put your animal pleasures above everything else?'

'You know that isn't true.'

'But you've just said—'

'I've tried to comfort you. I've tried so bloody hard, but you won't have it, will you? You don't want to be comforted. Well, maybe that's why I turned to Jeannette.' He appeared to be trying to control his temper, but his voice was getting louder. 'She was upset and she let me comfort her. And do you know what? It felt good. Yes, I know you don't want to hear this, but you can't keep putting your hands over your ears like a child. You're going to bloody listen this time. It felt absolutely bloody marvellous to have a woman's arms around me, to feel the warmth of human flesh for the first time in years. My God, I don't know how it didn't happen sooner.' He turned away from her and muttered, 'I need a drink.'

She stood in the middle of the kitchen, his words lapping around her. For some reason she suddenly became acutely conscious of her breathing and the beating of her heart; proof that she was alive. So why couldn't she *feel* it? Ted went into the dining room and she heard him wrench open the sideboard door. He came back holding the bottle of whisky she'd forgotten was there.

As she looked at him, images flashed through her mind: the way they'd once danced together, winning trophies because they were so perfectly in sync that it seemed as though they weren't even consciously moving their own bodies; the softness in his eyes as he slipped the gold band on her finger; the tear on his cheek when he held Eleanor for the first time; the way he'd beamed when she told him she was expecting again. It was all a lifetime ago. Now his face bore deep grooves; his mouth was turned down and his whole body looked weary.

'You know,' Ted put a tumbler on the table and half filled it, then screwed the cap back on the bottle and sat down. 'At one point, when I was with Jeannette, I tried to imagine it was you who was holding me.' He took a big gulp of his drink and then gave a sour laugh. 'Can you imagine that? Can't be many men who fantasise about their wives when they're with someone else.' His smile was bitter. 'What a lousy adulterer.' He took another mouthful. 'All I've ever asked is for you to let me in, to let me *love* you, properly, like a man should be able to love his wife.' He finished the whisky in one more gulp. 'Jeannette was only doing what a wife is supposed to do.'

The room was silent apart from that insistent drip, the sound much louder than it should have been.

A thought rolled into her mind quite suddenly: the idea that she could forgive him, that she could still stop all this if she tried. All she had to do, she realised, was to walk across the room, put her arms around him and tell him that she loved him. If she could only go to him now and tell him that she understood, that things would change and she would be able to give herself to him again one day … She tried to make herself take a step towards him, make herself speak, even, or move, or something. But it was as if she was frozen as she stood there, feeling the opportunity seep away and knowing it was too late.

Eleanor, summer 1982

'Mum, whose baby is it?' she repeated, surprised at her own bravery. Any minute now she would get told off for looking through her mum's stuff, but she had to know if she was right.

Her mum held the photo. She was chewing her lower lip and a tear spilled out of her eye and dropped down her cheek.

'Is it . . . was it ours?'

'Peter. His name was Peter.' Her mother put her fist up to her mouth but a sob escaped anyway. Then she turned away to pull a tissue from the box on the sideboard. She held it to her face briefly, then blew her nose and turned back to Eleanor. 'He died. He was eight months old.' She turned away again, plucked out another tissue and mopped at her eyes.

'But Mum, why . . . I mean, what did he die of?'

Her mum stared at her, and for a moment she thought maybe she hadn't heard her correctly, that he hadn't died. But then her mum shook her head. 'He wasn't very well.' She sighed. 'I'm sorry, darling, but I'd really rather not talk about it any more.' And with that, she walked out of the room.

Eleanor followed her into the kitchen. 'Why didn't you tell me?' She could hear the undercurrent of anger in her voice. Of course she understood that it was upsetting; it must be terrible to lose a baby, but surely she had a right to know? He was her brother, after all.

'Eleanor ...' Her mum looked at her, then her eyes flicked away again. 'Hang on.' She rummaged in her handbag and pulled out her cigarettes and lighter.

The little tortoiseshell cat from up the road was lying in a patch of sunshine on the veranda. Sometimes, if the French doors were open, the cat would come in and purr vigorously while she stroked it. She wished she could open the doors now. Her mum lit her cigarette and drew on it, her face turned away. Her shoulders were shaking. After a minute or so, she took a deep, shuddering breath and turned back to Eleanor. 'We ... your dad and I, we thought it would be for the best if ... Well, talking about it couldn't change anything, and sometimes it's not good to ... I don't know, dwell on things, I suppose.'

'But—'

'Eleanor, I just can't talk about it now. I have a terrible headache and I need to lie down.' She stubbed her cigarette out, sighed and went out of the room, closing the door firmly behind her.

*

If only Peggy were here; but she and Ken were visiting Michael in Bristol, where he was at university, so it would be a week before Eleanor could ask her anything. In the picture, which her mother now had in her handbag, the baby looked tiny, and her mum had said that Peter was eight months old when he died, so Eleanor must have been four at the time. The photo was proof that she had one day sat next to her mother in the living room, smiling at her baby brother and holding his hand. In her efforts to remember more, she felt as though she was physically squeezing her brain, but the harder she tried, the more her brain rebelled, feeling emptier every time she tried to conjure up a memory.

It was a few days later when she was ambling home through Ladywell Rec that an image jumped into her head from nowhere. A pram with a shiny ivory-coloured base and a dark hood parked out in the hallway; it had big silvery wheels, and there was a yellow chick hanging on a ribbon from the fringed hood. She tried to bring more from that memory, but nothing would come. Then one morning, early, and before she was properly awake, she had a vivid recollection of seeing her mother standing next to a wooden cradle, rocking it to and fro and looking anxious. Was the baby inside crying? She wasn't sure, because the scene evaporated as she became fully conscious, like dreams do, only she knew this wasn't a dream.

Sometimes, when she was thinking about something else entirely, a fragment, a glimpse of something not quite formed, would skip through her brain but it never stayed there long enough for her to read it properly. Her memories of the time before she started school had always been poor, whereas she knew quite a few people who claimed to remember things that happened when they were tiny. Ray said he could remember his first day at nursery – he'd have been three and a half, according to his mum. And his mum said she could remember being three, as well. Her family lived in the country in the thirties, and she remembered her older brother taking her by the hand and leading her to the end of the garden where he had something to show her. He'd pointed to an enamel bucket with a lid and told her to look inside. When she raised the lid, she'd wondered for a moment what the black things bobbing around in the water were, then her brother lifted out one of the dead kittens to show her. Eleanor was horrified, but Ray's mum said it was only the first of several litters she saw drowned. It had to be done, she said; it was something you got used to.

*

She almost wished she hadn't finished her exams, because at least then there would be something to distract her. The need to know more about Peter was driving her mad. She could barely think of anything else. Ray had suggested they go ice-skating that afternoon. That would help to take her mind off it, but she couldn't really afford it. What she should be doing, if she was being honest, was to be out looking for a temporary job – it was another three months before she started university, a good opportunity to build up some savings before she immersed herself in English literature for the next three years. But her mind kept returning to the fact that she'd once had a baby brother, and even though she couldn't remember him properly she felt as though some part of her remembered missing him. The feeling was deep down, not just on the surface. When Elvis Presley died a few years ago, she'd read somewhere that he'd felt his entire life was blighted by the loss of his twin brother, who died before they were born. She understood that now. Poor Elvis. It was worse for him because he was there, right next to his brother in the womb when he died.

If only she had the photo; but her mum had stuffed it away somewhere, and whenever she raised the subject of Peter her mum looked devastated and left the room.

Restlessness danced around inside her like an itch. For the sake of something to do, she made herself some cheese on toast, shook a few drops of Lea & Perrins on top and took it through to the living room. There were plenty of snaps of her as a baby, so surely there were some of Peter as well? She could understand her mother not wanting to be reminded every day by having pictures of him in frames about the house, but she wouldn't have destroyed them, surely? Maybe she'd put them away somewhere, like the wedding photos. As she ate, an image popped into her head. She put her plate down on the hearth and tore down the stairs to her mother's room.

The moment she crossed the threshold, she once again had the feeling that she was being watched, and even though she knew there was no one else in the house, she moved quietly and carefully, tiptoeing across the carpet. This time she knew where to look; the other shoebox, the one full of papers. She found her parents' marriage certificate; her father's birth certificate; some papers referring to his National Service. Then there were several vaccination cards. She opened a white A5 envelope and inside was another birth certificate. This would be it. She unfolded the paper carefully and there it was: *Twenty-second of October 1967, Lewisham Hospital, Peter Maurice, boy, Father, Edward John Crawford, Mother, Marjorie Elizabeth Crawford, formerly Lewis* . . . So she'd been nearly three and a half when he was born. She thought about Ray's little cousins Lisa and baby Lucy. Lisa was three, and was very aware of her baby sister, almost obsessed with her, in fact. The idea that if anything happened to Lucy Lisa would forget all about her was inconceivable. She tried to force her mind back, but her memories were so misty she wasn't even sure if they were real memories, or if she'd conjured them up because she *couldn't* remember. Then she realised there was something else in the envelope, another certificate. This was his death certificate. It was a different sort of paper; thicker, yellowish, and the lettering was in bold black type. There were several things written under *Cause of death*, but only one word jumped out at her: *Drowning*.

For a fleeting moment, she thought she'd made a mistake; maybe there had been another Peter Maurice Crawford. But no, the age was recorded as eight months. *Drowning*. But her mum said he was ill, and that's why he died. Kneeling on the carpet with the certificate in her hand, she tried to make sense of it. An image flashed through her brain, too fast for her to examine it properly. A naked baby doll in the water; surely just a doll? Then her mother, screaming ... No, it must be her imagination. But then, if she couldn't remember standing next to her mother and holding Peter's hand, which she knows happened because she's seen the photographic evidence ...

'What the devil do you think you're doing?'

Her whole body jumped. She hadn't heard the front door, hadn't even heard her mother coming down the stairs. She could feel the certificate in her hands. She wanted to fold it up and put it back in its envelope, but it was as if she'd been turned to stone. She wasn't sure whether what she saw on her mum's face was absolute fury, or ... She looked almost frightened. 'I ...' She swallowed, then got slowly to her feet. She'd been kneeling too long and she had pins and needles in her right leg. 'Mum, I know this is upsetting for you. It's ... it's awful, and I'm so sorry to upset you by bringing it all up. But—'

'You've no idea, Eleanor,' her mum said quietly, shaking her head.

At first she was going to say sorry again, but instead, feeling a surge of confidence, she said, 'Why did you lie to me?'

'What do you mean?'

'You said he was ill, or he had "problems", or something like that. But it says here that he drowned.'

'He wasn't well. He had—'

'But that isn't why he died, is it? She looked at the death certificate again. 'This says—'

'I know what it says.'

'So why didn't you tell me?'

Her mother sighed. 'What good would it have done?'

She felt a rage building up inside her that she'd never experienced before. 'He was my brother; I was his sister. Didn't I have a right to know? It's as though you tried to wipe him out completely.' She wasn't actually shouting, but she could hear her voice getting louder and she could feel her face turning red. 'You've never even *mentioned* him. I didn't know he'd even been born, never mind that he drowned.'

Her mum was crying again now, and for some reason that made Eleanor even more angry.

'Eleanor, he was ... There were a lot of things wrong with Peter. I—'

'Oh, so it was all right that he died, was it?'

Her mum slapped her cheek. 'How dare you?' she shrieked. 'You know nothing about it, nothing.'

170

For a second, Eleanor was speechless. She'd never seen her mum in this state before, eyes blazing, face contorted with anger and tears pouring down her cheeks.

Then she screamed back, 'How *could* I know anything about it? You didn't bloody tell me!'

Her mother was at the door, her fingers on the handle. She half turned, and Eleanor thought she was going to shout again, but she spoke quietly, her voice half choked by tears. 'It was you who put him in the bloody water, if you must know. That's why we didn't tell you.'

Eleanor, summer 1982

Eleanor lay on her back, staring at the ceiling. She wasn't sure how long she'd been awake, but it felt like hours. Her neck felt hot, so she sat up and turned her pillow over, briefly soothed by the coolness of the cotton against her cheek. She closed her eyes and tried again to empty her mind.

It had been a horrible few weeks, and she'd never felt so strange. It was as though she didn't know herself any more. She kept reflecting on the expression people used so often when they were unwell, *I'm not really myself.* That was how she felt, not herself; disconnected from who she had always thought she was. Before she'd found out about her brother, she was Eleanor Crawford, an ordinary, reasonably popular girl with a steady-but-not-serious boyfriend, a place on the English BA course at Reading University and what her careers adviser called a 'well thought-out life plan': degree, PGCE, teaching at primary level until she was ready to have her own children, and then a few years off to raise a family before considering the next phase of her life. Now she was Eleanor Crawford, one-time psychotherapy patient, responsible for the drowning of her baby brother. She'd put him in a paddling pool full of water, they told her. She vaguely remembered the shouting, people coming to the house, and her being sent up the road to stay with Peggy. And she remembered being taken to see Mr Greenfield, who had made her put her memories in a dustbin. Thanks to him, she didn't remember actually doing it, or what had been going through her mind beforehand. Her memories of Peter were so fleeting, she had no idea whether she was just playing or whether she'd meant to hurt him, maybe out of jealousy. Whatever the reason, no primary school in its right mind would let her anywhere near small children. And even if no one ever found out, how could she possibly trust herself to be responsible for thirty-odd children? Part of her knew that such thoughts were irrational, but the fact that she still couldn't remember exactly what had happened that day scared her. If she wasn't in control of her own self, how could she possibly be responsible for anyone else?

Her mum was distraught after she'd blurted it out, and didn't stop apologising for almost a week. When Peggy returned from Bristol, Eleanor had barely been able to bring herself to speak to her; she couldn't remember ever being angry with her before. Peggy had always been her ally, the one she turned to when things weren't going

SUSAN ELLIOT WRIGHT

well with her mum, so knowing that Peggy had kept something so momentous from her all these years ... it was hard to take. 'I'm so sorry, sweetheart,' Peggy kept saying. 'It was what your mum and dad thought best, you see.'

Peggy had been there when it happened, it turned out. At least, she'd arrived almost immediately afterwards. She'd walked into the garden to find Eleanor hysterical because Marjorie had shouted at her and Marjorie herself practically catatonic with shock. It had been Peggy who'd called the ambulance, and then she'd taken Eleanor home to stay with her in the days after it happened.

Her mum and Peggy were being extra nice to her at the moment. They both kept telling her it wasn't her fault: she was four years old; she couldn't possibly be held responsible. 'If it was anyone's fault,' her mum kept saying, 'it was mine. I fell asleep when I should have been watching you. Everyone knows you don't leave children unattended near water.'

Which was all very well, she thought as she turned over to try to get comfortable for the umpteenth time, *but it was me who put him in the water.*

*

She woke, as she had done every morning recently, feeling as though there was a heavy weight crushing her chest. It must be quite late, because the sunlight pouring through the open curtains was already hot, strong and

174

bright. Her mother would probably have gone to work by now, and she was mildly relieved at not having to make conversation. She levered herself up onto her elbow to look at the clock, and as she did so, she felt a strange popping sensation on the back of her head. She felt a tickle as her hair brushed against her cheek and she instinctively put her hand up to sweep it back behind her ear, but as her fingers touched it, it came right away from her head. She sat up. Strands of loose hair covered the pillow. There was some on her nightdress, too. Tentatively, she reached up to touch her head and yet another strand came away. There was a fluttering sensation in her stomach and all at once she became acutely conscious of her own heartbeat. For some reason, she felt as though she shouldn't move too quickly, so, slowly and carefully, she turned back the covers and eased herself out of bed, becoming instantly aware of clumps of loose hair falling from her shoulders as she did so.

She could feel the sun-warmed carpet beneath her bare feet as she walked over to the wardrobe mirror, taking great care not to make any sudden movements. She barely recognised her own reflection. Maybe it would have been better if her mother had hacked off her hair as a punishment; at least it would just be too short. But this was a horrible, uneven mess. On the left side of her head, the side where she usually slept, there were great clumps missing: large, bald patches where obscene white skin showed through. She turned her head. On the right-hand side, her hair looked almost normal – mousy blonde, still long and slightly wavy. She put her hand up to touch it; it felt normal, too. Carefully, she took a tendril between her thumb and forefinger and gave it a gentle tug. It felt okay. She tugged a little harder; still fine. She selected another, which also appeared to be firmly attached, and began to wind it around her finger like a corkscrew as she sometimes did when she was trying to encourage more waviness. She didn't even feel the roots come away from her scalp; she was only aware of the sudden disconnection, the definite separateness of what was in her hand. She was shaking. She put her hand out to the dressing table to steady herself as she looked at the long, detached skein of hair that was now twisted around her finger, then she looked in the mirror again. She was like a witch, an ugly hag, a crone; she half expected her teeth to start falling out as well.

She should do something; see if her mother was still at home. But she stood still, as though rooted to the spot, staring at her reflection in horrified fascination. She turned her head slightly to the left and looked again at the bald patches on the right side of her head. There were three areas that were about the size of a ten-pence piece, and two much bigger patches. They were disgusting to look at; the skin of her scalp was almost bluish white. She felt embarrassed to see this skin exposed; it was intimate skin that should never be on public display, as though she was walking around with her private parts showing. How could she even leave the room looking like this? She edged slowly back to her bed. There were strands or clumps all over the bedclothes. She held her hand in front of her, unwound the detached hair and laid it out on her bedside cabinet. Then she began to collect up as much hair as she could. As she bent to pick up a couple of lengths off the rug next to her bed, a tendril that was still attached fell across her face and she absent-mindedly tucked it behind her left ear, only to realise that doing so had loosened it, and now it too came away in her trembling hand. Slowly, she made her way to the door and out into the hallway. Her knees were shaky. She put her hand on the banister and her foot on the bottom stair and, barely raising her voice above its usual level, called up to her mum. There was no answer. She could see from here that the door to the upper hallway was closed, but she felt frightened to walk up the stairs. Her teeth were beginning to chatter, despite the late August warmth. She had to try to get upstairs. Moving as slowly and smoothly as she could, she took the next step, and then the next, until she was at the top and able to open the heavy door to the upper hallway. 'Mum?' She called into the kitchen, but then she noticed that her mum's car keys weren't in the pot. Still moving slowly, she walked along the shared hallway and opened the door to the main front porch. Her heart sank when she saw that Peggy's front door hadn't been left on the latch, so she too must have gone to work.

She fought the tears as she stood there in her nightie, barefoot in the hallway. If she cried, the very action of doing so might loosen more hair. Eventually, moving as though she was carrying a glass of water on her head, she managed to get herself into the living room so she could phone her mother at work, then she sat as still as a stone on a hard chair and waited for her to come home.

'Mum,' she half sobbed as soon as she saw her. 'What am I going to do?'

*

Over the next few days, more hair came away from her scalp. Then her eyelashes fell out, as did her eyebrows. So far, her pubic hair and the fine hairs on her arms and legs remained intact.

The doctor washed his hands. 'Alopecia areata. Not uncommon.' He was sympathetic, he said, and there were certain lotions that claimed to help, but he didn't want to mislead her, and he didn't hold out much hope that they would be able to halt the process. 'You can try this one.' He tore off a prescription. 'But don't get your hopes up, Eleanor. It might grow back in due course, but there are no guarantees, so in the meantime we need to get you fitted with a wig, okay?' He smiled a big, broad smile.

No, Eleanor wanted to say, of course it's not okay. I look like a freak. I'm eighteen; I don't want to wear a wig like an old lady. What she actually said was, 'How long will it take to grow back?'

His eyes flickered and he looked back at his prescription pad. 'As I say, best not to get your hopes up. I'll see you again in three weeks and we'll take it from there.'

Eleanor: the present, Scalby

Everything's fine, Peggy says when she phones. Marjorie has been no trouble at all; quite a few 'good days', in fact. The downstairs ceiling just needs a skim of plaster, then it'll be ready for painting; the floorboards have dried out without warping and once the decorating's finished, everything will be tickety-boo. Eleanor is reassured, but makes Peggy promise to call immediately if there are any concerns.

After dinner in the farm kitchen, most people drift over to the main sitting room, but she notices that Dylan has brought his sketch pad and drawing materials with him. He often spends his evenings here scratching away with pencils or charcoal, and in the past, if he's drawing outside, Eleanor has gone with him to the clifftop to watch as he sketches the coastline or the view along to the ruined castle. She's fascinated by the way he captures the whole feel of the seascape with a few careful strokes of his pencil. Sometimes, they walk along to the south bay so he can sketch families on the beach or the boats in the harbour, or they just hang around the farm while he draws what he sees, the comings and goings of the swallows that nest in the eaves, or the hens pecking around in the dust.

Tonight he wants to outline her head, her new hair. She protests gently but is secretly pleased. If it falls out again, as she fully expects it to, at least she'll have a picture, something more than the rather blurry shots Jill took with her phone.

He raises his eyebrows in silent enquiry as he reaches for her head. She nods her permission and tips her head forward so he can touch her hair. 'It's such an interesting texture,' he says, feeling around the roots with his slender fingers. 'It's almost feather-like. And the colour. There are so many different shades.'

'It's much lighter than it used to be. It was a horrible colour before. Mousy.'

'I bet it wasn't horrible. Women are always so self-critical. Now, sit here.' He pulls the other bentwood chair away from her desk and places it in front of his own. He has positioned them by the window so he can make the most of the light. She likes watching him work, and as she listens to the sound of his pencil as it rasps over the page, she reflects on how he's matured, and how they've both aged since they first met thirteen years ago. She is glad he's filled out a little, thickened at the waist; her own waist is bigger than it was, too, though the daily physical work has kept her body strong and firm. Dylan's face is more lined than most men of his age, probably because of all the time he spends outdoors, but it suits him. There are heavy creases around his eyes. Laughter lines. He laughs a lot; he always has. She wonders how he'll portray her own wrinkles, which, while still minimal, are definitely starting to take hold.

This isn't the first time she's sat for him. She has a particularly vivid recollection of that time a few years back, when they'd been sitting in bed talking about memories and how they sometimes got lost. He'd started running his fingers over her scalp again. 'Just think,' he'd said. 'It's all in there somewhere. It may be submerged, but it's there, even if you can't remember.' She'd felt the warmth of his smooth hands, gentle and deliberate at the same time. She liked him touching her head; maybe he was the only one apart from herself who did touch it.

'Have I ever mentioned that you have the most beautiful head I've ever seen?'

She'd laughed. 'Once or twice, yes.'

He trailed his fingertips down the back of her skull and stroked the hollow at the nape of her neck. 'It blows my mind to think that everything you've ever known, every colour or shape you've seen, the conversations you've had, the music you've heard; it's all there beneath the surface like a secret under the skin. The whole *essence* of you.'

'You don't half talk a load of crap sometimes.'

'Hang on.' He threw the covers back and sprang out of bed. 'Don't move. I want to draw you, the you that's there underneath.'

Eleanor groaned. 'Oh, no, come on, you don't really.' She'd never forgotten the year he was first here, when he'd got all excited about painting her head and she'd looked in the mirror and thought she looked like some freaky hippy weirdo.

'No, don't worry, I'm not going to splash paint all over you again.' He grinned. He snatched up his sketch pad and was standing by the window, flicking over the pages to get to a fresh one. 'I was obsessed with colour back then, but I'm more into monochrome these days. Light and shade; sheen and shadow.'

He grabbed a pencil and began making sweeping strokes across the page, glancing up at her every few seconds, his eyes now shining with a different light, an artist's appreciation rather than a lover's.

'Dylan—'

'Hold still a sec.' His brow furrowed in concentration, and she could hear the pencil scraping and swishing across the page.

'I think—'

'Shush. Tilt your head to the left a little. That's it; perfect.' Scrape, scrape.

She stifled a laugh. 'Dylan, listen, if you're going to stand right in front of the window, put some bloody clothes on!'

'Oh, shit. Right.' He looked around the room.

Eleanor reached under the covers. 'Here.' She tossed his boxers across to him.

'Cheers.' He grinned and waggled his bottom at the window – but not before surreptitiously checking there was no one nearby, she noticed – then pulled them on. He grabbed the wooden chair from the corner and settled himself a few feet away from her. 'Okay, now can you turn the other way, right round so you're facing away from me, and lean up on your elbow. Yes! Perfect.' Scrape, scrape. 'Now turn over and rest your head down on the pillow, face upward . . . and close your eyes. That's it, great.'

She'd lain there, eyes closed, enjoying the warmth of the bed, the golden autumn sunlight on her face, the rasp of his pencil.

That first sitting only took about half an hour, because he was concentrating on getting the basic shape. When he'd finished, he'd taken out his tobacco tin and set about rolling a spliff – he smoked a lot in those days. He always passed it to her, but she always refused because it messed with her memory, which was fragile enough already.

He understood, he said. It was one thing to choose to wipe out unhappy memories, but it was another thing altogether not to be able to recover them even if you wanted to.

He was thoughtful for a moment. 'Eleanor, how would you feel about . . . You see, I've got this idea for the piece.' He nodded towards the sketch pad. 'The head.' He turned to her. 'Sorry, that sounds a bit cold. I mean, *your*

183

head. I was thinking, I'd like to try and, I don't know, show your life by sort of . . .' He reached up to her head again and ran his hand over it. His palm felt smooth and dry. It would lose its smoothness again after a few weeks' work here, she reflected, but his artist's skin would soon recover once he returned to his usual life. Unlike her own hands, which were now as tough and calloused at those of any seasoned farm labourer.

'What I was thinking was, I could put in some of your memories, show them in your head, the contrast between the rich texture of what's inside and the smooth clearness of what shows on the surface.'

Eleanor laughed. 'What, the cool exterior and the turmoil within?'

'Yeah, that's the sort of thing. Glimpses of your life, you know? The precious moments, the flashes of childhood . . .' He gestured with his free hand, and he appeared to be focused on a point in the middle distance, as though he could see his idea taking shape in the air. 'Maybe even the sadder moments?' The question was in his eyes.

'Whatever,' she shrugged. 'I don't mind revisiting sadness once in a while. And anyway, it may be my head but it's your art.'

*

She'd sat for him a couple more times that summer, on this same bentwood chair, first with her head slightly tilted down and her eyes closed, then with her head turned to the side and her eyes open. He'd stood at the makeshift easel he'd knocked up out of spare wood, hands sweeping down the page with his pencils, shading and smudging, swearing when it went wrong. He was working on a much larger pad by that time, having ditched his original outline. He disappeared into his cabin most evenings to work on the picture. He was taking this one quite seriously, she'd realised; and he'd been quieter than usual while working on it, unusually reflective.

She'd stopped asking to see it eventually, and until today, had forgotten all about it.

The sky is growing darker now, and a smoky raincloud hovers above, blotting out what is left of the sunshine. There is a spatter of rain on the window. She looks at Dylan but he doesn't appear to notice. His eyes are sharp with concentration, his brows drawn together. 'Dylan, do you remember that drawing of me you started a few years ago? You did the outline quite quickly, then I sat for you a couple of times, but you said you wanted to try and draw—'

'Your memories. Yes, I remember.'

'Only, to be honest, it had completely slipped my mind until just now. Did you ever finish it?'

He doesn't answer immediately, just carries on moving his pencil. Then he glances up at her. 'I did, as a matter of fact.'

She waits, but he is leaning in to his drawing, making tiny movements with the pencil. 'So . . . ?' When he still doesn't answer, she says, 'Oh, for God's sake, Dylan! Don't be so mysterious. Was it any good? Were you pleased with it?'

At last he puts his pencil down, leans back and sighs. 'I was pleased with it, but I didn't show it to you because in the end, after I'd finished, I wasn't sure if ... Well, the thing is, I thought it might upset you. You know, some of the things ... the stuff that happened when you were younger, before you came here.'

'What about after I came here? Did you put any of—'

'Oh, yeah, it's not only about the bad stuff.' He is looking at her properly now. 'Would you like to see it?'

'You still have it? I thought for a minute you'd ... But where is it?'

'It's at a mate's place. In Shepherd's Bush. I usually crash there if I'm in London. My old schoolmate, Lloyd. I must have told you about him.'

She shakes her head. She knows very little about Dylan's life outside of the summers he spends here. Every now and again he'll tell her something, mention a name, somewhere he's stayed, and she feels like he's feeding her titbits as rewards for not asking.

'He's a good friend. Totally fucked up, mind, but a lovely bloke – do anything for you. Anyway, he lets me store stuff in his back room, so it'll be there somewhere. If you don't mind waiting, I'll bring it next year.'

'I don't mind waiting, but you won't be here next year, remember? You'll be in Italy, finally making some money.'

He laughs and shakes his head. 'I forgot. I suppose it still hasn't sunk in yet that I'm going to be doing a proper job.'

She smiled. 'Quite something, isn't it? And anyway, I don't even know where I'll be next summer, what with my mum and everything.'

'Shit, yeah.' He shakes his head again. 'I hope it's not too traumatic.'

'Thanks.'

'When do you have to go?'

'I don't *have* to.'

'You know what I mean.'

'Sorry, I didn't mean to snap. I'll probably go again quite soon. The redecorating's more or less done, and Peggy says my mum's quite lucid at the moment.' She sighs. 'I don't know what I'm even hoping for, really. Just . . . *something.*'

He picks up his pencil again.

'So, the memory drawing; I could post it, I guess?' He smiles. 'I'm glad you want to see it.'

Eleanor: the present, Scalby

Eleanor stands on the clifftop, watching a fragile light pushing through the clouds as dawn breaks over the North Sea. This is it: her last day here for who knows how long. The gale that's coming in off the sea moves her hair and flattens her jeans and t-shirt against her skin. There's something about the Scalby wind that she finds both comforting and invigorating. She loves the clean, sharp saltiness it brings with it, and the gentle sounds it makes as it ripples through the late crop of rapeseed that stretches from the clifftop right back to the farm. When she first arrived here all those years ago, she immediately became aware of the sound it made as it buffeted the cabins: an almost constant moaning in the background like some poor spirit trapped within the earthly walls of the farm buildings. Jill said it put some people off. They found it creepy, as though the place was haunted. But Eleanor has always liked it; it keeps her company without demanding anything in return.

There's a movement in the darkening sky above her, and she looks up just in time to see a bird of prey, a red kite by the look of its enormous wingspan, pass overhead. Maybe it's hurrying back to its nest before the rain comes. When she and Dylan walked along the cliff path to Scarborough yesterday, she thought it felt distinctly summery; there wasn't so much as a hint of a breeze, and the sea and sky were as blue as a Mediterranean postcard, diamonds of sunlight twinkling off the tiny waves. Today, though, the sea is dark and moody, a deep granite colour; only a flash of red from a single sailing boat breaks up the grey. She stands there for several minutes, mesmerised as always by the undulating, muscular waters below. How quickly and dramatically things can change.

As she walks back to the farm, she is aware of a heaviness settling about her, as though her body is waterlogged, saturated in melancholy. When she leaves here tomorrow morning, it's likely to be for quite a while; several months at least, possibly longer. She's driven up and down a couple of times since the flood, but it's proving to be impractical and expensive, so she suggested to her mum that she move back down properly 'for a while'. They both know what that means. Or at least, *she* does – there's every chance her mum will have forgotten they've even had a conversation, never mind what they've discussed.

She trudges up the track that runs alongside the fields and directly to the farm. She's lived here longer than she's lived anywhere else. Can she really walk away from this place that has become her world? She could change her mind ... But, no, how could she even consider it? Her mother is her mother, and now she is fading, disappearing. Just as the sea is gradually eating away the cliffs at Aldbrough, changing the coastline beyond recognition, the Alzheimer's is claiming more of her mother every day, eroding her brain and washing away her memory until there will be nothing left but a smooth, barren surface to which nothing will adhere.

The rain comes suddenly, blowing in great drenching gusts towards her and making frothy, coffee-coloured puddles on the ground. She hurries back to her cabin, wrenches the door open and slams it quickly behind her before too much water can follow her in. It's gloomy in here. She flicks on the light, grabs a towel, rubs it over her face and then gingerly blots at her hair. Her jeans and t-shirt are soaked through at the front but oddly dry at the back. She pulls the t-shirt off over her head and peels off her clammy jeans. The shock of cool air on her damp skin makes her shiver and break out in goosebumps. She switches on the oil-filled radiator and hangs her sodden clothes over it. Even her bra is wet through.

As she walks into the bathroom, she can hear the rain battering the ground outside and pummelling the roof, but by the time she's showered and dressed in dry clothes, the sun is coming out, making the raindrops that drip down outside her window sparkle prettily in the silvery light.

She's just made coffee when there is a familiar musical rap on the door. 'Come in, Dylan. That was good timing.' She takes another mug from the hook on the wall, spoons coffee into it and adds hot water and milk. He bounces in, smiling and holding a cardboard tube about three feet long.

'Got something for you. I didn't say anything because I wasn't sure it would get here in time. I could have got Lloyd to post it to your mum's, but ... but I wanted to give it to you myself.' His smile starts to fade. 'I hope you like it.'

'Is this ... ?' She hands him a mug of coffee.

'Sorry I didn't manage to get it framed, but, well, I suppose you might not even want it framed.' He drops his gaze. 'I just hope you like it,' he says again.

As she takes it from him, her hand trembles slightly. She isn't sure what to expect, but after what he'd said when they talked about it a couple of weeks ago ...

'Here, let me.' Dylan takes the plastic lid from one end of the tube and carefully slides the picture out.

'I hadn't realised it would be so big,' she said.

'I wanted to do it properly. Do it justice, I suppose. I used those sketches as a guide. He looks around for somewhere to unroll the drawing.

'Hang on.' She begins moving things off the desk. She'd been sorting out some admin work to take with her. She shifts the box files, ring binders and cardboard folders onto the bed, moves the tea-making tray onto the floor and wipes the desk with the towel she used when she came in from the rain.

Dylan lays the drawing on the desk and begins to unroll it. The paper is thick and heavy.

She feels a ripple of apprehension. What if it's awful? She's seen quite a lot of his work now, but she's never really known him to draw people. Well, only if they're in the distance, part of the landscape – a walker on a hill, maybe, or children playing on a beach. She's never known him do portraits, actual faces. And if he's made a good job of it, how will she feel about seeing herself as she was – how many years ago was it? Four? Possibly five. And she remembers him being worried it might upset her; what if it does? She steels herself. No matter what she feels when she sees it, she'll find something nice to say. Dylan is so much more than a lover now; he is a friend and she trusts him.

'Well?' He is smiling, but he sounds nervous.

Her gaze travels over the page. There are actually two drawings of her head on the paper. At the top the view is of her face and head from the front, and the one underneath is from the side. She looks at the front view, and although she can see the tiny sketches he told her about, all she can take in at first is the overall effect. Somehow, despite her horrible baldness, he has made her look serene and mysterious, almost beautiful. 'It's very flattering,' she says. 'You've given me cheekbones.'

'You *have* cheekbones,' he replies. 'I just draw what I see.'

Is this really how Dylan sees her? The face is tilted downwards, presumably to allow more room to show the head above as slightly oversized. He's drawn her with her eyes closed, lashes resting in such a way that you know she isn't sleeping. Even with the eyes closed, there is so much expression in the face, something to do with the set of the jawline and the way he's shaded the slight creases in the forehead. 'You've got those earrings exactly right!' She points to the dangly spirals of stainless steel with chips of polished glass positioned to catch the light as she moves. One of the helpers made them for her when they first started running the jewellery-making classes.

She looks more closely now at the area above her face. He's used soft pencil lines to divide it into six compartments, each of which contains a detailed miniature drawing. She smiles as she recognises the home-made red pottery lamp that even now stands on the bedside table. And there are herself and Dylan, entwined, deep in a nest of rumpled covers, his long hair spilling over their naked shoulders and her own smooth, bald head. She lets out a breath and, still smiling, shakes her head in admiration. 'I don't know how you can make such a small drawing so accurate; it's brilliant.'

'Thanks,' he mutters.

The other five compartments all contain scenes from life on the farm. She recognises the view from the clifftop of the scalloped coastline with the ruins of Scarborough Castle in the distance; beneath that is herself feeding the chickens in front of a polytunnel bursting with heavy-fruiting tomato plants; the picture next to it is of a group of helpers, some playing guitars or bongos, all sitting around the wood burner in the main house. When she looks closely at the final two pictures, both featuring herself and Dylan, she laughs out loud. In one, she is looking in a mirror and grimacing at the weird patterns Dylan has painted on her head, and in the other she is brandishing a sledgehammer as she chases a caricature of Dylan around the farm.

Still laughing, she turns to him. 'That's brilliant, really. You're so clever.'

'Thanks,' he says again. He looks almost as if he's blushing. 'You'd better look at the other one, though.'

Smiling, she turns back to the side view. Again, the shading is stunning, giving the contours of her face a depth that makes it seem three-dimensional. It's hard to believe he's achieved all this with nothing but a pencil on white paper. 'It's . . . it's incredible,' she says. It's only then that she focuses properly on the rest of her head. All she notices at first is that the large skull area is divided in a different way to the first drawing, where all the sections are defined by soft grey lines. In this picture there are eight sections, five of which curl around the outer edge of her skull, starting just above her forehead and finishing right round at the base near the nape of her neck. The shape reminds her of a question mark. In the middle, an inverted triangle that looks roughly heart-shaped is divided into three, and it is when she sees the drawings in this section that her throat constricts and tears rush to her eyes. She bites her bottom lip and hears herself draw in a breath.

Dylan is looking at her with concern. 'Are you okay?'

She nods, but can't speak. She forces her eye away from the middle area; she'll have to come back to that. Instead, she looks at the pictures that surround it. The first one, above her forehead, shows a woman and a girl, both wearing aprons, turning a cake out of a cake tin. She'd mentioned several times how much she loved making cakes, and that she'd started baking as soon as she was tall enough to reach the cooker. He probably assumed he was drawing a representation of her mum here. The next section shows a man and a little girl on a riverbank: her dad with his fishing rod, herself with a net. In the next one, the girl – herself – is older and stands smiling, holding the hands of the two women either side of her. 'Is that . . . ?'

'It's supposed to be your mum and the woman upstairs, Peggy. A bit of poetic licence there, really. I drew it like that because you sort of had two mums, in a way.'

'Yes, I suppose I did,' she murmurs.

He watches her anxiously as she scrutinises the next picture, which comes almost at the base of her skull. It's recognisably herself, even though she has long hair in this one: it shows her sitting at a table, crying as she looks at a photograph in her hand. Just behind her, to the right of the picture, stands her mother, also crying.

She looks up at Dylan. She'd forgotten telling him how

she'd first found out about Peter. Still nodding slowly, she leans in to look more closely at the last of the outer sections. He's shaded around an uneven area that seems to glow white and empty. Beneath the vacant patch is the tiny figure of a little girl, and just above her head, a cluster of question marks. To her right stands a man in a white coat, holding a clipboard; to her left, a man and woman – her parents, presumably. 'Your memory must be bloody good,' she says. 'I told you all that the first year you were here.'

'It's not the sort of thing you forget, is it?' Then he jerks his head up. 'Shit, I wasn't saying . . . I meant, I wouldn't forget you telling me something like that.'

She puts her hand on his arm. 'It's all right; I know what you meant.'

And now that she allows her eyes to rest on that inverted triangle, her heart starts beating harder as her eyes focus. In the top right-hand compartment is Doris, the old camper van that had been her home for almost two years; the left-hand section shows a teddy bear made entirely of flowers, and the final picture, the one at the bottom, is of herself, her bald head lowered towards the naked newborn in her arms. These last three drawings are all surrounded by raindrops. Or maybe tears.

Eleanor, October 1982

After her initial wobble about starting university with no hair, Eleanor decided the only way to cope was to grit her teeth and get on with it. She told Ray about the little patches coming through on the back of her head, but he didn't want to look. 'You're worrying too much,' he said. 'I reckon it'll all grow back soon, and in the meantime . . .' He glanced at her head and she thought she saw a look of distaste flash across his features, although maybe she imagined it. 'You can only tell it's a wig if you look closely.'

That was their last night together before she left. His mum and dad were away for the weekend, and she assumed he'd want to sleep with her. They'd slept together a few times now, and she was starting to get the hang of it, so she was mildly disappointed when he said he'd better call a minicab to take her home because he had to be up early the next day.

When the cab arrived, he walked her to the door and kissed her deeply. 'I'll miss you,' he said. 'We'll get together in a couple of weeks, once you've settled in.'

As she turned to go down the path, he patted her on the bottom. It was gentle, but it felt like he was pushing her towards the cab.

They'd only seen each other twice since then, meeting up in a pub in Paddington on both occasions because it was easier than him coming to Reading or her going back to Lewisham. The first time, a couple of weeks into the term, they'd eaten ham-and-mustard sandwiches washed down with a couple of bottles of lager, then they'd walked around Norfolk Square, holding hands and talking mainly about the books they were doing. He asked how her hair was coming along, and she laughed. She wasn't sure why.

The second time, a few weeks later, they sat in the pub again. Culture Club were on the jukebox, Boy George asking 'Do You Really Want To Hurt Me' over and over. Ray didn't want any lunch, he said, so he just had a packet of peanuts while Eleanor ate her cheese and tomato roll. He was going camping during reading week, he told her, with a few mates from Queen Mary's. They planned to go to North Wales, do some cycling, maybe some walking. He told her a bit about David and Tom, who were going with him. She listened attentively, smiling and nodding in the right places, determined not to let him know she was disappointed. Then, when he sat back and lit a cigarette, she told him about the girls she was sharing a house with: Diane, who was tall and thin and smoked black Sobranie – she was the student union rep for their year; Wendy, who came from County Antrim and was the eldest of nine children. She reminded Eleanor of a milkmaid, and was forever making toast or pouring bowls of cereal for the others and clearing away the plates afterwards. Then there was Kathy, who looked like a blonde Kate Bush and claimed to be sleeping with one of the lecturers, though she wouldn't say who; and finally Joy, who kept herself to herself and gave the impression that she hated sharing her living space. Apart from Joy, who barely spoke, the other girls were friendly and easy-going.

Ray seemed preoccupied, and hardly said two words the whole afternoon. When he looked at his watch for the umpteenth time, Eleanor drained her glass, stood up and said, 'Sorry, I'm obviously keeping you from something more important,' and walked out. She felt quite pleased with herself. He'd been a bit off with her on the phone last time, too, and if she was going to make the effort to come all the way here to meet him, he could at least pretend to be interested in what she was saying.

She was halfway down Praed Street when he caught up with her. 'I'm sorry, Ellie. I'm just a bit distracted, that's all. I've got an essay on Swinburne and Tennyson due in on Wednesday and I've barely started it. I should have told you I couldn't make it today, but I really wanted to see you, especially as we won't see each other during reading week.'

He did look genuinely sorry. 'Okay,' she said after a minute. 'But you should have told me before.'

'I know. I'm a shit.'

'Yeah, you are a bit.' She looked at her watch. 'You might as well get off home, then. I can get a train in about half an hour.'

He smiled. 'Listen, I'll make it up to you next time, okay?' He took hold of the collar of her jacket with both hands, pulled her towards him and kissed her firmly on the lips. 'I'll phone you,' he said, then he turned and walked away.

*

When reading week came around, she'd planned to stay in her room and do exactly what she was supposed to be doing – reading. But Diane, Kathy and Wendy insisted on dragging her to a party up the road. She resisted at first, but she was flattered by how keen they seemed to be for her to go with them. It was while they were all in the living room getting ready that she decided to bite the bullet.

'There's something I'd like to tell you all,' she said. Kathy was putting on her mascara in front of the mirror above the fireplace, Wendy was using a hand mirror propped up against a ketchup bottle on the dining table. Diane was sitting on the arm of the sofa, smoking and watching them with mock disdain.

'Oh, yeah?' Kathy muttered, still layering on the mascara.

'Something about myself.' She could feel her heart beating faster. Shit. She couldn't back out now.

'You used to be a man.' Diane said, straight-faced.

Eleanor laughed, feeling the tension starting to evaporate. 'No, it's not quite that dramatic.' She reached up to her head then lowered her hand again and took a breath. 'I ... This is a wig. I lost my hair a few weeks before I came here.' They were all looking at her now, all completely still.

Diane was the first to speak. 'What, it just fell out? All of it?'

She nodded. 'It happened over a few days, but, yes, all of it. Some people lose their body hair as well, but it's only on my head.'

'So,' Kathy paused, the mascara wand in mid-air. 'So under that wig ...'

'I'm almost completely bald, yes. There are a few patches growing back, but not much yet. And it's uneven, anyway, so ...' She shrugged.

Then they were all talking at once, asking questions and being sympathetic and telling her they had no idea it was a wig and had she thought of shaving her head like that lecturer, the one who specialised in Chaucer and Middle English. 'You could pull it off, you know,' Wendy said. 'Your head's a nicer shape, and you're much prettier than she is.'

By the time they set off for the party, Eleanor felt as

though she was properly part of the group now; one of the gang. She wondered why she hadn't told them before; they were her mates, after all.

She almost forgot about Ray and his camping trip, and when she phoned him the following weekend, she was gratified by the surprise in his voice when she told him about the party and what a great time she'd had.

Eleanor, 17 December 1982

It was the end of term, and they were getting ready for another party – in their own house, this time. They spent all afternoon decorating the rooms with paper chains and fairy lights. Eleanor was looking forward to it. It was a last chance to have a good time before going home for Christmas. Her stomach lurched at the thought. Ever since she'd found out about Peter, it had been virtually impossible to enjoy herself while she was at home. It felt wrong to laugh or be too happy, considering what she'd done when she was little.

The payphone in the hall rang while they were putting their make-up on in the living room. Kathy went to answer it. 'Hang on,' Eleanor heard her say. 'I'll get her.' She came back into the room. 'It's for you, Ellie – Ray.'

'Ray? Wonder what he wants.' She took a sip of her Bacardi and Coke and went into the hall. 'Hello?'

'Ellie, it's me.'

'I know. How's it going?'

'I, er, I thought I'd give you a bell.'

She waited.

'How did you get on with your essay?'

'Which one?'

'Weren't you doing something on Swinburne and ... ?' He sounded strange; nervous.

'Tennyson. Yes, I got it in on time. Haven't got it back yet, though. I think it'll be all right.'

'Thing is, Eleanor ...'

Ah. Now she knew what was coming.

'I don't want to hurt you, but I've been thinking about it, and I think we should split up.'

Her initial reaction was annoyance. How dare he assume she'd be hurt. But then she realised she *was* hurt. Not devastated, not heartbroken, but yes, a little hurt.

'I was thinking, it's not practical, is it? With me in London and you in Reading. I mean, it'll be months before we see each other again, won't it?'

'Not really. I'll be home for Christmas next week.'

'Yes, but I meant after—'

'It's my hair, isn't it? My lack of it, I mean?' She hadn't known she was going to say that. Not so boldly and bluntly, anyway.

There was a telltale moment's hesitation. 'No, it's just ... You're a really nice girl, Ellie. And I still want to be friends, but ...'

She was aware that things had gone quiet in the living

room. She tried to make her voice brisk. 'It's all right, Ray. Let's just call it a day, shall we?'

'I knew you'd understand.' The relief in his voice was unmistakable. She didn't know why she was so bothered. He was nice enough and he made her laugh, but it's not like she wanted to get engaged to him or anything. He'd seemed okay about her hair at first, but now she thought about it, she realised that every time they spoke, he asked if it was growing back yet. 'Yeah, well,' she said. 'See you around.'

When she pushed the living-room door open, there was a sudden flurry of activity as everyone pretended they hadn't been listening. 'Fuck him,' she announced as she walked back in. Joy and Wendy were doing their make-up at the table; they both looked up. 'You okay?' Wendy said.

'I think so.'

'You weren't massively keen on him, were you?'

She shook her head. She could feel tears brimming and she didn't trust herself to speak. Why on earth was she so upset? She *wasn't* massively keen on him. 'You know,' she murmured, unzipping her make-up bag, 'I'm sure it was because of my hair. I think the only reason he didn't split up with me straight away was because he thought it would have grown back by now.'

'Bastard!' Kathy said.

'Yeah,' Wendy agreed. 'You should have told him to go fuck himself.'

Even Joy, who rarely joined in their conversations and

who never swore, added, 'It'll be the only fuck he's getting tonight.'

They were all giggling now, and she had that feeling again of being one of them, a cherished part of their group.

*

She was on her third or possibly fourth drink by the time people started arriving, and she was already starting to feel a bit pissed. She made a point of adding a lot of Coke to her next Bacardi, and as she was putting the cap back on the bottle, she was aware of someone at her side. He held out a glass. 'Can you splash a bit in there please?' It was Simon Adams from her post-colonial literature seminar group. Tall, smiley, the sparkliest green eyes she'd ever seen and ridiculously golden curly hair – he looked like a grown-up cherub.

'Thanks.' He clinked his glass against hers. 'Helena, isn't it?'

'Eleanor. Ellie.'

'Thanks, Ellie.' He didn't bother to introduce himself – he probably guessed everyone knew who he was – and with another dazzling smile, he faded away into the huddle of people bobbing around to 'Our House'.

Eleanor's plan to slow down on the Bacardi and Cokes fell by the wayside fairly quickly, and she soon lost count of how many she'd had. She was sitting on the floor between Diane and Wendy, their backs against the wall, legs stretched out in front of them, watching some annoying bloke perform his juggling 'act'. While Eleanor and Wendy could barely conceal their amusement, Diane remained stony-faced. When he'd finished, clearly expecting more than the trickle of weak applause, Diane took a drag of her Russian cigarette, exhaled and pronounced in a voice heavy with contempt, '*Riveting.*'

Eleanor and Wendy caught each other's eye and grinned.

'I need a bloody drink after that,' Diane said. 'Anyone else?'

'S'okay,' Eleanor said, getting to her feet. 'I'll get my own.' She made her way to the drinks table, aware that the room was starting to spin. She'd better slow down. She'd just picked up the Bacardi when Simon appeared at her side again. 'Allow me,' he said, taking her glass from her and sloshing in a generous amount of Bacardi followed by a splash of Coke. 'You don't want to drown it, you know.'

To her horror, she felt tears spring to her eyes and start spilling down her cheeks. Simon's expression instantly changed to one of concern. 'Oh, fuck, what is it?' He took her glass and put it on the table, then put his arm round her. 'Come on, let's get some fresh air.' He steered her out of the room and along the hall, through the kitchen and out the back door. The landlord kept promising to clear the garden, which was overgrown and full of junk, but with everything dusted with white frost that sparkled in the moonlight, it looked enchanting.

'Now,' he put his hands on her shoulders and turned her to face him. He seemed to be searching her face, then he gently placed his thumbs under her eyes and swept her tears away. 'Tell Uncle Simon; what's making you cry?'

'Sorry. I don't know, really. I've had a bit too much to drink and I'm being silly.'

He nodded. 'Too many bevvies can do that. I was at a party a couple of weeks back and someone put "Without You" on the stereo. I fucking hate that record – always have, but there I was, blubbing like a baby.'

Eleanor smiled and wiped her eyes. The garden appeared to spin for a moment before settling again. 'Sorry. I'm fine, honestly.' Maybe she was more bothered about Ray than she'd thought. 'It might be because, well, I split up with my boyfriend earlier.'

'Your choice or his?'

'His. But I'm not—'

'He's a fucking idiot.' He looked at her. 'You're shivering. Come here,' he pulled her into his arms. 'Let me warm you up.'

She allowed herself to snuggle against him. Everything felt a bit spinny when she closed her eyes, but at least she wouldn't fall over because Simon was holding her.

'So, who's this dickhead ex of yours? Anyone I'd know?'

'No, he's at Queen Mary's in Mile End. We were at the same school.'

'You don't want to get back with him, do you?'

She shook her head. 'No, actually. It feels weird because I've been going out with him for a year. But, no, I don't want to get back with him.'

Simon's arms tightened around her and she felt his warm lips on her neck. It flashed through her mind that he was touching her wig. Would he notice? But then he was kissing her on the lips and she closed her eyes and the spinning started again.

She wasn't quite sure how that snog in the garden had led to them squeezing into her single bed while the party carried on downstairs, but here they were, squished together in the dark. She couldn't remember walking up the stairs or even getting into bed. The light from the street lamp outside fell on her gypsy skirt hanging over the back of the chair; she didn't know what had happened to her top, but she was still wearing her bra and knickers. Simon had taken his thick jumper off but he was still wearing his t-shirt and she could feel the rough fabric of his jeans against her bare legs. He was kissing her neck. She was about to push him away when she remembered that as of about eight o'clock this evening, she didn't have a boyfriend any more. She was free. But did that mean this was okay? She closed her eyes to try to gather her thoughts, but everything was spinning madly out of control and she felt as if she was falling. She opened her eyes again and felt a bit better. Simon was fumbling with the clasp of her bra, and in no time he was sliding the straps down over her arms and tossing it onto the floor. He leant up on his elbow and looked down at her, tracing the outline of her breast with his fingertips and bringing them to rest on her nipple. 'You look beautiful in the lamplight,' he murmured, and then she felt his weight on top of her and he was kissing her roughly.

She was aware that things were happening fast, and she hadn't decided she definitely wanted to sleep with him, but on the other hand he *was* nice, and she wasn't tied to Ray any more, so why not?

It was over more quickly than she expected. He hadn't even asked whether he should use anything, so it was a good job she was on the pill, although she kept forgetting to take it at her usual time – there didn't seem much point. She knew she'd remembered it tonight, though, because she'd only just taken it when Ray phoned.

Simon pushed back the covers, sat up and swung his legs round so he was sitting on the edge of the bed. He pulled a pack of Rothmans out of his jeans pocket and held it up. 'Oops.' He smiled. 'Bit squashed.' He buttoned his jeans then lit two cigarettes and handed one to her, then he leant over and gave her a peck on the cheek. 'Must get some water. I'll leave you to sort yourself out – see you downstairs.' And he was gone.

She took the ashtray down off the windowsill and lay there smoking for a minute, but then she began to feel queasy so she stubbed her cigarette out. When she stood up, the room started spinning again. God, she must be really, really drunk. She pulled her skirt on, found her top and pulled that on too, then she grabbed her bra and knickers, took her towel off the back of the door and hurried along to the bathroom.

*

After she'd brushed her teeth and washed her face, she felt much better, so she headed back down to the party, picking her way through the couples snogging on the stairs. A remix of 'I Feel Love' was playing on the stereo, with a few people dancing drunkenly in the middle of the room. She should find Simon. Was this just a one-off-party thing, or did he want to go out with her properly? Now she'd sobered up a bit, she wasn't sure that was what she wanted; she wasn't sure she even fancied him that much.

She suddenly felt desperately thirsty, so she went along to the kitchen for a glass of water. She was about to go in when she recognised his voice. She heard him say, *That Eleanor.* She hung back in the shadows, half smiling, expecting him to say something nice. But when the other voice said, *Isn't that the one who's bald as a coot? Wears a wig?* Simon replied, in an unnecessarily coarse tone, she thought, *You don't look at the mantelpiece when you're poking the fire, do you?* And then they both laughed loudly.

Eleanor, 18 December 1982

She wanted to get a head start on the books for next term, so she'd planned on reading *Things Fall Apart* on the journey, but as soon as she was settled in her seat she realised she was in no condition to read, even though they hadn't started moving yet. She wasn't even sure how she'd managed to pack her stuff, get to the station and get herself on the train. She was probably still hung-over, but she suspected the nausea and slightly dazed feeling had more to do with what she'd overheard last night. She couldn't seem to think about anything else. She sighed and put the book back in her bag. Simon was in at least one of her seminar groups; how was she going to be able to look at him across the room, knowing what he thought of her? After she'd heard that horrible conversation, she'd turned and run back up to her room, climbed into bed and cried herself to sleep. She woke with a humdinger of a headache, and when she went into the kitchen in search of aspirin, she found Wendy and Kathy sitting at the kitchen table nursing mugs of tea and smoking Diane's Russian ciga- rettes. Wendy stood up and moved towards the kettle. 'Tea and painkillers?'

She nodded. 'Please.'

Was it one of them who'd blabbed about her hair? Or was it Diane or Joy? When she'd asked them to keep it to themselves, every one of them had immediately mut- tered something like, *Of course*; and, *Goes without saying*. And she'd trusted them.

'So.' Kathy grinned. 'I saw you canoodling in the garden with that Greek god.' She pretended to swoon. 'But I think I must have passed out after that. Did you get off with him in the end? Come on, spill the beans!'

'Not really. He's a bit of an arsehole when you get talk- ing to him.'

'Is he? How come?'

She'd stood up then, told them she'd decided to go home a day early and was off to pack. They were clearly surprised by her change of heart – it was no secret that she hadn't been looking forward to Christmas at home, but there was no way she could risk bumping into Simon. And she didn't think she could face spending time with her housemates either, not now she knew that at least one of them had betrayed her trust and friendship. She felt a lump in her throat and tears prick her eyes. *Don't cry*, she told herself; think about something else. She huddled down into her coat and tried to blink away the tears as the train started to move off. She was vaguely aware of a hippyish-looking boy in an afghan coat settling himself in the seat opposite, but she kept her face turned firmly to the window. Out of the corner of her eye, she saw that he was doing exactly the same. Good. The last thing she wanted was to get into a conversation.

She was trying very hard to stop thinking about Simon, but then she kept wondering which of her so-called friends had blabbed about her hair. And if she managed to stop thinking about that, she started worrying again about how she was going to cope with Christmas at home with her mum. It wouldn't be so bad if they'd been going upstairs for the day like last year, but Peggy and Ken were spending Christmas with Ken's parents this year, up North somewhere, so they wouldn't be back until New Year. Her stomach was in knots. How on earth was she going to get through this? She couldn't possibly tell her mum about what had happened last night, even if she left out the sex bit. Her mind zipped back to that look on her mum's face the last time she'd seen her, the morning she'd set off for Reading. She'd still been in bed, her head uncovered, when her mum had come in to say goodbye before she went to work. Eleanor hadn't missed the double-take, the way her mother's eyes fluttered in embarrassment while trying not to look away. There was no avoiding the fact that a bald head first thing in the morning was a shocking sight.

She was doing her best to get used to the way she

looked now, and some days were worse than others. This morning, when struggling to confront her own reflection, she'd remembered not only Simon's vile comment, but also her mother's expression that day, somewhere between embarrassment and revulsion. As she'd forced herself to look in the mirror, she was reminded of some of the things she'd heard about in history or English at school, and more recently in the reading she'd been doing for her degree, stories of women whose hair had been shorn as a punishment, usually just before they were strapped into a ducking stool and drowned for being witches.

Conscious again of the boy sitting opposite, she bit her lip in an attempt to control her misery, but every so often a tear or two ran down her face. She wanted to wipe them away but that would draw attention, so she kept her tissue scrunched in her hand, ignored the tears and hoped the boy wouldn't look in her direction. After a few minutes, she noticed he was sniffing quite a lot, then she caught the movement of his hand up to his face. She risked a glance. It looked like *he* was crying! She tried to concentrate on looking out of the window, but then, without moving her head, she turned her eyes towards him again. He was younger than her, sixteen, maybe, possibly seventeen, and his face was red and blotchy – he was definitely crying. She didn't want to embarrass him, but his sniffing was hard to ignore and the next time her gaze crept towards him he caught her eye. Her own face was probably equally blotched, she realised. 'Sorry,' he said, wiping his eyes one at a time with his thumb. 'A

215

right pair we are, aren't we?' He sniffed again, and felt in the pockets of his coat.

Eleanor held out a travel pack of tissues.

'Cheers.' He took one from the pack, wiped his face and then blew his nose. 'You must think I'm such a wimp, blubbing like a kid.'

She shrugged. 'Happens to us all.'

'But it's not so bad if you're a girl, is it?' A look of panic flashed across his face. 'Sorry, I shouldn't have said that, it was sexist. My mum would kill me if she heard me.'

'It's okay. It doesn't matter, does it? I don't know why people get so annoyed about things that don't even bloody matter.'

He was looking at her closely. 'Are you all right?' he said. 'You look quite upset.'

'So do you.' She hadn't meant it to sound like some sort of accusation. 'I mean, are *you* all right?'

'Yeah. At least, I will be. Parent trouble.'

'Oh. Have you had a row with them, or something?'

'Just my dad. They split up. I usually live with my mum, but for the last couple of months I've only been with her at weekends and in the holidays, because she's ... oh, it's complicated. Anyway, I'm on my way to see my mum now.'

'So you're with your dad but he—'

'No, I don't live with him. Thing is, he doesn't think Jill – that's my mum – should do what she's doing. And even before that he didn't like where we were living.' He sighed, and it still sounded a bit shaky, as though he'd been crying quite a lot. He looked nervous. 'We're not weirdos, right? But we live in a commune. Well, I do, anyway; my mum's at Greenham Common at the moment, helping out at the peace camp. I've got O levels in May, so I need to get to school or I'd be there myself. Until they chuck me off for being a bloke, anyway.'

'Your mum's at Greenham? What, you mean she's one of those women who camp there?'

He nodded. 'For a while, anyway. She says she's going to do six months, then come back to the house. It's this massive old place in Camberwell, and there's usually nine of us, including my mum, and twelve if you include the kids. There's Andrew, he's ten, Tom, who's nine, and Dawn, she's only three. She's my sister. Her name's really Misty Dawn, but I call her Dawn. I'm Alex, by the way.'

'Misty; that's an unusual name. Pretty, though. There was girl at my old school called Rainbow but she made everyone call her Ronnie. So why doesn't your dad live with you?'

'He did at first, but they kept having rows. Jill says he was only interested in the "free love" side of it, and when he realised it wasn't an excuse to screw everyone in sight . . .'

'Your mum told you this?'

'Yeah, she tells us loads of stuff; I wish she wouldn't sometimes.' He paused. 'Do you mind me telling *you*?'

'No, not if you don't.'

'So, anyway, my dad said he was fed up with sharing stuff and wanted to go back to it being just the four of us. But Jill said no. See, my dad's a lazy bastard. When we lived with him, he never did anything to help Jill, just expected her to wait on him hand and foot. But it's not like that at the house. Everyone shares everything. We care more about people than *things*. And it's like, you realise that all this bourgeois shit, right, it just doesn't *matter*.' His voice had gone a bit strange, and she suspected he was repeating something someone else had said. 'D'you get what I mean?'

'Yes, I definitely get what you mean.'

'I go to his flat sometimes, but today he was in a really bad mood and he was saying all this nasty stuff about Jill and Lisa – she's one of the other mums from the house who's at the camp with Jill. Dad said they're all a load of lesbians, and if I want to live with them he doesn't want to see me or Dawn again. And that's shit, because Dawn hasn't done anything wrong and she isn't even old enough to decide things.'

Eleanor sighed, her own tears now at a safe distance. 'That sounds horrible,' she said. 'I bet he doesn't mean it, though. Perhaps he'll change his mind when he realises.'

'No, I don't think so. He's always been like this. I put up with it because he's my dad, but I'm not going to any more. I think that's why I got so upset. Before now, I've always thought something would change, but when I walked out of his flat today, I sort of knew I wasn't going back. Do you get what I mean?' He was looking at her intently.

'Yes,' she said. 'Yes, I think I do.' She felt a sudden pang for her own dad, how he used to call her Ellie-belly and ruffle her hair when she was little. Maybe if he were still around, things with her mum would be easier.

'Anyway, shit – I'm sorry,' Alex was saying. 'You're upset too, and all I've done is go on about my own problems. How you feeling? Are you okay?'

She nodded. 'Funny how someone else's problems can make you forget about your own. Sorry, I didn't mean "funny" in that way.'

'I know. You meant funny peculiar, not funny ha-ha.'

She smiled. Peggy said that sometimes. She felt another wave of sadness as she remembered Peggy wouldn't be there for Christmas.

'So, what are you upset about?'

She sighed. 'It's all a bit complicated.' She certainly didn't want to tell him the whole story, but he seemed nice, and he'd told her why he was upset, so she gave him an edited version. She found it surprisingly easy to tell him about her hair, maybe because she assumed she'd never see him again after today. She saw his eyes flick up to her scalp. 'This is a wig,' she explained. And then she told him that she'd split up with her boyfriend over it, and then soon after had overheard someone at a party making a nasty comment. And what was more, she was now on her way home a day earlier than planned to spend Christmas with her mother, who didn't really want her around, and she was dreading it.

'Shit, man. That's really, I mean it's—'

'Yeah, like you said, it's shit. I haven't even phoned her yet to tell her I'm coming today instead of tomorrow. I'll have to phone her from the station.'

He nodded. 'Where do you live, anyway?'

'Lewisham.'

'Lewisham? But ... you're going the wrong way for London.'

She looked at him. 'What?' She looked out of the window and then back at him. 'Isn't this the Paddington train?'

'No, this is going to Bedwyn.'

'Bedwyn?' She didn't even know where that was.

The train started to slow. 'This is me.' Alex stood and picked up his rucksack, and at the same moment a ticket inspector appeared at the other end of the carriage.

'Shit! Do you think he'll make me pay?'

'He might. Why don't you jump off here with me?'

'But where are we?'

'Newbury. Quick.' He glanced towards the ticket inspector and then reached up to the luggage rack for her suitcase.

'Tell you what,' Alex said as she stepped down onto the platform behind him. 'If your mum isn't expecting you, why not come up to the camp with me instead of going straight back? It's a bit of a walk, but you could have a coffee or something. Then you can meet Jill – I mean, my mum. She's really cool.'

Eleanor's mind was in a whirl. Thank goodness she hadn't ended up in Bedwyn, or wherever it was. She'd still have to get back to Paddington somehow, but if she went with Alex now, she wouldn't have to worry about that until later. 'Okay then,' she said.

Marjorie, December 1982

On the morning of 12 December, when they were due to get the coach, Peggy rang down on the extension to say that she felt like death warmed up and could barely lift her head from the pillow. Marjorie made her a cup of tea and hurried upstairs with it. Peggy was still in bed, her face pale and waxy-looking. There was a sheen of perspiration on her forehead.

'You'd better get going,' she told Marjorie.

'You've got to be kidding.' Marjorie frowned as she looked at the thermometer. 'It's a hundred and two – I can't possibly leave you on your own while you're like this.'

Peggy closed her eyes and gave a small, dismissive wave before her hand fell limply back onto the covers. 'I'll be fine, honestly. It's just a cold.' Her teeth chattered as she spoke.

'Are you feeling shivery?'

'A bit, yes.'

Marjorie pulled the quilt up and tucked it around her bare shoulder. 'It's probably that flu that's been going around. I'll stay here. You need looking after.'

'I'll be fine, Marje, honestly. I'm not planning to do anything other than lie here and feel sorry for myself. And Ken's due back tonight, anyway.'

'Yes, but that's not until much later.'

'Marjorie Crawford,' Peggy shook her head, and with some effort levered herself up onto her elbow. 'Go. Go for the sake of our kids, like we said. And their kids; that's if no one's blown the planet to bloody kingdom come by that time.'

Marjorie frowned as she tried to decide what to do. She wanted to go; at least, she *ought* to go because, as Peggy said, it was important. But it was one thing for the two of them to go together, and quite another for her to go on her own. Could she really do this by herself? She looked at Peggy again and rested a hand on her forehead. 'You're clammy. And you look dreadful.'

'Sod what I look like.' Peggy flopped back onto the pillow. 'Honestly, Marje, you won't forgive yourself if you don't go. Look how you felt last time, after Aldermaston. Just bring me some water and a couple of aspirin and I'll be fine.' She pointed to the dressing table. 'In the top drawer, that photo I was going to take – can you take it and put it up for me?'

Marjorie hesitated, then nodded. 'All right. If you're absolutely sure you'll be okay.' She opened the drawer and took out the photo of the twins. The organisers wanted everyone to take some memento, a symbol of peace or love. What better symbol of love than a photo of your children? The boys were about a year old here, sitting one at either end of a Silver Cross pram and grinning at the camera. They'd both left home now; Michael was in his final year at university and Martin, who'd left school at sixteen and trained as an electrician, was working in Saudi Arabia for a year and making lots of money, apparently. She knew Peggy missed them more than she let on.

'I'm still not sure what I'm going to take. I only have the one photo of the two of them. I hadn't looked at it for years when Eleanor found it, but now I don't think I can bear to part with it.' She glanced at Peggy, whose eyes were closing again. 'I'll think of something. I'll bring you water, aspirin and a flask of tea before I go. And a flask of soup as well.'

'Lovely,' Peggy murmured, and closed her eyes.

*

It was someone Peggy knew from her yoga class who'd told them about it and organised seats on the coach. She was a nice enough woman, but she wasn't really Marjorie's type – always going on about things she'd read in *Spare Rib*. Peggy had got talking to her about this because it turned out they'd both been on the Aldermaston march in 1960. Marjorie hadn't gone on that one, although she and Peggy had been friends by then – they'd started nurse training together a few months earlier. And after the march, when they'd talked about wanting a better world to bring their future children into, a world without the H-bomb, Marjorie thought maybe she should have gone after all. It was 'an incredible experience', Peggy had said, and Marjorie wished then that she'd been part of it. But despite all the passion and determination surrounding that march, here they were, over twenty years later, and the threat of nuclear annihilation felt just as close now as it had then.

What they hadn't known when they had had that conversation was that Peggy was already pregnant. And now they were both mothers – although Marjorie sometimes wondered if she deserved the title – and they'd intended to make their protest as mothers, as custodians of the future. We should think not only of our children, the organisers said, but of our children's children.

Marjorie almost ended up missing the coach because she spent so long looking for a suitable memento. She'd hidden things so well that she had to get the step ladder out of the old scullery so she could reach the boxes at the back of the top cupboards. She hadn't kept much because it was painful to have too many reminders in the house, but there was a little white romper suit with embroidered blue rabbits scampering across the chest that Ted's mum gave her just before Peter was born. There were two of these; the other one, the one he was buried in, was blue with white rabbits. Also in the box was a fluffy yellow chick that was part of a gift set from the other nurses when she left to have Eleanor. It had a ribbon loop made of yellow and white gingham so you could hang it from the pram hood. Eleanor had loved it, barely taking her eyes from it as she lay on her back gurgling and kicking her legs. When Peter was born, the chick hung in exactly the same place so he could see it all the time. He never looked at it, though.

She wrapped Peggy's photo, the romper suit and the chick in an old cardigan and put them carefully in her bag, along with some string and a handful of safety pins. Then she packed her sandwiches and a flask of Bovril before letting herself out into the dark morning. It had been raining all night, but now the rain turned to sleet as she hurried through the quiet streets to join the other women on the coach.

They'd been told it was definitely a women-only protest, but apparently not everyone had heard because two of the women came with their husbands, and she thought it rather a shame when the men were turned away. Surely this was something everyone should be protesting about?

Most of the women on the coach were Marjorie's age or younger. There were a few typical CND types with short hair and mannish clothes, no doubt concealing unshaven armpits from what she'd heard. But they turned out to be very nice. There were a couple of ladies who must have been in their sixties or even seventies. One of them, Betty, proudly announced she would be seventy-six next birthday, and cheerfully handed round deliciously chewy, oaty biscuits at regular intervals. There were so many requests for the recipe that she ended up calling it out rather than write it down so many times. The atmosphere on the coach was friendly and optimistic, and it was clear that the protest would go ahead despite the appalling weather.

The trip to Thatcham took longer than expected, partly because the driving rain made visibility difficult and everything was moving more slowly, but also because, as they neared the base, the roads were choked with coaches and minibuses from the all over the country. There were CND symbols in many of the windows, and peace slogans and flowers painted on some of the smaller vehicles.

It was sleeting again when they got off the coach, and the recent rain had turned the ground into a muddy bog. The bottoms of her trousers were already soaked about six inches up and the mud was sucking at her shoes; but as she allowed herself to be swept along with the others, she realised that no one else seemed to care about the mud, and with so much going on around her she soon forgot about it. There were lots of policemen milling around, and several Black Marias parked at odd angles, but it was hard to credit there'd be any trouble when you looked around and saw all these women, some with children, all smiling, all calmly determined.

She wasn't sure what she'd expected, but was surprised to realise that there was very little organisation.

She knew the plan was to 'embrace the base'; you were supposed to link arms, apparently, to form a human chain around the whole nine miles of the perimeter fence. She felt a flutter of nerves; she wished Peggy was here. Peggy was so much better at this sort of thing.

No one knew when they were going to actually start making the chain, but it didn't seem to matter because there were so many women here that everyone felt sure someone would know what to do when the time came. In the meantime, she wanted to pin the tributes she'd brought with her to the fence, which was already half covered. There were lots of coloured balloons, banners calling for peace, CND symbols, a collage of a rainbow with BAN THE BOMB written across it; and once she'd scrambled up the grass verge to add hers and Peggy's contributions, she was able to see the array of photographs, children's drawings and poems that adorned the wire, not to mention the Babygros, booties and matinee jackets, the teddy bears and dolls. The sleet was easing off now, but everything was soaked. Swallowing the lump that had formed in her throat, she reached into her bag for the things she'd brought with her. There was another rainbow banner along to the left, heavily decorated with embroidered flowers and appliquéd white doves. It was beautiful; the amount of work that must have gone into it! She pinned the romper suit and Peggy's photo just beneath it, then tied the little chick by its ribbon close to the romper suit.

She was still looking at it when she became aware of

someone standing next to her. 'Sorry.' She stepped back automatically. 'I'm in your way.'

'No, no, did mine further down. Just having a look, really.'

Marjorie recognised her from the coach, probably because of her severe pudding-basin haircut and tweedy appearance. 'Bloody moving, isn't it?' The woman gestured along the fence. 'Damn good turnout, too.' That was when Marjorie realised just how many people must be there. She turned to the left and then to the right; the lines of women were three or four deep for as far as she could see in both directions, and more were arriving every minute.

*

By the time they were all back on the coach that evening, Marjorie was cold, her feet were wet and she was shattered. As they'd driven away from the base, lit up in the darkness by hundreds of candles, she'd felt almost as if she wanted to stay, to be with those women who'd left their other lives behind to focus on the continuing peaceful protest. But much as she admired them and was glad she'd been there today, she didn't think she'd be up to sleeping in the mud under a sheet of plastic with people she didn't know. At first she'd been worried about the lack of organisation, but somehow the thousands of women had organised themselves and they'd made their point. They'd linked arms and formed a circle around the enormous military base, then later some of them had lit candles and sung Christmas carols. Had Peggy been there, they'd have probably joined in with the singing, but although Marjorie had got talking to one or two of the others, she'd mainly hovered on the peripheries of the bigger groups. She'd always liked Christmas carols, and there was something about them being sung in this cold, bleak place that made them particularly affecting. What moved her to tears, though, was when dozens of women, possibly even hundreds, began singing 'Imagine'. As she stood there listening in the darkness, she felt hot tears sliding down her freezing face. She knew it was a good song, but it always made her sad because she only ever focused on the first line, and she didn't want to imagine there was no heaven; she liked to think there was one, and that there was someone up there – Ted, or her mother, maybe – taking care of Peter. And poor Maurice, of course. She felt a familiar wave of guilt when she thought about Maurice, as though she were disobeying her mother by even allowing him into her mind.

On the way back, she sat at the rear of the coach next to Hilary, the woman she'd talked to earlier in the day. The return trip was a quieter, more subdued affair, probably because everyone was so tired and emotionally drained. Hilary's daughter, Carole, who was about the same age as Eleanor, was dozing with her head on her mother's lap. Hilary talked quietly to Marjorie, absent-mindedly stroking the girl's hair as she did so. After a while, Marjorie couldn't concentrate on what Hilary was saying; it didn't seem to require any response, anyway.

Her mind spooled back to one morning in the spring, before they'd had that dreadful row about Eleanor spending so much time upstairs. She'd gone in to wake her up for school, and had paused to look at her sleeping face, which was illuminated by a sliver of early morning sunshine that fell through a gap in the curtains. Eleanor was almost eighteen, but she looked younger when she was asleep, her skin smooth and glowing with childlike peachiness, hair spread messily over the pillow. It was long then, still blonde but darker than when she was a child. It came halfway down her back, and the sunshine picked out golden highlights. Marjorie moved nearer to the bed. She'd have to wake her soon, but for just a moment she wanted to pretend that they were a normal mother and daughter. She gently reached out and stroked her hair, which was thick and healthy, and fell into envi-able waves around her shoulders. When was the last time she'd touched it? When Eleanor was tiny it had been fine and silky, always a mass of tangles in the mornings, and she'd stand between Marjorie's knees, biting her lip and trying to be brave as Marjorie brushed the knots out and then plaited her hair into two pigtails before tying on ribbons. She would probably have plaited her hair on that morning, oblivious to the fact that it was something she'd rarely do again. While she was in hospital, Peggy had taken over getting Eleanor ready for school, and had carried on dealing with her hair, plaiting it, tying rib-bons in it, whatever Eleanor wanted, long after she came home. That familiar sense of regret bloomed inside her again. Ted had been right about that – she should never have abdicated motherhood so completely, but she hadn't realised there would be no way back.

Now, as she watched Hilary stroking Carole's mousy head, she tried to recapture the sensation as she'd carefully lifted a strand of Eleanor's silky blonde hair and allowed it to slip over her fingers like a waterfall. 'Oh, Eleanor,' she murmured, 'why wasn't it *my* hair instead?'

'What's that?' Hilary said.

'Oh, nothing,' Marjorie replied, surprised to realise she'd said it out loud.

Eleanor: December 1982, Greenham Common

It was a long, uphill walk from Newbury station to the camp, but Alex told her it was better to get off here rather than Thatcham or Aldermaston, because both those stations would still be crawling with police.

It had been misty even when they got off the train, but as they trudged up the hill past the dark, dense mass of trees that loomed on either side, the mist became thicker and it was difficult to make out much apart from what was immediately ahead. Even though it wasn't raining, the air felt heavy with moisture and the dampness somehow managed to creep through her clothes, creating a chill that reached her very bones.

The walk was arduous, but they talked more on the way and, before long, she was considering the possibility of staying at the camp for the night. 'Jill will sort you out somewhere to sleep,' Alex said. 'Then you can decide what to do in the morning.'

Her legs were tired and her feet were getting sore, and just when she thought she couldn't bear to walk any further, Alex pointed ahead and said, 'There it is. Still a way to go yet, though.'

The base seemed to appear from within the mist, giving the whole place an eeriness that sent a shiver though her. Being so close to it made her think about nuclear war, and thoughts like that tended to stay in her head for days at a time, the same as when she thought about what had happened to Peter. As they got nearer, she could see the perimeter fence. 'Is this where they pinned teddy bears and Babygros and things?'

'Yeah,' Alex said, pausing for a moment to look. 'They took it all down a few days ago.'

'Took it down? Why?'

'Not the women; they didn't do it.'

'Who did then?'

'The MOD mainly, but there were local volunteers as well. Some of them brought their children, and that was really sad, seeing all those little kids shoving everything into black bin bags as though it was just rubbish.' He shook his head. 'There are a few bits left where the women have put them up again, but you should have seen it the day after. It looked brilliant. Especially all the kids' things, the clothes and toys and that. Dawn did a picture – just crayon scribbles, really, but we put it up anyway.' He looked thoughtful for a moment. 'We lit candles when it got dark, and when you saw all that stuff on the fence in the candlelight, all the toys and the baby things – it was a bit, what do you call it? Tear-jerking.'

'I can imagine.' She put her suitcase down and looked up at the fence. 'Can I have a closer look?'

'Sure.' He shrugged. 'Not much to see now, though; just a lot of wire fencing.'

She scrambled up the verge and tramped over brambles. There were scraps of string here and there left tied to the wire, a shrivelled balloon that had been missed. On the news on the night of the protest, the camera had panned along the fence, past all the banners, mementoes and photographs, and zoomed in on a section where someone had woven strands of green fabric through the wire in the shape of a Christmas tree and pinned on little gold CND symbols to look like baubles. There was tinsel, too. Many of the protesters would be here over Christmas – Alex and his mum were definitely staying, he told her.

'Shall we carry on?' Alex said. 'It's still quite a way to where my mum and her mates are.'

'Okay, sorry.' She was negotiating her way back down through the brambles when she spotted a mud-spattered scrap of yellow and white gingham caught on a thorn. It looked like ribbon, obviously from something that had been pinned to the fence, and she felt an unexpected ripple of sadness as she passed it.

The camp was vast, and the expanse of cold, grey concrete on the other side of the wire fence only added to the bleakness. Parts of the site were just a sea of mud-covered plastic. There were Calor gas bottles everywhere; bundles of clothes, crates and dustbins filled with tinned food; pots and pans hanging from nails banged into planks of wood. There were tents, most of them tiny, and a few caravans, but Alex said they sometimes had to sleep under plastic sheeting. They passed a teenage girl sitting on the step of one of the caravans, reading to three small children, who were sitting on upturned buckets and looking up at her with rapt expressions. There were plumes of smoke coming from a campfire which was surrounded by groups of women talking quietly. No one seemed to be particularly bothered by the cold or the damp, but Eleanor could feel the mist clinging to her clothes already. There were lots of police around, but they weren't doing anything, just watching or talking to each other.

What would it be like to spend Christmas here, she wondered? Alex said she could stay as long as she liked; he said she would be more than welcome, and they had a spare sleeping bag. At first, she'd laughed and told him not to be silly. But now she found the possibility of not going home growing larger in her mind. After all, there was no law that said you had to spend Christmas at home, was there? Last Christmas, she'd eaten turkey and all the trimmings with her mum and Peggy and Ken, then they'd all sat by the fire watching a James Bond film while eating chocolate Brazils and crystallised ginger. But this year would be different; it would be just her and her mum. And if all these women were giving up their cosy family Christmases to make their point about the horror of nuclear war, maybe she could, too . . .

'Here we are,' Alex said as they approached a cluster of tents and caravans. The door to an orange-and-cream camper van slid open and out stepped a tall, smiling woman with her hair in a plait that reached down to her waist. She enfolded Alex in her arms and closed her eyes as she hugged him. 'I'm so glad you're back, sweetie,' she said. 'How did it go with your dad?'

Alex's cheeks pinked as he glanced at Eleanor while extricating himself from his mother's embrace. 'Yeah. It wasn't great. I'll tell you later. Anyway, this is Eleanor. She got on the wrong train and she doesn't want to go home, so she might stay for a bit.' He took her arm and pulled her forward. 'El, this is Jill, my mad mother.'

Jill's smile broadened even further and she cuffed Alex playfully on the shoulder. 'Eleanor,' Jill put her arms out and pulled her into them as though she was a long-lost friend. She smelt of bonfires and slightly of motor oil and that green gunge Ray used to clean his hands with after he'd been tinkering with his car – Swarfega, that was it. 'Eleanor, welcome, welcome. The more the merrier. Excuse the state of me.' She released her and held up her hands, which were smeared with black oil. 'I've been trying to sort out this fucking camper. I swear to God, she's for the scrapyard if she keeps this up.'

Eleanor had no idea what to say, and looked helplessly at Alex.

'Forgive my foul-mouthed mother,' he said, half smiling. 'She's just showing off.'

'No, it's fine.' She smiled. 'I mean, I'm not ... I don't ...' In truth, she was mildly shocked that someone's mother should swear so freely in front of her. But on the other hand, she liked it, because it made her feel instantly accepted and welcomed. She laughed. 'Sorry, I'm trying to say I really don't mind. I swear all the time.'

'Yeah, but probably not within two seconds of meeting someone.' Alex grinned.

'I'm sorry,' Jill said. 'I do try, but when something vexes me ...' She turned towards the camper. 'Like Doris here.' She aimed a small kick at the wheel arch. 'Who *keeps* refusing to start, no matter how nicely I speak to her ... then I just can't help myself.'

'I told you, El.' Alex rolled his eyes. 'She's a nutter.'

*

If anyone had told Eleanor she would end up sleeping in a tent in the middle of winter and living on eggs, beans and soup, she would have found it hard to believe. But it was amazing how quickly you could get used to something when everybody else was doing the same thing without complaining.

There was a Quaker meeting house not far from the camp where the women could use the telephone, so she'd phoned her mum to let her know where she was and that she wasn't coming home for Christmas. Her mum was upset, of course, but probably secretly relieved. And when they spoke again two weeks later, she wasn't at all happy at Eleanor's news that she definitely wasn't going back to Reading. She didn't like upsetting her mum, but she was an adult now; this was her life.

She didn't see much of Alex on the weekends – he was here because he was always in demand as a babysitter, and was often around the camp somewhere, entertaining groups of kids while their mums were busy organising things or having run-ins with the police. His little sister – everyone called her Dawn but Eleanor thought 'Misty' was much prettier – adored him and could usually be found clinging to his legs or sitting on his shoulders. No trace of sibling rivalry there. Some of the children were here all the time, and some came for visits, dropped off by their dads after breakfast and collected again later. A couple of times, Alex asked Eleanor if she fancied baby-sitting with him. She might have been okay with the older children; she could see herself turning a skipping rope or kicking a ball around. But when it came to the babies and toddlers, she couldn't imagine trusting her-self enough. Would she ever be able to hold a baby in her arms? 'I'm not very good with little kids,' she told him. 'Never have been.'

*

The first time she saw Alex driving the camper, her mouth dropped open. He'd been up to the main gate to pick up some firewood. 'You can drive!' she said like an idiot when he slid the door back and jumped down onto the grass. 'How come you can drive?'

'Jill taught me.'

'But ... I didn't think you were old enough.'

'Well, I'm not old enough to take my test yet, so I can't actually drive it off the site, but I passed my moped test before Christmas, so I know a bit about the road already.' He lifted a sack of firewood down onto the grass. 'And Jill's taken me out in Doris loads of times – only round car parks and wasteland and that, but enough for me to get the hang of the gears. Obviously, I'll need a few proper lessons as well, but Jill's paying for those for my birthday. She was going to give me Doris when she gets a new camper, but I want to save up for my own car.'

'That'll take a while, won't it?' She helped him haul down the other sack of wood.

'Probably. But when we go back to the house, I'll be able to get a weekend job, and it won't be that long before I leave school anyway. I'm going to get a second-hand Ford Escort.'

'I wish I could drive. I was having lessons before I started at Reading, but I'd only had four and then ... then my hair fell out and, I don't know, I chickened out, I suppose. My instructor was lovely, but he'd have noticed and I didn't want to have to explain.'

'Get Jill to teach you. You can drive Doris round here, easy. You still got your provisional licence?'

'Yes, it's in my bag.' She'd planned to take lessons again at some point, and she didn't want to be like her mum and leave it until she was over thirty before she passed her test, and only then after Peggy had nagged her into it. Peggy said all women should learn to drive as soon as possible, because then you didn't have to rely on men to give you lifts. 'Do you think your mum would mind?'

'Course she wouldn't. Jill's always teaching people to do stuff.'

Eleanor, the present

Exhausted, Eleanor climbs into bed at half past nine, thinking about Scalby and wondering what they're doing on the farm right at this moment. It's Friday night, so probably some wine, maybe a bit of a sing-song in the main house. She thinks about Dylan, about the feel of his bed-warmed skin against hers, and to her astonishment she finds a tear on her cheek. She flicks it away immediately. For God's sake! What is the matter with her? When has she ever even thought about Dylan when they weren't together? A handful of times over the whole year, maybe, and usually only when it's nearing the time when he's likely to show up. He'll only be in the country another few weeks anyway, so there's no point thinking about him. But then her thoughts stray to the picture he did of her head. She'll get it framed eventually, but for the moment, she's keeping it in the wardrobe so it doesn't get damp. She still can't quite get over the amount of thought he put into it, not to mention the work. All for her; all because he is interested in her and what goes on in her head. She'd like to look at it again, but she doesn't want to damage it by pulling it in and out of its cardboard tube. She sighs. She can't get comfortable. The pillow is hard and lumpy. She sits up and punches it a few times but it doesn't make much difference. She lies down again, but it makes her ear hurt. This bloody mattress is so ancient she can feel the springs. She turns onto her back and makes a conscious effort to try to relax.

Her mother has been fine over the last week or so. Well, fine-ish. She accused Eleanor of stealing her handbag when she'd actually left it upstairs in Peggy's kitchen, and she's started emptying cupboards again, but apart from that, it hasn't been too bad until today. Today, her mother has driven her nuts; following her around, asking the same irrelevant questions over and over again. Jenny is much better at handling this sort of thing; she seems to have endless patience with Marjorie, no matter how annoying she's being. 'Believe me,' Jenny told her, 'I've come across a lot worse.' Then she'd put an arm around her waist and given her a squeeze. 'You're doing all right, you know. And don't get me wrong, it's only because I'm trained to do this and I've got no personal connection. If it was my flipping mother . . .' and they'd both laughed.

She tries to focus on that now. It's to be expected, and it will get worse. Tears prick her eyes again, but this time she realises that they aren't because she is missing Dylan or the farm – well, not entirely, anyway. They're because she feels so bloody frustrated. Her body is awash with it all, full up with it. She nearly shouted at her mum this afternoon but stopped herself, thank God. It wasn't her mother's fault. She is beginning to see Alzheimer's as a living creature, an entity who has taken possession of her mother's mind and body and is moving around the house taunting them with its conquest. It flashes through her mind that she doesn't have to do this; no one is making her stay here. Then she shakes that thought out of her head. She finds herself thinking about that couple of years when she lived in the camper. It was so soothing to be certain that no one knew where she was unless she chose to tell them, that she wasn't responsible for anyone but herself. Apart from that, though, she remembers very little about that dark time.

Eventually her body stills, her breathing slows and she starts to sink down into a deep pool of sleep. Then she is upstairs standing by an open window; the night darkness has quite suddenly adjusted itself so that she knows it is early morning, a heartbeat or two before the dawn. In that enticing almost-light, she sees that Doris is parked right outside the house, looking like she had thirty years ago, only cleaner, shinier; she is fully operational and raring to go. In fact, her engine is running and her headlight seems to be winking at Eleanor as if to say, *Come on, hurry up*. So Eleanor climbs in and drives off, still in her pyjamas, running away again, escaping. Guilt starts to gnaw at her, as though acid is burning her stomach. And then she sees her mother, walking by the side of the road in her nightie, but she drives past. She keeps thinking she should turn around and go back, but she cannot move her foot from the accelerator, so she drives and drives and drives, and she knows she has done a terrible thing. She starts to cry and soon she forgets what the terrible thing is, but that makes it worse. If only she could turn around and go back . . .

She wakes with actual tears on her face. The image of her mother walking along the side of the road was so vivid it takes her a moment to accept that she's been dreaming. So far, her mother hasn't started wandering, but it's quite common in people with dementia, and there's always a first time. Maybe she heard something while she was asleep, and this is her brain's way of alerting her. She gets out of bed and moves quietly along the hallway to her mother's room. Heart thumping, she slowly turns the handle and pushes the door open. Thank God; her mum is there, snoring softly.

She creeps back to her room and climbs into bed, falling asleep quickly this time and sleeping soundly until her eyes spring open a few hours later. A soft bluish light seeps through the curtains, which means it must be around five. But it isn't the light that woke her, she's sure. She can feel her heart beating, and all her senses are on high alert. She throws the covers back and is out of bed and at the door in seconds. She smells it before she gets even halfway to her mother's room – gas. She spins round and hurries back along the hall, up the stairs and into the kitchen. Marjorie is sitting at the table with two trays of jam tarts ready for the oven in front of her. 'Something's wrong with that blasted cooker,' she says as Eleanor leaps across the kitchen to turn the gas off. 'It's not getting anywhere near hot enough. Oh, don't open those doors, darling, it's far too chilly.'

When Eleanor explains, Marjorie is horrified. 'Oh my goodness, I could have killed us,' she says. 'I'm not to be trusted, am I? I could have killed us all.'

*

It's a beautiful day. Peggy has taken Marjorie to Bromley to look for some summer clothes because even the things she bought recently are hanging off her now. They'll be back any moment, so Eleanor is preparing lunch for the three of them to eat in the garden. She wanted to try out the new cooker – electric this time – without her mother leaning over her shoulder. Marjorie didn't want an electric cooker, and when Eleanor explained why they needed one, Marjorie said she'd made the whole thing up.

She is pleased with her morning's work. She's made a quiche, a few fairy cakes and her famous – famous on the farm, anyway – Guinness and chocolate cake. She is just spreading the buttercream on top when she hears voices as her mum and Peggy walk along the side alleyway into the garden. They're both carrying bags and smiling as they come into view and make their way up the veranda steps.

'Successful trip?' she asks.

'Very,' Peggy says. 'I bought a red dress and a top, and your mum's had a real old spend-up. Show her, Marje.'

Her mum looks happy. 'Yes, Debenhams had some tops on special offer, two for fifteen pounds. Only cheap little t-shirts, but ever so useful, so I bought four.' She starts to look in her bags. 'I bought two nice cotton dresses as well, only simple, but fine for around the house. And a skirt, I think, and . . .' She looks at Peggy. 'What else, Peg?'

'That yellow blouse from M and S.'

Her mum seems about to say something, then doesn't. She looks distracted all of a sudden, as though she is no longer quite following the conversation.

'You look tired, Mum. Do you want lunch now, or would you like some tea first?'

'Yes, tea. Please.' She nods towards the bags she's holding. 'I'd better take these downstairs before they get wet.'

Eleanor and Peggy exchange looks. Sometimes it's best to ignore things like this. Eleanor switches the kettle on. 'You go and sit in the garden, Mum. I'll bring your tea out, then I'll pop down and put these in your room.'

When she opens the bedroom door, her heart sinks. The contents of the wardrobes and cupboards are once again strewn all over the floor as though they've been thrown. Marjorie still insists she's 'looking for something', but although Eleanor has helped her go through most of the cupboards now, she still can't find what she's looking for or remember what it is. Eleanor

246

dumps the carrier bags on the bed and kneels down to start tidying the mess of papers, boxes, towels and bed linen that are all jumbled together along with the odd shoe or bottle of body lotion. After a moment, she sits back on her heels and wonders why she's bothering. It'll only end up on the floor again in a few days' time. She bundles up the sheets and towels and shoves them back in the cupboard, then heaps the papers into empty shoe-boxes. Even though she's been through everything with Marjorie more than once, she always seems to find one or two photos that she hasn't seen before, which is why she still hopes she'll stumble across that photo of Peter she found when she was a teenager. She leafs through a handful of pictures and pauses over an old shot of her mother aged about ten, sitting on a blanket on the grass with her parents. She vaguely remembers her maternal grandfather. In this photo he was probably only in his mid-forties, tall and elegant with slicked-back hair and a full moustache. Her grandmother, who died when Eleanor was tiny, looks tired here, and old. This was taken in Mountsfield Park; there's the old bandstand in the background. If you stood right in the middle and shouted or stamped your feet, you were rewarded with a fabulous echo. Had her mum done the same thing as a child, she wonders? Maybe she'll ask her. She puts the photo to one side and looks again through the others. The last time she went with Marjorie to the dementia café, a fortnightly drop-in session run by the church, the woman from the Alzheimer's organisation talked about using photographs or other prompts – objects, perhaps, or music – to stimulate memories. Eleanor immediately downloaded loads of music onto her laptop and it worked brilliantly – her mum hummed along and tapped her foot and told detailed and entertaining stories of the days when she and Ted had won prizes for their dancing.

But she had to be careful with photographs; photographs had caused trouble in the past. Somewhere in this house there is a little black-and-white snap of Peter, maybe even more than one. She can't remember whether she'd asked her mum back then if there were more hidden away somewhere, but she was convinced they'd have taken more than one picture of him. And it was hard to believe they'd have thrown photos away. She wonders what would happen if she were to find that snap and show it to her mother. Not that she has the time to look for it properly these days.

She glances at her watch and sighs, then selects a few pictures from the pile, including one of her mum and Peggy as teenagers in their very new, very stiff-looking nurses' uniforms. There are a couple of herself here, too – a school portrait taken when she was perhaps nine or ten. She has thick, wavy hair here, held off her face with an Alice band, and she's wearing her favourite navy polka-dot dress. There aren't many of her taken after Peter died. True, her parents didn't actually take this one, but at least they kept it. In the other, she is little more than a toddler. It's taken at Christmas, in the living room upstairs. A tall, tinsel-draped tree stands to one side of the fireplace, every branch bearing a bauble. She is tearing open a present amid a sea of discarded wrapping paper while her mum kneels just behind her on the rug in front of the fireplace, smiling fondly. Eleanor swallows, gathers up the photos and heads back upstairs.

*

The gentle breeze that kept them comfortable while they ate lunch has disappeared, and the sun is so fierce that even though they're shaded by the big parasol it's far too hot to sit outside any longer. The Guinness and chocolate cake is melting after only ten minutes out on the table, so between them they gather up what's left and make their way inside.

'So,' Peggy places the cake carefully on the worktop. 'What are you two up to this afternoon?'

Marjorie looks blank and turns away.

Eleanor keeps her voice low. 'Actually, Peg, I was wondering if you were free for a bit of a memory session. She's been emptying cupboards again, and I found a few photos to show her, but to be honest, I'm a bit ... well, I'm not sure if it's a good idea. What do you think?'

Peggy glances at Marjorie, who is noisily opening and closing the kitchen drawers.

'Anything's worth a try, I suppose.' There's a note of hopelessness in her voice that Eleanor hasn't heard before.

'I've got nothing on until this evening,' Peggy says, 'so I'll stay for an hour or so. I'll put the kettle on again.' She turns to Marjorie. 'What are you looking for now, Marje?'

'A cutting thing,' Marjorie says. 'For that beer cake.' She tuts. 'This is my own kitchen and I can't even remember where we keep the ... the cutting things.'

*

Marjorie takes the photograph and studies it. 'Ellie-belly,' she says. She glances at Eleanor, then looks at the photo, then back at Eleanor. 'That's you, isn't it,' she says.

'Yes, Mum, that's right.' Her mum had never used the pet name for her before; only her dad ever called her that. She hands her the next picture, the one of her and Peggy in their nurses' uniforms. Marjorie turns to Peggy. 'That's you and me, the day we started.' She looks back at the snapshot and sighs deeply. 'We saw some shocking sights in that place, didn't we?'

Peggy sighs, too. 'It wasn't a barrel of laughs, was it?'

Eleanor waits, but it's soon clear that neither of them plan to say any more. She knew they'd done part of their training in a residential home, helping to look after children with profound physical and mental disabilities.

'I don't know how you stuck it for so long, Marjorie, I really don't. I had to leave when I had the twins,' she tells Eleanor. 'But although I knew I'd finish my training later, I couldn't ever go back to that sort of nursing. Your mum was much more dedicated than me.'

'Had to do something,' Marjorie mutters. 'Next one,' she holds out her hand impatiently.

Eleanor passes her the sepia photo. 'Do you know who these people are?'

Marjorie peers at it. 'I'm not bloody stupid, you know.' She looks at it for a good thirty seconds, then taps it with her finger. 'We used to go there every Saturday afternoon. There was a lovely little tea rooms there in those days.' She glances up. 'Your dad and I used to take you there, Eleanor, when you were tiny.'

'Did you?' She tries not to show how desperate she is for any morsel of information about the early part of her life.

'You used to ask for the same thing each time, pink ice cream. Of course, it's gone now, the café.'

Peggy leans over to look. 'Your dad was a handsome chap, wasn't he? Quite a catch.'

Marjorie smiles. 'Yes, everybody said so. My mother was very beautiful too, before she was married. Wasn't surprising she lost her looks, though. What with Maurice and everything.'

'Who's Maurice?' Eleanor and Peggy say in unison.

Marjorie looks up warily. 'Not supposed to say.'

Eleanor smiles, trying to make light of it. 'It doesn't matter now, Mum. You can tell us. Who was Maurice?'

'No,' Marjorie shakes her head. 'Mother made me promise, you see. She said I was to forget all about it. I was never, ever to tell anyone, not even my father.'

Peggy gives Eleanor a wry look. 'Was he a friend of

your mum's, then, this Maurice? Is that why you weren't supposed to say anything to your dad?'

To Eleanor's horror, tears spill down her mother's face. 'No one must ever know, that's what Mother said. She wouldn't let me see him unless I promised.'

'She took you with her?' Eleanor tries to process this. Her grandmother, wife of an undeniably handsome and reputedly charming man, taking her daughter along to some clandestine tryst? Is that what her mum is saying here?

'I wasn't supposed to tell *anyone*,' Marjorie sobs. 'Don't you see?'

'Don't upset yourself.' Peggy takes Marjorie's hand. 'It can't hurt anybody now, can it?'

Eleanor catches Peggy's eye and knows they're thinking the same thing, that when Marjorie is like this it's hard to reason with her, so the only way to move on is to change the subject, distract her. 'Tell you what, Mum, shall we have a look at your new clothes now?' Marjorie wipes her eyes. 'What clothes?'

'The summer things you bought this morning.' She can still see the tears on her mum's face, although she's stopped crying.

'No,' Marjorie says, 'I've not moved from this chair all day.'

'Yes, you have,' Peggy says. 'We went to Bromley. Remember? We had coffee at that Italian place in The Glades. You bought those four t-shirts in Debenhams. One in navy, one in—'

'So I did.' Marjorie turns to Eleanor. 'A bit on the cheap and cheerful side, but they'll do for indoors.'

*

The next day is one of Jenny's days, so Eleanor takes the opportunity to go to the hairdresser's. She isn't complacent about her hair, but even though it's still short, it's definitely beginning to look like a normal style and she's sure no one will stare at her this time. As she's unlocking the car, the main front door opens and Peggy comes out wearing her new red summer dress and her red sandals.

'Ooh,' Eleanor smiles, 'you look nice. Where are you off to?'

Peggy looks slightly coy. 'I'm off to meet my gentleman friend for lunch, if you must know.'

'I didn't know you had a gentleman friend.'

'His name's Dennis – he helps out at the food bank with me on Fridays.'

'Come on, then,' Eleanor teases, 'tell me all about him.'

'It's early days yet, but he seems a decent man, and it's nice to get out a bit more. It's much easier now you're around, and Jenny's a godsend, isn't she?'

Eleanor doesn't say anything for a moment. 'You've done so much for us, Peggy. I'm sorry, I forget sometimes how much you've given up.'

Peggy waves her words away. 'Don't give it a thought. Like I've said before, your mum was there for me when I needed her.' She takes her car keys out of her handbag.

SUSAN ELLIOT WRIGHT

'Before I forget, did you find out any more about the mysterious Maurice?'

'No. I asked her again last night who he was, but it seemed as though she genuinely didn't know what I was talking about. You know, I'm never surprised when I find out things she hasn't told me, but I'm amazed she's never mentioned him to you. I thought you two didn't keep anything from each other.'

Peggy smiles. 'Yes, we used to tell each other pretty much everything. Although we all have our secrets, I suppose. I kept your secret from her for quite a while, didn't I? Even though, in the end . . .'

Eleanor feels her eyes fill. She nods. 'I don't know what I'd have done without you back then. I owe you so much, Peggy.'

'Nonsense. Now, off you go and get your hair cut and let me go and meet my chap.'

Eleanor: February 1983, Greenham Common

Eleanor's stomach was doing somersaults as she dialled Peggy's number for the third time. Engaged again. She hung up and waited a few moments. Rain was lashing the phone box and she didn't even have her cagoule, so she was glad there was no one waiting outside. At least she was getting used to the pissy smell. She counted to a hundred, then dialled again. At last it was ringing. Then there were the pips and her stomach turned again as she pushed her coins into the slot.

'Six-nine-zero two-eight-nine-four?'

'Hello, Peggy, it's me. Eleanor.'

'Ellie! Sweetheart, how are you?'

She felt her face crumple. She'd imagined this conversation over and over in her head last night. She must have slept at some point because she remembered dreaming, but for most of the night she'd been planning what she would say. Now all of that, all the sentences she'd carefully practised as she'd walked here, it all poured out of her head, disappearing like water down the plughole.

She let out a weird wheezing noise and tears started streaming down her face. She bit her lip and dug her nails into her palm to try to get a grip on herself but she didn't dare try to speak in case she couldn't help crying out loud. She hadn't cried about it at all yet, so why, when it was so important for her to be able to speak sensibly, was she in floods?

'Ellie? Are you still there, pet?'

She tried to say 'yes', but a horrible choking sound came out.

'Oh, sweetheart, what is it? Whatever's happened?'

Again she attempted to speak but was completely overtaken by a sob.

'Ellie, darling, where are you?'

She could hear the rising note of panic in Peggy's voice.

'No,' she managed to force out. Peggy probably thought she'd been attacked or something, and the last thing she wanted was sympathy. 'Sorry,' she said quickly. 'I'm all right.'

'You're not hurt? Are you safe?'

'No, I mean . . . Yes, I'm safe, I'm just . . .' She was taking great shuddering gulps of air now, trying desperately to control herself. The sheer force of her body's reaction had taken her completely by surprise; she couldn't ever remember crying like this before, not even when she found out about Peter or when she lost her hair; not even when her dad died.

'Thank heavens,' Peggy murmured. 'Now, take your time, pet. Take some deep breaths and try to calm down.'

'I . . .' But before she could say any more, she heard the pips again.

'Quick, Ellie, read the number on the dial. Or ring back and reverse the charges.'

She only got halfway through reading the number, so she dialled 100 for the operator and waited for the call to be put through. 'I have a reverse-charge call from an Eleanor Crawford,' she heard the operator ask. 'Will you accept the charge?'

She heard Peggy's 'Yes, of course' and then the operator saying, 'Go ahead, caller.'

The break in the conversation was enough for Eleanor to regain her composure. 'Peggy, I'm sorry I scared you like that. It's so embarrassing – I don't know what came over me.'

'You never mind all that. You're obviously breaking your heart about something, so come on, tell your auntie Peggy.'

She felt tears building up again. 'Please, stop being so nice to me. I've done something really stupid.'

'You're pregnant.'

Eleanor gripped the receiver. Her heart seemed to be beating in her abdomen. 'How . . . how did you know?'

'Lucky guess. Are you certain? How far gone are you?'

'Just over two months. I did a test.'

SUSAN ELLIOT WRIGHT

She heard Peggy sigh. 'Okay. I thought you and Ray had split up.'

'It's not Ray's.' Shame flowed through her entire body. What on earth must Peggy think of her? 'It was some-one who ... It was a mistake. It's not that I was sleeping around. I was stupid. Drunk and stupid. I don't want to see him again.'

Another sigh. 'Have you thought about what you want to do? Because if you're only two months gone, you could still—'

'No. I can't have an abortion. I couldn't. I ... I want to have it, and I think I want to keep it.'

Peggy didn't say anything for a moment. Then she said, 'Well, that's a brave choice, but you don't have to decide for certain yet. I take it you're ringing me because you haven't told your mum?'

'Yes. I can't tell her.'

Peggy sighed again. 'You want me to tell her for you. All right. Now, I think—'

'No! No, sorry, that's not what I meant. I meant I rang you because I wanted to tell someone who would understand.'

'I do, darling, of course I do. But your mum will, too. She was the one who helped me, don't forget.'

'It's not that. It's ...' Tears were rising again; what the hell was the matter with her? 'It's just that I can't tell her I'm going to have a baby, can I? It would be like rubbing her nose in it.'

'Oh, no, Ellie, that's silly, of course it wouldn't. Your

258

mum'll want to help you and support you, you know she will.'

Not for the first time, Eleanor wondered whether Peggy knew her mum as well as she thought she did. 'No. She might *want* to, but she wouldn't be able to. I know she wouldn't. I really can't tell her. Please, Peggy. I know it's a lot to ask, but I don't want her to know, certainly not yet. Maybe, in a year or two, if we're getting on a bit better.'

'A *year* or two? Oh, Ellie.' There was a sigh. 'How can you get on better with your mum if you're not here?'

'Please don't be cross with me. I know you're right, but I can't face her. Not properly face-to-face, anyway. I've talked to her on the phone a few times, but she still . . . The thing is, I know she's better off with me not there.'

'No, that's not—'

'It is. As I say, in a year or two. If I can get myself straightened out a bit, perhaps then I can meet her again and, maybe, tell her about the baby.'

'So let me get this straight. You want me to pretend to your mum – and bear in mind I see her most days – that I don't know anything about the fact that her daughter's having a baby?'

'I know it's a lot to ask.'

'Too bloody right it is.'

She didn't say anything. Maybe she really was expecting too much. She hadn't thought this through properly at all. 'Peggy, I'm sorry, I didn't think about that part of it. I know that sounds ridiculous, but I didn't. I'm being selfish, aren't I? It's just, well, Jill said I should tell someone at home, and when I said I couldn't tell my mum . . .'

'Sweetheart, it's not that I don't want to help you, but you're putting me in a terribly awkward position. Look, tell you what: I won't say anything yet, but you really need to think about this some more. I don't see how you can *not* tell her, that's all I'm saying. And, anyway, you can't stay there, can you?'

'That's what Jill said. She said I should ask your advice.'

There was silence for a few moments, then Peggy said, 'Leave it with me. But Ellie, promise me you'll give this a lot more thought.'

'Okay. Thanks, Peggy, and . . . and sorry.'

*

Jill had been taking her out in the camper almost every day since she'd told her about the pregnancy, and then a few days ago, as they came to the end of another successful lesson, Jill astonished her by telling her that the old camper was hers if she wanted it. 'She's old and knackered,' Jill said, 'but she still goes. She'll get you from A to B, and, let's face it, you'll be stony broke for a while once the baby comes. At least if you've got Doris you'll know you can take off for a few days' holiday somewhere when you need to. Alex has made it clear he wants a car instead, so . . .' She shrugged.

'It's very kind of you, Jill, but—'

'Look,' Jill said, putting her arm around her shoulders, 'I've already bought a new one, actually. I'm fond of this old heap, and I was hoping Alex would want her, but it's ridiculous to keep her purely for sentimental reasons. You can make use of her. It's a different life once you can drive; more freedom, more opportunities. You don't want to be stuck in a room on your own with a small baby for weeks on end.'

'But how am I going to . . . I mean, I'm—'

'Put in for your test now. You want to get used to driving before you get too big – and definitely before the baby comes. I know women who've passed their tests but have been too busy with babies to get behind the wheel. They end up losing their nerve and having to start all over again.'

And with that, she'd handed Eleanor the keys, kissed her on the cheek and told her she'd drive to Chislehurst with her as long as someone there could give her a lift to Bromley, where she was picking up the new camper.

So now they were leaving Greenham, Jill to return to the commune in Camberwell, Eleanor to move into a place Peggy had sorted out for her. She was surprised at how easily she took to driving again. The trick was to wait until mid-afternoon, by which time the morning sickness had subsided. When she wasn't feeling sick, she quite enjoyed driving.

The journey from Newbury to Chislehurst took just over two hours, and it was the furthest she'd ever driven but she knew she'd done well. She still struggled with parallel parking, though. 'Right, now turn the wheel back a touch, forward a bit, then straighten up. That's it.' Jill slid the door open and looked down at the kerb. 'Not bad at all,' she closed the door again.

Eleanor turned off the ignition and took a proper look at the house. *Laburnum Lodge*, the sign said. *Friendly, Family-run Hotel.* They were early. They'd arranged to meet Peggy and Ken at eleven thirty – Ken had agreed to drive Jill to Bromley and was coming in his own car. Peggy had been thrilled to hear that Eleanor had been given the camper, and she'd immediately volunteered him.

She looked in the rear-view mirror and pushed some strands of hair behind her ear but they just sprang back again. 'It's no good,' she muttered. 'It's so obviously a bloody wig.' Part of her wanted to tear it from her head, throw it on the floor and stamp on it, but she'd have to get into the habit of wearing it again. At the camp she'd only worn it for the first week or so, partly because it wasn't practical but also because after a couple of days no one seemed to notice, so she'd worn woolly hats to keep her head warm. But on the drive down here, when they were briefly stuck in traffic, she was conscious of other drivers looking at her, so she pulled into a service station, clambered into the back and found the wig, now tatty from being shoved to the bottom of a carrier bag instead of sitting neatly on a polystyrene head as it had at home.

'It looks fine,' Jill said. 'Stop worrying.'

'Sorry.' She sighed and looked at her watch. It was still only five past eleven.

She hated having put Peggy in such an awkward position. According to Peggy, though she said it in a jokey way, she and Ken had *nearly ended up in the divorce courts over this carry-on*. Ken had come round now, though, Peggy assured her. But it was Peggy who saw Marjorie two or three times a week for coffee; went grocery shopping with her whenever they had the same day off; chatted with her in the garden as they pegged their laundry out on the shared washing line. It was she who was being forced to be economical with the truth. 'Still,' she said when she told Eleanor what she'd arranged, 'as long as when you do tell your mum, you make it clear all this was on the understanding that you'd tell her eventually.'

She'd agreed, although she suspected Peggy meant *before* the baby was born. She assumed she would tell her mother at some point, but she doubted it would be for quite some time. She looked at her watch again. 'They should be here in a minute; it's gone twenty past.' A white Ford Escort was turning into the road. She froze. 'Oh, God, no. It's my mum.' She reached for the ignition, but Jill put a hand on her arm.

'Hang on, you can't just drive off. If it is your mum . . .'

But the Escort sped past, Abba blaring out of the open windows. She relaxed, then became anxious again. It didn't mean Peggy hadn't told her mum, did it? It hadn't occurred to her before, but they were very close, after all. Then just as she was working herself up into a state, Peggy's little red Mini drew up behind the camper and Peggy, only Peggy, got out. Seconds later, Ken, also alone, pulled up in his Rover.

*

She thanked Jill again, promising to keep in touch as she watched her climb into Ken's car. Ken gave her a cursory smile and said he'd see Peggy back at home. He was clearly more uncomfortable with all this than she'd realised.

The house was warm, and she noticed immediately how plush the carpet felt under her feet. There was still a faint smell of toast and bacon lingering in the hall. She hadn't eaten since before they set off, and she was starving. Maybe she could ask for a slice of buttered toast in a minute. Or maybe that wasn't the done thing, since she was technically staff.

'It's only a box room, really,' Rita said, 'but we'll be able to move you to the big room up the top when the baby's born. Roof's leaking like a sieve at the moment, and the roofers can't start until July, so you'd get rained on in your bed. And the plinking and plonking of water dripping into buckets would probably drive you crackers. Anyway,' she straightened the pink-and-white bedspread and smoothed away a crease. 'This'll be a bit cramped, but it's only for a few months, so . . .'

'Compared to where I've been sleeping for the last few weeks, I can assure you, this is luxury!'

'Oh, yes, you've been at Greenham, haven't you?' Rita smiled. 'I want to hear all about that. Anyway, like I say, we'll move you up to the top as soon as the roof's done.'

'Thank you. It's so kind of you.'

'It's a nice big room, so the two of you should be fine up there. When you've recovered, we'll expect you to put in twelve hours a week for your bed and board. Anything over will be money in your pocket. Does that sound fair? Hours flexible to fit in with the little one, of course.'

'It's very fair. And I'm ever so grateful, I really am.'

'Don't be too grateful.' Rita laughed. 'It's bloody hard work. Ask Peggy – she did it for a while when we first started.'

Peggy nodded. 'I couldn't go back to nursing when the boys were babies because of the shifts, but I used to bring them here with me while I did a few hours' work. I did it for almost a year, didn't I, Rita?' She turned back to Eleanor. 'And it is hard work. But you'll be in good hands.' She smiled as she nodded towards Rita. 'My little sister can be a pain in the nether regions, but as long as you pull your weight, she's fair and she'll help you out whenever she can.' Eleanor noticed how Rita flushed with pleasure at the praise. It must be nice to have a big sister.

Eleanor, the present

Eleanor stands by the French doors sipping her coffee and watching the rain. It's been hot and dry for weeks, but her mum has been keeping everything watered. It's odd how her ability to make things grow seems entirely unaffected by the Alzheimer's. It's as though her hands remember when to water, how often to add plant food and what needs pruning or tying back, even though her brain can no longer identify the flowers she grows, or the fruits they pick from the trees.

The house is blissfully quiet today because Peggy has taken Marjorie for her routine check-up so Eleanor can have a break. They're unlikely to say anything different at the hospital – an adjustment to her medication, maybe, or more information about residential care. Even with Jenny coming in every weekday now, and a carer twice a day at weekends, things are tough and getting tougher.

There is something about heavy rain that Eleanor finds

almost as mesmerising as the sea. Raindrops chase each other down the glass doors; circles appear and disappear in the puddles surrounding the pots on the veranda. A sparrow lands on the watering can and cocks its head to one side as though it's looking at her. She blinks and allows her gaze to travel past the wrought iron railings and out across the garden. Everything is growing vigorously; the rain varnishes each blade of grass and makes the colours brighter, fresher. It's a shame the inside of the house doesn't match up to the garden. At least the basement rooms are nicer since the redecoration after the flood, although the dark, heavy furniture means it still feels oppressive.

Her phone beeps. A text from Jill: *Is now a good time to call?* She's been expecting this text – even telephone conversations have to be prearranged, or there's bound to be some drama or interruption from Marjorie.

Yes, she texts back, *free for an hour or so*. She waits, looking at her phone. 'Come on, Jill,' she murmurs, just as the doorbell rings. Taking the phone with her, she hurries to the front door and opens it.

'Surprise!'

She feels her mouth actually drop open then change to a grin as she flings her arms around Jill, then Dawn. 'Oh my God, I can't believe . . .' She looks back to Jill. 'Why didn't you tell me you were coming? Oh, never mind. Come in out of the rain.'

'I'll grab the baby,' Dawn says. 'Didn't want her to get too wet.' She runs back down the steps to the car.

'I can't get over this,' she says as Jill follows her into the hall. 'What a lovely surprise.'

'I like surprising people,' Jill replies. 'Listen, just quickly – if your mum comes back early, or if it's awkward at all, we'll clear off. I'm staying with Dawn until the weekend, so if you get a chance, perhaps we could have coffee or a drink or something.'

'That would be brilliant – the sitter's here tomorrow and Friday, so yes, definitely!'

'Great. Now, where's that grandson of mine? Come on, Charlie.' Jill turns to look down at Dawn's eldest, who is standing shyly behind her. He's just turned three, if Eleanor remembers rightly, still strawberry-blond and cherub-like.

Dawn hurries up the steps with the car seat in one hand and an umbrella in the other. 'Phew! Think we managed that without waking her up.' She puts the car seat on the floor and closes her umbrella.

Eleanor looks down at the shawl-covered bundle. 'So this is the new arrival, is it?'

Dawn smiles. 'Flora. She's sound-o at the moment, thank God, but I'm sure she'll wake up soon for a cuddle.' She looks round. 'Charlie, stop hiding behind Granny and come and say hello.'

He jumps forward before his mother can finish. 'Hello, Ellie,' he says, beaming. He can't quite manage her full name yet, but she is touched and flattered that he even remembers her. Dawn used to bring him over to the farm a lot before they moved down here, but it's months since they last came up to Scalby, and although Eleanor has been meaning to meet Dawn for coffee, things have been so hectic with her mum that she just hasn't got round to it. She smiles at Charlie. She always talks to him, but she's aware that she never really plays with him or reads to him or cuddles him. She wonders why he bothers with her.

'My goodness, who's this big boy?' She looks back at Dawn. 'And what have you done with Charlie?'

Charlie giggles. 'It *is* me!'

'Is it really?'

He nods vigorously until she acknowledges that, yes, this big boy must be Charlie after all. 'Silly Ellie!' he says, and everyone laughs.

*

Eleanor makes tea and gets out plates for the flapjacks and carrot cake Jill has brought. Charlie only wants half a flapjack; he's busy running his Thomas the Tank Engine back and forth in front of the French doors and making train noises quietly, so as not to wake the baby.

'So,' she hands a plate to Dawn. 'How are you feeling? You look wonderful for someone who gave birth less than two weeks ago.'

'She does look well, doesn't she?' Jill says, turning to Dawn. 'I was still in hospital at this point when I had Alex; two weeks was standard for a first baby, and even when I had you, it was nearly a week.' She turns back to

Eleanor and shakes her head. 'Do you know, they kick them out the same day now?'

Dawn smiles. 'I'm fine. Sleep-deprived, exhausted, desperate for a moment to myself, but apart from that ... How about you, Ellie?'

'Much the same, to be honest – completely knackered.'

Jill is shaking her head. 'It must be so hard to cope with. It's normal to be knackered when you're a new mum, but when you've got to look after your own parent ...'

'Jenny comes in for a few hours every day now, so that's a help. And Peggy is absolutely brilliant with her. But yes, when it's just me and her, it's ... well, it's pretty hard going.'

'You sounded so down on the phone the other night.'

'Did I? Probably just feeling sorry for myself. The weekends are tough, especially when Peggy's out with her bloke.' She smiles as she sees Jill's eyebrows go up. 'I'll tell you all about that later.' She pauses. 'My mum seems to be getting worse, but it comes and goes. I never know how she's going to be from one day to the next. Every now and again – although less and less frequently, to be honest – she seems completely normal. To the point where you wouldn't know there was anything wrong. And the next minute ...' She shrugs.

'David's mum was the same. She lived in the past a lot towards the end.'

'Yes, my mum's doing that. I knew she'd gradually

lose her memory, but I didn't realise it would go backwards. This morning I reminded her she was going to the hospital, and she'd forgotten that within ten minutes. I doubt she'd be able to tell you what she did yesterday. But then the other day, she said she was in a hurry because she had to take Peter for his polio vaccination.' She turns to Dawn. 'Peter was my baby brother, the one who died.'

'Bloody hell,' Jill says. 'Didn't you tell me once that she never used to even mention his name?'

She nods. 'All those years I was desperate for her to tell me about him, and now, if she mentions him, I don't know what to do. I can't tell her the truth, can I? I mean, she thinks she's about to go and pick him up from his nap. But on the other hand, I feel cruel if I go along with it.'

'So what did you do in the end?' Dawn asks.

'Nothing. I was just trying to work out what to say when I saw her face change, then she burst into tears and ran out of the room.'

'How sad.' Jill shakes her head. 'Poor woman. Imagine just going about your day thinking you're still a young mum and then suddenly remembering you lost your . . . Shit, sorry, El.' She reaches across the table for Eleanor's hand and whispers again, 'Sorry.'

'It's fine,' she says, 'really.' At the same moment as she becomes aware of the look on Dawn's face, Jill puts both hands to her mouth and says, 'Oh, God, sorry Dawn, this is not the sort of thing you want to hear, either.

Sometimes my idiocy surprises even me.' This breaks the slight tension that is threatening to settle.

There's a snuffling from the car seat. 'Ah,' Eleanor says, 'sounds like someone's waking up.'

Dawn is already halfway across the room, making shushing noises. She picks up the car seat, brings it over to where they're all sitting and sets it down by her feet. 'Here she is,' she says. 'Meet Flora. Flora, meet your auntie Eleanor.'

'Her name is not called Auntie Ebbener.' Charlie sounds indignant. He's sprung to the baby's side and is now stroking her hair perhaps a touch more firmly than he needs to. Does he resent his little sister, Eleanor wonders, even if he loves her too?

'Her name is called Ellie.' He looks at Eleanor and rolls his eyes in exasperation. 'Silly Mummy.'

She smiles at him and then looks back at Flora, trying to ignore the zip of pain that always flashes through her when she's in close proximity to a new baby. 'Hello, Flora.' She hears the croakiness in her voice as she leans closer. She clears her throat. 'She's beautiful.' She strokes the baby's downy cheek and smiles at Dawn, whose face glows with love and pride.

Flora's fingers curl and uncurl, she twitches a little, makes a snuffling sound and opens her eyes.

'Hello, my angel.' Dawn bends down to unbuckle her. 'I think you're going to be in demand for cuddles, young lady.'

Eleanor's stomach shifts. She stands up and starts to

collect the mugs. 'I'm sure she is. I bet Granny'll spoil her rotten with lots of cuddles.' She fills the kettle and switches it on. 'Let's have another cup of tea.'

Charlie, who has now moved to his mother's side so he can continue his earnest hair-stroking, looks uncertainly at Jill, who immediately leans over and scoops him up in her arms. 'Only when I've had enough cuddles from my Charlie Farley.' She buries her nose in his neck and blows raspberries on his skin until he squeals with delight. 'My little Mr Man; my cuddly bear. Give Granny a ginormous cuddle,' she says. 'No, more ginormous than that! No, even more ginormous.'

Eleanor feels frozen, a fixed smile on her face as she watches Jill rescue the situation she almost created. She is useless with small children; why didn't she notice immediately that Charlie was feeling left out? She becomes aware of Dawn preparing to hand her the baby.

'Eleanor?' Dawn is right beside her with Flora. 'Would you like a hold?'

'I . . . er, I should wash my hands.' She turns to the sink, knocking a mug off the countertop. 'Oh, sh—' She glances at Charlie. '—sugar.' She grabs a cloth from under the sink and mops up the dregs of the tea. Fortunately the mug isn't broken. Just then, she hears the front door close and then voices in the hall. 'That must be my mum back.'

Everyone stops talking and waits expectantly and, she thinks, a little nervously. 'We're back,' Peggy calls, and they hear Marjorie mutter something and the click of the bathroom door opening. Then Peggy comes in, still talking over her shoulder to Marjorie. 'All right, but hurry up or I'm going to wet myself. I'll put the kettle on. Oh—' She stops dead as she turns and sees the packed kitchen. A smile spreads across her face. 'Well, now everyone knows I need a wee! I'm Peggy.' She looks around. 'Who are you?'

Eleanor introduces them, not forgetting Charlie.

'Actually,' Jill says, 'I think we did meet once, very briefly. In Chislehurst, many moons ago. I came with Ellie from Greenham, before she passed her driving test. Your husband kindly gave me a lift to pick up my new camper.'

'Of course!' Peggy claps her hands together. 'Ex-husband, now. You're the clever lady who runs that farm. It's lovely to meet you properly after all this time – I've heard so much about you.'

'Likewise,' Jill says. 'I feel we know each other already.'

'So,' Peggy says, smiling, 'what brings you from your lovely seaside air down to this polluted hellhole?'

Jill takes the baby from Dawn and holds her for Peggy to see. 'New grandchild. And I'm usually down every couple of months anyway, to see senior grandchild.' She ruffles Charlie's hair. 'And daughter, of course. Dawn lives in Greenwich.'

'More Woolwich, really, Mum,' Dawn mutters.

'I have a son, too – Alex. Did Ellie tell me you have boys?'

'Twins, yes.'

'Wonderful! Any grandchildren? I have another four, but they're in Australia now. Alex and his partner are very happy out there, but I miss them all terribly.'

'I know what you mean,' Peggy says. 'All we want is for our kids to be happy, but sometimes that means we have to suffer.'

Jill nods. 'Absolutely. That's the way it goes, doesn't it? They're the centre of our lives, but we're no longer the centre of theirs.'

Peggy smiles. 'Not fair, is it? So, tell me about your lot.' And they are off, chatting as if they've known each other for years. It's never occurred to Eleanor before how alike they are in some ways, but now it seems obvious, and she realises she is smiling with sheer pleasure at the knowledge that these two women have met properly at last and clearly like each other.

When the door opens again, her breathing quickens slightly. She can never be sure which Marjorie is going to walk in. Her mum is often unsettled by things being different. Will this invasion of her kitchen trigger some drama? Jill would understand, obviously, but it still wouldn't be pleasant.

But after an initial moment or two of confusion, Marjorie appears to relax. She wears an open smile, says hello to everyone and seems to understand when Eleanor explains who Jill and Dawn are. She takes over making the tea, although as she hands it out, it becomes clear that she's made two cups too many, and while she remembers to ask everyone if they take sugar, she forgets to add it to the tea or bring it to the table. She doesn't talk much, and she asks Jill several times if she's married and what her husband's name is. But then she kneels down on the floor with Charlie and nods and smiles as he chats away to her and shows her his Thomas the Tank Engine and his plastic figure of the Fat Controller.

Eleanor is taken aback slightly by the tenderness on her mother's face. She supposes her mum must have played with her like that when she was little, but as she watches them now, the easy connection between them, the obvious lack of any tension, she is embarrassed to feel a childish stab of jealousy.

*

Much later that evening, after they've watched Marjorie's favourite film – *The King's Speech* – on DVD for maybe the fourth or fifth time in as many weeks, Marjorie turns to her and asks, 'Who was that girl?'

At first, she thinks her mum is referring to something from the film, but Marjorie tuts. 'No, the one who was here. In the kitchen.'

'Oh, you mean Dawn? You remember her being here today? That's really good, Mum.' Shit; that sounds patronising. 'Anyway, Dawn is Jill's daughter. You remember Jill? From the farm where I . . . where I used to live.'

'Yes, yes,' her mother says, irritably. Then she leans forward and looks Eleanor right in the eye. 'She took the

276

baby, you know. I saw her. Put it in that carry thing and walked right out of the house with it.'

Disappointment seeps through her. 'Mum,' she sighs. 'The baby . . . it was Dawn's baby. Her own little girl. She was just taking her home.'

'Well, where's your baby, then?' Her expression is one of curiosity and her face looks completely normal, as though she's just asked a perfectly reasonable question.

Eleanor, September 1983

Eleanor, September 1983

Eleanor woke slowly from a long, dreamless sleep, possibly the best and deepest sleep of her entire life. She still felt exhausted and there was a raw soreness between her legs. She knew something momentous had happened, but for a second or two she was uncertain about where she was and why she was here. She could hear a soft beeping noise that sounded vaguely familiar. She opened her eyes and saw a cream-coloured ceiling that looked bright and freshly painted. She turned her head to the left, registering as she did so that her head was completely bare. The steel trolley by the wall was stocked with surgical gloves, tissues, things sealed in little square packs and a stack of disposable nappies. Now she remembered. Carefully, because her body felt battered and ripped, she managed to turn over. There, a few feet away, was a transparent box that looked rather like a fish tank, and inside it a tiny scrap of orangey-pink in a white nappy that was almost as big as she was. Her pink-and-white gown seemed to be made from a J-cloth, and the miniature cream-coloured hat, which had slipped over one eye, looked as if it were made from a bandage. The baby was lying on her front, eyes closed, knees curled and bottom sticking up. The baby, she thought. *My baby; my daughter.*

She lay there for a minute or two, trying to assimilate this new reality. She was a mother; she had a child of her own, a real, actual person for whom she was solely responsible. The surge of fear that rushed through her almost made her gasp. Ever since she discovered she was pregnant, she'd tried to avoid thinking ahead to this point, but whenever her mind had hovered over or settled on this moment, she'd felt afraid. The fear she'd felt then was nothing compared with what she felt now. This was her daughter, a new and separate human being, and Eleanor was the one she would rely on to love her, feed and clothe her, keep her safe. It was her responsibility to gently float this new life into the world.

Despite her fears, she was in no doubt about her ability to love this child – she'd begun to do so even before today, before she actually met her. It was the rest of the package that she wasn't so sure about. Babies were much more fragile than most people realised. One careless action, one wrong move, a slip of the hand, a moment's loss of concentration – any of these could be catastrophic.

A pain started to spread across her middle, a raw,

tightening cramp, not unlike the pains of labour she'd endured all night. The midwife had warned her about 'afterpains', but Eleanor saw this as a physical manifestation of her fear. How could they possibly allow her to take this precious living, breathing child out into the world on her own? How could she be trusted? She watched the little chest moving up and down, reassured by the evidence of life. The midwives had told her the baby was jaundiced and a little cold. 'We'll just pop her in an incubator to warm her up a bit.' They talked as if she was a leftover casserole. With some difficulty, Eleanor swung her legs over the side of the bed and stood up, then took a few hesitant steps closer to the incubator. She could feel tightness where they'd stitched her up, and she was incredibly sore. She could hardly even walk – how on earth could she look after a baby?

She felt her throat constrict as she looked at the tiny creature behind the glass. She mustn't cry; she was a mother now. *I am somebody's mother*, she told herself, and was momentarily caught off balance by the tide of panic that rose inside her at the thought. The name she'd decided on was Aimee Sarah, but her daughter, with her serious little face and sleek dark hair, didn't look like an Aimee at all. She leant over the incubator and looked into her daughter's eyes for a few moments. Sarah; that was better. Sarah Aimee.

As she stood there with her hand on the incubator, she could feel tears welling up. Sarah seemed even more vulnerable from this angle. She was sucking her thumb, her tiny fingers with their delicate pink nails curled around her nub of a nose. God, this child was beautiful; she had never seen a baby more perfect, more exquisitely proportioned; not that she'd allowed herself to be close to many babies before now. She ached to show her off to her mother: *Look what I did, Mum; look what I made.* But how could she possibly go to her mother and flaunt her own live child? Peggy and Ken said she'd have to tell her mum at some point, because she couldn't keep the baby a secret forever. But she'd argued that it didn't have to be just yet. It would only upset her mum, she felt, and it would make things even worse between them.

As she stood looking down at the plastic crib, the door swung open and a large, motherly-looking nursery nurse in a plastic apron came in carrying a tray. 'Had a good rest, Mummy?' She was smiling broadly. 'You slept through lunch and tea, but I saved you a jam sandwich from the trolley and I've made you a cuppa.'

'Thank you,' Eleanor said, taking a step back towards the bed. At that moment, the baby uttered a small cry. Eleanor froze.

'Oh, listen, Baby's awake too.' The nurse beamed as she set the tray down on the table at the end of the bed. 'Let's see how she's doing, shall we?' She looked expectantly at Eleanor, who was still standing halfway between the incubator and the bed. Then she turned back to the baby. 'She's warmer now, but make sure she keeps her hat on while she sleeps. The jaundice is looking better but we'll do more blood tests tomorrow.'

'Thank you.' She eased herself back into bed. She hadn't realised how hungry she was and how desperate for that cup of tea.

'Okay, little one,' the nurse was saying, 'let's take you to your mummy.' She lifted Sarah out of the incubator and turned to Eleanor. 'You're breastfeeding, yes?'

'Yes.' She'd thought about bottle feeding, but she didn't want to take the risk. She'd read a lot about it. Apparently, you had to be ultra-careful to measure exactly the right amount of powder when you were mixing the milk, and if you got it wrong, the baby could be very ill or even die. What if she was distracted while she was measuring?

'Good. Much better for Baby. Now, she must only have breast milk or boiled water for the first four months, okay?'

Eleanor nodded. *Only breast milk or boiled water for the first four months.* She must write that down; she must not forget.

The nurse brought Sarah over to the bed. She was really crying now, juddering, grizzly cries, and her fists were clenched as if she was absolutely furious. With the nurse's help, Sarah latched on, and Eleanor gasped at the strength with which the little mouth clamped to her nipple. She hadn't expected it to hurt that much.

'Good, good,' the nurse muttered. 'She's latching on nicely. It looks like you're a natural.'

Eleanor, September 1983

She was glad she'd managed to get into Greenwich District Hospital. The only other option was Lewisham, where her mum was a nursing assistant. But even though she didn't work on the maternity ward, there was a risk of bumping into her. She hated that dismal old hospital anyway; this one was still fairly new and much more bright and modern than Lewisham. Ken came in with Peggy the first day and took some photographs. He'd get them developed straight away, he said, and send them in tomorrow with Peggy. After they left, Jackie, the girl in the next bed, leant over to speak to her. 'Was that your mum and dad?' she asked.

'No, my dad's dead and my mum ...' She didn't finish because Jackie's baby had started crying and she turned away to attend to him, and then soon after that it was the mothers' rest time. The nurses came in and drew the curtains around each mother and baby, then they turned off the main ward lights so there was just an orangey glow above the beds. This quickly became Eleanor's favourite time of day; the warmth of the ward, the soft, golden lighting, the comforting hush which was disturbed only by an occasional newborn's cry and the soothing murmurs of its mother.

Peggy came in to see her every night, and even Rita managed to pop in during the afternoon, but the only time she could get away from the guest house was right in the middle of the mothers' rest time, so she was only allowed in for ten minutes.

'Was that your mum, then?' Jackie said when Rita left.

*

When she and Sarah were discharged, Peggy and Ken came to pick them up. Ken carried the baby down to the car in her carrycot while Peggy helped Eleanor with her bags. Everyone was quiet on the drive to Chislehurst. Sarah slept and Eleanor was still feeling a little stunned; she was slightly surprised to have been allowed to take Sarah with her when she left the hospital. She kept thinking someone was about to pop up and say no, you can't actually keep her. When they pulled up outside Laburnum Lodge, Ken said sorry, but he wouldn't be coming in. 'I hope you won't take this the wrong way, Ellie, and I hope you know I wouldn't want to see you upset, not if it could be avoided.'

'Ken—'

'No, Peg. I've got to say what's on my mind. I know it's nothing to do with me, and you're a grown woman now and all that, but I'm sorry, Eleanor, I don't hold with keeping all this from your mother. It's not right.'

'I know,' she said quietly, her hand hanging limply over the edge of the carrycot so that her fingers rested on Sarah's warm little body. 'And I'm sorry. I know I've put you in a difficult position, but—'

'Difficult position? I think that's understating it somewhat, don't you?'

From the back seat, she saw Peggy's hand move over and touch Ken's arm. 'All in good time, Ken.'

'I can't condone it, Peg. There. I've said my piece, and that's all I wanted.'

'Yes, well,' Peggy said, in a tone that made Eleanor think they would probably 'have words' later. 'You'll take the carrycot upstairs for her, won't you?'

He didn't reply, but got out, opened the back door and carefully lifted the carrycot off the back seat.

*

Peggy and Rita had moved her things up from the box room while she'd been in hospital. Peggy had told her that her new room would be ready when she got back, but when she actually walked in and looked around, she immediately felt choked at the trouble they'd gone to. The bed was made up and covered with a new patchwork quilt in blues and reds; there was a bowl of fresh fruit on the drop-leaf table they'd found in the cellar, and a white vase filled with pink carnations and baby's breath.

Compared to the room downstairs, this one was enormous. They'd turned it into a temporary bed-sitting room, and although the big walk-in cupboard that led off the main living area could hardly be classed as a nursery, it was big enough for the cot and a small chest of drawers, so at least she'd be able to put the baby to bed and still watch TV or listen to music in the evenings. Rita suggested she still have most of her meals downstairs, especially at first, but with her own kettle, toaster and a single electric ring, at least she wouldn't have to keep running up and down to the main kitchen every time she wanted a cup of tea or a snack. The only other room on this floor was a small bathroom, so she was completely self-contained up here, separate from the guest bedrooms and from Rita and Alan's quarters on the floor below. There was a cardboard sign that said SARAH'S ROOM hanging on the door to the walk-in cupboard. The lettering was pink and the words were surrounded by lilac butterflies. 'I know it's not really a room,' Peggy said, 'but at least it makes it a bit more ...' Eleanor opened the door to find a musical mobile had been fixed to the cot, and an assortment of teddy bears and a large pink rabbit were sitting on a shelf above. Hanging on the edge of the cot was a tiny woollen dress, duck-egg blue with a scattering of yellow chicks. A night light in the shape of a fairy palace stood on the chest of drawers.

Eleanor found herself in tears yet again. She cried easily at the moment.

*

The baby bath looked like a little yellow boat. It stood on the table, half filled with water. Eleanor added a squirt of Johnson's Baby Bath and used a thermometer to test the temperature. It was still too hot, so she added more cold a little at a time until she managed to get it between the ideal range of 90 and 98 degrees Fahrenheit. Now everything was ready. Beside the bath was the changing mat with a yellow towel spread over it so she could wrap Sarah in it immediately if she got cold. Next to that was a clean nappy, a nappy liner and nappy pin and a pair of rubber pants. She'd also laid out an envelope-sleeved vest and one of the white cotton nighties that Peggy had given her, the ones with the pink and yellow flowers and sweet little bluebirds embroidered across the chest.

Peggy took a week off work and, having told Marjorie that she was helping her sister with the guest house, which, she said, wasn't actually lying, she was staying here to help Eleanor get settled. She was downstairs at the moment, making spaghetti Bolognese for dinner. 'I'm here if you need me,' she'd said. 'But you won't. You'll be absolutely fine.' Eleanor found Peggy's quiet confidence reassuring, but she was acutely aware that her fear of lowering a baby into water was, in her case, rather more than simple new mother nerves.

SUSAN ELLIOT WRIGHT

You were supposed to bath your baby while you were still in hospital, but the midwives and nursery nurses were so busy with a flood of new admissions that the first bathing session had to be cancelled. The second time, when she and Jackie were summoned to the nursery with their babies, she panicked at the last minute and pretended to feel faint and dizzy, so she'd got out of it on that occasion. Another bathing session was set for the following afternoon, but she'd been in hospital for almost a week by then and had asked if she could go home. The doctor took a look at her stitches in the morning and said that she was 'healing nicely', so he would be happy to discharge her.

So now Sarah was nine days old, and Eleanor still hadn't bathed her. The home midwife had visited every day since she was discharged, and she seemed to be happy enough, but Eleanor didn't feel confident at all.

'Right,' she said aloud as she carefully undressed Sarah and removed her nappy, 'nothing can go wrong.' She tried to sound firm with herself. 'She's my baby and I need to be able to give her a bath without making a fuss about it.' She looked at her tiny daughter, whose eyes were wide open and fixed intently on her own as though she were actually listening to her. She smiled. 'Don't I?' The baby kicked her legs in response. She slid her hands under Sarah's back and lifted her, one hand cupping her head, the other cupping her bottom. Her skin was dry and warm with a softness that felt like raw silk. Her hands trembled just a little as she lowered her daughter into the bath. Sarah gave a slight shudder as her skin made contact with the water. Eleanor's grip tightened in fear and for an awful moment she worried she'd grabbed her too tightly, but then Sarah began kicking her legs, blinking and opening and closing her mouth as if she was trying to taste the water.

Eleanor had attended every antenatal appointment and parentcraft session, and she'd concentrated extremely carefully on the bathing demonstration so she could commit the whole process to memory. Remembering what she'd been shown, she rested her right hand, the one holding Sarah's head, against the base of the plastic bath. That felt quite safe until Sarah kicked her legs, but then her whole body swayed and Eleanor was worried she would let go. She tried to slow and steady her breathing, tried to calm herself enough to slide her other hand out so she could swish the foamy water gently over her baby's shiny, slippery skin. But she couldn't bring herself to let go; so instead, still supporting Sarah with both hands, she moved her gently back and forth in the water, so it was as though tiny waves were washing over her skin. Sarah watched her the whole time, eyes wide open and full of trust.

Marjorie, October 1983

Marjorie knew there was something wrong as soon as she saw their faces, but she pretended not to notice. They'd probably had another row; she knew things were strained between them. She filled the kettle and switched it on. 'Tea or coffee?'

'Whatever's easiest,' Ken said, as usual.

'They're both easy, Ken, it's instant coffee or teabags. Which would you prefer?'

'Tea,' Peggy said, not meeting her eye. 'We'll both have tea.'

They pulled out chairs and sat at the kitchen table while she got the tea things out of the cupboard, but no one said anything. Usually, Peggy would be chatting away from the moment she walked in the door, especially when they'd not seen each other for a few days. Marjorie tried to think of something to say but the longer the silence went on, the harder it was to break it. The kettle was taking ages to boil, too.

'So.' She smiled. 'To what do I owe the honour?'

'Wait till you sit down, Marjorie,' Ken said. 'We have something to tell you.'

They're getting divorced, she thought as she put the mugs on the table. *Poor Peg.*

She sat down and looked from one to the other. She hoped her expression was suitable; Ted always used to say she wasn't very good at arranging her face.

'It's about Ellie,' Peggy said.

She felt her heart jump. 'What is it? What's happened?'

'Don't worry,' Peggy said quickly, 'she's not hurt or anything.'

Marjorie noticed that Peggy still seemed to be avoiding looking her in the eye. She slid her hands around her mug. It was colder today than she'd realised.

'What, then? You've heard from her?' She felt the familiar sting of jealousy, then a wave of guilt for feeling like that; after all, it was her fault Eleanor had become close to Peggy as a child. Her own detached mothering had pushed her daughter away and she had never known what to do to draw her back.

Peggy and Ken glanced at each other. Ken sighed. 'I'm going to come out with it, Marjorie, because I'm not happy with all this deception. She's ... we've seen Eleanor, and—'

'You've seen her? I thought she was still at—'

'No,' Peggy murmured, 'she's been back for a while.'

'Back? Back where?'

Ken leant forward. 'She's staying with Peg's sister. Thing is, Marjorie . . .'

And then she thought he said something like, *Eleanor's a sad young lady.*

'Well, yes,' she said, but then the words started to form a different shape. 'Sorry, what did you say?'

'I said, Eleanor has had a baby.'

Marjorie just stared at him, wondering what stupid attempt at a joke this was. Then she saw Peggy's face, the tears on her cheeks. There was a roaring sound in her ears and she thought she might faint. She still had her hand around the mug of tea. It was beginning to burn now, but she felt temporarily paralysed and she had to force herself to move her hand away.

Ken looked embarrassed, less confident than he was a moment ago. 'It must be a shock. She didn't want you to know about it, but as I said to Peg—'

'But I'm her *mother*!' It was almost a wail, full of anguish. She stood up. 'I can't . . . Hang on a sec, I must have left my cigarettes in the other room.'

The living room smelt cold and damp. She rarely used it now Eleanor wasn't here, but she'd been talking to Ted's mum on the phone this morning – Vera had no one now, so Marjorie rang her every few weeks. Her hand was trembling as she picked up her cigarettes and lighter from the phone table, but she managed to light one and take a few calming drags before she went back into the kitchen.

Peggy was crying. 'Marjorie, I was in such an awkward position. I only agreed to this because I thought she would have told you by now. I kept telling her she should talk to you.'

Marjorie drew shakily on her cigarette. 'Wait, I'm not quite sure what you're saying. Agreed to what? How long—'

Ken put his hand up to stop Peggy speaking. 'Peg's fond of Eleanor – we both are – but she's put us in a tricky position here, and I thought, well, I said to Peg, enough is enough. I mean, what you do about it is up to you, but I just thought you should know, that's all.' He stood up. 'I'll leave you to it.' He put his hand briefly on Peggy's shoulder, but she shook it off. 'I'll see you upstairs, Peg.'

Peggy ignored him. He hesitated for a moment, then nodded and quietly let himself out.

'I'm sorry, Marjorie. I didn't know what to do for the best. She asked me for help and she made me promise—'

'When? When did she contact you?'

Peggy took a scrunched tissue from her sleeve. 'God, I wish I still smoked. It was a while ago. She begged me not to tell you, but—'

'But I'm her *mother*, Peg,' Marjorie said, her voice catching on the tears in her throat. 'And you're supposed to be my friend. How could you?'

Peggy was nodding, tears streaming down her face. 'I know,' she said. 'I'd be livid if you kept something from me like this. I've agonised over it; I told her right at the start she'd have to tell you eventually, and I really thought I could get her to talk to you about it, but she's adamant she doesn't want you to know yet.'

Marjorie stood up and started walking back and forth as though moving might help her to deal with what she was hearing. She'd never been as close to Eleanor as she'd have liked, but the thought that Eleanor felt she couldn't come to her at a time like this, the thought that it was still Peggy she turned to ... It hurt almost physically; she could feel it around her middle, somewhere between her heart and her navel. 'And why? What does she think I'd say? Surely she didn't think I'd behave like some Victorian—'

'It wasn't that. She thinks you'd be upset because of Peter; she said she thought telling you she was having a baby would be ... Oh, never mind. The point is ...' She blew her nose. 'Now you do know, what do we do?'

'Where is she?'

'At Rita's. You know, my sister who runs the bed and breakfast. Rita's keeping an eye on her. We all are.'

'You all are; everyone's helping my daughter except me.' She took a long draw on her cigarette. 'There's so much I need to ask, but I can't even think straight.'

'Maybe tomorrow.' Peggy mopped at her eyes with the already sodden tissue. 'I'm truly sorry I went behind your back, but I was worried about what would happen if I said I wouldn't help her. She'll come round in the end, especially once she feels more confident with the baby. I know this is hard, Marjorie, but I think we should bide our time. I'm sure I can get her to—'

'Go away, Peggy.' She stubbed out her cigarette and took another from the pack. 'Just go. I don't want to talk to you any more.'

Peggy looked as if she'd been slapped.

'Not today, anyway.' She lit the cigarette.

*

She sat on her bed with the ashtray beside her, smoking her way through the remaining half-pack of John Player Specials. She looked at the half-smoked one in her hand and then squashed it into the ashtray; they weren't even helping any more. Peggy was probably right; she should wait until Eleanor felt ready. And though it hurt to acknowledge it, Peggy was the best person to bring her round; she always had been. Peggy was her best chance of seeing Eleanor sooner rather than later. And the baby – she kept forgetting that the fact there was a new baby meant she was a grandma now. A grandmother; she thought about it. Perhaps she could make a better job of that than she'd made of being a mother – if she was ever given the chance, of course. How long would it be before she was allowed to meet this grandchild, she wondered? And then it occurred to her that Ted would never know he was a grandad. 'Oh, Ted,' she murmured, her vision swimming as her eyes filled up.

It was only when her stomach started to rumble that she remembered she'd made herself a sausage hotpot this afternoon. It was almost cooked when Peggy and

Ken came down to drop their bombshell, so she'd put the oven on low but then forgotten all about it. She dragged herself off the bed and traipsed wearily upstairs. The smell of burnt sausages and tomatoes hit her as soon as she opened the door on the landing. She turned the oven off and opened the French doors to let the smoke out, then she took the charred hotpot out of the oven, carried it down the steps into the garden and threw the whole lot into the dustbin, casserole dish and all.

Eleanor, the present

Eleanor goes to bed smiling. She talked to Dylan on the phone for almost half an hour tonight. It's possibly the first time they've ever had a telephone conversation, but he's off to Italy next week, ready to start his job the second week in October. He'll be gone for at least a year, and he wanted to be sure she knew he'd been serious about her coming out and staying for a while. 'It depends on how things go with my mum,' she'd told him. 'But, yes, I'd like that.' It's odd to be making plans with Dylan, even such loose, holiday-type plans, but she feels surprisingly good about it.

She dreams that she's back in Scalby, standing on the clifftop with the North Sea wind blowing gently over her face. The waves are thudding onto the beach below, but instead of enjoying the sound as she usually does, it irritates her. She has to get down there and stop it, stop that annoying bumping sound. Her brain readjusts itself as

SUSAN ELLIOT WRIGHT

she wakes to a cool breeze on her face and the sound of her bedroom door bumping against the door frame in the draught. Funny; she could have sworn she'd closed the window before she went to bed. It's turned much chillier this last week, and so blustery it feels quite autumnal. She throws back the covers and swings her legs out, and as soon as her feet touch the carpet she feels a definite breeze. She walks across to the window and moves the curtain, but the window is closed. It is only a moment before her puzzlement turns to alarm and the adrenalin starts to flood through her body. She doesn't even need to look in her mother's room to know she isn't there; she can sense it.

A memory rushes into her head. She was sixteen or seventeen and had wanted to stay out late at a party, but her mum said she had to be in by eleven. Reluctantly, she came home on time, said goodnight to her mother who was watching the late night movie and went down to bed. But then she rolled up her dressing gown, a spare bedspread and a couple of jumpers and arranged them carefully under the duvet so that it looked like she was in bed. Leaving the door ajar so her mum would see the shape under the covers, she quietly let herself out of the lower front door, tiptoed up the steps and went back to the party. She was smoking a No. 6 and dancing with a skinny boy in a studded denim jacket when her mother appeared in the doorway of the darkened front room. 'Home, young lady,' she said. 'Right now.'

She can't remember what punishment she'd been

given, but much later, when they were on better terms, she'd asked what it was that had given her away. 'It wasn't anything you did,' her mum said. 'I sensed you weren't there.'

She'd forgotten that until now.

Sure enough, as soon as she steps outside her bedroom, she can see that the basement front door is wide open. 'Shit!' she says aloud. 'Shit, shit, shit!' Barefoot and wearing only her pyjamas, she bounds up the area steps and out through the gate into the street. 'Mum!' she shouts instinctively. 'Marjorie!' She looks up and down, but the road is completely deserted. Oh, God, what now? Her heart is thudding and she can't think straight. Police. That's what she should do. Call the police. She hurries back down the steps and is about to dial when she thinks about what they'll ask. They'll want a description – what she's wearing, where she might be likely to go. Details, they'll want details.

She takes a breath and consciously tries to calm down. Then she goes into her mum's room to try to work out whether she got dressed or not. There are no open drawers or wardrobes, but her mum's dressing gown is on the back of the door and her slippers are still there. She can't have gone outside barefoot, surely? She was only wearing a thin cotton nightie. Just then, she hears the click of the door at the top of the stairs. Her heart leaps. She's been up to Peggy's; of course. But then Peggy appears on the stairs in her pyjamas and dressing gown. 'What's going on? I heard you shouting outside.'

'She's gone.'

'Oh, Christ. Have you called the police?'

*

She drives up and down every road on this side of the high street between Lewisham Park and Davenport Road. It's surprising how many people are out and about at four in the morning. Every time she sees a figure in the darkness her hopes shoot up for a millisecond, only to plummet again immediately. She doesn't need daylight, because after being back here for almost six months, she knows the way her mother moves; she would recognise her by her walk.

She tries the other side of the main road, behind Lewisham Hospital. She slows as she passes the entrance to the rec, or Ladywell Fields as it's called now, thinking she sees someone at the side of the path. She used to stand on that little bridge with her mum when she was small, throwing twigs into the Quaggy and rushing to watch as the current carried them under and out the other side. She strains her eyes searching for the person she thought she saw. Big, fat drops of rain start to fall on the windscreen. 'Shit,' she mutters, remembering the forecast is heavy downpours overnight. Thank God they've built floodplains here now – the Quaggy was forever bursting its banks when she was a child, turning the rec into a vast lake. There is another movement, but she realises that what she thought was a person is in fact a large branch, broken but not entirely detached from the tree, moving in the wind.

She sighs and drives on. She's been out for an hour now, and she has no idea how long her mum had been gone when she woke up. She heads back to the house. There's been no call on her mobile, but maybe Peggy's heard something.

'No luck?' Peggy says, moving to the sink and filling the kettle. She's dressed now, and her Sudoku book is open on the kitchen table.

'No. I keep trying to think where she might have gone, but it's hard to know how her mind works now. I mean, would she head for a particular place, or would she be walking aimlessly?'

'Your guess is as good as mine, I'm afraid.' Peggy pours steaming water into mugs and brings them to the table.

Marjorie lives in the past these days, so perhaps she'd go somewhere she knew from when she was younger. But it's so difficult to imagine what goes on in a brain ravaged by Alzheimer's. *Plaques and tangles*, the consultant told her. She'd looked it up: *Abnormal clusters of protein fragments (plaques) and twisted strands of another protein (tangles) are prime suspects in cell death and tissue loss in the Alzheimer brain*. She thinks about the gap in her own memory, the empty space in Dylan's drawing occupied by question marks. It seems nothing in comparison to what's happening to her mum. What would Dylan draw if he could see into that crumbling brain, she wonders?

301

Sometimes she visualises her mother's mind as a many-roomed cellar, its chambers now empty and swathed in cobwebs, Miss Havisham-style; sometimes she remembers an image from a conversation with one of the farm helpers, a great house of a man who could lift sacks of potatoes or onions as if they were bags of flour. He was a keen scuba diver, just back from a diving trip off the West Coast of Scotland, and he was furious about how the practice of dredging was devastating the seabed. 'I last dived up there four years ago,' he said. 'It was teeming with life, then: flatfish, crabs, scallops – all sorts. But this time . . .' She remembers how his voice caught in his throat and his eyes glistened briefly. 'The ocean floor was empty and lifeless, nothing but a few broken shells lying around. It was an underwater desert.'

There is an ominous smattering of rain on the window. She takes a hasty mouthful of tea and grabs her car keys. 'I'll call if I find her, and obviously—'

'Of course. And I'll call you if the police phone.'

The rain is cold on her head as she hurries down the steps. Marjorie is wearing nothing but a nightdress; she has to find her quickly. Just as she reaches the bottom step, a police car pulls up in front of the house and the driver's door and rear doors open at the same time. Her heart crashes against the walls of her chest as two uniformed officers climb out. Time seems to stand still for a moment, and then she realises one of the officers is talking to someone in the back seat. He leans in and helps Marjorie out onto the pavement.

'Mum, thank God. Are you all right?' Her mum is dressed in a long white nightdress and there's a blanket draped around her shoulders. She is barefoot. Eleanor can't remember the last time she saw her mother without shoes or slippers, even in the house, and there is something about her bare, blue-veined feet that makes her appear terribly vulnerable. Her heart contracts.

'She's a bit upset,' the taller of the two officers says, 'but she seems okay. Better get her inside, though, before this rain gets any worse.' He takes Marjorie's hand. 'Come on, love, let's get you in the warm.'

Marjorie doesn't move; she looks terrified. Raindrops sparkle on her hair.

'It's all right, Mum,' Eleanor soothes, taking her other hand. 'These are policemen.'

Marjorie looks from one to the other. 'Policemen? Why are they here again? Told them already, I can't remember.'

'They brought you home, Mum. They know you can't remember – I told them when I phoned.'

Marjorie looks puzzled, but allows them to lead her up the steps.

Peggy opens the door as they reach it. 'Oh, Marjorie, where on earth have you been? We were worried sick.'

Marjorie doesn't answer, but her features start to relax as soon as she is in the living room, and she settles herself in her usual armchair.

'I'll nip down and get your dressing gown,' Peggy says. 'And then I'll put the kettle on. Would you like some tea or coffee?' she asks the officers.

'Yes, please, love. Tea, please. We was nearly at the end of our shift when we got the call, so we're well ready for a cuppa now. Two sugars for me, but young Steve here reckons he's sweet enough.'

The younger officer smiles.

'So,' Eleanor says, turning to Marjorie, 'where were you, Mum? Didn't you realise it was the middle of the night?'

'The middle of the night,' Marjorie repeats.

'Yes, for goodness' sake. Anything could have happened. Do you realise—' She stops herself. She can hear the exasperated tone in her voice and she can feel the older officer looking at her. 'I'm sorry. It's just that I was so worried about you.'

Marjorie's expression is blank; she's shutting down again.

The older police officer clears his throat. 'Has this happened before, at all?'

'No. At least, I don't think so. Not unless she's gone out and come back without me knowing.'

'You don't double-lock the door, then? It might be an idea, you know, from now on. They do this quite a lot. Your mum's not the first one me and Steve have picked up, is she, Steve? Sometimes we know who they are because the family's called them in missing, sometimes we just find 'em wandering. Found an old boy walking down the middle of the Sidcup bypass a few weeks back. Family didn't even know he'd gone.'

'Oh, God,' Eleanor murmurs, 'I see what you mean.'

Peggy comes back in with the tea, and while she's

helping Marjorie into her dressing gown and slippers, the officer speaks quietly. 'It's not a nice situation, is it? My gran had it, and my old auntie. My mum coped at home as long as she could, but there comes a point when they're better off somewhere where they have experience, you know.'

She nods. She needs to think more about this, but not now. 'So, where did you find her in the end?'

'Verdant Lane, up by Hither Green cemetery.'

'The cemetery?' Peggy says. 'Oh, Marje, why didn't you ask me to take you?'

'Nearly frightened the life out of young Steve here, she did.' He looks over at Marjorie and smiles. 'Hanging round the cemetery in a long white frock – we thought you was a ghost, Marjorie.'

Marjorie looks up and smiles for the first time. 'Thought you was a ghost, Marjorie,' she mutters.

Eleanor, December 1983

Eleanor forced herself to consciousness and tried to focus on the clock – almost twenty to six; she'd have to get up soon to give Sarah her first feed, but it had been another pacing-the-floor night, so maybe she could have just a few more minutes. After all those months at the camp, a warm, dry bed was a comfort she still appreciated every day.

Some of the women kept their babies with them in their tents or caravans, and at the time she'd had no idea how difficult that must have been. If only she'd paid a bit more attention to how they settled their babies at night. She must be doing something wrong, but she couldn't work out what it was. And she was constantly worried that her pacing or Sarah's crying would disturb Rita and Alan, whose bedroom was directly below this one. She'd tried feeding Sarah whenever she cried, but she still found it quite painful, not to mention exhausting.

Sometimes Sarah appeared to have dozed off, curled into the hollow of her neck, but then Eleanor would try gently to put her back into her cot and her little arms and legs would jerk suddenly, she'd fill her lungs, screw up her eyes and begin crying in earnest. Having Sarah in bed with her didn't work either, because Eleanor was far too afraid of suffocating her to allow herself to sleep. She'd tried singing to her, humming along to the Brahms lullaby or rewinding the cot mobile over and over again so that there was no break in the tinkling music, but as soon as she crept back to her own bed and allowed the music to slow, Sarah would open her eyes and start crying again.

The health visitor said babies often 'turned a corner' at nine or ten weeks, so maybe things would get better soon. She'd mention it at the baby clinic today. Peggy was finishing work at lunchtime and was going to drive over and go with them, then they were going to put Sarah in her pram and push her around Chislehurst village, where the Christmas lights made it look like some sort of fairyland. Even though she was still nervous, she loved taking Sarah out. It made her feel special: the admiring glances of older women as they asked how old the baby was; the way they held doors open for her and helped her on and off buses; it made her feel like some sort of VIP.

She snuggled further into the pillow. It was soft and comfortable under her bare head. The weather was getting chillier by the day, though, so she'd soon have to start wearing something on her head at night. One thing that delighted her was the realisation that she didn't have to explain her baldness to her baby daughter. It was a completely unexpected joy to discover that Sarah seemed to recognise her instantly – and be pleased to see her – whether or not she was wearing a wig or a scarf.

She sighed and turned over. It was so unusual for her to wake before Sarah that she couldn't quite relax. She was half listening for the familiar first cries that always started as little mewling sounds but quickly became fully-fledged yells if Eleanor didn't get there quickly enough. Sarah was such a hungry baby. She hadn't gone more than three hours without a feed since she was born, which meant that Eleanor hadn't had more than three hours' unbroken sleep. It must have been almost four this morning when she finally got her back down, and now it was ... She reached for the clock, and this time, as her eyes focused properly, she saw that it was not twenty to six, but almost half past eight. Sarah had slept for over five hours! Last night's long crying session must have tired her out. Or maybe it was just that the health visitor was right and that she had turned that corner.

Eleanor stretched and sat up, feeling quite decadent. Who'd have thought she'd ever consider five hours' sleep to be such a luxury? She yawned as she pulled her dressing gown on and padded across the carpet to what she now thought of as 'Sarah's room'. She'd started to look forward to picking her daughter up in the mornings; she was no longer quite so afraid of dropping her, or stabbing her with a nappy pin. When she thought back to how determined she'd been not to have children, she went cold inside, as though an icy sea was rolling in over her stomach. She couldn't imagine life without Sarah now. True, she had a long way to go in terms of trusting herself completely, but she felt more confident with each passing day. She particularly loved the mornings, and found herself anticipating the wonderful baby smell that wafted over her as soon as she lifted Sarah up out of her cocoon of blankets. There were few things more precious than the warm, salty-sweet smell of her baby's hair, still sweaty-damp from sleep. Every now and again she felt a pang as she imagined how her mother must have loved that smell too; how she must have missed it.

The only light in the tiny narrow space came from the electric night light, the base of which revolved, casting an ever-moving scene of fairies, elves and bobtailed bunnies in shadows on the wall. Eleanor turned the handle and gently pushed open the door to allow a little daylight into the room. The hush of early morning rushed up to greet her, and the shadows of dancing fairies faded back into the night.

There was no sound or movement from the cot.

*

Even before she'd touched the tiny form in the centre of the cot, she knew Sarah wasn't breathing. Instantly, she snatched the baby up into her arms and yelled for Rita.

The changing mat was still on the table in the main room, surrounded by baby clutter; she swept everything else onto the floor in one movement and laid Sarah down on the mat. It had happened; the thing she'd most dreaded, the reason she hadn't wanted children, the thing she'd somehow known was going to happen but in her complacency had stopped being on the alert for. 'Rita!' She yelled again at the top of her voice. 'Anyone! Help me, please.' She stamped her foot on the floor as hard as she could. Please let someone come soon, someone who'd know what to do. She tried desperately to recall the basic first-aid training she'd had at Girl Guides all those years ago, but panic was filling her mind. It was different for a baby, she knew that much; somehow she *had* to remember how to do it, she had to get a grip. Instinctively, she leant over and covered her precious daughter's tiny mouth and nose with her own mouth. It started to come back to her: she could see the training woman in her St John Ambulance uniform, standing at the front of the guide hut with the life-size dolls they had to practise on. The adult one was called 'Resussie Annie', and there was a baby doll, too ... That was it: gentle breaths, only for a second or so, and light chest compressions using just two fingertips.

She heard someone on the stairs. 'Help me!' she called, between breaths. The door opened.

'What ... Oh my God!' It was one of the guests, wearing a long black nightie, hair all over the place. She stood frozen in the doorway.

'Ambulance,' Eleanor screamed between breaths. 'Get an ambulance.'

She carried on with short, steady breaths; turn away, light compressions, inhale, repeat.

She heard the woman hurrying down the stairs and, in no time, someone else running up them. Alan burst into the room, closely followed by Rita. 'What's happened?' Rita said, her face ashen.

'Not breathing,' Eleanor said. She could hear the panic in her own voice, then she heard the woman shout something up the stairs. Alan went running down but was back almost at once.

'Ambulance is on its way,' he called from the doorway. 'They're still on the phone. They want to know exactly what happened.'

Inhale, steady breaths, turn away. 'Went to get her up ...' Inhale, count the breaths ... three, four, five, turn away, light compressions. 'She wasn't breathing.'

'Right.' He shouted down the stairs. 'Baby wasn't breathing when her mum picked her up.'

He paused. 'Ten weeks, I think.' He looked at Eleanor for confirmation, then went back out to the stairs. Yes, she heard him say, they were doing mouth-to-mouth, and, yes, the baby's mother knew how to do it. Then there was a pause. 'Hang on a sec,' he said and put his head round the door again. 'Eleanor! You do know how you do it, don't you? The bloke on the phone says they can talk you through it.'

Eleanor was struggling to keep the panic at bay. She

nodded. 'Did first aid.' She mustn't cry, mustn't cry mustn't cry. If she cried, she wouldn't be able to do this properly. Breath, breath, breath, breath, breath, turn away. Inhale.

The ambulance men arrived within minutes, although she could have sworn it was several hours before she finally heard them clattering up the uncarpeted stairs to her room. One of them took over the mouth-to-mouth immediately while the other prepared a tiny oxygen mask and held it over the baby's face. There was something about seeing these two tall, capable-looking figures attending to Sarah that allowed Eleanor to stop trying to hold it all together. One of the men was young, not much older than she was. But the other reminded her of Ken, and was about the same age as her dad would have been if he was still alive. She allowed herself to cry now, and when Rita put her arms around her, she felt herself crumple as though someone had just removed her innards. Rita held her and tried to comfort her while the ambulance men worked silently. Alan stood unmoving by the door.

She had no idea how long they tried to bring her baby back; she was only aware of the fact that they'd stopped. When the two uniformed figures straightened up, sighed and shook their heads, something inside her snapped. *'What are you doing?'* she shouted. 'Don't stop!'

The older of the two looked at her, his face a picture of compassion. 'I'm sorry, love.'

'Try again!' she yelled, breaking away from Rita's embrace. 'You can't stop, you *can't!'* She began hitting the younger man, who turned towards her with tears in his eyes. 'It's no good. I'm sorry, but she's probably been—'

'Try again,' she sobbed. 'Please try again.'

'No, Eleanor,' Rita said softly as she tried to stop her from hitting the poor man again. 'Come away, now.'

'Come on, love.' The older man put his hands on her shoulders and gently but firmly steered her away from the younger man, who looked devastated. 'I think we all need a cup of tea now, don't you?' He turned towards Alan, who was still standing by the door, his face stricken. 'Would that be all right, sir?'

Alan swallowed. 'I'll put the kettle on.'

Downstairs in the kitchen, the older man pulled out a chair and guided Eleanor, still sobbing, into it. 'What's your name, sweetheart?' Eleanor was crying too much to speak. She put her arms on the table in front of her and slumped over so her head was resting on them.

The man sat down in the chair next to her. He put his hand over hers and turned back to Rita. 'What's her name, love?'

She told him.

'Now listen, Eleanor,' he said, leaning in towards her and speaking softly, still covering her hand with his, 'I know this is going to be difficult, but I need to tell you that in cases like this, I'm afraid we have to inform the police, love, okay? It's nothing to worry about.'

Rita, who was pouring milk into mugs for tea, spun round. 'The police? Why on earth do you need—'

'It's routine, I promise you. It doesn't mean anything

else, it's just that it's technically an unexplained death, which is why we have to report it.' He sighed, then squeezed Eleanor's hand and nodded towards Rita. 'Your mum can stay with you.'

'That's not her mum,' Alan said, then he turned to Eleanor and said gently, 'Eleanor, I think we should phone your mum.'

'No,' she said quickly. 'I don't want her to know.'

'Why not?' This was the younger ambulance man, who'd gone over to help Rita with the teas. 'Surely your mum—'

'It's all right, Danny. Young lady can decide later.' The older man accepted a mug of tea from Rita. 'Thanks, love.' There was a pause, and it seemed to Eleanor as if everybody in the room was stirring their tea too loudly and for longer than was necessary. 'Is her boyfriend . . . ?'

'No,' Rita said.

'She'll need someone with her.'

'My sister'll go. They're very close.' Rita leant down to Eleanor and put her arms around her shoulders. 'I'll ring Peggy at work in a minute, all right? She'll be here in two shakes, I'm sure. Are you absolutely determined for us not to fetch your mum?'

At that moment, although she knew it would pass, her longing for her mother was so powerful it almost hurt. A fresh wave of tears prevented her from speaking, but she shook her head again, more vigorously than was really necessary. She began to feel light-headed, as though she might faint. She put her head down on the table again.

Maybe this wasn't actually happening; perhaps it was just a nightmare, brought on by sleep deprivation and worry about Sarah. In a minute, she'd realise she was still in bed and that Sarah was crying for her six o'clock feed.

Then she heard someone sighing, and the older of the two men asking if he could use the telephone.

There were various comings and goings during the rest of the morning, and she lost track of what was happening. Then Peggy arrived, her eyes already red and puffy, her eyelashes still wet.

'Ellie,' Peggy said, shaking her head, 'I can't believe ... Oh, Ellie ...' She sat next to her, taking her other hand and holding it between both of her own. The three women sat in stunned and tearful silence until the young police constable arrived. He had a freshly scrubbed, not-old-enough-to-shave look about him, and he appeared so upset and awkward that Eleanor felt sorry for him. He took his hat off and sat on a chair opposite while Rita got up to make another pot of tea. He was so sorry for her loss, he kept saying. He understood how difficult it was, but he had to ask these questions and he hoped she would forgive him. There would have to be a post-mortem, he said, usually within a few days so she could get on and organise a funeral. At that point she became aware of a strange noise, like an animal in pain. It was only when Peggy put both arms around her and Rita came rushing back in that Eleanor realised the noise was coming from her own mouth. The constable had gone very red in the face and was mumbling apologies again. The coroner might order an inquest, he explained, and she was not to worry. It was the same thing that the ambulance man had said – routine in these cases, where the death was unexplained.

'It's a cot death, surely?' Peggy said. 'Why put the poor girl through this? Christ, you can see she's distraught.'

The policeman nodded, then sighed. 'I'm sorry, madam. I understand how upsetting this is, but it's only a formality, I can assure you.'

Peggy tutted, muttered something under her breath and then said, 'Okay, but this had better happen quickly. Look at the state of the girl.'

After the police officer left, a doctor arrived. He gave her an injection to help her sleep, and some pills, which he left with Peggy. She couldn't face going up to her own room, so Rita made up the bed in the box room for her, and Peggy tucked the quilt around her body just as she had when Eleanor was little. A flood of tears engulfed her. She ached for her mum, but she was emphatic when Peggy suggested contacting her. She couldn't bear to imagine what her mother would think of her now.

Her head began to feel heavy and she was sinking. It felt like she was dying. Part of her wanted to fight it, but another part of her was relieved that she didn't have to bother any more, so she let herself sink down and down with the hope that she might just dissolve into the ground and never wake up.

Marjorie, January 1984

Marjorie had cried so much her eyes felt sore and dry; it hurt even to blink. It happened five weeks ago, Peggy said. Five weeks! And Eleanor didn't want her to know because she thought it would remind her of what happened with Peter. Her insides seemed to liquefy when she heard that. She was still angry with Peggy and Ken for not telling her about the birth straight away; she should have made them take her to Eleanor, but she'd been afraid of scaring her away again. She couldn't possibly go to work, so as soon as she was able to compose herself, she telephoned the ward sister and said she had the flu and would call again in a week or so. Her heart ached to think of her poor, grieving daughter. She wanted Eleanor home, she told Peggy now, here in this house, where she could look after her. 'I don't care how you do it,' she said, a steely edge to her voice, 'but you are to bring my daughter home. You owe me that much.'

*

Marjorie sat holding the photograph Ken had given her a few days after they told her about Eleanor and the baby. He'd taken it in the hospital – Greenwich District, apparently. She was glad she had that piece of information, because until then she'd been picturing Eleanor in Lewisham, where she'd given birth herself long before she worked there. It was a grim place in those days, and you could see it had once been a workhouse. And the idea that she could have been at work one day while her own daughter was giving birth in the same building . . .

She looked down at the photo. All she could see of Eleanor was her arm and hand as she cradled her new daughter. The sleeping baby had a mass of dark blonde hair, the same as Eleanor had when she was born, and she was dressed in one of those little pink-and-white hospital gowns that look as if they're made out of J-cloths. She looked perfect, just perfect. Marjorie swallowed. Poor, poor Eleanor.

She glanced at the clock. They'd be here soon. She put the photo back in the envelope, opened the sideboard drawer and slipped it under the cutlery tray. She'd find somewhere else for it later. Eleanor didn't know she had this picture, and she certainly didn't want her stumbling across it unexpectedly.

The phone gave a single ring – Peggy calling down from upstairs. Since they'd had that big row after they'd told her about the baby, Peggy tended to ring first rather than just coming down like she used to. Things had been strained between them, but if she was honest, she wouldn't be able to get through all this without Peggy.

'Hello?'

'Rita's just phoned. They're about to set off. She said Eleanor's quiet and a bit tearful but she seems okay about coming.'

Marjorie didn't say anything.

'Rita's driving her, and she said – Rita, that is – that she hopes you won't mind but she'll need to get straight back because she's short-staffed. Ken's going to run her back.'

According to Peggy, Eleanor could drive herself now, although not at the moment, obviously. Apparently, she had an old Volkswagen camper that someone at Greenham gave her, and Rita was bringing her over in that. A birth, a death, driving a big van; it was as though they were telling her about someone else's daughter.

'Fine.' She hesitated. 'Do you fancy popping down for coffee?'

'Put the kettle on.'

*

She tried not to glance at the clock every two minutes, but her eyes were drawn to the damned thing. 'Shouldn't they be here by now?'

'Sit down, Marjorie. You're making yourself more agitated. They'll be here when they get here.'

'You don't suppose she's changed her mind, do you?' She could hear the anxiety in her own voice. 'It doesn't take that long to get here from Chislehurst.'

'It's rush hour,' Peggy said.

Even after she sat down her heart was beating so fast it was making her breathless, so she stood up again to distract herself. This was Eleanor, she kept telling herself. This was her own daughter. True, she hadn't seen her for over a year; they hadn't even spoken on the phone since the summer and even that had been a ridiculously brief conversation. Now she thought about it, Eleanor had sounded odd that day – vague, distracted – she'd assumed it was because of what was happening at Greenham. There was quite a lot about it in the papers, and she'd read somewhere that the women took it in turns to get arrested. For a moment she'd wondered if that was why Eleanor sounded so strange, but when she asked, Eleanor had said of course she wasn't in trouble with the police, and then she said she had to go. She'd have been six months' pregnant at that point. Marjorie felt another swell of sadness at the thought that her daughter had felt unable to tell her she was expecting, unable to tell her she'd given birth and, worst of all, unable to tell her when this terrible thing happened. She felt her eyes fill with tears, but she had to hold them in. Compared to what had happened to Eleanor, she had no right to cry.

She swallowed. 'What am I going to say to her, Peg? What do you say when your child can't even come to you—'

'You need to trust your instincts,' Peggy said. She was making tea again, even though they'd only had one half an hour ago.

'After all, you know exactly what she's going through. And even if you didn't, you're still her mum. It's not too late to make things right, you know.'

Marjorie nodded. Peggy could be wise sometimes, but she had a tendency to approach life in a black-and-white way, and things were seldom that simple. For one thing, she wasn't sure she even felt like Eleanor's mother any more. She'd been thinking a lot lately about when Eleanor was little, and how she'd been so afraid of damaging her by saying the wrong thing after Peter died that she'd actually avoided being with her. What sort of mother did that make her? She remembered Ted telling her once that she seemed to have given up being a mother: *It's as though you've abdicated responsibility*, he said. And even though she knew he was right, she hadn't made any attempt to change things. Was it surprising Eleanor had pulled away from her?

'This is them.' Peggy lifted the corner of the net curtain.

Marjorie heard the engine judder to a stop, then a sliding door opening and closing, then another. After a few moments, the doorbell rang. She was frozen for a second. Why wasn't she using her key? But then she went to the door.

She expected Eleanor to look different, but not quite this different. She was heavier, and she appeared slumped; she looked pale and tired, with brown circles around her eyes, and while her skin was still firm and unlined, there was something so careworn about her face you would have thought she was a woman of thirty or more, not a girl just coming up for twenty. Her wig looked awful, as though someone had mopped the floor with it. She made a mental note to buy her some new ones as soon as she felt up to trying them on.

'Come in,' she said. 'The kettle's just boiled.' *How ridiculous*, she thought, *as if she gives a damn whether the kettle has boiled*. 'Go and sit yourself down, darling,' she added, aware that Eleanor wasn't meeting her eye.

'How are you, Marjorie?' Rita's smile looked uncertain.

Marjorie tried to smile back as Eleanor walked past, head lowered, and as she tried to focus on Rita, she sensed that behind her Eleanor was almost certainly being enfolded in Peggy's arms before going into the living room. Why had *she* not embraced her distraught daughter?

'Rita, I want to thank you for what ... for taking care ...' It stuck in her throat. She had to thank this woman for doing what *she* should have been doing.

Rita waved away her words. 'Only too glad I could help. And I'm sorry it's been so ... and, you know, the way things turned out.'

Marjorie nodded. There was an awkward silence, and she wondered if she should invite Rita to stay for tea, but then Ken appeared in the hallway jangling his car keys, and Rita said she was sorry she had to dash off but there were new guests arriving soon. Most of Eleanor's things were in the camper, she said, but Peggy was going to pick up anything that was left, and there was no hurry.

Marjorie thanked her again, and stood by the front door with Ken while Rita went to say goodbye to Eleanor.

'How are you bearing up?' Ken said.

'Okay, I think. Just about.'

Rita came back out, Peggy following, and when they'd said their goodbyes, Peggy put her hand on Marjorie's arm. 'I'll leave you to it.'

Marjorie went back into the living room. Eleanor sat hunched on the sofa, a battered canvas bag at her feet. She had her arms crossed over her chest and was hanging onto her own shoulders as though she was trying to hold herself together.

'Would you like a cup of tea?'

Eleanor shook her head without looking up.

Marjorie sat tentatively on the sofa next to her. She'd thought about this moment a thousand times over the last few days, but now that it was here, she was dumbstruck. Why did everyone but her know what to say to Eleanor, how to *be* with her? A memory dropped into her mind of a similar feeling she'd had years ago when she'd not long been out of hospital and was still having very bad days. Eleanor would have been about six because she'd been staying at Peggy's for a couple of days before they moved in upstairs. Peggy had persuaded Marjorie to let her perm her hair with a Toni home perm – it would perk her up, she said. She brought Eleanor home at lunchtime and settled her with some colouring at the dining room table while she did Marjorie's hair, and at the end of the afternoon when she was ready to go, she called through to the dining room, 'I'm off now, Ellie. Be a good girl for your mum.'

There was a clatter and the sound of a chair being scraped back, and then Eleanor came tearing out into the hall and threw her arms around Peggy, who lifted her off her feet in a tight hug.

Marjorie watched her daughter's face, her eyes closed and a blissful smile on her face as Peggy hugged her. The smile turned to resignation as Peggy set her back down, dropping a kiss on the top of her head, and opened the front door.

When she'd gone, Eleanor sighed, then turned away and trudged back along the hall. Marjorie took a step towards her. She wanted to say something, something about having missed her while she was at Peggy's. As she opened her mouth, she felt as though the words were all there, gathering in her chest, trying to push their way up and out into the open, but she was still standing with her hand on the door frame when Eleanor settled herself at the table and became engrossed in her colouring once more.

She'd felt inadequate then, but that was nothing compared to how she felt now as she sat watching her grown-up, newly bereaved daughter pull aimlessly at loose threads in her jumper.

'I've made a shepherd's pie for dinner. I only need to heat it up, and I thought—'

'Thanks, Mum, but I'm not hungry. In fact, do you mind if I go down to bed in a minute? I can hardly keep my eyes open.'

'Of course I don't mind.' Should she offer to go down with her? Would that be intrusive? She'd risk it. 'I'll come down and get you settled, shall I?'

To her surprise, Eleanor murmured, 'That would be nice.'

She was glad she'd put the heating on this morning, because the bedrooms had a tendency to damp and could be chilly this time of year. Eleanor sat down heavily on the bed and bent over to unlace her boots. She seemed to be struggling, and Marjorie was about to offer to help when Eleanor muttered something and managed to pull both boots off without undoing the laces. She pulled back the covers and lay down, fully clothed.

Surely she'd be more comfortable if she undressed? Instead of mentioning it, Marjorie took the folded spare blanket from the bottom of the bed, shook it out and laid it over her daughter.

'Thanks, and thanks for not asking loads of questions. I'm sorry I haven't been in touch.'

'We don't need to talk about that now. You just try and get some sleep.'

Eleanor, February 1984

It was the same almost every morning; she'd wake with her face wet with tears and the front of her nightdress soaked. At least it tended to happen only at night, now, usually when she'd been dreaming about Sarah, but that was most nights. She pushed away the covers and put her hand up to her breasts. The wet fabric still felt warm, but it would cool quickly now it had made contact with the air. She levered herself up slowly and sat on the edge of the bed, thinking about Sarah. On the one hand, she wanted the milk to dry up completely, because every drop that leaked from her nipples was a reminder that her baby was no longer there to receive it. But on the other hand, this was her last connection with Sarah, the living proof that she had existed.

Tears were trickling slowly down her face, but she didn't bother to wipe them away because it wasn't as though she was actively crying. Weeping was a better word, but even that didn't describe this feeling of ... of *seepage*; that was probably the nearest she could get. It was as if she was so full up with grief and sadness that some of it was seeping out along with the tears and the wasted, useless breast milk.

With a clean nightdress on, she got back into bed and lay down. It was 5.02 a.m., so all that dreaming had only lasted a few hours at the most. It felt like weeks. She dreamed about being pregnant, the hugeness of her swollen belly, the strange intimacy of Sarah shifting position inside her; she dreamed about being in labour, the intensity of the pain and the smell of the rubber mask; she dreamed about the birth, the feeling that she couldn't take any more and then that searing sensation as her skin tore and Sarah finally pushed her way out.

A tear ran across her cheek, down past her ear and into the hollow of her neck. She would take the pain of childbirth again every day of her life if it meant she could have Sarah back. During the day she tried to push these thoughts to the back of her mind, but her dreams were so real that while she was here, alone and safe in her bed, she allowed herself to think it all through repeatedly, to relive those moments of motherhood that she would never experience again. She turned over, wiping her face on the pillow, and revisited the memory she cherished the most: Sarah is less than one minute old and she is lying with her feet on Eleanor's stomach, head resting against her breast. She doesn't cry. Eleanor says, 'Hello, baby,' and her daughter opens her eyes and looks right back at her; the connection is made. They stare at each other for a few moments, soaking up all they can, then Sarah blinks, looks away and begins to root.

All this, she thought now, all this was her mother's experience, too. Did she lie in bed in the mornings reliving Peter's birth, or was she still too haunted by his death? What had his funeral been like, she wondered? She wished she could remember Sarah's more clearly, but the main thing that stuck in her mind was the floral tribute she'd ordered, a two-foot-high teddy bear made entirely of yellow chrysanthemums. It sat with the other flowers outside Rita's, and as she walked from the house to the funeral car, a young mother walked past with her child in a pushchair. 'Look!' the little boy pointed excitedly. 'Look at the big teddy!' The mother, crippled with embarrassment, hushed the child and wheeled him quickly away.

There were no photographs of the flowers, but now she wished she'd asked Ken to take some, then perhaps, at some point, when the time was right, she could show her mum. She hadn't even mentioned Sarah so far. Everyone else – Peggy, Rita, the policemen that came that day, even the doctor – they all kept telling her it wasn't her fault, that cot death can happen to any baby, any mother; she even found herself starting to believe them. But her own mum hadn't said that.

She turned over and looked towards the window. It was beginning to get light outside, thank God. The nights seemed endless sometimes, and even when she tried to comfort herself by recalling the feel of Sarah in her arms, it never lasted because her thoughts would soon become darker and heavier. *It'll get better*, the doctor told her. *It may not feel like it now, but I promise you, you will find a purpose in life again*. And then he'd said, *And you're young – you'll have more children*. She wouldn't, of course. And a purpose? What was the point of a purpose?

She must have drifted off to sleep again, because it was some time later when she became aware of a soft knocking on the door.

'Eleanor?' Her mother's voice was quiet.

'Come in, I'm awake.'

'I've got to go to work in a minute, so I thought I'd bring you breakfast in bed.'

Her mum set the breakfast tray down on the bedside cabinet. There was a boiled egg, bread and butter cut into soldiers, a slice of toast with marmalade and a cup of tea.

'How did you sleep?'

She hesitated. *I relived my pregnancy and my baby's birth and my breasts still ache and leak and I felt as though I was crying all night long in my sleep.* 'Not too bad, thank you.'

Her mum opened the curtains. 'Jolly good. Now, as I say, I'm working today but Peggy's home so she's going to look in on you later. She says to phone up if you need anything before that.' She paused. 'You're getting your colour back, at least; you don't look quite so peaky.'

Yesterday, her mum said she looked as though she was on the mend. Please don't say that again, she thought. It's not a broken bone that's going to knit together.

329

'Okay, thanks,' she said, sitting up. 'Mum,' she said after a moment. 'I don't know how long it's going to take for me to feel better.' She felt her courage waver. 'I mean, it's not as though I'm actually ill, is it? I was wondering if we could maybe talk about—'

'There's plenty of time for that, darling.' Her mum turned towards the door. 'You just concentrate on getting better for now.'

'But—'

'Sorry, darling, I . . . I don't want to be late.'

Marjorie, June 1984

Marjorie put two slices of bread under the grill. Eleanor's cup and plate were on the draining board, so she'd obviously been up and had breakfast quite early. That was a good sign. The first few weeks, she rarely came up before ten, and even then she looked as though she still needed more sleep; perhaps she was picking up a bit now. Marjorie had been the same herself after she lost Peter. The doctor said it was the brain's way of coping, the idea being that you couldn't feel the pain of grief while you were asleep. It wasn't true, of course; the grief that came to her while she slept was even more painful. While she was awake, she had a certain amount of control over her thoughts, even if some of it was on a subconscious level, whereas when she was asleep, her unconscious threw up images that demolished her.

The Times was still on the doormat, and when she picked it up, the date jumped out at her. How could she not have realised? Usually, she was prepared a few days before, but today it just popped up and slapped her unexpectedly in the face. Would Eleanor remember the date? She hoped not. Where was she, anyway?

The phone rang – the single tone that indicated Peggy's extension. Peggy always remembered. She picked up the receiver. 'Morning, Peg.'

'Just thought I'd see if you were feeling all right.'

'I'd forgotten what day it is.'

'Not surprising,' Peggy said, 'what with Ellie and everything. Does she—'

'I haven't seen her yet. She's been up but I think she's gone back to bed.'

'Shall I pop down?'

'You not at work today?'

'Not until two. Put the kettle on.'

Peggy was there within a couple of minutes. She pulled out a chair and sat down. 'Still no sign of Eleanor?'

'No,' Marjorie placed two mugs of coffee on the table. 'I thought I'd let her sleep. She must need it.'

Peggy nodded. 'Are you going to the cemetery today?'

'I'm not sure. I want to, but I don't know if it'll upset Eleanor.'

'Marjorie,' Peggy's voice was hesitant, 'I know it's not really any of my business, but I was thinking maybe you should ask Eleanor if she'd like to come along with you.'

'Come with me? Don't you think—'

'Then you could offer to go with her to the cemetery at Chislehurst.'

'No. No I don't think that would be a good idea.' She got up to see to her toast.

'Why not think about it for a bit? I know things haven't been easy between you two, especially since she found out.'

She meant when Eleanor confronted her with the death certificate and she'd ended up telling her she'd put him in the water. She flicked her head to loosen the memory.

'But when you think about what Eleanor's been through, and what you went through with Peter, well, it seems to me . . .' Her hand strayed towards Marjorie's cigarettes, then she pulled it back. She was determined to give up this time, she'd said. Marjorie admired her but half hoped she'd fail – she liked to smoke in company. 'It seems to me you've both suffered a similar thing. A mother losing a child – it's such a terrible loss, and only someone who's been through it can really understand. I thought, if the two of you went to Peter's grave together, you could go with her to see Sarah's. And I'm sure things could be easier between you if—'

'Peggy, I know you think everyone should talk about everything bad that's ever happened to them, but it's not always the best way.'

'That's not what I'm getting at.'

'No, listen. I know you mean well, but sometimes it's better not to bring everything out in the open. She's not long lost her baby; if I start trying to drag her along to visit her brother's grave, it's bound to upset her. She's only just started to eat again, don't forget.'

'I know, but you need to reassure her.'

'What do you mean?'

'I mean that not only does she blame herself for Peter, she blames herself for this as well.'

'But it was a cot death.'

'For heaven's sake, Marjorie. Have you not been listening? *Was the room the right temperature, should she have put her on her back instead of her front, should she have fed her more often, less often.* The poor girl's going mad with it, and you haven't said a word.'

'But I've done whatever—'

Peggy shook her head. 'You're looking after her marvellously, but you haven't *said* a word, and sometimes you actually try to shut her up when she mentions it.'

'That's not true!'

'It is, Marjorie. The other evening when you both came up to me for dinner, she asked if you thought it was possible that there was something about her milk that the baby could have been allergic to and you pretended you hadn't heard; you got up and started clearing the dishes.'

Had she really done that? But then the memory crept back. 'I just thought . . . I thought it would upset her.'

'But Marjorie,' Peggy spoke gently, 'I'd bet a month's wages it's upsetting her more that you won't talk about it. And I don't think you've talked to her about Peter, have you?'

Marjorie felt the tears behind her eyes.

'You've both lost a baby; you don't have to lose each other as well.'

Marjorie didn't move. Had she avoided talking to Eleanor because doing so forced her back into her own memory of that day? Her recollection had always been slightly hazy, possibly because of the sedatives she'd been given so soon afterwards. And she'd never wanted it to be clearer; it was easier, more comfortable not to remember, and she assumed it would be the same for Eleanor. But perhaps Peggy was right; perhaps she'd done more harm than good. And now she had a chance to try to make things better between them. Maybe she should ask about the baby; she could ask to see a photograph – Eleanor didn't know she already had one.

'Marjorie?'

She looked at Peggy. 'You're sure I should ask her to come to the cemetery? You don't think it'll upset her terribly?'

'Of course it will – it *is* upsetting. It's a terrible, terrible tragedy. But when something hurts that much, not bringing it out into the open won't make it hurt any less. In fact, keeping it festering away inside probably makes it hurt more.'

She thought about it, imagined going down to Eleanor's room, knocking on the door. She tried to think how she would start, how she would phrase it.

'Just try it.' Peggy stood up. 'I need to go. Ken's coming home tonight, though God knows why. I'm not used to dealing with him midweek.' She pushed her chair in. 'Talk to her, see what she says.'

Marjorie sighed. 'Maybe you're right. I'll go down now and see if she's awake.'

Peggy smiled. 'I think you'll feel better afterwards. See you later.'

Marjorie made Eleanor a fresh mug of tea. The house felt unusually quiet as she walked down the stairs; there was an increased sense of emptiness. Maybe she'd gone out already; she sometimes went out walking very early and then had a nap later. 'Eleanor?' She knocked and opened the door.

The room was empty. The bed was neatly made and an envelope with *Mum* written on the front sat waiting on the pillow. She took out the folded A4 sheet. The writing was messy, nowhere near as neat as Eleanor's usual hand, but Marjorie had always been good at deciphering near-illegible handwriting.

17th June 1984
Dear Mum,

Sorry to leave without saying goodbye but I wasn't sure how you'd react. You have been very kind, and I'm not sure how I would have got through the last few months without you. I was annoyed with Peggy when she said she'd told you, but now I'm glad, and I'm sorry I didn't tell you myself. I know it must have been difficult for you to have me living here again, especially under the circumstances.

It's exactly six months since I lost Sarah, and I know it's also fifteen years today since Peter died. You've

*always said you never blamed me, and I'm sure that, in
your head, you don't. But in your heart you know that if
it hadn't been for me, he'd still be alive. Since Sarah died,
I've wanted to die too, and I don't know how I would
have coped if I'd had another child to care for, as you did.
I'm amazed you were able to do anything for me at all.
As I'm sure you must know, I blame myself for Sarah's
death, despite what the inquest said. I keep telling
myself they were just being kind. The thing is, I was so
nervous, so worried about being responsible for her, that
I'm sure I must have made a mistake with her feeds or
something. That's bad enough to cope with. But I keep
wondering how I would feel if it had been someone else
who was in charge of her, and I think that even if it had
been someone I loved, and even if it had been absolutely
clear that it wasn't the person's fault, a tiny part of me
might still blame that person. Do you see what I mean?
I might not be able to help blaming them, even if I loved
them, and even if I knew it couldn't be their fault. So
what I'm saying is, I don't blame you for blaming me, if
that makes any sense.*

*I wish we could have talked about Peter and Sarah.
Maybe we will be able to one day. But at the moment,
I think it's because we have this same experience that –
well, not the same, but you know what I mean – that
makes things so difficult. It feels like a double dose of
grief. I know you don't like to talk about Peter and
what happened because it upsets you. It upsets me, too,
and talking about Sarah upsets me even more. But I*

do want to talk about her. I don't want to pretend she never existed, even though she wasn't meant to exist – I would never have deliberately chosen to have a baby, not after what happened with Peter. But Sarah lived for ten weeks and five days and for that time, she was my daughter and your granddaughter. I am still her mother, and I need to allow myself to be her mother, and when I meet people, I want to be able to tell them about her, show them photos of her. I don't want to feel guilty for remembering my baby – I feel guilty enough already.

Anyway, sorry, I didn't mean for this to be so long and I didn't mean to ramble on. It was meant to be a quick note! I'll drop you a postcard to let you know I'm okay. I'm not sure when I'll be back, but I need to get away and be on my own for a while. Thanks again for all you've done and please say thank you to Peggy for me, and tell her I'll never forget everything she did for me.

Love,
Eleanor

Marjorie felt as though her insides had been hollowed out. Still clutching the note, she allowed herself to collapse onto Eleanor's bed. Again she was too late. She'd missed her chance; possibly her last chance.

Eleanor, the present

'Well, she settled more easily than I thought she would,' Eleanor says when she gets back to the house. Peggy is in the hall, waiting for Dennis to pick her up. She's wearing an elegant black dress with a cream linen jacket, and she's bought a new black leather weekend bag specially for the trip. 'You look lovely, by the way – just right for Paris.'

'Thank you, sweetheart. So she was all right about it in the end?'

'Absolutely fine. I'm not sure she'll remember that I'm picking her up on Tuesday, but she seems to understand she'll be sleeping there for a few nights.'

'That's a relief. I was sure she'd be okay once she got there, but I wouldn't have been able to relax completely if I thought she was upset.'

'I left her chatting with one of the residents about dancing. Rock and roll – they were taking about the jitterbug, of all things!'

Peggy grins. 'She used to do that, you know, she and your dad. Everyone else used to move off the dance floor and stand round watching them.'

'I wish . . .' Eleanor half laughs. 'Silly. I was going to say I wish I'd known her then.'

'Not silly at all. I wish you'd known her then, too.' She glances at her watch. 'Dennis'll be here any minute. Now listen, you make sure you have a rest while you get the chance, all right? Do as your auntie Peggy says.'

Eleanor smiles. 'Don't worry about me, just have a brilliant time. Did you say it's his birthday tomorrow?'

'Yes, he'll be sixty-five.'

'And you're—'

'Old enough to know a good thing when I see it.' She laughs. 'My last chap was even younger, you know, but I think I was a bit much for him.'

'Your last chap? Peggy, you dark horse. I didn't know you'd been seeing anyone.'

'Well, that was a long time ago now, before your mum got ill.'

Again Eleanor thinks about how much Peggy has sacrificed. 'I've been a bit self-absorbed, haven't I?'

'Rubbish,' Peggy says as the car horn toots outside. 'You're entitled.' She picks up her bags. 'There's my fella. If I wear him out, I'll trade him in for a younger model.' She kisses Eleanor on the cheek. 'Rest!' she says.

*

Eleanor goes into the living room and flops onto the sofa, savouring the silence. It's strange, being in the house without having to worry about her mum, or even think about Peggy. She has four whole days to herself, and it feels like the ultimate freedom. She'll just sit here for five minutes to get her head together, then have an early lunch and read for a while, maybe give Jill a call a bit later.

She doesn't remember resting her head on the arm of the sofa or tucking her legs up underneath her, but when she wakes, she has a crick in her neck and her cheek feels bobbly where the rough fabric of the sofa has left an imprint on her skin. She sits up, disorientated, and wipes the corner of her mouth where she's dribbled. When she looks at her watch, she has to blink, rub her eyes and look again. She has slept for four hours solid. She swings her legs down and groans aloud as she moves her neck. Her back hurts, too. How can she have slept that long? Suddenly, adrenaline rushes through her body making her heart thump and her fingertips tingle. Her mum. Where ... ? And then she remembers: her mum is in respite care for the weekend, being looked after by someone else. She breathes out and her heartbeat starts to return to normal, but she still feels uneasy until she checks her phone to make sure there are no messages.

Yawning, she goes into the kitchen, makes herself some toast and a cup of black coffee. Rest, Peggy said; well, she's certainly done that. And she'll probably sleep more, but one thing she definitely wants to do while her mother isn't around is go through all those papers and photographs properly. Somewhere, she is sure, there is at least one snap of Peter.

She goes down to her mother's bedroom and stands in front of the cupboards. Her father built these when they first moved here, apparently. She's stopped tidying things back properly every time Marjorie pulls them out because it happens so often, so it's all in quite a mess now. She opens the lower doors, takes things out and starts sorting them into three piles – photographs, papers that need to be looked through later and stuff that's obviously rubbish. There are electricity bills so ancient they bear the London Electricity Board's LEB logo, gas bills from SEGAS – both companies long defunct. There are old shopping lists, letters from Lewisham library about overdue books, even old bus tickets. She hadn't realised Marjorie had become such a hoarder. But that made it even more likely that the picture was still here.

After a couple of hours, she considers the three distinct piles. There aren't as many photographs as she thought, and although the pile of papers to be gone through is substantial, it's nothing compared to what can be thrown away.

It's almost six. She stands up and stretches, pleased with what she's achieved. She rubs the back of her neck which still aches from sleeping awkwardly this after-noon. As she moves her head to try to ease the pain, she realises she hasn't looked in the top cupboards yet.

God knows what's in there. They probably haven't been opened for ages, though, because you need a set of steps to reach them. She grabs the chair from in front of the dressing table, climbs onto it and manages to open the cupboard door, but she can't even see what's on the bottom shelf, never mind the top one. She'll have to get the ladder. A break first, though. Still revelling in the novelty of being responsibility-free for the first time in six months, she grabs her jacket, walks round the corner and buys a bottle of wine. She deserves it.

Her brain is so full of her mother's paperwork and photos that she finds herself completely unable to decide what to have for dinner, so instead she makes cheese on toast, opens the wine and takes it all downstairs to her mum's room, resting the tray on the bed while she fetches the steps from the utility room.

Even on the top rung she can only just about reach the highest shelf. The first cupboard contains yet more blankets and a couple of sleeping bags; the shallow cupboards across the alcove are completely empty, and the other deep one contains suitcases, two on the bottom shelf and one on the top. She pulls tentatively at a handle. This one is light, clearly empty. The next one has something in it, but she suspects it's a smaller case. She reaches up to the top shelf, where there's another small suitcase, heavier this time. She needs both hands to lift it out and has to steady herself as she climbs down. When she opens it, her heart sinks. More of the same. Old payslips, rates bills, recipes. But there are some photos here, too. Maybe this is where she'll find what she's looking for. She carries the suitcase over to the bed, pours herself some wine and picks up a piece of cheese on toast, which is cold now, but she's hungry enough not to care. As she eats, she takes things out one at a time and makes another three piles. There are photographs here that she hasn't seen before, but still not the one she's looking for.

She is about to call it a night when she spots a folded piece of paper with the word *Mum* written on the front. As she unfolds it, a colour photograph slips out. She freezes, glass halfway to her lips. 'Sarah,' she whispers aloud. 'My Sarah.' She puts down her glass and touches the picture with her fingertip. How come her mother has a photo of Sarah? Could she have given it to her and forgotten? Surely not. She looks again at the note but struggles to read her own handwriting. It snakes all over the place; she must have been in quite a state when she wrote this. Some of what she'd written sounds young and naive, but she is surprised by how articulately her nineteen-year-old self has expressed her feelings; it's easier to write about these things than talk about them, she supposes. The photograph is similar to the one she keeps in her purse, taken a minute or so later, or perhaps earlier. She has only ever had five photographs of Sarah, four taken on the day she was born – she was forever grateful to Ken for bringing his camera to the hospital – and another one that Rita took the day Sarah started smiling. In that one, she's wearing the brown and yellow striped Babygro that Peggy gave her. She remembers showing Dylan that photo; he'd smiled and said she looked like a little bumble bee.

Apart from the photos, the only proof she has that her daughter existed is her birth certificate, the hospital bracelet that had encircled her tiny ankle and the rust-coloured booklet they gave her at the clinic. The cover had become detached from the other pages, and only the first few lines were filled in, recording a steady, healthy weight gain.

She still keeps these things all together in a thick plastic wallet that stays next to her bed wherever she sleeps. In fact, that plastic wallet is probably the only thing apart from money and a few clothes that she took with her when she left that day. She remembers putting that note on her bed, then going to the back door with the intention of slipping out quietly through the side alley. But as she'd walked through the utility room, she heard her mother and Peggy in the kitchen upstairs, their voices louder than usual, so she went back along the hallway and let herself out through the downstairs front door.

That was in June 1984. Even now, she has little recollection of what happened between that day and the day, around two years later, when she ran into Jill again at some open-air music thing in Brighton. They hadn't kept in touch for more than a few weeks after they left Greenham, so the first thing she had to do when they met up again was to explain about Sarah, a task that never got any easier. Jill immediately put her arms round her and cried with her, an experience she found profoundly moving. Eventually, they talked about other things. It turned out Jill and David had just bought the run-down farm buildings and surrounding land up in Scalby and had what they called 'a crazy idea' of turning it into a community farm. With love and attention, they said, it could be transformed from a hopeless wreck into something new and alive and productive. She hadn't taken much persuading to go with them, and she remembered those first few weeks on the farm: the cuts and splinters she got from clearing piles of rubble and broken machinery; the pain in her back and shoulders from whole days of digging; the tiredness that was so extreme she felt almost tearful with it. But she also remembered becoming aware that for the first time in two years, she cared about what she was doing, and that she started to feel as though she was being put back together.

But most of the couple of years in between is still a blur even now, a jumble of images and half-memories that she still struggles to put into any sort of order. She knows she did lots of bar work because you could usually live in if you worked in a pub, but when she was waitressing or serving in cafés, she just slept in the camper. That post-card she found in the sideboard upstairs, the one saying she was working in a pub in Derbyshire, is postmarked August, so it must be one of the first places she'd worked after she left here. But even now she has absolutely no recollection of how she got there. She drove the camper, of course, but had she known where she was going, or had she just driven aimlessly? Her only solid memories from those first few weeks are of watching people going about their business. Men working on building sites, whistling; women chatting with the checkout girls as they packed their shopping and planned what to make for dinner; children skipping or playing football in parks and playgrounds; and, worst of all, television presenters wearing nice clothes and heavy make-up, smiling, being witty and entertaining. And she remembers being incredulous that these things were still happening, that all around her people were going to work or peeling potatoes or reading newspapers, as if nothing had happened.

*

It is gone midnight when she goes back upstairs. That long sleep earlier must have fortified her – she's usually ready to fall into bed by ten. She makes a mug of hot chocolate to take to bed, then goes around switching off the lights. In the living room, her phone flashes in the darkness. Shit. She'd forgotten to take it downstairs with her. She unlocks the screen; five missed calls. The voicemail icon is lit, and her heart thumps as she waits for the message to play.

Eleanor, the present

The doctor reassures Eleanor that she has nothing to feel guilty about. 'In fact,' he says, 'if your mother had been at home when this happened, she wouldn't have received medical attention so promptly and the damage may well have been more significant.' They'll need to keep her in hospital for a while, he says, but he's optimistic.

Marjorie was in the residents' sitting room taking part in a singalong when it happened, and the staff recognised the signs immediately. A nurse was by her side within seconds and the paramedics arrived in seven minutes. 'All our staff are thoroughly trained,' the matron says when Eleanor calls the home the next day to thank everyone for their quick actions. 'The first half-hour or so is crucial, you see. Do you know about FAST?'

'Yes,' Eleanor says. 'They gave me a leaflet.'

'Good. Remember, time is of the essence.'

*

Later, when she calls in to pick up her mum's suitcase, the receptionist apologises. 'We usually make sure ladies' handbags go in the ambulance with them,' she says, 'but it might be because it all happened so quickly. Or maybe it was because the clasp is broken.' She looks at the handbag as she hands it to Eleanor. 'They'd have been worried something might fall out, I suppose. Anyway, it's been in the safe, so everything should be there.'

Eleanor assures her it's not a problem, and thanks her again. She puts the suitcase containing the four days' worth of clothes, toiletries and medication in the boot and places the open handbag on the passenger seat. All her life, her mother's handbag has been sacred. It was drummed into her as a small child that she was not to touch it, much less look inside, and here it is, tantalisingly open next to her. As she's driving back across Blackheath, a young fox appears out of nowhere and darts across the road in front of her. She slams on the brakes, shooting everything off the passenger seat and into the footwell. The terrified animal freezes, yellow eyes flashing in the headlights; they stare at each other for a second before it runs off across the heath into the darkness.

After a moment, she sets off again, sticking rigidly to the speed limit and concentrating on not allowing her mind to wander. She pulls up outside the house, takes the suitcase out of the boot and then bends to pick up the contents of her mum's handbag. She shoves everything back rather haphazardly, half expecting to be shouted at for touching it. There is a battered leather wallet that she doesn't recognise. Maybe it belongs to someone else at the home and has accidentally got in with her mum's things. She opens it, and there is the black-and-white photo she hasn't seen for thirty years – the one she was looking for at the exact same moment her mother was having a stroke.

*

After the first week or so, Marjorie seems to be recovering well, and she appears reasonably lucid today, so Eleanor takes advantage, handing her a series of photos, one at a time, the safe ones first: herself as a child, Marjorie as a child, Peggy, her mum and Peggy together. Marjorie smiles and nods, occasionally mutters, 'Peg,' or 'That's me.' She slips in one or two of her dad and Marjorie still smiles and nods. 'Your dad,' she says, then looks puzzled. 'He's not been in today.' Eleanor says nothing. She hands Marjorie the photo she found in her bag. 'Who's in this one?'

Marjorie smiles. 'That's me.' She points. 'And there's you. And poor Peter.'

Eleanor's heart starts to thump. 'Can you remember what happened to Peter, Mum?' She braces herself.

'Drowned,' she says, matter-of-factly.

'Yes, that's right. It was very sad, wasn't it? Can you remember the day it happened? Was I ... was I playing with Peter?'

Marjorie is staring at the photo, no longer smiling. A tear runs down her papery cheek. 'Same as Maurice.'

'Maurice?' That name again; the one she said she'd been told never to mention. She'd forgotten all about that. 'Mum, who was Maurice?' Marjorie closes her eyes and begins to rock back and forth, more tears trickling down her face. 'Ohhh,' she wails, louder and louder.

'Mum, it's all right.' She reaches out, but Marjorie snatches her hand away and begins pulling at her hair. The noise she's making is terrible, like an animal caught in a trap.

Eleanor looks around frantically for a nurse. She should never have shown her that picture. Further along the ward, another elderly lady starts to shout and pull at her clothes in distress. Oh, God, what has she started? 'Nurse!' she calls, and a tiny nurse who looks about fifteen walks calmly towards them. 'What's the matter, Marjorie?' she shouts, taking hold of her hands. 'Stop pulling your hair, now. Come on, stop that! And look now, you're upsetting the other ladies.'

One of Marjorie's hands flies out of her grasp and she raises it as though she's going to hit the nurse.

'Oh, Mum, stop it, please.' Eleanor moves nearer to try to help but the nurse shakes her head. 'It's fine. Don't worry. Best if you wait outside the ward for a minute.'

SUSAN ELLIOT WRIGHT

She hesitates. Is there something she doesn't want her to see? Is she being a bit rough? You hear about these things in hospitals. But then it dawns on her. She's being asked to wait outside because her presence is making her mum worse. Another nurse comes hurrying past her to deal with the old lady three beds down who is now swearing heartily and throwing anything she can lay her hands on.

She hovers near the nurses' station but Marjorie is already calmer, and the nurse is making soothing noises and asking if she'd like a drink of water. 'Yes, please,' she hears Marjorie say, 'you're very kind.'

She walks along the corridor and out into the car park. She'll give her mum five minutes to calm down, then go back in. What did she mean by *Same as Maurice*? She studies the photo again. There's a framed shot of her dad on the wall in the background; could that be what she meant? But before she can think about it any more, she spots Peggy walking across the tarmac towards her.

'I'd thought you'd be gone by now,' Peggy says. 'Everything all right?'

'Bit of a drama just now, but I think she's calmed down again.'

'Oh, no, really? This is happening quite a lot now, isn't it?'

A couple of days ago, Eleanor arrived at the hospital to find Peggy outside the ward in floods of tears. Peggy had taken in some of the fresh strawberry ice cream that Marjorie liked so much to try to encourage her to eat, but

Marjorie had grabbed it and thrown it at her, screaming at the top of her voice that Peggy was trying to poison her.

She sighs. 'Yes, it seems to be.'

As they go back into the ward together, she wonders whether her mum will remember she's here. Marjorie looks up as they approach. 'I won't stay now Peggy's here,' she says, taking her car keys out of her pocket, 'but I didn't want to leave without saying goodbye.'

Marjorie appears not to have heard. 'Peg.' A smile spreads across her face as Peggy sits in the chair opposite. Then she looks at Eleanor, leans towards Peggy and whispers, 'Who's that woman?'

Peggy looks mortified.

'Mum, it's me, Eleanor.' She waits. Before now, it has sometimes taken a moment for her mum to recognise her, but never this long. 'Your daughter,' she adds. But there is no hint of recognition in Marjorie's eyes.

*

That evening, unable to face being downstairs on her own, she sits in Peggy's kitchen, sipping the generous gin and tonic Peggy has poured her.

'At least she recognised you when you went back in the evening.' Peggy pours herself a more modest amount.

'True, but—'

'Sorry, that's not much comfort, is it? I hate seeing you like this, Ellie.'

She gives a small smile. 'Thanks. Even I'm quite shocked at how upset I was; I knew it would happen at some point, and it's not as if she and I were ever close. But it was the way she looked at me, so *politely*, as though I was a total stranger.' She sighs. 'I suppose this'll start happening more often.'

They sit in silence for a moment. Then Peggy says, her voice unusually low and quiet, 'I miss her, Ellie; it feels like she's already gone. Sometimes I wonder if it wouldn't be . . .'

She pulls a tissue from her sleeve and dabs at her eyes. Eleanor feels her own throat tighten, then Peggy blows her nose and shakes her head. 'If I ever get this bloody Alzheimer's, shoot me, would you?'

Eleanor

She feels guilty thinking it, but she's quite glad Marjorie hasn't been discharged yet, because it means she can have a leisurely lunch with Jill, who's down on one of her regular visits to see Dawn. Usually she only just about has time for a rushed coffee, so this is a real treat. 'The rehab's gone well, so they want to discharge her soon.'

'What about the dementia?' Jill says.

Eleanor sighs. 'It's getting worse. Apparently, it's not unusual for that to happen after a stroke. Physically, though, she's almost there.'

'Have you thought any more about homes?'

'I've seen a couple, and the place she was in for respite is brilliant but I'm not sure she's quite at that stage yet.'

'I'm not just saying this because we want you back – although we do, of course – but don't give up your life entirely. No one can say you haven't done your duty.'

'Well, anyway . . .' She reaches for the wine bottle and

tops them both up. 'It's all gone well, but she's still having trouble walking. She'll never manage the stairs, so I'm going to turn the dining room into a bedroom, for the time being at least. It needs redecorating anyway. I'm dying to get rid of that gloomy wallpaper – I'm sure I remember my dad putting it up, so that's how long it's been there.'

'Sounds like a good idea,' Jill says. 'Dawn and I can give you a hand if you want to make a start tomorrow.'

'Seriously? Oh, Jill, that would be brilliant, but what about Dawn? I don't want to eat into your visit.'

'To be honest, I think she'll be more than happy to come over to you for a few hours.' She smiles good-naturedly. 'She doesn't know what to do with me after the first couple of days, especially now Flora's settled into a routine.'

'How old is Flora now?'

'Three and a half months. I thought I'd spend the best part of my visits looking after her so Dawn can get on with things, but she's as good as gold; sleeps like a little lamb.'

'That's good,' she murmurs.

Jill looks at her. 'I'm sorry,' she says gently. 'I sometimes forget how much it still hurts.'

'Don't apologise. It still surprises me at times how raw it feels. It passes, though.' She takes a breath and smiles. 'Anyway, if you're sure Dawn won't mind, it would be wonderful to have you there, even if it's just moral support. There's so much in that house that has stayed the same for donkey's years, I feel like if I move anything I'm going to disturb some sort of, I don't know, dormant misery.'

Mostly, the house has become more comfortable and familiar over the last six months, but every now and then, she touches or looks at something that zooms her back to childhood. She shudders now as she remembers her mother's dark days, when black despair seemed to flow from her and seep into the carpets and up the walls.

'Don't worry, I can do moral *and* practical support! We'll be round first thing.'

The following morning, she gets up early to move the smaller items of furniture into the living room. The dining table and sideboard will have to stay put for now, but she can push them into the middle and cover them with dust sheets. The oak sideboard is heavier than she thought, so she needs to empty it before she can move it. She takes out the drawers, still stuffed with papers, and is just carrying them through to the living room when the doorbell rings. That'll be Jill and Dawn. As she sets the last drawer on the coffee table, she notices a piece of paper caught at the back. It's slipped through a gap where the wood has split, probably from being pushed up against the radiator for so many years. She plucks it out – it's a plain white envelope, sealed but with nothing written on it – and tosses it on top of the other papers to look at later.

'Here we are,' Jill says when Eleanor opens the door. She's holding a plastic bucket full of decorating equipment in one hand and a broom in the other. 'Team Charlie, ready for action.'

Charlie bounces in, carrying a miniature wooden

toolbox with a red handle. 'I putted my old clothes on,' he says, 'so I can be a helper.'

'Wonderful.' She smiles. 'I certainly need some help today.'

'Daddy's looking after Flora,' he continues, walking into the dining room. 'She can't help because she's too little. Only big boys can do working.' And with an air of great importance, he places his toolbox on the floor.

'Right,' Jill says, hands on hips. 'We've brought some stuff with us, but we need one more wallpaper scraper, a couple of brooms and some buckets or bowls of water. My father was a waste of space in many ways but he showed me how to strip wallpaper before he buggered off and left us – without repapering the room, I hasten to add.'

Eleanor goes down to the utility room to fetch what they need, and then Jill shows them how to use the scrapers to make criss-cross scores all over the wallpaper to allow the water to soak in properly.

'Now comes the fun part.' Jill points to the buckets and bowls of water. 'What you do is take your broom,' she pauses to pass a handbrush to Charlie. 'Here's yours, sweetie. And then you dunk it and slosh it up the wall as far as you can, like this.'

Charlie squeals as water splats onto the floor.

'We give it a good coating, then leave it about ten minutes, then do the same thing a couple more times. After the final soak, we'll go and have a cup of tea and by that time it'll have soaked right through the layers and it'll scrape off easily.'

'Give us a broom,' Dawn says, holding her hand out.

'You don't have to help, Dawn,' Eleanor says. 'You're a new mum; your job is to chat to us while we're working to keep our spirits up.'

'No, I came to help – I've been looking forward to this. When else do you get the chance to chuck water all over the place, eh, Charlie? And it's a good excuse to leave Madam with her dad for a few hours so we can have some Mummy and Charlie time, isn't it, pickle?' Charlie nods, already dunking his handbrush and happily sloshing water over the lower part of the wall, the floor and much of himself.

The water running down the walls is the colour of tea, Eleanor notices. According to Peggy, Marjorie only gave up smoking a few years ago, so the paper is probably suffused with forty-odd years' worth of nicotine.

Half an hour later, the radio is on and Jill, Dawn and Charlie are singing along to the theme from *Frozen* as they start on the final soak. It feels good to have her friends here, laughing and singing; maybe some of this cheerfulness will soak into the walls, too.

Peggy, who's come down to help in a 'tea-making and supervisory' capacity, appears in the doorway, brandishing a large white paper bag with telltale grease spots at the bottom. 'Who's for tea and doughnuts?'

'Me!' shouts Charlie. He's drenched from head to foot.

'Me, *please*,' Jill says. 'Good grief!' She laughs as she looks at him. 'You're like a drowned rat! Good job Mummy brought some other clothes.'

'Come on, Charlie Farley,' Dawn says. 'Let's get you into some dry things.'

Dawn takes Charlie off to the bathroom, while Jill goes into the kitchen to help Peggy with the tea. Eleanor is about to join them when the landline rings. She hurries through to the living room, trying to negotiate a path through all the extra furniture crammed in here. In her haste she bangs her knee hard against the corner of the coffee table. 'Shit!' she rubs her knee with one hand and manages to grab the phone with the other, just in time to hear yet another automated message telling her she can make a personal injury claim if she's had an accident at work. She swears loudly, slams the handset back in its cradle and is picking her way back through the room when she spots the white envelope that was caught in the back of the drawer. She'd almost forgotten it. She picks it up, sits down on the sofa and turns it over in her hands. The envelope is dusty and feels brittle with age, and there is definitely something inside. Tentatively, she opens it and slides out several folded pages. It's a letter, dated 17 June 1984:

Dear Eleanor,

I'm writing this in the middle of the night because I can't sleep, and I don't know if you'll ever read it. At the moment, I wouldn't know how to get it to you, and even if I did, I'm not sure I have the courage to actually hand it over, but I am going to write it anyway so the words will be here, on paper, and perhaps you'll read them at some point.

*I see now that I have done so many things wrong. I
came down to see you this morning but you'd already
gone. This may be hard to believe, but I was going to
ask how you'd feel about coming along to the cemetery
with me. I thought maybe we could go to Peter's grave
together, and then, perhaps, to your Sarah's.*

Tears well up instantly behind her eyes. So her mum
really had wanted to talk back then. Even though this is
what Peggy has been telling her these last few months,
part of her still hasn't quite been able to believe it.

*Peggy suggested it, and at first I thought she was
wrong, especially so soon after your own loss. I have read
your note several times, and each time it makes me cry.
I don't say that to make you feel guilty; I'm the one who
should feel guilty. I'm so sorry I didn't talk to you about
your baby, your Sarah. I wanted to comfort you so much.
Every time I looked at you I could see your grief, not
only in your eyes but in your whole body; I could see it
underneath your skin, and in the way you moved; I could
hear it in your voice when you talked. But I am a coward.
I thought that if I brought it up, you might start crying
and never stop. I was terrified of stirring up my own
grief for Peter, too, and I didn't know how to deal with it.*

She turns over the page. There are several sheets of
paper here, all covered on both sides with her mother's
elegant handwriting.

It was heartbreaking to read what you said about
being desperate to talk about Sarah and not wanting to
pretend that she never existed. Of course you wouldn't
want to pretend such a thing, and I'm so sorry you
thought that's what I was trying to do. It seems so
obvious to me now that you would have thought that,
given that I didn't speak of Peter at all until you found
that photograph when you were eighteen. I know
now we made a terrible mistake in taking you to Mr
Greenfield, but what he said seemed to make sense to
your dad and me at the time, that if you were able to
completely forget what happened that day, you would
grow up more easily and happily. We were wrong.

You see, I made you think it was your fault because
you'd put him in the water, and by covering it up, by not
telling you anything at all, I made it worse. You said in
your note that you thought I'd always blamed you, and I
cannot tell you how sorry I am that you've thought that
all this time. I have never blamed you. When I shouted
at you that day, it was a reflex reaction; I didn't mean it
was your fault, Lord forgive me. You certainly weren't
trying to hurt him. You were little more than a toddler,
playing with your dolls. Even if it was as simple as that,
you couldn't possibly be blamed. But that isn't all there
was to it.

She feels a thud deep in her abdomen, as though her
heart has dropped down from her chest into the pit of
her belly. Hadn't her mum said something like this fairly

recently? *There was more to it*. What did she mean? She turns to the next sheet of paper.

I've been sitting here all night – it's starting to get light outside – forcing my head back to that day. You've said you can't remember exactly what happened, and neither could I, not properly anyway, not until tonight. As you know, Peter was born with a lot of problems. They still called it 'retarded' then, and they wanted me to put him in a home, but I refused. I'd seen what went on in those places – I worked in one before you were born, as you know; I wanted to try to make things better. Now, this is something I've never told anyone before, not even your father. I had a brother, Maurice.

Maurice! Eleanor's hand shoots up to her mouth involuntarily. So that's who he was!

I didn't even know I had a brother until I was fifteen, because he'd been in a home more or less since birth. It was a dreadful place. My mother never told me exactly what was wrong with Maurice, but when I met him, he had the mind of a two- or three-year-old, but he was thirteen. There was something wrong with his heart, too, and his lungs, I think, because he couldn't breathe properly, and he had fits. He wasn't expected to live past his teens and my mother decided I should visit him just once, but she made me promise I would never tell anyone. I was especially not to tell my father

SUSAN ELLIOT WRIGHT

*we'd been to see him, because Father thought it best to
forget all about him and move on. When we arrived,
Maurice was strapped to his bed with what looked like
leather belts and he was moaning and crying. Mother
asked the matron why, and she said it was to stop him
falling out of bed and hurting himself. Mother insisted
they remove the straps, and they did, but I'm ashamed
to say I was so frightened I wanted to run out into the
street. I'd never seen anyone like him before, you see.
You didn't, in those days, because they were all shut
away in homes. Anyway, I made myself stay and look
at him, even though I was scared. His head was big
and round and his eyes were tiny and much too far
apart. He was wearing short trousers that looked too
big for him because his legs were so skinny, and when
he moved his feet I could see that there was webbed
skin between his toes. Mother talked to him as though
he was perfectly normal, but he couldn't talk back, he
just made a horrible grunting noise. It made me think
of what the bus conductor had said to my mother when
we got off at the stop just outside the home. 'Visiting,
are you, love? Poor wretched creatures.' Once I'd got
over the shock, I started to think I might go and see him
again, not least because I wanted to make sure they
weren't still strapping him to the bed. But he died soon
after our visit, from an epileptic fit, Mother said. She
had a little cry, but then she said she was glad he wasn't
suffering any more. Anyway, what all this is leading up
to, Eleanor, is that I need to tell you something I hadn't*

364

properly remembered about the day Peter drowned. You see, the moment I first held Peter in my arms, I knew he was like Maurice.

Eleanor leans back on the sofa. She can hear Peggy and Jill talking and laughing in the kitchen, Charlie chattering away to Dawn in the bathroom. Part of her feels she should be hiding away to read this, but being up here in the daylight, hearing laughter and chatter around her, makes her feel safe. She reads on.

It's only a couple more pages, but it takes her several minutes because she has to keep rereading bits to make sure she's got it right. It is the final sentence, *Can you forgive me?* that brings on the tears she's been holding back.

It is a moment or two before she becomes aware of Charlie standing next to her, his head tilted to one side. 'Have you got a tummy ache?' he asks, his huge, clear eyes full of concern.

She quickly wipes her eyes and shakes her head. 'No.' She rummages in her jeans pocket for a tissue and tries to smile. 'Just feeling a bit sad, that's all.'

'Do you need a cuggle?' He moves closer and puts a hand on her knee, as though ready to climb onto her lap. Her whole body tenses, the same reflex reaction she always has around young children. But this time, she feels her muscles relax again.

'Yes,' she manages to say without sobbing, 'I think I do need a cuddle.' For the first time, she lifts him onto her lap and leans her face against his silky hair. It is still damp and smells of Johnson's baby shampoo, a smell she'll never forget. Charlie slides his chubby little arms around her neck; he is warm and solid and soft, and the feel of his tiny hand patting her back is so profoundly comforting that she isn't quite sure what she'll do when it stops.

Marjorie, June 1968

Marjorie pushed the pram up and down the pathway that ran alongside the lawn for a good half-hour before Peter finally closed his eyes. His breathing sounded dreadful and his little face still bore the signs of his distress. He'd been restless and wheezy all night and awake since five, snuffling and grizzling the whole time. She'd known caring for him would be difficult, but she hadn't realised quite how difficult; she'd had some vague idea that simply being his mother would help her to ease his discomfort, but she felt every bit as inadequate with her own child as she'd felt with those poor, doomed creatures she'd cared for during her nursing days.

He seemed to be asleep now, thank the Lord, so she parked him in the shade of the pear tree and went back inside to check on Eleanor, who was still sitting on the settee, cuddling the Tiny Tears Peggy bought her for her birthday.

'Oh, has *Playschool* finished?' She moved to switch off the television.

'No!' Eleanor said, pointing to the screen. 'I want to see that big girl.'

'But darling, that's just the Testcard. It's not a programme.'

'Please may I watch Testcard?'

'But ... Oh, very well.' Why argue if it kept her quiet? 'I'll be in the kitchen.'

'Okay.' Eleanor put her thumb in her mouth and sat back on the settee.

She walked wearily into the kitchen, her arms weak and aching from holding Peter and a dull, ominous pain in her back. Her heart sank at the sight of the piles of washing that were still on the floor. The laundry seemed to have more than doubled since Peter arrived, and all she'd managed to get through so far today was the nappies. How she was going to tackle the rest of it she didn't know, especially with her hands still feeling raw. She must remind Ted about getting that twin-tub – Peggy said hers had changed her life.

She filled a tumbler with water, threw two aspirin into the back of her throat and washed them down in one gulp.

'Mummy?' Eleanor appeared in the doorway with the huge plastic box of Lego bricks. 'Can I play with my Lego?'

'Yes, of course you can. Just take it back into the living—'

But before she could finish her sentence, Eleanor tipped the bricks out onto the lino with a crashing noise that seemed to smash Marjorie's fragile, aching brain against the inside of her skull.

'Ooh, Eleanor.' She put her hand to her forehead. 'Darling, Mummy has a terrible headache. Try and play quietly now, there's a good girl.'

Eleanor immediately started trying to be quiet, but as Marjorie stood at the sink, attempting to muster the energy for the next batch of washing, the constant chinking of the Lego bricks became almost too much to bear. How could those little plastic bricks make so much noise? Eleanor had become more demanding lately. Probably normal for a first child who suddenly has to share her mum with a new baby, but in this case, the baby took so much there was nothing left. Poor Eleanor – she'd been promised a baby brother who would be fun, who would gurgle and chuckle and admire his big sister. What she'd got was one who drooled and never smiled; who needed constant attention and who used their mother up completely; a brother who may never be able to sit up unaided, never mind play with his sister.

But Eleanor tried, bless her. She never tired of leaning over the cot, shaking a rattle in front of her brother's unmoving eyes or waving a fluffy toy in a desperate bid to get his attention. 'Look, baby. Look at the chicky-chick.'

She sighed and leant against the sink. 'Eleanor, how about you put the Lego away for a while and play outside in the garden?'

Eleanor shook her head. 'No thanks.'

'Oh, come on, darling. You love playing in the garden.'

Eleanor frowned. 'Don't want to play in the garden.'

Typical. If it had been pouring with rain or freezing cold, you could bet your last shilling she'd want to play outside. Marjorie sighed. There was no point in being cross with Eleanor; it wasn't her fault.

She wiped her hands on her apron and crouched down to Eleanor's level. 'Tell you what, how about if I come with you?' The washing would have to wait; she was too tired to stand at the sink for hours anyway. 'Auntie Peggy's coming round later, so we could just wait for her in the garden.'

Eleanor looked mildly interested but was still reluctant.

'It's lovely and sunny; how about we get the paddling pool out? You can give your dollies a bath.'

Eleanor was already on her feet, selecting dolls from the toybox in the corner.

*

Eleanor's swimming costume was still pegged on the line from yesterday, but it was perfectly dry now, so after she'd got Eleanor into it and persuaded her to wear the matching yellow sun hat, she opened the shed where she'd thrown the paddling pool, still inflated, yesterday afternoon. When she'd left it out the other day, the wind had got up overnight and blown it right down to the end of the garden where it had got caught in the forsythia. They were lucky it hadn't punctured. She uncoiled the hose and turned on the outside tap, keeping half an eye on the pram as she filled the pool. *Please don't wake up yet, please don't wake up yet.*

Eleanor was in the pool with two of her dolls before Marjorie had even finished filling it. She turned the hose off and wound it back onto its wheel, then she opened the fold-up chair, picked up her copy of *Woman's Realm* and settled down to read, now and again glancing at the back gate for Peggy. At least once Peggy was here she didn't have to worry so much about Eleanor, who would be all over her the minute she arrived.

She wasn't aware of her eyes growing heavy, and she hadn't even realised she'd dozed off until she felt Eleanor's wet hand on her arm. 'Mummy! Wake up!'

She opened her eyes, but her vision swam. How stupid, to fall asleep in the sun, and with Ellie playing in the pool, too.

'Mummy! Peter's too slippy.'

'What, darling?' She tried to get to her feet but a wave of nausea knocked her backwards. As she steadied herself, her vision cleared. Eleanor was standing beside her, looking as though she'd been caught doing something she shouldn't.

'I did taked his nappy off all by myself. He wants to get out now but he's all slippy.'

At first, it didn't quite register. She looked over to the pool. She could see the dolls in the water, wet patches on the grass, the folded towel she'd left in readiness.

Then she saw Peter's vest; then his rubber pants with the nappy still inside.

She froze for a moment as the realisation dawned. *'What have you done?'* she screamed as she sprinted across the grass. 'You stupid, stupid child!' She was vaguely aware of Eleanor's face crumpling and her running back towards the house as she fell to her knees beside the pool. Two of Eleanor's dolls floated on the surface, but Peter, barely bigger than the Tiny Tears even at eight months, lay on the bottom, completely submerged.

Although she had heard the expression 'time stood still' many times before, she hadn't properly understood what it meant. But now it was actually happening; it was as if a whole day's worth of thoughts and sensations were happening simultaneously. This was what she was aware of, all within a fraction of a second: Peter was completely still and his face, with its twisted mouth and vacant, too wide-apart eyes, looked more relaxed than she'd ever seen it; no sound came from him, not a grizzle or a whimper, no laboured, whistling breaths that forced his chest into impossible exertions. She could feel the dry grass prickling her knees; she could hear a lawnmower somewhere in the distance. Peter was quiet at last. As she gazed at him, marvelling at how peaceful he looked, his hand moved, then his eyes flickered and his face began to contort. And then something very strange happened; she felt herself separate into two. The next moment she was hovering a few feet above the ground, looking down on her other self, still kneeling on the grass. She watched as her own hand moved slowly through the air, over the surface of the water, towards her drowning child. Even from up here, she felt her hand break the surface – the water was pleasantly warm; she was glad of that – warm water could sometimes soothe him. She saw her hand rest gently on his tiny, inadequate chest, the fingers splayed.

Something wasn't right; she should be snatching him from the water, giving him mouth-to-mouth; she'd done it before on one of the little mongol boys in the home. He'd got an electric shock from a loose socket and his poor weak heart had almost given up, but she'd brought him back, he'd coughed and spluttered into her mouth and he'd carried on living . . . not that anyone noticed.

But there was her hand down there, resting on Peter's chest, holding him gently in place until eventually his face relaxed again and the faint fluttering under her fingers finally stopped.

Everything started to jumble up in her head. A fat bumble bee landed on her arm and brought her crashing back into her body and then she had Peter up and out of the water and in her arms and he felt so much heavier. She should do mouth-to-mouth; why was she not doing mouth-to-mouth? Again she slipped out of her body and looked down at herself; she could see the back of her own head and the top of Peter's, his hair darkened by the water, as she held him against her. She was rocking him.

And then Peggy was there running towards her, dropping her shopping bags which spilled out, sending oranges and potatoes and tins of things rolling over the grass, and Eleanor was coming back down the path, wiping her tear-stained face which was already smeared with dirt and grass stains.

'Oh my God! *What's happened?*' Peggy cried.

Marjorie carried on rocking her baby.

Eleanor started to cry harder. 'I putted him in the paddling pool,' she sobbed. 'I did want to get him out again but he was all slippy.'

Peggy put her arms around Eleanor. 'Shush, sweetheart,' she said. Then turned to Marjorie. 'Is he ...?'

Marjorie didn't seem to hear.

'I closed my eyes,' she said eventually, still clutching Peter as she rocked back and forth. 'It was only for a moment ... I shouted at her ...'

*

The rest of that day was a blur. Peggy called an ambulance and neighbours started to gather, and soon Marjorie was aware of there being a lot of strangers in her house and garden. Someone made tea and someone else thought to contact Ted at work, and then a policeman came and went. After all the fuss had died down and Peggy had taken Eleanor back to stay with her and Ken for a while, a grim-faced doctor arrived. She didn't know him, but she was grateful because he gave her a sedative that worked quickly and made her feel as though she was retreating, just falling away from everything that had happened, as though it hadn't really happened at all.

Eleanor, the present

Eleanor blows her nose and attempts a smile, then kisses Charlie on the head. 'Thank you, Charlie.' She sets him gently back on the floor. 'I feel a bit better now.' She folds the pages again and slips the letter into her back pocket, where she can simply touch it and feel the reassuring thickness of the paper. She still can't quite believe what she's read, although reading her mother's account – her confession – has finally opened the door to her own memory of that day. For over thirty years she has desperately tried to recall that little pocket of time leading up to the moment when she put her baby brother in the water; she has agonised repeatedly over whether she'd been angry with him or felt jealous of him. But although she's remembered fragments over the years – waking her mother up, being shouted at, running back down the garden and into the house – nothing else has come back to her until today.

Now, though, she can conjure up that morning, crisp and clear, there in the garden on that sunny June day. Peter was crying and she'd tried to wake her mother, but when that failed, she went back to the pram and tried jiggling it about like her mother did and saying, *Shush, shush, Peter Poppet; what's all this in aid of?* But his cries only became louder, and the smell coming from his nappy suggested that it was very wet indeed. She'd reached in and lifted him as carefully as she could. As she thinks of this now, she can feel his overheated forehead against her chin, damp and salty with baby sweat, and the stench of ammonia coming from his sodden nappy. She'd pulled that nappy off in one go along with his rubber pants, and she remembers the weight of it as she threw it on the grass. Then she laid him gently on a towel and entertained him for a while by blowing raspberries on his bare tummy. But he soon started crying again, and so that was when she decided to try putting him in the paddling pool. As she lowered him into the sun-warmed water, he stopped crying instantly and, pleased that she'd found a solution, she climbed in with him so they could play a game together. She would be the mermaid, she decided, and he could be the water baby, just like in her book.

She is aware of Charlie still looking at her with great concern. They've called from the kitchen a couple of times to say that the tea's ready, so she stands up now and finds she is holding Charlie's hand and allowing him to lead her back to the others. She has remembered, finally. And the truth is that not only had she not intended to harm her brother, but she now knows that it was her mother who ... at least, she knows her mother contributed to his death.

Before they can ask about her tear-streaked face, she tells them what she's just found.

'Really?' Peggy says. 'Do you think that's what she's been looking for all this time?'

'Yes, I think it may be.'

'What does it say?' Jill says. The way she and Peggy are looking at her makes it clear they expect her to produce the letter. Instead, she tells them about part of the content, the part where her mother acknowledges that talking about their shared grief may have helped, and where she talks about Peter and Sarah, finally able to use their names. 'I know it's made me cry,' she says. 'But they're good tears, and I think I understand her a bit more now.' She turns to Peggy. 'She wrote it the day I left, apparently, when I took off in the camper.'

'That makes sense. She was devastated that she'd missed you that day. She was genuinely shocked when she realised how much worse she'd made things by not talking about it all.'

Eleanor nods. 'A lot of what she says is exactly what you've been telling me, but this feels ... I don't know, almost as if I'm hearing it from her own lips.'

'And that helps?'

'Massively.'

Peggy smiles and gives Eleanor's arm a comforting

rub. 'Good. I think you going away was good for her in the long run. It gave her the shake-up she needed, made her face up to things she'd tried to wipe out.'

'Maybe.' She lets her gaze linger briefly on Peggy's face. Might Peggy know the truth? According to her mum's account, she'd pulled Peter out of the water by the time Peggy arrived. But wouldn't she have confided in her best friend at some point in four and a half decades?

'What a shame she never found it,' Peggy says, 'so she could give it to you herself.'

'Yes,' she agrees. 'All that searching.' But would she have given her the letter if she'd found it? Maybe; maybe not.

As they gradually drift back to stripping the wallpaper, Eleanor makes a decision. She will never show this letter to anyone, ever.

*

That evening, tired and aching from a day's physical work – something which, six months ago, wouldn't have phased her at all – she goes to the hospital to visit her mother. Her breath catches slightly when she sees the bed neatly made and the surrounding area cleared of all signs of occupancy. As her eyes scan the ward, one of the orderlies she's spoken to a few times spots her. 'Your mum's been moved, love. Down the end there, see? She being discharged soon?'

'Thanks. Yes, a day or two, I think – soon as we've sorted out her room.'

'That'll be why, then. They move 'em when they don't need to be so near the nurses' station no more. Good luck with it all, love.'

'Thank you,' she says again, and makes her way down the ward.

'Hello, Mum.' Marjorie is sitting in her chair, holding one of her slippers, pulling at the stitching. 'What are you doing?'

Her mum carries on plucking at the threads, pulling them looser and looser.

'Mum? Can you look at me?'

There is no response. Looks like it's bad today. Slowly, she reaches for the slipper her mother is worrying at. She lets her fingers close around it but doesn't try to take it away yet, because it's the sort of action that could set her mum screaming as if she's being murdered.

'Mum,' she says again, 'it's me, Eleanor.' The fingers slow a little in their movement, and she pulls gently on the slipper. Marjorie grips it more tightly. 'No,' she mutters, but she looks up and there seems to be a glimmer of recognition in her eyes. 'Eleanor. Ellie-belly.'

'That's right, Mum.' She smiles. 'Listen, we've started decorating your new bedroom. Jill and Dawn came to help. Do you remember them? Jill is my friend from the farm, and Dawn is her daughter, the one with the little boy and the baby girl. Remember?'

'Baby girl,' Marjorie says. 'Baby girl. Baby girl. Baby girl. Baby—'

'Mum!' She takes her hand quite firmly, which usually breaks this needle-in-the-groove repetition. She has no idea whether any of this is going in, but she carries on anyway. 'We've started putting up the lining paper, so I expect we'll finish that tomorrow and start the painting. I thought a soft, forget-me-not blue might be nice. Do you think you'd like that?'

Marjorie smiles. She doesn't say anything, but Eleanor takes this to mean that yes, she would be happy with the forget-me-not blue. Still holding the connection with her mother's eyes, she says, 'When we moved the sideboard, I found your letter, the one I think you've been looking for.' She waits for a moment. 'You wrote it a long time ago, when I'd been staying with you after my baby, Sarah, died. Do you remember?' The smile is still there but it wavers now. She continues. 'I'd been with you for a few months but then I left, and I wrote you a note, saying I wished we could have talked about Sarah . . .' she pauses, '. . . and about Peter.' At this her mum's eyes flicker and she knows for sure something is going in. 'You wrote the letter that night, after I left, and I don't know if you remember this, but in it you explained everything.'

Is it her imagination, or are her mum's eyes a little glittery? She's still holding onto the slipper with one hand, so Eleanor takes the other in both of hers. 'You told me exactly what happened when Peter died, and you asked if I could forgive you.' She pauses. 'Mum, I understand why you never told anyone the truth.' She is still looking into Marjorie's eyes, and for the briefest of moments, there is something, a sparkling of understanding, of perfect and absolute connection between them that reminds her of the moment she first laid eyes on her own daughter. She blinks, shaken by the intensity of the experience. She wants to say this quickly, before the connection disappears. 'I'm grateful, Mum. And there's nothing to forgive.'

*

Jill and Dawn come again the next day and, with the three of them working flat out, the lining paper is up by lunchtime, and by mid-afternoon there's an undercoat on the woodwork and a first coat of emulsion on the walls. The colour is warm and restful, and while this room will never be particularly light, it now feels soft and cosy rather than dark and gloomy. Before she goes to the hospital, she photographs the almost finished room so she can show her mum.

The ward has a slightly abandoned feel today, with so many of the other patients having been discharged. She spots Marjorie making her way back to her bed with the aid of a walking frame. Her mobility is improving every day, but progress is still slow. She notices that her mum's nearest 'neighbour', who also appears to have dementia, although not so far advanced, is wearing a coat and outdoor shoes. Her husband is there, holding her bags and listening to instructions from the nurse as an orderly helps her into a wheelchair. 'Hello, love,' the woman calls out when she sees Eleanor. 'I'm off home today.'

'That's nice.' Eleanor smiles. 'I expect you're looking forward to it.'

'Oh, yes. Can't wait to get out of this place.' She grips the arms of the wheelchair, tips her head back and yells, 'It's a fucking shithole!' at the top of her voice.

'Jean! For heaven's sake!' Her husband looks mortified, but no one else takes any notice.

Marjorie is standing by her chair now, watching with a vague smile. As Jean is wheeled out of the ward with the nurse in attendance, she waves and calls, 'Good luck, love, hope you get out of here soon.' Marjorie, still smiling, lifts her hand and waves back.

'How are you today, Mum?' Eleanor pulls up a chair. 'You're looking fairly bright and cheerful.'

'Hello.' Marjorie smiles as she settles herself in her chair, but Eleanor isn't sure she recognises her.

'Look, Mum.' She takes out her phone. 'I took a picture of your new bedroom. Remember, we're moving your bed up to the dining room so you don't have to cope with the stairs. Isn't it a lovely colour?'

Marjorie takes the phone and looks at the picture. She is still smiling, but Eleanor can't tell if she knows what she's looking at, or if she remembers – or understands – that she's coming home. 'This is taken from the door, so your bed'll go on this side here, see?' Marjorie nods but her smile has gone. She lets out a low moan and puts her hand to her head, screwing up her eyes. 'What is it, Mum? Have you got a headache?' There is a slight tremor in Marjorie's other arm which Eleanor only notices a split second before the phone falls to the floor. Her mum appears to move forward. 'Don't worry, I'll get it.' She bends down and picks it up, examines the screen. 'It's okay, it's not broken.'

Her mum is looking at her but her expression is blank. Her skin is pale, and there's a sheen of perspiration on her forehead. 'Are you feeling all right, Mum? It's ever so warm in here, isn't it? Let me get you some water.' She pours water from the plastic jug into a beaker, but as she holds it to her mum's lips, Marjorie moves so suddenly that the water spills down the side of her dressing gown and onto the floor.

'Never mind.' Eleanor stands up and grabs a handful of paper towels from above the washbasin then stoops to mop up the puddle by her mum's feet. Marjorie doesn't move. It's not a lot of water and she manages to get most of it up, then she puts the paper towels in the bin and sits back down just as Marjorie slumps forward in her chair. The grunting noise she makes sounds a bit like a snore, and for a moment, Eleanor thinks she has dropped off to sleep – it wouldn't be the first time. But then she notices Marjorie's left arm hanging limply by her side and it comes back to her straight away: the acronym, FAST, the doctor explained after the first stroke. She'd googled it and printed it out for Peggy: Face, Arms, Speech and Time, as in, *Time is of the essence.*

She lifts Marjorie's head so she can see her face. Sure enough, one side looks as if it's collapsed. The left eye is half closed and the left side of her mouth is turned down; a dribble of saliva runs down her chin.

'Oh, God ... oh, shit ...' She looks down the ward but there's no one around, and she can't see the nurses' station from here. 'Hang on, Mum, I'll get the nurse.' She starts to get up then jumps as her mother's good hand clamps around her wrist. 'Mum, I need to find someone.'

Marjorie's grip tightens. Her lips are moving as if she's trying to speak, but there's barely any sound, more a thin stream of air.

'What is it, Mum?' She leans in close, straining to make sense of the wisps of sound coming from her mother's pale lips. 'I'm sorry, I can't quite ...' She shakes her head. She rests her hand over her mother's, which is still clasped claw-like around her wrist, and moves round so they're facing each other. Marjorie's face now appears completely frozen on one side.

'Mum,' she whispers, 'I think you're having another stroke. We need to get some help.' As she looks into her mother's eyes, she becomes aware of her own heartbeat, louder than usual, but suddenly sluggish and cumbersome, as though it is dragging in her chest. At the same moment she has a sense of time slowing, stilling almost. She looks again into her mother's eyes. Once a deep, strong blue, the colour has faded now to a watery grey, and yet there is still something, some hint of memory that flickers behind them.

'Mum,' she whispers, 'are you ... are you trying to tell me ...?'

Marjorie's hand falls back into her lap as her grip on Eleanor's wrist loosens. She searches her mum's face; she can't absolutely swear to it, but she is as sure as she can be that she is reading those eyes correctly. The look that passes between them right then carries more meaning than should be possible in those few brief moments, and she feels almost hypnotised as she sits unmoving while her mother's brain cells die at the rate of two million per second.

After several seconds, maybe minutes, she looks along the ward again, down towards the nurses' station. There's no one behind the desk, but she can hear voices and she knows they're there, just round the corner, out of sight. If she were to shout for help, they would hear her straight away and would probably come running. She has no idea what the emergency treatment for a stroke is, especially a major one. This is a major one, she's pretty sure of that.

But she does not shout for help. Instead, she takes her mother's hand in both of her own. 'I'm here, Mum,' she murmurs, trying to shut her ears to that horrible rasping sound.

Someone will notice eventually, of course, but she doesn't turn her head to look along the ward to see if anyone's coming. She wonders what they'll do when they realise what is happening, and she wonders what, if anything, will happen to her afterwards. But she remains sitting there, holding Marjorie's hand, while the brain cells continue to die.

EPILOGUE

Six months later

There are forty or so guests at the wedding. Everyone is friendly and smiling and the warm glow surrounding the bride and groom seems to suffuse the whole wedding party with happiness. The ceremony is simple but moving, and Eleanor's eyes are moist, partly because she wishes her mum were here to see this woman who has loved and cared for them both so selflessly, finally finding the happiness she deserves.

They make a handsome couple. Peggy's hair is a delicate silvery blonde and the soft style frames her face perfectly. Her 1940s-style dress is oyster pink, decorated with seed pearls; Dennis is even more dashing than usual in a cream linen suit and a dazzling white shirt. They're honeymooning in Italy, apparently – a bit of a coincidence, given that she'll be flying there herself in a couple of days. Peggy and Dennis are going to Florence, though, whereas Eleanor is heading for a little town just north of Genoa, where Dylan has settled for the time being. She can stay as long as she wants, he said when they spoke on the phone – he's 'given in', as he puts it, and bought a mobile. For good, if she'd like to. That took her aback slightly, and she still isn't sure what she feels about the idea. But in the meantime, she's told him she'll definitely stay for a few weeks, and after that, she'll see.

She's been back at the farm since she cleared the house, and she assumes that's where she'll stay, at least for the present. She isn't too old to train as a primary school teacher, she's discovered, so that's an option. Although now she feels able to trust herself in that role, she's no longer sure she wants it. She'll probably follow Peggy's advice and not make any decisions for a while.

She enjoys the wedding more than she expected to, and it's been especially nice to see Peggy's sons again, but once the happy couple have left in a shower of confetti, she says goodbye to Martin and Michael and their partners and heads back to the house.

When Peggy told her the sale was about to complete, she wasn't sure if she wanted to see the place again, but it's her childhood home, after all, so she decides to have one last look before she hands over the keys. She and Peggy cleared it soon after her mum died. They'd chosen mementoes – she kept photos, a pair of pearl earrings that belonged to her grandmother and a pair of gold cufflinks that must have been her father's, and Peggy kept a couple of pictures, a pretty glass vase and a few pieces of jewellery. When they'd finished packing everything up, and Peggy went upstairs to 'put the kettle on and open the brandy', Eleanor had walked slowly from room to room, keenly aware of an almost tangible weight to the air. This house was the centre of so much unhappiness – for her, for her mother and no doubt for her father, too. Even with the rooms emptied, it still felt heavy and oppressive, and yet it was hard to say goodbye.

She expects to feel that heaviness again as soon as she opens the door, but this time, as she walks from room to room, she feels lighter than she's ever felt here before. She can't understand it, because on the surface, the place seems so bleak. It's been empty for months, and although Peggy's been popping down to air the rooms, there's still the unmistakable smell of damp. In the living room, the light patches where the pictures and mirrors used to be only emphasise the extent of the nicotine stains on the already dark wallpaper. In contrast, the dining room still looks newly decorated, albeit in a rather bedroom-y colour.

Down in the basement, the damp smell is so bad she can taste it, so she's not surprised to see black mould on the wall of the utility room and the revolting scuttle of the strangely prehistoric-looking silverfish as she unlocks the back door. It was raining this morning, and a deep puddle has formed in the area at the bottom of the steps leading up into the garden. She'd forgotten how it floods down here in heavy rain, and how her mum or dad would have to come down and fix the stormboard across to stop it coming in under the back door. She goes up the steps and takes one last walk around the garden. Peggy looked after it at first, but she's been so busy with the wedding and selling her own place that it's now quite overgrown, and Eleanor has to push back some of the foliage in order to walk down the path.

When she first found out about Peter, she used to wonder why her mum wanted to spend so much time out here, the very place where her baby died. But now she understands her mum's need to make things grow, to keep propagating new life and nurturing and tending it to maturity. She does a similar thing herself with her work on the farm, she supposes.

It's only when she's back upstairs and taking a last look round before locking the door that she realises what it is that feels so different. The ghosts of the past are no longer trapped in this house; they've gone, finally laid to rest.

ACKNOWLEDGEMENTS

The first round of thanks must go to my wonderful editor Clare Hey and my agent Kate Shaw, for their perceptive, honest and insightful feedback on the various drafts of *What She Lost*. I am profoundly grateful for their continuing support, encouragement and understanding, and their unwavering belief that I would eventually make a silk purse out of the sow's ear that was the first draft of this novel.

Huge thanks also to the fabulous team at Simon & Schuster for all that goes into preparing a novel for publication, including proofreading, copy editing, and the beautiful cover design.

This book has been the most difficult to write so far, and it would be impossible to thank by name everyone who has supported me, so I'd like to express my gratitude to all those who read early drafts and later drafts, helped me explore plot ideas, soothed my insecurities, poured wine down my throat, and reassured me that I was getting somewhere. My very special thanks to Russell Thomas (who's done a lot of insecurity-soothing) and to Marian 'Dill' Dillon. Hoorah for wine and feedback! 'When shall we three meet again?' A special mention also to Ruby Speechley, Iona Gunning, Sue Hughes, and the Hallam Writers.

Authors need a place to write, a space conducive to concentration and creativity, where you can lose yourself in your story without interruption. Thank you to the past and present teams at Couch for keeping me supplied with green tea and coffee while I bash away at my laptop.

When I need to get away from domestic responsibility completely, I rely on the wonderful Annie McKie's writers' retreats, which offer a room-with-a-view, gorgeous food, and oodles of encouragement. Thank you for all that, Annie, and for the wine and friendship.

In researching this novel, I read several accounts of women's experiences at the Greenham Common Peace Camp in the early Eighties, and I found *Orange Gate Journal* by Ginette Leach particularly useful. My thanks also to Jeremy Holden-Bell, chairman of the Newbury Society, for information on the geography of Greenham Common and access routes to the peace camp at that time.

Before settling to fiction, I wrote a number of health-related books including one on dementia. I was in the slightly unusual position of turning to one of my own books for research, and I'd like to reiterate my thanks to the Alzheimer's Society, and all those who contributed their personal stories to *When Someone You Love Has Dementia*.

Finally, not only for the reading and proofreading, the tea-making, dog-walking, wine-pouring and other activities incumbent upon an author's spouse, my biggest thanks go as always to my husband Francis – I couldn't do this without you.

**SIMON &
SCHUSTER**

IF YOU ENJOY GOOD BOOKS,
YOU'LL LOVE OUR GREAT OFFER
25% OFF THE RRP ON ALL
SIMON & SCHUSTER UK TITLES
WITH FREE POSTAGE AND PACKING (UK ONLY)

Simon & Schuster UK is one of the leading general book publishing
companies in the UK, publishing a wide and eclectic mix
of authors ranging across commercial fiction, literary fiction,
general non-fiction, illustrated and children's books.

For exclusive author interviews, features and competitions log onto:
www.simonandschuster.co.uk

*Titles also available in **eBook** format across all digital devices.*

How to buy your books

Credit and debit cards
Telephone Simon & Schuster Cash Sales at **Sparkle Direct** on **01326 569444**

Cheque
Send a cheque payable to *Simon & Schuster Bookshop* to:
Simon & Schuster Bookshop, PO Box 60, Helston, TR13 OTP

Email: sales@sparkledirect.co.uk
Website: www.sparkledirect.com

Prices and availability are subject to change without notice.

Susan Elliot Wright grew up in Lewisham in south-east London. Before becoming a full-time writer, she did a number of different jobs, including civil servant, cleaner, dishwasher, journalist, and chef. She has an MA in Writing from Sheffield Hallam University, where she is now an associate lecturer, and she lives in Sheffield with her husband. She is the author of *The Things We Never Said* and the *Secrets We Left Behind*. To find out more, visit her website: www.susanelliotwright.co.uk or follow her on Twitter @sewelliot.

Praise for *The Things We Never Said*:

'Passionate, intriguing and beautifully written, *The Things We Never Said* deserves to stand on the shelf next to Maggie O'Farrell's books. A powerful and talented new voice' Rachel Hore, bestselling author of *A Place of Secrets* and *A Week in Paris*

'If you love Maggie O'Farrell, you will love this' Veronica Henry, bestselling author of *The Long Weekend*

'A brave and moving story about how much can be lost and what happens next. A compelling and impressive debut' Alison Moore, author of the Booker-shortlisted *The Lighthouse*

Praise for *The Secrets We Left Behind*:

'[A] tense and emotional drama' *Daily Express*, Best Summer Reads

03/17
D
LB of Hackney
91300001023189

Also by Susan Elliot Wright

The Things We Never Said
The Secrets We Left Behind